DEFEATED

The watermots who had survived the battle were running for their lives. Those who turned to fight were slain almost immediately. Thru ran up an alley all alone. He stopped. With no visible pursuit, he ducked into a pigsty and pulled himself up on the beams and wedged himself under the narrow eave. Hauling himself up with his damaged left arm was agonizing, but the place was quiet. The pigs were gone, but it still stank of them. His arm ached horribly. He wondered if it was broken.

Two men looked in, missed him in the eave above their heads, and went running on. He scrunched back into the narrow space, but couldn't get both legs inside. His left arm was turning numb again.

His mind was awhirl. Disaster had befallen the land. The army of Sulmo had been defeated. Thru had no idea how badly the rest of the battle had gone, but he was certain that the Meld had been driven from the field, and now four regiments were gone. Slaughtered to the last mot.

And then his exposed foot was seized and he was pulled down into the mud below and struck repeatedly with heavy objects. He was trying to get to his feet when he lost consciousness. . . .

THE SHASHT WAR

The Second Book of Arna

Christopher Rowley

A ROC BOOK

ROC
Published by New American Library, a division of
Penguin Putnam Inc., 375 Hudson Street,
New York, New York 10014, U.S.A.
Penguin Books Ltd, 27 Wrights Lane,
London W8 5TZ, England
Penguin Books Australia Ltd, Ringwood,
Victoria, Australia
Penguin Books Canada Ltd, 10 Alcorn Avenue,
Toronto, Ontario, Canada M4V 3B2
Penguin Books (N.Z.) Ltd, 182–190 Wairau Road,
Auckland 10, New Zealand

Penguin Books Ltd, Registered Offices:
Harmondsworth, Middlesex, England

First published by Roc, an imprint of New American Library,
a division of Penguin Putnam Inc.

First Printing, February 2001
10 9 8 7 6 5 4 3 2 1

Cover art by Duane Myers
Design by Ray Lundgren

 REGISTERED TRADEMARK—MARCA REGISTRADA

Printed in the United States of America

PUBLISHER'S NOTE
This is a work of fiction. Names, characters, places, and incidents either are
the product of the author's imagination or are used fictitiously, and any
resemblance to actual persons, living or dead, business establishments, events,
or locales is entirely coincidental.

BOOKS ARE AVAILABLE AT QUANTITY DISCOUNTS WHEN USED TO PROMOTE
PRODUCTS OR SERVICES. FOR INFORMATION PLEASE WRITE TO PREMIUM
MARKETING DIVISION, PENGUIN PUTNAM INC., 375 HUDSON STREET, NEW YORK,
NEW YORK 10014.

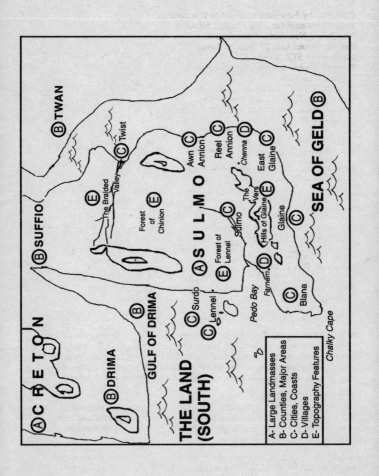

THE LAND
(SOUTH)

A- Large Landmasses
B- Counties, Major Areas
C- Cities, Coasts
D- Villages
E- Topography Features

Prologue

Basth received the call at the usual hour, just before dawn. It came as a little flutter in his mind, almost as if a voice were speaking into his ear. There were no actual words, but he understood nonetheless. The Master wanted him.

Outside the temple, the great city of Shasht was still asleep. Basth glanced out the window over the rooftops toward the sea. The city was so huge! Even after two months young Basth was still thrilled to be a part of it all. Sometimes when he looked at his shaven head, now painted gold instead of red, he had to pinch himself to believe his good fortune. He ran light-footed up the stairs to the Master's sleeping chamber and lit a lamp before hurrying inside.

In the low light the Master's skin had a waxy sheen to it. Later, he knew, this waxiness would fade and be replaced by a more lifelike color. Sometimes, when he had an attack of chest pain, the Master's skin would go grey and the veins would be visible as a network of blue threads under the skin.

"I had a dream, Basth."

"That is wonderful news, Master."

The Old One's eyes glittered for a moment. "Once I had a dream, and ten Gold Tops died the next day."

"A powerful dream, Master."

"Very powerful, Basth. But the dream I had this morning was not like that."

At the tone of his Master's voice, Basth wished he was still a Red Top back in Ectuma.

"I dreamed that my greatest enemy was coming here,

but I would fail to see him. And one day he will drive a sword through my heart."

"Heaven forfend, Master! May He Who Eats destroy them who think this could ever happen."

"Yes, that is a good thought. May He Who Eats destroy them all. Help me up, Basth. My legs aren't responding well today."

Chapter 1

Feeling sticky from the heat, Brigadier-Colonel Thru Gillo watched his regiments forming up on the parade ground after another long day of drilling with the new weapons.

The long lines represented the peoples of the Land: mostly grey-furred mots, of course, but with a few tall brilbies and brown-furred kobs among them. All wore the woven chain armor and grey trousers of the Sulmese army. Together they made up the Sixth Brigade of the Sulmo Army, composed of the twelfth and sixth regiments. Their shields, all bearing the fierce lion head of Sulmo, made a smoothly uniform front.

Since the invasion of men from Shasht the year before, the peoples of the Land had been forced to learn soldiering, or face extermination. The men of Shasht offered them nothing but the edge of the blade. Industrious folk, the mots had taken a very thorough approach to the job. Thru Gillo had been sent south by General Toshak during the winter, to help create the new army of the South that was being formed in Sulmo. Toshak remained in the north, at Dronned, where the seasoned army of the North continued to train fresh recruits.

Thru watched from a hillock directly overlooking the flat parade ground, set outside the walls of the town of Glais in southern Sulmo. He'd been impressed that day by his mots' improved abilities. Even after a long day, their formations were still crisp and their movements precise.

His personal staff stood beside him: Major Ilb, a kob from the Glaine Hills, Sergeant Burrum, a wry-humored mot from Glais, and Private Kipes, his personal secretary. All different characters, but they worked well together.

Even better, they were not prejudiced against Northerners, at least by Sulmese standards.

Down below, at the head of their battalions, were his regimental commanders: Colonel Ter-Saab, a tall kob standing clear of his other officers, and the Grys Glaine, a plump mot wearing the blue coat of his social rank. Both of them had the red dot of their rank marked clearly on their helmets.

Thru sighed. Both of these colonels were difficult to deal with, and their endless wrangling was enough to try the patience of a saint. And underneath all of that was Thru's Northernness. Toshak had warned all the volunteers that Sulmese pride would give them plenty of trouble.

The Grys Glaine had the Twelfth Regiment, raised from the streets of Glais. Ter-Saab had the Sixth Regiment, country mots from Glaine. Both regiments had come a long way since Thru had first joined them in the depths of winter. Back then they'd been little more than enthusiastic but undisciplined mobs. Now they were halfway toward their goal of being a well-drilled pair of military formations capable of taking the field against any foe.

The lines stood there absolutely still, the regimental flags flapped slightly in the breeze. Thru lifted his right hand.

Immediately the Grys snapped an order, followed by Ter-Saab, and the stentorian voices of the regimental sergeant majors bellowed the commands for attention, presenting arms and stand at ease.

Finally the regiments were dismissed and the formations broke up as everyone turned and headed off to the rows of tents pitched along the farther edge of the parade ground. Dust swirled up above the mass of helmets, and the neat lines of pikes, spontoons, and spears dissolved into chaos.

Thru turned away from the parade and headed for his own tent, set up beside the command post. He pulled off the hot, uncomfortable helmet made of wicker and painted with several coats of lacquer. New, the helmets were an important addition to the army, for they deflected arrows and saved warriors from all but the most direct blows with club or sword. Still, they were decidedly uncomfortable on a hot day.

Inside, he unbuttoned the stiff brown wool tunic, rubbed down his fur, and washed his face and hands before heading to the command tent. As expected a pile of message scroll awaited him. With a weary sigh he sat down and dug into it.

Most were reports, usually of nothing, from coastal observers. All along the Glaine coast outposts maintained a constant watch on the sea. At the slightest sign of an enemy sail, they lit their beacons and sent runners to Glais. However, for the past several weeks there had been little enemy activity off the coast. Other scrolls were letters; these he piled to one side before sorting them out.

He had hardly begun when both his regimental commanders entered, boiling with another quarrel.

"I must register a protest!" said the Grys.

"Ah, must you, now," murmured Thru, used to the Grys and his ways.

"You saw it. You saw what happened," continued the Grys, speaking in a high-pitched voice.

"I did? Both regiments performed very well. The Quarters wielding pikes have learned how to use them. The mots with spears filled the gaps very well."

Ter-Saab smiled and nodded politely. The Grys bounced up and down on his heels with visible impatience while Thru spoke, then exploded.

"We were supposed to be the lead regiment on returning to the parade ground. Yesterday the Sixth were the lead; today it was our turn. But instead the Sixth moved in front of us as soon as we turned back from the flank-maneuver practice."

"My dear Grys," said Ter-Saab. "We were positioned right beside the road. You wanted us to wait until you had all marched past?"

"And why not? It is our right."

Thru closed his eyes for a moment. It was easy to understand how the Grys had earned his nickname, the Pook of I'm Right. Endlessly prickly, always insisting on receiving the respect due him for his social rank, he was hard to work with.

Ter-Saab, however, wasn't as much help as he might have been. Endlessly condescending and quietly sarcastic, the kob from the hills could be just as difficult as the Grys.

Still, Thru comforted himself, he wasn't there to be friends with these colonels; he was there to command them. He had battle experience and they did not.

"Then, tomorrow you will exercise your right. And I will be informed before either regiment begins to march back to the parade ground so that I can be sure the Twelfth are in the lead."

The Grys smiled tightly and bobbed up and down.

"Thank you, Brigadier."

Ter-Saab's mouth drooped in resignation.

"Are we to inform you every day now, Brigadier?"

Oh, such a wily old kob, trying to set traps like that for Thru's feet.

"Of course not. From now on you will conduct the regimental etiquette without these little conflicts. We will all do our utmost to cooperate, so we function smoothly as a unit."

"Well, of course, Brigadier, I always strive for that."

"Thank you, Ter-Saab, I'm glad to hear that. Let's see that we avoid offending the sensibilities of the fine Twelfth regiment from here on."

The Grys bristled a little, but wisely kept his mouth shut.

"Now, my comments on today's drill." Thru looked them both in the eye. "The pike line of the Twelfth did very well in the close-order movements."

The Grys perked up immediately. He flashed Thru a grateful look.

"And the slanted echelon attack actually worked. When ordered to weight up the right flank, the Twelfth was easily the better regiment today."

Ter-Saab's droop became further pronounced. He stirred himself to respond. "Well, it seems I must offer the congratulations of the Sixth Regiment to the Twelfth. They have finally done something better than us."

The Grys's eyes bulged once more.

Thru thought to himself that between himself and Ter-Saab, they were capable of playing the poor old Pook like he was some kind of instrument—up, down, up, down. But Thru had more pressing demands on his time. A mountain of scrolls still awaited his attention.

"Well, then, if that's all, I'll see you at dinner. I have work to do."

And indeed, he wasn't the only colonel within five miles who had an intimidating pile of paper awaiting his attention. Command of eight hundred individuals, three quarters of them mots, the rest kobs and brilbies, produced paperwork like polder produced waterbush. Both Ter-Saab and the Grys hurried back to their own command tents.

After they'd left, Thru marveled once again just how far they'd come in the last few months. With those two as regimental commanders, it might have been a disaster. In the beginning they could barely form a column without falling into chaos. Now they could march at the double in a slanted echelon with pike units to the front. Even in mock combats the formations held up.

Of course, the main question remained: how would they hold together when they went into battle against men. Men were better at battlefield maneuver. They had trained all their lives for it, while these mots were just country folk. But at least they hoped to prevent the kind of mob chaos that had ruined all their attacks at Dronned.

They'd won that battle, but only because they'd been lucky. Luck and the sheer arrogance of man had saved the day for the army of Dronned.

He checked the coastal reports. There wasn't much of any import. A fishing smack reported some sails off Lilli Point, about ten miles to the east. There might have been sails seen in a report from another fishermot, the cog "Garvas" out of Brinilhome. Other reports were vaguer still. A shepherd near Glais had seen figures in the distance that might have been men. A farm mor on the coast had found tracks on the shore. So they went, but he read them all, just in case.

Things had been quiet since the early spring, with only three large scale raids in Glaine. By dint of fast marching and a little luck, the Sixth Regiment had actually arrived at Brinilhome in time to stop the burning of the town and to drive the attackers back to the beach. A dozen men had paid with their lives, while mot casualties had been less than five. But that had been months before, and since then there had been nothing more than these reports of sails on the horizon and mysterious tracks on the shore.

With a sigh he shoveled the message scrolls into a sack. Just then Major Ilb came in with another bag of messages.

"Oh, wonderful, just what I needed."

"Sorry, Brigadier, this lot just arrived."

"Thank you, Major. And, by the way, what is the situation regarding the Lady Alvil?"

The Alvil of Parunte was a famously wealthy old mor who owned extensive fields and wood lots along the Parun River.

"She still wants a royal indemnity for her trees. She says the orchard is one of the best in the whole valley."

Thru sighed. Getting a royal permit meant someone had to slog all the way up to Sulmo, get in line at the palace, and wangle the indemnity out of the royal bureaucracy.

If he just sent a simple written request, it would be a month before he heard anything. And by then the brigade might well have moved somewhere else and no longer need to camp in the Lady Alvil's damned orchards.

If he'd thought Ilb could be spared he might have sent him to Sulmo, but the major was dealing with a thousand things a day. Ilb was essential here at camp.

Sergeant Burrum was likewise necessary to the running of the brigade. And in Sulmo, when dealing with the desk clerks and the doorkeepers, he would not be as effective as the wily and efficient Ilb.

Kipes? But Kipes, too, was essential. He knew where all the paperwork was.

Thru put it out of mind for a moment as he examined the next report, which was about a shipment of new weapons from Sulmo: two dozen more of the small pikes, called spontoons, which had hooks as well as spearheads. The hooks allowed the spontoon bearer to pull an opponent off balance before thrusting home with the spear. The spontoons were proving popular with the mots, who were training enthusiastically at the one-two motions of pulling and stabbing.

He set it down. Well, there was progress in some directions anyway.

But, he sighed inwardly, it never seemed like enough. There would be war this summer. It was inevitable, and if the army they had built was defeated, then millions of folk could die. The men had shown that they were out to exterminate all the peoples of the Land, even the helpless chooks.

Something about a scroll farther down the pile caught his eye, and he reached and pulled it free.

His eyes widened as he saw the writing and recognized the hand. He fumbled for his knife and slit the seal.

Nuza had not written for more than a month. She had been in Lushtan when last he'd heard, still working on the production of bandage and splints for the coming campaign season.

The words swam into view as he read. She was in Sulmo, having come south with a donkey train of war supplies. She included an address in the Outer Ward of the great city. She would be there for a while, perhaps all summer; it depended on what orders came down for her. She hoped he was well, sent love and kisses, and prayed that they would see each other soon, somehow.

At once all his responsibilities, his regiments, his lines of Quarters vanished from his mind and were replaced by the thought of her. Nuza in her acrobat costume, tumbling and leaping with amazing grace. Nuza, in his arms, her body pressed close to his.

He stepped out of the tent and stared off northward toward the hills. She was just on the other side of those round purple knobs. A day's march away.

Chapter 2

The thought of Nuza so close by gnawed at him all evening. He could make it to the city in a night's hike if he pushed it. All he was doing here anyway was watching the regiments drill. And for one night he and Nuza could be together again, like in the old days, before the war destroyed their lives.

He wrote out orders for Ter-Saab and the Grys and handed them over personally. He would be back within three days. While he was gone, Ter-Saab would assume brigade command because he had been a colonel for three months longer than the Grys. The Grys made a sour face at this news, but accepted it. Ter-Saab gave the usual weary shake of his shoulders.

Thru ate a hearty breakfast an hour before dawn, then set off with a small pack, his bow and his staff, just as he might have traveled in the days before the war.

He pushed himself through the day, reached the hills in the early afternoon, and began to climb. That night he rested briefly while he ate a meal of dried bushcurd and twice-baked bread. Then, after a drink of cold water from a spring, he resumed the march under the light of the half-moon. The white chalk of the road glowed, and he followed it northward while the heavens wheeled above.

It had been almost a year now, a year like a giant wound in his life. Ever since that dismal day in the village of Sonf when she'd gone south and he'd gone north to join Toshak and the war. The coming of the men of Shasht had changed everything. The easy life of the Land had ended in a moment and been replaced ever since by war, terror, and preparation for more war.

It was hard being sundered in this way, and when time hung heavy on his hands, Thru had to fight mean and petty thoughts. Why did he have to serve in Sulmo? Why couldn't he join the bandage makers in Lushtan? Then he would be with Nuza all the time.

But then Toshak's words would come back to him and stiffen his resolve.

"Our lives are over, the lives that we knew. Until this war is over we are nothing but soldiers."

So, he wasn't "Seventy-seven-Run Thru Gillo" anymore. He was a brigade commander and he bore a heavy responsibility.

And yet, now had come this opportunity for them to be together. During a time when there was little happening in the field.

He kept up a hard pace, and long before morning he was going downhill. He stepped lively, marching for mile after mile, something he'd grown accustomed to during the past year. Something hard, almost like iron itself came up in the body and gave him the strength to go on, one foot after the other.

At dawn he stopped to drink from another cold spring and splashed some water on his face and down his back. Then he took up his staff once more and continued. By late morning he was in the farm country just south of the city. In late morning he passed through the village of Ka- chiesek and over the first of the bridges that spanned the many channels of the Sulo. The high outer walls of Sulmo were soon in view.

The white stucco buildings glowed in the southern sun. The harshness of the midday light still struck him as strange, even after spending half a year in the southern land. A long pennon flew from the gate tower, white- checked with red squares. Culpura was in the city. Anyone who needed to speak to an Assenzi was free to call on him. The Assenzi were beings of an ancient kind, smaller than mots, with lives that stretched back into distant antiquity. In most parts of the Land they were regarded as founts of wisdom. Only in Sulmo was there widespread suspicion of the Assenzi, a legacy of the reign of King Ueillim long ago.

The sight of the city spurred him on, driving his boot heels down the road. In the heat of the day, he'd removed his jacket and shirt and tied them up in his pack, so when he reached great South Gate, he stopped just long enough to rinse his fur off under the pump and put his uniform back together.

He was Colonel Gillo now, commander of the Sixth Brigade of the Sulmese army, and he had to look the part even though his uniform was tattered after sixth months of active service. His grey outer coat was newer issue and still had its nap, but the brown inner tunic was a ruin, as was his shirt. Still, he tied it all together as best he might and hoped his coat would cover the worst. Finally he adjusted the red wooden peg that he wore in the top buttonhole of his coat, which marked his rank as a brigadier colonel.

Inside the outer gates was the visible evidence of Sulmo's decline. The Outer Ward had returned to vegetable gardens for the most part. What buildings were left were scattered about like small villages inside the outer wall. The real city had retreated back inside its original walls, which were still ahead of him, two miles down the road.

The road now ran between gardens and small fields. It could as easily have been countryside as part of a great city with trees along the road, small green fields with young crops, and strips of houses, or perhaps a larger building. But everywhere, in the fields or in the houses, the old city clung to its sleepy southern rhythm. At noon, by ancient tradition, everyone ate a big lunch and then took a nap. The city didn't get going again until the middle of the afternoon. Nor was this restricted to the city itself, it was the habit throughout the Sulmo Valley.

In the winter, when he'd first taken command of the regiments, he'd had problems in getting Southern recruits back on the parade ground right after the midday meal. They'd cussed a lot about "Northern ways" back then. But they were volunteers and after a while accepted the necessity of discipline.

The only traffic he passed consisted of a few donkey carts until he entered the inner gate. Inside the old city the air bustled. Sulmo had not been able to entirely escape the upheaval produced by the invasion from Shasht.

On the Street of Charms he pushed through crowds of soldiers and workers and made his way to the warehouse on Dock Street, which was the headquarters of the new army. Fourteen thousand mots had responded to the King of Sulmo's muster. Eight thousand had now been trained and deployed across the southern counties from Blana to Reel Annion. Six thousand were still training in Sulmo. Inside he found the usual hum of bureaucracy. He handed over a small sack of letters from the mots of his regiment. Then he dug out his request for the indemnity and hunted for his friend Meu of Deepford.

Meu was now an important officer of supply, in charge of feeding the vast establishment of professional soldiers that filled the streets outside. Finding him took a little work, since Meu was hidden behind several layers of booths and offices, but he emerged immediately when he heard that it was Brigade-Colonel Gillo waiting to see him.

They embraced, took the time to look each other up and down. Both still bore the scars of their encounter with pyluk in the Farblow Hills some years before. Indeed, few mots who had come so close to armed pyluk, had lived to tell the tale. The green-skinned lizard men of the eastern deserts had a well-deserved reputation for ferocity.

"How did you find the time to come up here?"

"Well, I was actually the only one who wasn't absolutely needed."

"How long can you stay?"

"I'm going back tomorrow."

"Ah." Meu nodded. "Well, that's quite a hike."

"We're all used to it now. Glaine's a big place when you're trying to cover all of it against raids."

Meu understood. He'd been out there in the field in the early part of the winter, before being posted to his current position.

"Here's my problem," said Thru, handing Meu the paper on the Alvil's orchard back at camp. Thru explained that he needed more space for his troops to set up tents. Meu nodded briskly; this was a familiar problem.

"I think we can get this indemnity written up pretty fast. I can put in with Major Huba, who feeds those requests to the royal legal department. Huba owes me a favor or two. The King does not need to seal it personally, since it is a document of the Second Tier, you see."

"Well, that's good to hear. I absolutely have to go back tomorrow morning."

"And one night of true love, eh?"

"You've seen her?"

"Yes, she sought me out when she arrived. Wanted to know all about your adventures."

"Such as they've been."

"You were there in Bilauk together weren't you?"

"Yes." Thru shook his head to dispel the images that name brought up. For a moment Thru was back there in that ruined village, smoke still swirling up from the blackened houses. He could see the mound of heads that the men had left on the jetty. Every person in the village, bar a tiny handful of survivors, had been beheaded and their bodies taken as meat. Meu shifted uneasily on his feet.

"Yes. Well, let's go find Major Huba and get this indemnity process in motion."

Huba turned out to be a charming old brilby with white side whiskers that grew down below his chin.

"Gracious," he said. "I know the dear old Alvil of Panute. Oh, yes."

The indemnity was written up in no time, then signed and sealed. Thru and Meu parted company with a hug and a promise to dine together the next time Thru reached the city. Then Thru headed for the Outer Ward.

Whiteflower Lane was a street he knew well. On that street were a few houses and three famous inns. During the previous winter when he'd been billeted in Sulmo, Thru had visited them often. Even in wartime these kitchens turned out food in the manner of the Land.

Gardens filled with lush vegetable growth went all the way up to the edge of the street. No space was wasted. The fragrance of gardenias filled the air. He found the house quite easily, two stories of wood on a brick foundation. His knock brought her to the door.

"Thru!" was all she had time to say before she vanished into his arms. They stayed that way, rocking back and forth in the doorway for a long time.

"Oh, my love, my darling, my only Thru," she babbled as they kissed and nuzzled and kissed again. After a separation of almost a year, it was almost overwhelming to be together once more.

They sat together on the little bench at the back of the whitewashed cottage. The garden was filled with blooming asteria and wild yellow foxgloves. Thru felt alternating surges of wonder and pure happiness. This was something he'd dreamed of for most of the last year.

He saw her examining him, seeing the red pin of rank on his coat, and the frayed edges and worn cuffs of most of his clothes.

"How did you do it?" she said, somewhere between tears and joy. "I thought you would be tied up in Glaine for months."

"I had business here." He grinned at her look of disbelief.

"Really. I had to get some legal paper signed. My brigade is jammed into a tiny camp barely big enough for one regiment. We have to have more space."

Well, I'm glad you have an excuse. But couldn't you send someone?"

"I had to see you."

"Oh, Thru."

Eventually they sat together in her room upstairs, wrapped in a sheet, backs against the wall while the sun threw long setting beams through the window onto the opposite wall.

"Did you know that this day last year was the day we left Tamf for the last time? Old Tamf, the way it was." Her voice caught. There were tears on her cheeks.

"No," he whispered. "I didn't. I haven't kept track, too much to do."

By the Spirit, their whole world had changed since that day. Lovely old Tamf had been burned to the ground by the invaders.

"It seems a long time ago now. Another world."

She rested her head on his shoulder. "Sometimes I think it will never end. We will be forced to live like this forever."

"Yes, I know that feeling."

"I want to pretend that we're in the old time, before they came, before the war."

"Yes," he said, bending his mouth down to kiss her lips.

They tried not to think about the war, just for a little longer.

Later, she told him about her trip down from Lushtan, using the coast road through Suffio to Twist in the Braided Valley.

"We brought six donkeys loaded with bandages, splints, and dried herbs for poultices."

His eyebrows bobbed up and down as he thought of all the work involved in making that much bandage.

"Sad to say, but we'll probably need them."

The war and its grim consequences was hard to shut out for long.

"They will come again, everyone says so."

"There have been raids all the way to Awn Annion. Sometime this summer they'll land an army," Thru predicted. "We will have to fight them again and defeat them so utterly that they are forced to flee this part of the world."

"Have you seen them?"

"Myself, no. But one of my regiments caught some raiders fair and square, before they could even burn the town. Killed some of them, too."

"I have heard that the wolves are helping the watch."

"Thanks be to the Assenzi. They have roused all the wolves, 'tis said. They helped warn the villages on two occasions."

"Do you have enough food?"

He laughed. "Barely, it's Highnoth rations for everyone these days. But none have died of starvation. We got through the winter. We ate turnips more than bushpod, but we ate."

Later, they went out in search of a meal and stopped in at the Whiteflower Inn. They dined on bushpod pie and crumbly beeks, a Sulmo specialty, and washed it down with some thin ale.

"What happened when you took Simona to her people?"

Thru's face grew solemn. He had fond memories of the human girl who had lived among the mots for a while the previous year. The circumstances in which she had returned to her own people had not been auspicious.

"The men can never be trusted."

"I know." She was still watching his eyes.

"They took me captive. They tortured her."

Nuza was left appalled at this thought. Indeed, the ways of men were hard to comprehend.

"I met her father. He helped me to escape. He is not like the rest of them, I think."

Afterward they strolled along the lane, enjoying nothing more than each other's company and the lush scent of the gardenias that were in bloom throughout the Outer Ward.

They spent the night in her room on Whiteflower Lane.

"I have to leave early in the morning. I left Ter-Saab in charge, and he's capable enough, but I should be there."

"Of course. And I will be here. We will build a new hospital."

"How I wish I could be posted here."

"Hush, my darling, don't talk anymore," she said, sealing his lips with her own.

Chapter 3

In the early morning they took breakfast at the army kitchen by the South Gate. It was simple food, bushpods and meal mush, but there was plenty of it. Thru ate with a mind on the long march ahead of him.

"I wish this didn't have to be the way," he said, holding her hand like a drowning mot clutching at water weed. One night together seemed but an instant in time. If he let his thoughts turn to self-pity then every second seemed like a fragile flower, passing away to dust before his eyes.

"Oh, my love, it is cruel, but that is the way of our world. So much cruelty, so little love." Nuza closed her eyes. In the long winter months of separation, she had found a way to accept their fate. He had to learn to accept it, too. "We will survive this war. I know it." She reached out to stroke his cheek. "We've been so fortunate, just to have this."

They wandered for a while along the great Street of Charms, deliberately avoiding the gate. The Street of Charms had five solid blocks of shops and emporia stocked with goods both usual and exotic.

There were many emporia selling high-quality floor mats. He noticed a window showing two beautiful Misho mats, one a "Brilbies at the Gate" the other a "Mots at Prayer." In many other windows he saw the usual "Mots at Prayer," plus the traditional style of "Brilbies at the Gate." He even saw a few mats with the old "Chooks and Beetles" pattern. The same handful of pictures, repeated over and over. Only the Misho stood out with its obvious brilliance of effect and technique.

And suddenly an idea blossomed in his mind. It frightened him so much that almost immediately he shrugged it away. But it had been there for a moment. A new pattern, introducing a new subject. "Men at War" he would call it. He could visualize the work, oh, so easily!

And then it was gone, banished from his thoughts as too heretical to even be considered. But though it was dismissed, it was not quite erased. Nothing could do that.

The craft of mat weaving was organized with the customary thoroughness of his people. A handful of designs, those that had first been produced and blessed by the Assenzi many thousands of years before, were all that were ever produced. It was much the same in the other crafts, from woodwork to painting.

"Are you all right?" Nuza was looking at him with concern in her eyes.

He shook his head as if to clear it. "Yes, yes, it's just a difficult time."

They found a dry goods store that was open despite the early hour, and Nuza bought some fine Fauste cloth.

"I will make you some new trousers. By the looks of those you're wearing you need new ones very soon. You see, my love? That gives you a reason to come back to Sulmo."

They laughed for a moment and then turned away, too sad all of a sudden to look each other in the eye.

Outside, walking along, getting closer to the gate and their good-byes, Nuza was drawn to a stall selling stylish little boxes, buttons, and brooches. It, too, was open very early in the day. The stall displayed rings and other pieces of jewelry, lovely things from Mauste and Geld. Thru found a brooch for her, an antique piece, a lily worked in soft gold, with an emerald as the flower.

She fastened it to her jacket, and they admired its brilliance for a moment. The green stone accented her pale fur and grey eyes.

"I've never had anything so lovely." And right out in the open she kissed him hard on the lips. The owner of the stall gave a gasp at such scandalous behavior, but Nuza was an independent-minded mor who went her own way, and at that time of day there weren't many people on the street.

When they parted at the gate, they both understood that

this might be the last time they would see each other. They hung back. Thru stared at the ground. The desperation was visible on both their faces.

Then time ran out. His regiments needed their commanding officer present in these times when a raid might come at any moment.

"Good-bye, my love."

He squared his shoulders and set off up the road without a backward glance. It was the only way he could do it. He covered fifty, then a hundred strides.

Suddenly there came a blast of trumpets from the direction of the Royal Palace. Thru stopped and looked back. Everyone was staring off toward the tower of the palace. The trumpets continued to call frantically. Distant figures were in motion. Mots scrambled to the top of the gate tower for a better view.

Shaking his head, Thru turned back. Something important had happened. He had to find out what this emergency was before he left the city.

"What can it be?" said Nuza as he rejoined her.

"Let us go to the palace and find out."

They hurried through the crowds to the palace gate, where they found a message board set up for all to see.

As Thru read the words, it felt as if a pit had opened up in his stomach. The enemy had landed in Reel Annion. At least three thousand men. This was more than a raid; this was the invasion they had expected all summer. They were at war and he was a day's march away from his command!

In huge red letters all soldiers were ordered to prepare themselves for an immediate march to the Annion coast.

From others in the crowd they learned that the news had come by messenger pigeon that very hour. More trumpets could be heard from the palace. The city of Sulmo was shaking itself awake to face the long-expected crisis.

King Gueillo published a proclamation that was read aloud by the city criers. He called on the folk of Sulmo to go about their work with determination and courage. Now was the time they had known must come when they must rise up and defeat the invaders. Many would be called to serve. It was imperative that everyone give everything they

could to the cause, for defeat meant only one thing—
complete annihilation at the hands of the men.

More birds and runners were sent out at once to carry
the news quickly throughout the kingdom of Sulmo. Other
birds were sent north by the Assenzi to take the word to
Dronned. Within two or three days at most the news would
have spread to the remotest parts of Creton and the north.

In the streets rumors swarmed like bees on clover as
Thru and Nuza struggled through the crowds to the military
headquarters. It was said that the invaders had been defeated by the local militia and chased back to their ships.
Then they heard that the men had captured a village and
devoured its inhabitants down to the last chook, and now
they were marching through the county of Annion slaugh-
tering anyone they captured. At the headquarters building
the crowds stirred anxiously while mots hurried hither and
yon in the effort to rejoin their units.

Thru had to report his presence. As a brigade-colonel he
might be needed for any force sent out from the city itself.
He saw Nuza for the last time there, on the steps outside
the buildings.

She waved, a curious little frown on her forehead, even
while she tried to smile. He waved back and then turned in
through the big doors. Immediately he was swallowed up in
the gathering storm. The confusion outside helped distract
him from the chaos inside his head.

Mots, brilbies, and kobs jammed the passageways. Voices
sent up a roar inside. Adding to it were the trumpets and
drums going on the parade ground behind the palace. The
trainee regiments were already forming up.

The Meld of Daneep was the commanding officer of the
Royal Army of Sulmo. He had been closeted with the King
and then with the officers of the trainee regiments. Communications had been sent north at once, but it would be a
day or more before a bird returned from Dronned. The
most immediate thing was to get an army into the field and
in motion toward Annion.

Orders had been sent to the units stationed in the South
Coast counties. Each brigade would send one regiment and
retain the other. Brigade commanders would accompany

the brigade sent to Annion and leave their seconds in command with the remainder. Something like six thousand mots were in the trainee regiments and with them would go eight hundred veterans of the Royal Guard of Sulmo. They would bolster the four thousand mots in the regiments already trained and in the field. Together this force would seek to surround and destroy the human army.

That at least was the plan, Thru knew, worked out in the winter conference when Toshak and the Assenzi had come south from Dronned to confer with King Gueillo.

When the Meld of Daneep finally found a minute to see him, Thru got a roasting for being absent from his own brigade at a time like this. Angrily, the Meld ordered Thru to travel with the Royal Guard units leaving that day and rejoin his own regiments in Annion.

Within the next hour, he was marching out the gate in a column of mots armed with everything from spears and swords to ancient tridents and round shields that had not seen use in combat for hundreds of years. The mots of Sulmo had no experience of war. Peace had been the rule in the southern land for a thousand years or more.

Now they marched to survive. Defeat was unthinkable.

Chapter 4

After three days of hard marching, the army from Sulmo reached the outskirts of Reel Annion. They began to meet columns of refugees, mixed groups of mots, chooks, brilbies, and kobs, all exhausted and hungry.

They spoke in terrified tones of Man the Cruel and the devastation that was being wreaked in the coastal districts of Annion. The terror in their voices brought back unwelcome memories for Thru Gillo: the fear of being hunted for food.

From the confused accounts of the refugees, Thru had pieced together a semi-coherent tale.

The men had landed close to the tiny village of Sea Cor, which they had plundered and burned. The population had fled at the sight of the first sails and were untouched. Then the raiders had not re-embarked as had been their usual course of action. Instead, an army of men was landed. This army then moved south along the coast burning villages.

The inhabitants of these areas had fled up the valley of the Punwell on the single good road in the area, the Punwell Pike. When the column of men reached the Punwell road, they turned inland and marched upstream, pressing behind the fugitive folk.

Fortunately the Meld saw the great danger of this advance. The enemy, by chance, was heading toward Chenna, where he would stand between the two halves of the army of Sulmo. Communications between those two halves were already poor, and with an enemy army in the middle they would only get worse.

The Grys Annion was sent back along the line of the march to hurry up the stragglers at the rear of the army.

The first thing was to get the army to Chenna as quickly as possible.

In the late afternoon when the army reached the small village of Demel, Thru received a summons from the Meld. Thru responded at once, determined to show that he was concerned only with the pursuit of victory.

"Ah, Gillo." The Meld's greeting bore overtones of unhappiness.

"When I spoke to General Toshak last, he told me to make good use of you. He said you were an exemplary type. And yet, I find you far from your own brigade headquarters in this time of trial."

"Sir, I know you don't want to hear excuses. So I will make none."

Thru could bring up the Alvil's orchards, but he didn't want to. What need did they have of the orchards now, anyway? Ter-Saab and the Sixth Regiment were marching for Annion, so Twelfth Regiment were alone in Sulmo camp and had plenty of room.

"I see." The Meld seemed surprised by Thru's forthright acceptance of the blame. He dropped the topic, but Thru felt his reputation taking a beating.

"Well, I hope that it never happens again."

"Yes, sir. It will not."

"You have known General Toshak in his private life, I believe."

"Yes, General, before the war. We were in a wandering troupe, lead by a tumbler."

The "wandering troupe" was an unfortunate revelation perhaps. The Meld seemed to take an even dimmer view of Thru.

"And you were close to him during the fighting last summer."

"I think the whole army was close to him during the battle at Dronned. He covered every regiment. I think he worked harder than anyone else."

The general looked away for a moment and took a breath. Toshak had been most insistent that this Thru Gillo was an excellent soldier, and the one to talk to. The Meld had to wonder if he had the wrong Thru Gillo here.

"What would he be thinking now, if he were in our position, do you think?"

"I wouldn't presume to speak for Toshak, sir, but I would guess that he'd be concerned first and foremost with reconnaissance. Where's the enemy? How many do they have?"

"Yes, of course. Well, I can tell you that the enemy have moved up the Punwell Valley. The new estimate of their number is six thousand. The most recent report put them on the south bank of the River Pun and heading for Shimpli-Dindi."

Thru felt a stab of anxiety. Six thousand strong! That was a larger force than they'd faced before. They would have to be very careful.

"And he'd also be concerned about meeting up with the other regiments."

"As am I. I was hoping to join up with Brigadier Colss at Shimpli-Dindi, but I don't know exactly where the other brigades are. And now it looks as if the enemy will get to the crossroads before we do."

"Well, if we're that close to them, then we have to accept that they probably know we're in the vicinity."

"How so?" said the Meld, alarmed.

"Toshak always insists that we remember that the enemy will be doing his own reconnaissance work and may know more than we like about our positions. He suggests that we always work with the assumption that the enemy knows something of our position."

"Mmmm."

The Meld looked around him at the forested hills with visible unease, then took another look at Thru. Maybe Toshak had been right about this fellow.

Thru was busy examining the map, already rather worn from being studied so much in recent days. "The roads all converge on Shimpli-Dindi and then run down to Chenna, correct?"

"Yes. Chenna has a new stockade around it, and it will be held by a small force of local militia. How long they can hold out is unknown."

Thru tried to calculate the time and the distances. He

cast a glance off to the south. About a mile from Demel rose a hill called the Sow. There was a notch where her neck was and then another smaller bump called the Head. The top of her Head was bare of trees, probably eight hundred feet above the plain. It was famous all over this part of Annion as a place where wolves liked to howl on nights of the full moon.

Over on the other side of that hill lay Chenna Forest and the vital crossroads. South of there, somewhere down the road to Glaine was the other force of four thousand mots, led by Brigadier Colss. Thru knew Colss only by reputation, since Colss had command of East Glaine and Reel Annion, but that reputation was a good one. Thru imagined therefore that Colss would have his own scouts abroad and would be aware of the existence of the Shasht army on the road ahead of him. Colss was most likely moving cautiously forward, seeking some sign of the Meld and the main army.

The two forces of mots, four thousand under Colss and the six thousand under the Meld, were separated by something like ten miles. In between, and close to Chenna was the army of men, six thousand strong—too big for either of the separated mot forces to handle. They had to coalesce, but the only road lay through Shimpli-Dindi and Chenna and was likely to be blocked by the enemy army.

Most likely the enemy knew he had this advantage, too. He would seek to draw one or the other of the two mot forces into an engagement and crush that force before the other could become involved. Then the men could turn on the remaining force of mots and destroy them, too. Thru had no illusions about the battlefield skills of the larger part of the army of Sulmo. The regiments under the Meld were capable of little more than holding a defensive line. Any maneuvers would soon turn them into chaotic mobs and such ill-disciplined units would be easy meat for the well-trained men.

Suddenly a plan just fell into place in his mind. Thru pointed to the hill.

"Sir, that is the Sow's Head. Take the army up there and fortify. Make him attack you on good defensive ground. He's between our two armies, and he can probably bring one or the other to battle before we can join. So we must make him attack our stronger force first. While he engages on your front, the other half of our army must drive in and take him in the rear."

"You think he will attack?"

"That is his best option. We have to hold him off, win time to allow us to combine."

The Meld licked his lips. The terrible weight of responsibility had never seemed so heavy before.

"And what of Colss?"

"Send me to Colss, and I can advise him about the situation as you see it."

"And what if the enemy chooses not to attack us all dug in on Sow's Head?"

"Then Colss and his army will have to find a way to reach you by going cross-country. There must be hunting trails through Chenna Forest. When we have the entire army together, then we will be strong enough to defeat him."

"Yes." The Meld clearly liked that idea.

"And what if the enemy attacks Colss?"

"Then Colss must move back into the forests quickly and avoid giving battle. He would be outnumbered and outclassed."

"What should my regiments do in such a case? In your opinion, Brigadier."

"Hold fast, sir. These regiments are not likely to hold together too well during attacking maneuvers. Use the better trained regiments for maneuver, once the army has been pulled together."

The Meld was nodding. His six thousand raw youngsters, stiffened with eight hundred veterans of the Guard, could be deployed in a defensive arc on the hill. They could hold a position like that and give a good account of themselves. To ask anything more of them was to risk a loss of cohesion when faced by men with swords in their hands.

"Go, then. I will write you orders and a message for General Colss. He is to press the enemy hard, but he is to be careful. We cannot afford defeat."

The Meld gave a series of orders, and shortly thereafter

the army turned off the road and marched along narrow trails up onto the flanks of the Sow. Soon they reached the top of her Head and formed a defensive arc. Scouting parties were sent out into the forested slopes of the hill.

Thru waited for the Meld's sealed orders for Colss. Far down the valley of the Shimp he could see the temple steeple of the village of Shimpli-Dindi. Down there were men and soon there would be war.

Chapter 5

Thru and two young mot soldiers, Beerg and Natho, kept to the rocky streambeds, under the hemlock and sycamore forest. They made little sound as they sprang from boulder to boulder, stone shelf to stone shelf.

They had left Sow Hill far behind and, after cutting down through stands of pine and birch, they'd reached the stream in the late afternoon. Thereafter they'd followed the wild dipping water and then the larger stream to which it soon joined. Somewhere ahead lay Chenna, through which the stream, by then a river, would flow.

As they traveled, they glimpsed the animals of the forest. Flocks of ducks took wing from a pond. Small groups of deer bounded away at another point. Beaver slapped water in alarm, and a blue heron watched them pass its pool without moving.

Above, through the trees, they glimpsed a clear blue sky. Under such clear conditions the Meld's army would be plainly visible to the Shasht generals. Thru was sure they would take the bait. The men of Shasht were very confident of their own strength.

As they moved on down the rocky riverbed, Thru let his thoughts wander. Jumping from rock to rock he chewed at a question he often asked: Why had the men of Shasht chosen this path? Was it something inherent in Man's nature? Was that why he was known to them only as Man the Cruel?

The Assenzi spoke of an evil force, a personage that lurked somewhere in Shasht. Thru had helped them send a special message to that person. He knew only that the

message contained great power, and he hoped it would
have the desired effect.

Bu Thru had fought men on several occasions now. He'd
seen the incredible determination that men exhibited, even
when badly hurt. There was some elemental drive in men
that drove them to make war. They were conquerors, en-
slavers. They seemed to have no sense of the harmony of
life and the way of the Great Spirit. Thru wondered how
they could possibly be so bereft.

The stench of the ship on which he'd been briefly kept
captive came back to him. Perhaps living in such a stink
had driven them mad. Perhaps that was how they always
lived, packed together in huge buildings, so close that they
had no privacy. The stench of their wastes in their nostrils
every day. They had no concept of the inner life of the
spirit. They had gone insane, locked away from the natural world.

Simona, his human friend, had told him many things
while they taught each other their respective languages.
The land of Shasht had once been green and fertile. A
dozen small nations had expanded to fill the arable land,
and as a result there had been endless war, which was only
curbed by the creation of the Empire. That had been the
work of the First Emperor, Kadawak the Great. Since then
the Empire had ruled all the lands of men. Its enemies
were always broken, always brought to the temple pyramid
and sacrificed to the Great God while the multitudes bayed
below, the priests tearing open their victim's chest to rip out
their still-beating hearts to offer to their cruel and blood-
thirsty God.

And yet, these harsh people dwelled in a high city,
carved in white stone, draped in the scarlet cloth that honored the Emperor. Great song festivals were held where
choirs and musical ensembles strove to produce great
music. They produced paintings and rugs and many other
beautiful objects.

It was all a huge puzzle to Thru. How did they turn from
the harsh world that Simona described to sing of love and
the caress of the infinite?

And again, just for a moment he had that thought of the entirely new mat design that had come to him in a flash of insight. The excitement he felt at this idea left him acutely uncomfortable, as if he'd done something completely forbidden. So he shrugged it aside, suppressing the idea once more.

They came out into a place where the stream broke into dozens of channels on flat ground. Dwarf pine competed with the birches here, and they watched a pair of storks fly up in alarm.

They were a good distance from the storks. And storks were never hunted or killed except when they raided seapond. All three mots exchanged a look, but after careful study of the ground ahead of them, they moved on through the dwarf trees, across the braids of gravel in which the stream wandered.

At the far side of the open space, the stream fell more steeply. Huge hemlocks towered up above, leaving only dimness on the forest floor. After the dwarf forest it was like walking into a quiet vault.

Suddenly, Beerg froze and raised a hand.

"Look!" he whispered.

Lying on the gravel bed, beside the stream, was an old mor. She was wrapped in a thick, homespun cloak and appeared to have died peacefully, most likely from exhaustion and exposure.

"Refugee," said Natho before offering a short prayer for the dead mor.

Beerg had found tracks.

"There are many, and some are not from mot or brilby foot."

Mot eyebrows flashed up and down in the universal sign of apprehension.

Men!

They studied the ground. Beerg pointed out the details that showed which marks were made by mots and which by something else.

"May the spirit be with us," whispered Natho.

There were at least ten men somewhere ahead of them.

Before that a party of mots, many mots, had passed across the streambed.

"Scouts from their army, I guess," muttered Thru as he studied the ground.

They went on down the tumbled stone of the streambed, then again they halted. They heard sounds from up ahead. Moving with extreme care, they drew back and shifted off the streambed and into the forest. After a while they peered over a huge fallen tree trunk and saw a party of men, lounging by the side of the stream. Thru saw the straggly dark beards, the metal helmets, their swords and spears. These men were completely at ease here in the forest of Chenna. The big noses, the fleshy lips were ugly to his eyes, and Thru felt hatred course through his veins.

Natho pinched him and pointed. Thru sucked in a breath.

Tied to a tree by a length of rope were two ragged-looking young mors, youngsters no more than ten or twelve years old. They looked exhausted, with mud and perhaps blood staining their fur.

The men suddenly stirred and called out, and then from the trees on the far side came more men, carrying wood gathered from the forest floor.

With cheerful banter that Thru could understand at least in part, the men built a big pile of wood. Then they set it ablaze with the help of a splash of oil. Soon smoke was rising, and flames were licking up from the wood.

Now, to the horror of the watching mots, the men seized one of the mors, cut her free from the tree, and dragged her, screaming, to the streambed where they smashed her head with a blow from a heavy club.

As the watching mots gagged, the men cut the mor open and emptied her body cavity into the stream. Then using their swords and dirks, they butchered her into pieces that were set on sticks and placed over the fire. The stench of burning flesh filled the air, and the mots crouched down and ground their teeth.

There were ten men. The three mots had no hope of defeating them. Moreover they carried vital information that had to reach Brigadier Colss. The entire battle hung on that. And on the battle depended the fate of all Sulmo, maybe even the Land itself. And yet, they could not leave the surviving mor to his awful fate.

They waited, watching with appalled eyes while the men went about their grisly feast.

The men kept only a single sentry and appeared unafraid despite being in hostile territory. They were all focused on the roasting meat.

The surviving mor sobbed quietly beside the tree.

Thru, Beerg, and Natho made their plan, then set it in motion.

The meat cooked while the men tested it with their knives. Then they removed some of the smaller parts and shared them out. They ate hungrily and loudly with little jesting until most of it was gone. Then sitting back and picking at the major bones, they conversed in comfort while passing around a canteen.

At that point they discovered the man posted as sentry was no longer standing on the high rock. They called to him and assured him they'd left him some meat. When he still failed to respond, they stood up and cast about for him. Now they noticed that the other mor was gone. With angry cries they examined the tree and the cut rope. And then there was a shout as someone else found the sentry's body, throat slit from ear to ear.

The men exploded into action with rage. They seized their weapons and searched for the monkeys who had stolen their prey.

Ahead of them, perhaps half a mile, ran the mots and the young mor. The little mor had forgotten her exhaustion, at least for now. They stayed in the streambed, keeping a good pace, springing along from rock to rock and then running in the shallows when possible to break up the trail.

But, fifty feet ahead of them downstream, they spotted more men, a smaller group. The mots dove for cover and then studied this new obstacle.

"Four only," murmured Beerg, who had pulled the mor down beside him and had a hand over her mouth to keep her absolutely quiet.

Natho was a little farther back, hidden in a clump of alders. He had drawn his bow and notched an arrow. Now

Thru risked another look downstream. The men were still there, unaware of the mots' presence, facing the other way, walking slowly through the stream. They appeared to be alone, a small scouting party.

Thru motioned to the others that they should avoid the men by leaving the streambed and cutting across through the hemlock forested bottom to the polder land of the Wirra River. Somewhere down there, they should find safety with the four thousand mots under Colss.

Quietly they left the stream and moved carefully through the litter on the forest floor. They moved up the steep side of the streambed into a forest of hemlock and oak. There wasn't much underbrush here, so they moved cautiously from tree to tree through the shadows.

Thru was just beginning to think they had left the men far behind when a spear lanced out of the dark and Natho went down on his knees with a grunt of pain. Thru saw the shaft jutting from between Natho's shoulders the instant before he dove to the ground, pulling the mor down with him.

Beerg had gone behind a tree, drawn an arrow, and was ready to return fire. Thru rolled to the base of the next tree, a sturdy oak with sprawling roots. The mor had slipped into a crack between two boulders.

Thru drew his bow, nocked an arrow, and searched the dark pools under the trees for some sign of the enemy.

Nothing moved except insects whirring among the vine flowers, and then a dark mass flashed on his right. A javelin sank into the tree trunk just above his head. He rose and aimed at the man now running toward him with a spear aimed point first at his chest. His arrow took the man in the right eye socket, and though he kept coming for another stride he was already dead when he crashed to the ground.

Another arrow snicked off the tree trunk behind him as Thru dove for cover again. He rolled over, got to his feet with short sword ready just in time because a man was only a few steps away with his own sword ready.

Thru drove forward and they met with a ringing slam of steel on steel. The man's sword broke as the Assenzi forged and hammered steel of Highnoth cut through the cheap casting from Shasht.

Thru spun around, the man was trying to draw a knife. Thru thrust at him. The man kicked up and deflected Thru's point. Thru dodged a second kick and slashed down at the man's leg, which brought a shriek, and the man fell awkwardly among piled branches.

Another man was there, his spear missed Thru's head by less than an inch and then Thru was borne back, chest to chest until he got a hand up and ripped at the man's face. The man turned his head, a small gap opened, and Thru stabbed him in the side and felt the sword go deep.

The man sagged to one side. Thru hid behind the tree again.

The one whose leg he'd cut had rolled free and pulled himself into cover. Thru searched the darkness beyond the trees. Were there more? They'd seen four men in the river. Three were dead in front of them, for Thru could see another man lying there with Beerg's arrow in his chest.

Thru knew the men behind them would not be slow in following.

"Come on," he said, and urged the mor out of the rocks and back onto a narrow deer trail through the forest. After a while the stream curved across its bed, and they found themselves running beside it, except that now it was no longer a stream splashing down on rocks and boulders, but a sinuous coil of water, thirty feet across and deep enough to make the bottom invisible.

Thru knew there would be a polder up ahead. There usually was on streams like the Wirra. That gave him hope. The valley opened out ahead, growing wider. Thru kept reliving that moment when the man charged with his sword raised, the flash of the blade and the crunch of the blow when Thru's sword met it full on. He felt for the hilt of his weapon. The Highnoth steel had proved the better.

Beerg came up suddenly in a hurry.

"I hear them behind us."

They redoubled their efforts. The trees were thinning out.

"Look," said the little mor.

The first outlying strips of polder were visible ahead. Bright green with ripening waterbush.

They came on a party of chooks working along a drainage ditch for beetles. Thru turned to them as he ran.

"Run, my brothers, run for higher ground. Man is coming."

"Man?" squawked a young bantam.

The rest stopped pecking in the grass and looked upstream.

"Run!" shouted Thru.

The chooks fled. When chooks put their minds to running, they were among the swiftest creatures of the Land, at least for short distances. In moments they were melting away back into the trees.

Thru rejoined the others in a few strides.

Beerg was still looking back every so often.

"They can't be far now. They know where we are, I think."

Thru agreed.

Now there was walled polder beside them, and dozens of small crayfish ponds for producing that staple of the Annion cuisine.

And just then the men broke into view at the far end of the cleared ground. They gave harsh whoops at catching sight of the three mots and broke into a sprint.

Now it was a race, and the mots were tired, particularly the mor, whose strength was finally beginning to fade.

Sensing her inability to continue, Thru stopped her with a hand on her shoulder, bent down, picked her up, and slung her over his back. He could still run, but more slowly than before. He shifted her weight, centered himself under it, recalling a long-ago class of Master Sassadzu's. He had to let her weight become part of his own. As he did so he found it easier to increase his speed. Beerg had fallen back a little to try and cover them with his bow, but some of the men had bows, too.

Thru drove himself on, each leg digging for purchase, accepting the weight and then driving forward. The roofs of the town weren't far off. Surely the mots of the southern force would be in Chenna by now.

Recalling again Master Sassadzu's teachings in kyo class,

he found the easy rhythm between a walk and a run, where his body worked most efficiently.

The roofs of Chenna seemed to float there forever, unattainably far away. There was a row of tall poplar trees planted along the canal running through the town. The trees seemed to go past with aching slowness. The men were only a couple of hundred yards behind. Their howling was horrible.

At the bend the canal curved back toward the main river channel, which it joined just above Chenna Bridge.

The roadway curved past the bend and entered the village. There wasn't a soul to be seen. Thru's heart sank as they stumbled past the houses.

At about the same time his legs started to give out. He was almost done. He looked about wildly for a place to hide. Beerg galloped up and pushed open the front door of a small house by the side of the road.

"In here."

There wasn't time for anything else. If they had to, they would make their last stand there. Thru promised himself that he would kill the little mor if it came to that. She'd not be taken alive.

He lurched inside, dropped the mor in the corner, then whirled back to join Beerg, who was in the doorway. Had the men seen anything? Breathless, they waited for a few seconds. But the spirit was still protecting them, for the men still had not rounded the bend. Beerg shut the door, and they retreated down into the cellar, where they pushed the mor into a narrow space behind a stack of root bins. They hid themselves behind a winepress in front of the bins.

A few moments later they heard the dull thudding of the men running by. The men were no longer whooping. They had lost sight of their prey.

Thru heard a hard voice say clearly, "Where are the fornicating monkeys?"

Another, louder voice shouted, "Fan out, search the houses!"

"They could be anywhere in this stinking warren," said

a third, opening the door upstairs and looking into the main room.

Thru tensed, hand on the hilt of his sword. Was this where he would die? In a dark cellar, like a cornered rat?

They listened to boots stomp across the floor above. They paused, each side listening acutely for the slightest sound. Then the boots stomped back. The door crashed shut again. The man had never even seen the narrow entrance to the cellar.

The mots crouched down and exhaled very slowly. The little mor wriggled out of the space behind the bins, climbed into Thru's arms, and pressed her face into his shoulder. She was trembling. They heard the men go on down the street. There came a loud crash somewhere, and some hooting and yelling. Then that second voice could be heard again, giving orders.

The young mor's eyes were glazed. She was breathing in little shallow gasps. Thru hugged her to his chest.

"What's your name?" he whispered.

"Issa."

"Issa, I want you to start taking long, deep breaths. . . . Start now . . ."

Thru showed her how to calm her breathing.

"Just think about the air you're breathing."

The mor's breathing began to deepen.

They heard more shouts. She tensed once more in his arms.

And then suddenly there was a loud increase in the shouting. She dug her face into his shoulder as if to block it out.

Then they heard feet running back the way they had come. There was a great urgency to the running, a voice shouted something that Thru did not understand, and then there was silence.

Seconds ticked by, then a minute. Thru crept up the steps and peered out the window in the front room. The road outside was empty. He whispered down to the others that the men seemed to have gone.

He pulled the front door open a crack.

And then there came other footsteps, stealthy, moving

along the side of the house. Thru closed the door, drew his sword, and waited behind it.

Figures were passing by the house. Thru peered through the cracks in the window shutter and saw mots, with bows drawn, cautiously moving down the street, scouts from Colss's force.

Chapter 6

Thru found Brigadier General Colss in a barn on the southern edge of the town. Beerg and little Issa waited by the door. Colss took in Thru's torn coat and ruined trousers with pursed lips and raised eyebrows.

"Welcome, Colonel Gillo. Your regiment will be glad to see you."

Thru had to accept that he deserved the implied rebuke.

"I hope so, General. I'm sorry I wasn't there when the call came. Here is a message for you from the Meld."

"And I'll bet the old Meld gave you hell, too," said Colss, taking the scroll.

As he read it, Colss's demeanor underwent a dramatic change. Before he'd finished reading he'd unrolled the map resting on the portable table to check various positions. When he looked up again, it was with considerably more respect.

"The Meld says you know the situation and can advise me."

"Yes, sir." Thru pointed to the map. "As you can see all the roads meet at Shimpli-Dindi. We ran into an enemy patrol about here." Thru pointed to the woods northwest of Chenna. "That leads me to think the enemy army is massed somewhere between here and Shimpli-Dindi."

Colss pointed to the Sow Hill. "The Meld is positioned here?"

"Yes. His regiments are too raw for anything more than defensive work."

"And the enemy may number as many as six thousand?"

"Some estimates put it that high. Possibly a second force was landed without our knowledge."

"Mmmm. So the enemy is in the middle between our forces. You think he will attack the Meld?"

"I thought so, but those scouts that chased us here will report your presence. That may change things."

Colss nodded thoughtfully. His big brilby brows were furrowed in concentration as he thought about the battle that was coming.

"The little mor?" He said with a glance over to the door where Issa waited beside Beerg.

"We found her in the forest The men had captured her and her sister."

Colss paled around the eyes, waiting for the rest of the story.

"They killed and ate her sister."

Colss stared off into nothingness for a moment while he tried to master his anger. "They shall have nothing from us except cold steel. I will take no prisoners."

They returned to study the map. After a few minutes Colss ordered more scouts to pick their way north along the road. He wanted to know the location of the enemy force.

Issa and Beerg, meanwhile were given food and medical care. Beerg had some cuts and scratches. Issa was very hungry, not having eaten properly for days. Thru stopped briefly beside the young mor, who was emptying a bowl of hot bushpod paste.

"Go with the spirit's blessing, young Issa."

"Thank you, sir. Thank you for what you did."

They clasped hands for a moment, and then he left her in the hands of the army cooks. Now he had to rejoin his own regiments.

Making his way through the army, he came upon his own mots at the side of the road just north of Chenna, where they were taking a quick meal. He found Ter-Saab and the other officers drawn up and awaiting his inspection. He'd been spotted approaching down the lane. The story of his encounter with the enemy in the forest had already spread, and he was cheered by many of the mots as he passed.

He responded with his best salute and then moved along the line of officers, each standing stiffly to attention, as if he'd never been away. He'd let them down by being absent

when the call came, but he was back in time for the fighting, and along the way he'd added to his reputation by
saving that young mor. The story of their flight through the
forest had spread wildly in the ranks. He could see a renewed pride for him, their brigadier, in every eye.

Ter-Saab was smiling broadly when it was done and they
could talk alone.

"They'll fight to the death for you now."

Thru was startled a little by that idea. Then he chuckled,
a little defensively.

"Well, we're all going to be fighting for our lives pretty
soon. There's six thousand enemy soldiers just up the road,
and they know we're here."

Ter-Saab whistled.

Thru turned back to more mundane matters, such as the
morale of the other regiment in his brigade, still back at
camp in Glais.

"So, how did the Grys take the news?"

"Ah," Ter-Saab tugged at his cheek fur. "Well, he was
somewhat indignant at having to stay in Glaine. He's waiting for the order to follow on."

"Mmm, well, we could probably use all the other regiments. We're not in a good position. They'll be getting the
call soon enough I'd wager."

"We outnumber the enemy."

"But he is between the two halves of our army. And
only half our army is capable of maneuver. The rest are raw
recruits. If the men get in among them, they might break."

"Well, we can do better than that."

"Yes, I'm confident in this regiment. But we're nowhere
up to the level of the enemy's training."

Ter-Saab tugged at his cheek fur. He knew there was no
answer to that.

"So," said Thru, "what's our strength now?"

"At the morning count we had 817 effectives, 12 in medical tent."

"That's pretty good considering you've been on the road
for days."

"These are hill mots and brilbies. Tough as old kob hide
they are."

"They'll need to be. Let me show you the dispositions."

Ter-Saab unrolled his own map, which covered the western half of Annion county.

An hour passed while Colss waited for better scouting reports. Thru sat under a tree and rested from the exertions in the forest. A meal of bushpod paste and dried biscuit was brought around with a pot of hot tea to wash it down.

A messenger arrived from the scouting parties. Colss immediately requested Thru's presence in the command post. When Thru got there, Colss had a larger scale map opened on a folding table.

"Well, Colonel Gillo, we have no positive sign of the enemy. Scouts went all the way up to Shimpli-Dindi, too."

Thru was surprised. "Then either I'm wrong about those scouts we met in the forest, or the enemy is already moving against the Meld."

"Which is what I'm thinking. He saw the Meld in position up there and decided to have a go at him. Our job is to move right up behind them and attack them from the rear, force them to split their force."

Little alarm bells were ringing for Thru. They were now engaged in the most deadly game, probing through these forests for an enemy capable of destroying either half of their army.

"The scouts saw nothing?"

"They saw signs of the enemy's passage, all the way up and down that road. But they didn't see the enemy."

"He could be withdrawn into the woods."

"I don't think so. I think he's going for the Meld, and we've got to hurry up that road and stop him."

"Yes, sir."

"Catch him between two stones and crush him!"

The orders went out, and the mots were up and moving, with an eager spring to their steps. This was what they had been trained for all winter. Now was their chance to avenge Creton and Tamf.

They advanced down a straight stretch of road with flat polder off to their right, bordering the river. They crossed the Chenna Bridge and went on through the village, which, though empty was untouched. Beyond the village the road ran between meticulously kept fields bounded by wooded hills. The enemy were not in sight; however, along the road debris of all kinds had been tossed aside. They saw scraps of clothing, plundered from a mot village, fragments of bushpod, and empty sacks that had once held dried apples.

The mot regiments moved up the road in a long column. The Sixth Regiment was in second place, with the Fourteenth in front and the Second right behind. The Fourteenth set a good pace. In fact, the Sixth were slowly losing ground.

Thru had dropped back to talk with Ter-Saab about this. The Sixth were tired, yes, they were all tired, but there was a fight coming today and they had to be ready for it. Thru wanted his mots to pick up the slack, at once.

Suddenly there was a shout; heads came up.

Scouts were running down from the nearest wooded hill, and were waving their arms wildly. Thru felt a sinking sensation in the pit of his stomach.

Bugles blew up and down the columns. The regiments crashed to a halt. Orders went out at once to turn to the right and form in defensive alignment.

Thru saw Colss hurrying past, flanked by worried-looking aides. He met the scouts halfway across the nearest field. There was a hurried conference and more orders came down. The men were coming; they were hidden in the trees off the road.

Thru felt a thrill of dismay. They had marched into an ambush. Worse, they were strung out on the road with the broad river at their back. The enemy hoped to trap them here and destroy them with his superior numbers.

And then the men broke out of cover from the trees. A long line of them, their armor glinting in the sunlight, their long red banners unfurled and flapping in the wind, and the sound of their drums throbbing through the air.

Thru felt the tension rise. Here they came. Now would be the decision. More flags appeared, dozens of them, as more regiments emerged from the trees. Thru realized that six thousand might be an underestimate. Skirmishers, peltasts with bows and javelins, were hurrying forward to make contact.

Mot archers were sent forward, too, and soon shimmering

arrows were whistling through the air. As the arrows fell among the ranks a mot here, a brilby there, staggered and fell.

"Prepare to receive the enemy!" came the command from Colss.

The pikebearing Quarter moved to form the front line. Behind them was a line of mots armed with two throwing spears. Behind them was the third line, mots armed with spear and shield who would move forward to engage when and if the pike line was ruptured.

In that event the big kobs and brilbies who wielded the pikes would move to the rear and form a new line with whatever weapons were available.

They had practiced these maneuvers countless times. Thru prayed that they could execute them now when their lives depended on it, when the chaos and the tension could make mots panic and run if their discipline broke.

The archers fell back and filed through the lines. The enemy skirmishers had retired as well. Now the long lines of men marched closer under the ominous scarlet banners with the white fist of Shasht raised high.

Mots waited, as calmly as they might, shields and spears ready. At the order they lifted their spears into place.

The men now gave a great shout and broke into a run. The drums were banging insanely behind them, and their war cry echoed off the forested hillsides.

Arrows began to fall among the mots, so they raised their shields. Mot archers were already pacing their ranging shots among the advancing horde.

Coming at a run now, the lines of men were still holding firm. They had their throwing spears at the ready, their shields bobbing as they ran. Spears flew between the closing lines, here and there a man fell. Mots sagged and crumpled as spears found gaps between shields.

Then the men came up against the pikes.

They swung shields and engaged with their spears. The pikes and spontoons were wielded by the strongest brilbies and kobs. They pulled and jabbed, keeping the men at bay. The momentum of the charge was dissipated. Thru felt a surge of hope. The lines of men piled up just at the outer range of the stabbing pikes. A huge clatter went up as men used shields and swords to try and divert those long, vicious pikes and get in close. Screams of agony and triumph announced the success of the pikebearers as they sought to hook or stab their opponents.

Here and there, though, the men got through. They were veterans and they'd fought against massed pikes before. A skillful parry of the pike, perhaps driving it aside with the shield and the spearman, was inside the range of the pikebearer. Another shove, a step or two, and the spear or sword could be buried in the chest of the pikebearer.

This was where the mots in the second line came forward to engage, pushing past the pikebearers. However, this tended to break up the pike formation, and that allowed more men to push in past the lethal pike points. Mots and brilbies died as the lines coagulated and the formation broke up.

Colss had waited too long to order the pikebearers to withdraw. In truth, they lacked time to execute any such maneuver. Pressed this hard by men skilled at turning aside a pike, they could do nothing except struggle to hold the front.

But after just a few minutes of this furious battering, the pikes had been abandoned, broken off or their bearers forced back into the general mass of mots. The pikes had proved a failure, despite the training.

The men were better trained, but their superiority was dissipated in the brutal slugging match that developed. So the battle teetered here, neither side gaining an advantage, while every so often a combatant would stagger back and sit down, stabbed too badly to continue.

Now the enemy began to use their superior numbers, concentrating the weight of their attacks at either end of the line of mots, forcing them back into a U that was anchored on the river. Inside the U was a stretch of polder, broken up by low stone walls across the fertile muck.

The ring of sword on sword was coming more and more often as spears were given up in the tighter press. Within the press it was becoming very difficult to move. The mots went back, step by step, but they were stubborn and exacted a toll from the men who pressed forward. The dead continued to accumulate.

Thru saw the danger of the slow movement backward. The U would contract until the mots were eventually crowded against the stone walls of the polder. Their formations would break up against those walls, and they would be slaughtered in the confined spaces.

He pulled Ter-Saab aside.

"Have to counterattack. Before we get crushed into those walls."

Ter-Saab had seen the problem as well.

"Get two hundred mots," said Thru. "We're going to surprise them."

"Easier said than done," said Ter-Saab, looking at the sprawling lines, locked in combat.

"Get it done!"

Thru turned away to organize a line of archers. He wanted a sudden storm of well-directed fire at a narrow part of the enemy line. The archers were to be thrust into the heart of the fight, where they could make sure of their targets.

As it happened, Thru and Ter-Saab were given a gift. For a moment there was a spontaneous separation of the lines, both sides drawing breath.

Ter-Saab used it to pull a Quarter into shape. His big voice was unmistakable as he bellowed orders to whip the mots into four short lines. Archers came forward to take up places at the ends of these lines. The order was given, and just as the Shasht drums started, the mots drove forward. The front line parted, the assault group burst through and attacked the enemy line.

The tip of the assault was borne by a dozen kobs and brilbies carrying spontoons. They hooked and pulled and stabbed and kicked their way through the opposing line. In a matter of minutes the enemy regiment was broken into two halves. The mot archers fired along the lines and took many victims.

The enemy horns wailed with a frantic edge, the drums thudded, and stentorian voices yelled orders, for the Shasht line was broken.

Another regiment came hurrying across from the center to fill the gap, but for the moment the intruding assault group was free to turn the lines on either side and break up the entire enemy formation.

Training had paid off. The attacking Quarter had kept a vestige of organization. The mots of the first line went into defensive deployment, while the rest turned on the men to their left and right and enlarged the breach in the lines of the enemy regiment.

Suddenly the whole fight broke open as the men's lines collapsed completely. The mots of the rest of the line pressed forward, spears stabbing into the confused and broken masses in front.

Men died in exactly the way that Thru had seen so many mots die on the field at Dronned when their formations broke up. The side in chaos, with soldiers getting in each other's way, was the side that took the casualties. But now the enemy's reserve regiment was ready to engage, and the mots of the Sixth came to a halt. Orders went out for them to fall back to preserve the main battle line.

Alas, as can happen with relatively untrained troops, the grand but terrible energy of battle had overwhelmed their discipline. Having the hated enemy on the run and vulnerable to their spears was so intoxicating that they could not be stopped. They kept pressing, moving farther apart from the main line.

The enemy reserve regiment was coming on fast and would envelop the assault group of mots in a few moments. Thru saw the disaster looming.

"Come on!" he roared, drawing his own sword and driving all the mots around him, into the fray. "Forward, we have to hold them off!"

About fifty strong, including Thru's own brigade staffers, they sprinted forward to bolster the assault group, arriving just as the enemy regiment took a grip. Thru found himself holding the left flank of the Quarter, and immediately engaged by spearsmen.

He had his sword but no shield and could only parry spear thrusts as they came in. A brilby joined him, and then another, armed with a stump of a pike that he wielded like a club, hammering a spearsman into the ground with a terrific overhand blow.

Thru knocked aside a spear thrust, then felt a shield slam into his chest. A powerful man heaved him back, the spear thrust came down. Thru knocked it aside, and got a hand over the edge of the shield and tried to pull it down. The man snarled and slammed his helmeted forehead down on Thru's fingertips.

Thru heard himself howling in pain, while he hit the man on the head with the sword, but the blow slid off the helmet. Still it dazed the fellow, and Thru was able to shove back the shield.

The brilby on his left suddenly crumpled, a spearhead erupting from his side. A man was trying to pull his spear free. Thru struck with his sword, took the man in the shoulder. There was a scream in his ear, the spearsman hit him with the shield again, and he felt the spear slice across his arm, but miss his ribs.

Something hit him hard across the back of the head, but his backhand with the sword took the spearsman in the face and the man fell away howling in a spray of blood.

Another man was in his place, another was thrusting at him. Thru dodged, struck back, was joined by more mots who thrust in on either side and reinforced the flank. The stabbing spears withdrew, the mots attacked.

Suddenly there came a change of phase, rippling through the enemy lines. They had lost the momentum of their thrust. With well-trained precision they drew back to regain their formation.

Running up and down in front of the mass of mots, Thru and Ter-Saab screamed, shoved, and even slapped at them with the flat of the sword to get them turned around and moving back to the main line of the regiment.

The mots were on fire with battle. They could barely hear the commands shouted into their faces. But after intense work by the officers, they gave way and tumbled back to the main line. The mot army's front was reknit: spontoon bearers to the front, spear throwers behind them.

Almost immediately the men on their front charged, hoping to catch them on the hop while the mots reorganized. They came in with a determined thrust, but the spontoons proved deadly; being smaller and lighter than the pikes, they could be worked more quickly and the best brilbies with the spontoon were unbeatable. Now the fighting became intense right along their line.

Thru was in the thick of it, unable to disengage and return to the command post. It was close work with sword and spear, hard, dangerous, and confusing. When the two sides drew back again for a breather, he noticed that he'd taken a hard blow to the right shin, which was bleeding freely. His fingers were also bleeding. He'd lost a nail.

Around him the lines of the Sixth Regiment reformed as everyone found their own unit commanders. What had been total chaos was reshaped into something resembling a regiment.

Thru saw that Ter-Saab was still alive, still fighting, still bellowing orders as the units coalesced once more.

Horns blew on the Shasht side. The men on their front withdrew to the limit of bow shot and stood behind a wall of shields. More men were in motion behind them as the enemy prepared another assault column.

It would be a minute or two before they were ready. Thru took the opportunity to run across to Colss's command position. It took him just a few moments to sprint along behind the regiments, but when he reached the table, set beneath the brigade and army banner, he found disaster.

Colss was on the ground, dying in the arms of a sergeant. A stray arrow had taken him in the neck, penetrating clear through to the other side.

Crouched down beside the dying Colss was a nervous-looking Colonel Floss, a Sulmese aristocrat now grappling with the reality of command in the middle of a battle.

Lieutenant Chillespi was also there, the efficient youngster who ran Colss's staff.

"Brigadier," said Chillespi as Thru came up. Thru took it all in with a single glance. Floss was floundering, but prickly; Colss was done for. The pool of red around him was overwhelming. Despite the efforts of two orderlies, he was dying.

"General Colss is unable to speak, sir."

"I can see that, Lieutenant." Thru turned to Floss.

"Colonel, we must fall back over the stone walls at once. We can't allow ourselves to be trapped against them."

Floss saw the walls, but was obviously afraid of trying to withdraw in the face of the Shasht army.

"How?"

"Now's the moment. They're reorganizing before they attack again. We will simply pull back and keep moving. The enemy stood down, they're getting their breath back and putting together a fresh attack. You hear those horns?"

Floss licked his lips. "Yes, what do they signify?"

"Those are regimental horns; I hear two different pairs. It's a big attack they're planning, but that means it will take a half a minute. If we hurry."

Floss stared at him.

"But if they're gong to attack, we should make ready."

"We need to be behind those stone walls. We don't want them at our backs."

Floss still hesitated. Thru didn't wait, but simply turned to Chillespi. "Orders for the army. Moving to the rear. All units are to withdraw over the stone wall into the polder. Understood?"

"Yes, sir."

"But, wait, who are you to take command?" said Floss.

"Someone has to, or we will all die here."

Floss stared back at him, the indecision writ large on his face.

Thru's order went out, and was obeyed. Thru was in effective command.

"Everyone, back behind the walls, at the double!"

And they went, at a run. Crossing the walls in a mass and forming up on the other side with the low wall in front of them now.

The Shasht army leaped forward after them, but too late to take advantage. The clash came when the walls were between the two armies and the fight stabilized there, the whole line ringing with the sound of steel on steel while curses and cries of pain rose up in two tongues.

The mot line held. There were incursions, but each time, the mots drew strength from other units and counterattacked and threw the men back over the wall. After a half hour of combat, the men drew back and the mots surveyed the scene behind an unbroken shield wall.

They had held, but they had paid a price. Both sides had left more than three hundred dead on the field. In places they were heaped up three or four deep.

As soon as the men had drawn back out of bow shot, Thru ordered the wounded to be evacuated. They were brought back through the polder lanes to the riverside and then ferried downstream in the boats of the watermots of Chenna.

Thru himself went to study the river. Around the bend the polder gave way to wild water, a patch of the river bottom left uncultivated. While he investigated, an old river mot came up from the polder to help.

"You soldiers can climb out through the reeds down there. They be very thick reeds in there now."

Thru nodded, the seed planted in his head.

"Thanks, old-timer, that's good advice."

Thru knew he had to get these regiments away from this battle. With their superior numbers the men would eventually push them against this river and annihilate them there.

He decided to risk everything on a footrace to the crossroads at Shimpli-Dindi. If they could get there first, then they could reach the Meld first, and then things would be different.

Of course there were no boats left, so they would have to swim. Even their carts would be thrown into the river and left to float downstream. Same with the donkeys. They might not want to, but it was better than being left for the men, who would probably eat them.

He called Chillespi to his side and began to set up the orders that would be required. The wild area began with a great growth of willows. The mots need only swim down that far and from there get on the road to Shimpli-Dindi. At a stroke they'd put a half mile between themselves and the Shashti men. After that it would be a footrace.

Chapter 7

Working in the mots' favor was the fact that the men had absorbed a lot of punishment in the fighting. Once they had penned the monkeys into a space alongside the river, they were ready to settle back and take a breather.

Cook fires were started. Wounded mots were dragged in and tortured to death to provide a little entertainment.

As darkness fell, the drumming began that signified the slaughter. While the men crowded around to watch the grisly rites, Thru set his plan into motion. Mots rose up quietly and began thinning out the lines. Thru was relieved to see that this was done with discipline and in almost complete silence.

With the screams of their comrades in their ears, the mots filed down to the river. There they handed their shields and spears over to the boats before setting out to float or swim around the bend to the wild water. Fortunately the river was calm and placid and easy to swim.

Once around the bend the whole nature of the land changed character dramatically. Instead of the uniformity of flat polder with small hedges and short walls, trees and mudflats abounded. A multitude of frogs filled the air with noise.

Here, under the trailing branches of the willows, the mots pulled themselves to the riverbank and hauled out onto the muddy shore.

One by one, the regiments, wet, muddy, but reunited with weapons and shields, eventually moved up the road, marching for Shimpli-Dindi as rapidly as they could go. All undetected by the Shashti, who were too interested in the gruesome fun that was being had around the fires.

Within a half hour the line at the polder wall had thinned to a handful. Thru watched anxiously for any sign that his maneuver had been detected. This was the vulnerable time; an enemy attack now would scupper his small force. But the men were too busy roasting the bodies of mots and brilbies for their supper to be vigilant.

Now the last line of mots fell back, leaving their shields and a few scarecrows set up as a final illusion. They ran down the narrow polder lanes and waded out into the cold water. Thru was one of the last. There was still no sign the enemy had detected anything.

He floated along, with an occasional kick to keep his head above water. Around him a dozen other mots swirled like the dead leaves of fall. His sword weighed him down somewhat, but his wicker armor buoyed him up. He kept an anxious hand on his sword handle, not wanting to lose it in the river.

Then came the bend in the river, and the willows. Thru reached up to the trailing branches, already stripped of their leaves by so many grasping hands. Carefully he halted his drift downstream and began moving in to the shore. At last he felt his foot ground on the muddy bottom. A few more strides and he splashed out onto the dark riverbank.

Like the others around him, he barely paused to empty his boots of water and then it was up the bank, through the bushes, and on along narrow trails through dense thickets.

At last they emerged onto more open space and found the road ahead, visible as a line of grey-and-white flint under the moonlight. A long line of mots and brilbies, wet, bedraggled, but alive and in motion marched toward Shimpli-Dindi.

Thru hurried up the road, trying to ignore his bleeding shin. Encountering Chillespi and the other junior officers of the staff, he learned that the maneuver had succeeded almost completely. They had lost some mots who'd been swept on around the bend of the river. But the army had survived, they were on the road and marching at a great pace for Shimpli-Dindi. However, there was no sign of Colonel Floss.

Of course, there was plenty of confusion, some units

were mixed up with others, but that didn't matter. They were all marching northward and they had lived to fight again another day.

Ter-Saab had the Sixth Regiment organized and marching well, toward the front of the column. When Thru came up to him, the tall, kob saluted and congratulated him on the success of the maneuver.

"Looks like it worked perfectly, Brigadier General. We've given him the slip."

"Mustn't count the chooks before they hatch, Colonel, but this is a good pace. If we can keep this up, we'll get to the Meld's camp before they can catch us."

"Everyone's well fed, we're strong enough now. Have to see how we respond in a few more days now that we've lost our food."

"Hopefully, the Meld can feed us."

The Sow's Head was visible now, a hump sitting in front of the larger mass of the Sow herself. The Meld's fires, glowed red on the smaller dark hill, inviting them to their warmth.

Chillespi came running up with a scout beside him.

"News from the enemy front, sir!"

"They are coming. They left everything, fires . . . everything."

"But we have a lead?"

"Two miles, sir."

Not much, thought Thru, but it might be enough. He corrected himself, it had to be enough!

Chapter 8

Through the long hours of that night the race continued, pitting the battered but defiant mots of the southern command against the veteran soldiers of Shasht.

In the space between the two armies, a fluctuating band between a mile and two miles deep, scouting parties sniped and ambushed each other in endless small tussles.

For the mots and brilbies of the southern regiments, the march was literally a race against death. Anyone who fell out, or collapsed, would die when the men came upon him. This kept many marching despite the agonies of exhaustion or wounds. A few, too badly wounded to keep up the pace, elected to hide in the woods. Others asked for the mercy of a sword thrust through the heart.

And then, at last, some time past the midnight hour, Thru was able to send his regiments off onto the sheep trails that lead up to the Sow's Head. Parties from the Meld's regiments were there to guide them. As they pushed, panting, up the rutted tracks they came under the protective cover of a larger force, drawn up to confront the Shashti.

When they reached the top of the hill, they found that the Meld had already dug a ditch and raised a rampart. The Meld's army was ready for the fight. As the exhausted ones marched into the camp, the Meld Army cheered. Their spirits lifted, the worn-out mots were given hot food and tea, though many simply sprawled headlong and slept like the dead.

Thru found the Meld waiting for him at a command post set up in a large tent. Just outside a fire burned, and someone pressed a cup of hot tea into his hands.

The Meld was red-eyed from lack of sleep. Thru could

see by the firelight the lines that had been etched into the Meld's face.

"Congratulations, Brigadier. It seems you've seen all the action today."

"We certainly have, General. I pray I don't have too many more days like this one. But, we'll be busy enough tomorrow, I'll wager."

"I was sorry to read of Colss's loss. He was a good soldier."

"The ambush caught us unawares. Our scouts passed up the road, but didn't pick up their sign. They used deer trails, or walked in streams."

"Casualties?" The Meld was bracing for the worst.

"Heavy, I fear. Maybe five hundred. We sent many wounded down the river in boats, but our total strength now is thirty-five hundred."

The Meld swallowed. Their advantage in numbers, already slim, had grown more slender still.

"And how many do you estimate the enemy has now?"

"At least five, maybe six thousand."

The Meld rubbed his chin. Thru could feel the older mot's unease.

"Will they attack?"

"Oh, yes, at first light. They will come right at us."

"What would Toshak do, do you think?"

"It would depend on the dispositions of your forces, sir. But he would expect an attack. The Shasht generals have always shown that they like to take the initiative. By attacking you he will keep you on the defensive."

"But he will waste his strength against our defenses."

"He will accept a certain amount of loss; however, he will also be confident in the abilities of the men. They broke our pike formations quite easily."

The Meld stared into the fire, rubbing his hands anxiously. Thru was reminded of a mouse.

"You have done well, Brigadier Gillo. I want you to continue as commander of the Southern Force, although for now your regiments will be used to reinforce mine. Understood? You will report directly to me."

"Yes, sir." Thru realized the Meld was naming him as a

successor to the command of the whole army in case the Meld should die. He exchanged a glance with the aristocrats who were in the ascendancy in the Meld's general staff. Would they accept an outsider as commander in chief if it came to it?

Thru went over the maps with the Meld, tracing out the line of the recent march. Scouts soon reported that the Shasht army had halted on the road and built a camp. Aggressive scouting was reported all around the Sow's Head position.

The army was laid out in a circular position, with the strongest line facing the road and the sheep tracks that lead up to the hill-top. The Meld sent scouts ahead with pickets to slow up the enemy's advance on the sheep tracks. Thru needed only to add words of encouragement. Whether they had any effect, however, was hard to say.

Eventually Thru reached his own command post, set up by Lieutenant Chillespi. The officers of his southern regiments were summoned.

"We are going to fight in the morning, I would say. The Meld wants us to hold back, maintaining a reserve force. We expect the enemy will come up at first light and attack from the direction of the road. Any questions?"

"I have some walking wounded who need surgery."

"Talk to Chillespi, he's been working to get help for our wounded."

"I have twenty mots without shields," said Colonel Ury of the Fourth Regiment. Thru made a note to ask the Meld's staff if there were any extra shields available.

"I have a dozen pikebearers with broken pikes. I need new spontoons," said another, Bekk of the Fifth. Thru made another note for the Meld's staff, all of which were swiftly taken away by a runner.

After a few minutes the meeting broke up and the officers returned to their regiments. The mood was grim, but still hopeful.

Thru finally found himself with some time to sleep. He lay down in a corner of the command post, wrapped in a blanket, and slept from the moment he laid his head on the ground.

All too soon he was shaken awake. A young mot in a very new uniform coat was leaning over him.

"Sir, the Meld wants to see you. The enemy is coming."

"Right, right," he muttered, struggling to sit up. "What is the hour?"

"Be dawning soon, sir."

"Thank you, soldier."

Thru pulled himself to his feet, pulled fragments of straw off his shirt and trouser and shrugged his coat over his shoulders. Ignoring the aches and pains from the day before he made his way to the general's command post.

The Meld had obviously slept in his chair, beside the map table. Now he was drinking cup after cup of hot tea while studying the reports coming in from the front.

"Good morning, sir."

"Morning, Gillo. The enemy are formed up, and they seem intent on a frontal assault straight up from the road."

"They are confident. They have good reason to be."

The Meld allowed himself a small smile. "Well, we'll have to see if we can change that, eh?"

They waited. More reports came in indicating that the men were marching directly up the slope, pushing through the thickets, trying to keep their formations organized, which would not be easy as the slope increased.

Now they could hear the war drums and horns, a steady thrub-thrubba-thrub that billowed up ominously from the direction of the road.

Thru went forward to the front line to see things for himself. He found the Meld's regiments waiting expectantly, somewhat nervous, resting on their shields with their spears to hand. He traversed the line moving from east to west and back and had reached the far eastern end when the first shouts told him the men were in sight. The drumming was louder, the horns suddenly brayed en masse, and the men of Shasht began to offer up their chilling war song.

Mot archers were visible, retreating, pausing to release an arrow, retreating again up the slope, through the boulders and scrubby trees and onto the open space on the top of the hill. Then they ran ahead.

Behind came the men, their shields forming a line of red

and gold, their helmets glittering in the early sun. Now a command rang out from the Meld. The pikebearers dropped their weapons to the ready, and the mots picked up their shields.

Showers of arrows slanted through the air between the two armies. Then the men stumbled onto the first of the Meld's surprises, a row of pits dug thigh deep with a sharp stake anchored at the bottom.

Their lines buckled momentarily, then came to a halt while orders were bawled and men adjusted. A line of skirmishers began to probe the ground in front of the marching regiments. They found the rest of the pits, and the regiments flowed over and around them.

Arrows glittered in the early light as they flashed high between the two armies. The men were coming at a steady trot, their shields held in front of them like a wall of pale eyes. The young half-trained mots in the Meld's regiments watched with dry mouths as they came on. Drums thundered behind them. At fifty paces the men erupted with their war cry and ran forward to engage. The roar of battle leaped up all along the northern side of the hill.

As before, the men used their shields and swords to deflect the pike heads and rushed inside to close with the pikebearers. The ditch and the low rampart added to their difficulties, but did not stop them. The pikebearers pulled and stabbed, and men fell. Bodies began to pile up in the ditch. But in time the men broke in close to the pikebearers, and their spears took a toll. Mots and brilbies tumbled back in the death throes. The pike line broke up.

Mots with spear and shield stood forward to form a fresh line.

The men pulled back to reorganize and then came on again with a renewed roar of drums, horns, and war chants. Once again the lines locked and the struggle continued. Back and forth it swayed over the low rampart, and down into the ditch. The men made minor breakthroughs, but these were always seen in time and the gaps filled from the reserve regiments. Every so often the fighting died down as the men pulled back to take a breath or two and reorganize their line.

Thru received a call to the Meld's command post. He found the general in a state of anxious excitement, standing over the map and rubbing his hands together. His staff busily received reports from the frontline commanders and passed on vital information. The mouse seemed much more confident now.

"General," said Thru.

"Ah, Gillo. Well, what do you think? Not bad, eh, for raw recruits."

"Done well, sir."

"But they keep coming."

"They can no more afford heavy casualties than we can, so they have to stop eventually."

"Was it like this at Dronned?"

"Very much so. They attacked us there, tried to break us. But we held them."

The Meld signaled for more tea. Thru was glad of a cup before he returned to his own post. There was little news from Chillespi. Ter-Saab was with his regiment. They waited, each separated in his own universe of concerns and hope for the day.

But now the Shashti general formed his men up into two huge battalions, shortening the line and then storming forward to smash into the two weakest areas of the Meld's line, places marked by collapses in the dug rampart and partial filling of the ditch. The men poured across, and slammed into the defense lines once again.

The mot line began to give.

A message came from the Meld ordering Thru to bring his regiments around the right end of the fortified line and to attack the flank of the nearest enemy column.

Thru had been waiting impatiently for exactly this moment. His own orders were ready and waiting to go. Immediately there came a bellowing of commands in the ranks, and soon the lines had turned to the right and were in motion.

"Hurry!" was the only word on Thru's lips as they moved off. Every moment was precious, and every mot knew it.

Within less than a minute the force was pulling around the flank and coming into view. The assault column had penetrated, but not completely broken through. There was fighting going on all along the ditch and rampart, and over it in the center.

The command for the charge was given, and the southern regiments flowed forward, hurling themselves across the flat ground beside the ditch. The Second and Fourth regiments were in the lead, with the Fifth and Sixth in support.

The Shashti spearmen on the left flank turned to face the new threat while other men fell in behind them with javelins and bows. Thru whistled to himself at the smooth way this maneuver was performed.

Then the gap closed and the leading regiments drove in and the fighting sent up a fresh roar of noise.

Thru was standing at the corner of the rampart and ditch. The ditch ended here, though the rampart had been continued around for another forty paces. He had a view right up the line of the battle. The Meld's entire army was now committed to that front.

Thru felt a momentary premonition. He commanded the last reserves. After his regiments engaged, they would have nothing to spare. He chewed his lip for a second, and then he sprang down and ran to catch up with Ter-Saab at the rear of the Sixth Regiment.

"Turn it around," said Thru. "Move the regiment back behind the right flank."

Ter-Saab's eyebrows rose. "What about the attack?"

Thru was watching the attack as it drove home into the enemy's column.

"The enemy is flanked all right, but he must have known we'd do this."

And indeed the assault column was extricating itself and retreating back and down the slope as Thru's attack went in.

Ter-Saab was standing there, glowering at him.

"My people have worked long and hard for this moment. We've trained for months on these maneuvers. Now we sit back and do nothing."

"The Sixth is the last reserve this army has. Look, see how the enemy are moving away. They were expecting this attack from us."

Ter-Saab bit back any further comments.

The Shasht assault columns were pulling back and forming a defensive shield wall. Thru's regiments had clashed with them and caused some casualties, but the men had disengaged with skill and were reformed and waiting.

The attack was stalemated, and Thru was about to order the regiments back, when a messenger, covered in blood and dust, ran up.

"The men!" said the messenger, eyes staring, obviously struggling to speak.

"What men?" said Thru, grabbing him by the shoulders.

"Surprise attack. The Meld is lost."

Thru whirled to see Ter-Saab and the Sixth marching back around the flanking works of the ditch and rampart.

"Back everyone, support the Sixth!" He grabbed Chillespi and bellowed in his ear. The lieutenant was quick on the uptake, and nodded agreement at once.

Thru ran for the Sixth.

A Shasht regiment had somehow crept up unseen on the far side of the hill. They had crossed the rampart facing that side unopposed and smashed into the Meld's command post and the rear of the main line of the army. The shriek of their horns was plainly audible now over a renewed clamor of war.

That was the signal the main body of the enemy was waiting for. Now the assault column on the right side of their line charged once more, slamming into the Ninth Regiment in the center of the Meld's line.

The Shasht regiments of the other assault column were held back, facing off with Thru's regiments. And now the southern regiments were turning away, pulled back by Thru's order to close up on the Sixth, which was marching back the way they'd come.

Thru caught up with Ter-Saab, who still hadn't received the word.

"Hurry! The enemy has broken at the rear!"

Ter-Saab stared at him blankly for a second, then he sprang into action. Orders were bellowed, and the Sixth Regiment surged around the end of the works.

"At the double!" Thru roared at one stunned lieutenant

that stared back at him with mouth hanging open. The mot gulped, then whirled and started shouting at his mots. Thru set off alongside Ter-Saab at a dead run.

Rounding the gap in the works, they saw a confused mob of mots broken out of the rear of the Meld's forces. Beyond them the Blitz Regiment of Shasht was driving hard into the rear of the Ninth Regiment, which was simultaneously receiving renewed attack on its front.

Complete disaster loomed, except for the presence of the Sixth Regiment.

With swords and spears at the ready, they drove through the fugitives broken away from the Ninth and other regiments and hurled themselves into the Blitzers, taking them in their right flank.

The Blitzers turned to fight, and the battle along their flank quickly became disorganized as men and the mots of two regiments fused into a chaotic mass of fighting.

Thru ran past the Meld's command post. The tents were down, bodies scattered here and there, but he saw no sign of the Meld himself. There was no time to search, the armies were still locked together in confused combat. The Ninth Regiment had been reinforced from the regiments on either side, and it had held the assault column at the rampart. But in the rear there was still a tense struggle in progress between the Sixth Regiment and the Shasht regiment. The men had done terrible harm to the Ninth Regiment, but the flank attack had prevented a complete breakthrough.

The situation continued to be fluid, however. The men had lost cohesion, but they extricated themselves from the fighting with skill. As they fell back, they instinctively began to dress out their lines and on the turn lock their shields and prepare to deliver a riposte. They were the crack troops of the Shasht army, and they came together with a clack and a crash and roars of their war cry.

Thru saw the danger. The Sixth had lost the impetus of its charge. The men were about to regain the initiative, and they might scatter the Sixth with a strong enough thrust.

Thru spun about and ran back to the confused mob of mots and brilbies that had been flung out of the way of the initial charge into the rear. They had stopped running once they'd been passed by the Sixth. Now they were standing there in several groups, unsure what to do next.

Thru jumped up on a broken, overturned wagon.

"Do you see those men?" he roared pointing toward Shasht soldiers. "If they win today, they will kill you all. They will kill your families. They will leave none of us alive. Do you understand?"

"For I was the broken pig!" shouted a voice. And every mot and brilby heard the first line of the ancient poem, and a collective shudder ran through them. Then anger exploded into a roar of rage.

Thru waved his sword toward the Shasht regiment and, yelling for the charge, he jumped down and started running at them.

He had no idea if the rest were following; he knew he didn't dare look back, didn't dare falter a step. This mad charge was it, the moment of truth, because if they didn't halt the men's advance here, then the whole army could be destroyed.

He passed the lines of the Sixth. They were reforming, but still not ready. He heard a swelling noise behind him, and he ran on. With two hundred or so mots behind him, he could only hope to slow the Blitz Regiment, but that would gain enough time for the Sixth to regroup and join them.

Thru heard an arrow whisper past his head and dodged a javelin that bounced on the ground and skimmed past his ankles. Then another javelin zipped past at waist height, and now he found other mots had caught up with him. They were possessed by the spirit of war, yelling continuously as they ran straight for the enemy. A moment later they joined battle with a smashing crunch that immediately sank beneath a swelling roar of screams, shouts, and the clatter and clang of weapons and shields.

Thru had only his sword, but he used it to deflect a spear thrust as he ran in and leaped up to stab over the nearest shield and down into the man's neck. His blade cut into flesh and bone and then slipped off armor. He felt something hard strike his shoulder, something else banged off his helmet. He got a foot up against the nearest shield and threw its owner back and off his feet. As he went down, another man in the second line was there, he thrust with the spear at Thru's head. Thru ducked, was hit from behind, tripped and went down on one knee.

A brilby with a broken pike had come in behind him, and he knocked the spearman down with a crunching blow from the pike handle. A mot went over Thru's bent back with a howl and a spray of blood as a sword found his unprotected chest. Something hard and heavy struck a glancing blow off the side of Thru's helmet, and he saw stars.

The big brilby was using the broken pike like a club, knocking men down, hammering their shields so hard they were driven back a step with each blow.

More mots came up, swords rang on swords, Thru was back on his feet, conscious that someone else's blood had soaked one side of his face.

He crossed swords with a snarling man, wide-eyed in battle rage. Thru tried to fight with the benefit of kyo, but in this frenzy there wasn't the room for kyo maneuver. In a tight press they simply hacked and stabbed at each other. Thru pulled the man's shield away, opening the man up for his sword. He stabbed, and stabbed again. The man toppled backward. Thru released the shield. Other men trampled their fallen fellow and thrust at Thru with their spears. He slipped, almost fell, and just managed to knock up a spear that would have gutted him. Mots on either side slammed up against the spearman. Wicker shields crashed against wood and metal. Swords, spears, and pikes clattered along the Blitzer's front.

Thru looked along that line and let out an exultant yell. It had worked. The Blitz Regiment of Shasht had plowed to a halt. And now he heard the Sixth Regiment coming on behind them. They had stifled the enemy's deadly thrust.

Something smacked him hard on the back of the head, and a moment later he found himself kneeling on the chest of the man he'd stabbed to death. The man's face was curiously peaceful in death, as if he'd died in his bed. Thru shoved himself back onto his feet. He felt distinctly strange. The Sixth Regiment flooded around them and struck the enemy front. The men of Shasht were thrust back a step, then another.

Thru felt arms around him. A voice in his ear. Chillespi.

"Are you all right, sir?"

Thru didn't know.

"Yes, I think so."

It's not my blood, he wanted to say, and then everything seemed to lose color and form, and Thru felt his knees buckle as darkness enfolded him.

Chapter 9

Thru awoke in a dark place with a sense of closeness and the smell of sweat and excrement. He turned his head slightly. He was lying under a blanket on a pallet. His clothes were gone.

He put a hand up to his head and found it wrapped in heavy bandages. He tried to sit up, but the pain in his head was sharp. Instead he lay still and listened to his surroundings. After a while he realized he was in a tent, in camp. Outside, he could hear the sounds of woodchopping and voices some distance away. The wind soughed in trees overhead.

Later a mor pulled back the flap of the tent and brought in a basin of water and a cup. By the red armband she wore, he knew she was with the volunteer medical corps. She gave him water to drink, and then she unwrapped the bandage and examined the wound.

"Your head is pretty hard, I'd say." She cleaned the wound area on the side of his head and began to rewind the bandage. "Should have broken your skull, but it didn't. You're lucky to be alive."

"Where is Ter-Saab," he said thickly, "and the Meld?"

"I don't know. I'll have to ask the surgeon."

"Yes, please do that. Quickly. There's a lot I need to know."

"Well, you won't be doing anything about war for a good while yet. That wound will take time to heal. They laid you open there, right across the back of your head."

He recalled dimly the feeling of blood running down his face. A wild melee came to memory filled with flashing swords and shields with eyes painted on them. The roar of battle left him shivering for a few moments.

"The battle was won, then?"

"Oh, that's what you want to know is it? Yes, your precious battle was won, but we'll be burying the dead for days to come."

The battle was won. Then he could rest. He'd done what he had to do. Released from immediate worry, he fell asleep after a while.

The next time he awoke the nurse looked in and then hurried away. Soon afterward Chillespi entered and sat cross-legged beside him.

"Congratulations on your survival. When we pulled off that helmet, we weren't too sure you would live."

"I think I must be pretty lucky from what the mor tells me."

"She's damned right. Anyway I thought I should tell you what's been going on the last few days. I knew you'd want to know."

"How long?" Thru started to say.

"The battle was four days ago now."

"The Meld?"

"Is recovering in the next tent. He was found after the fight was over. He took a knock in the surprise attack. He'll be up and about pretty soon, not as badly hurt as you."

Thru supposed that was good news.

"Who's in command now?"

"Colonel Ter-Saab. But the Meld will reassume command when he returns."

"That's good. Where are the enemy?"

"They ran for it to the coast. Ter-Saab took the army in pursuit. I came back yesterday to help organize our supply train."

"Any chance that he'll catch them?"

"No. Our mots were tired after the battle. I think the enemy are already at the coast. They will escape."

"That's a pity. We had a chance to finish them."

"But we did hurt them. They left six hundred dead here. And there were more than four hundred found on the site of the first fight near Chenna."

"And what of our own losses?"

"Not sure yet of the totals. They have found eleven hundred bodies here. Probably another five hundred at Chenna."

Thur winced. "Too high. We can't sustain those kind of numbers."

"Nor can they."

It was small comfort, but alone again in the darkness Thru grasped at it. The enemy expedition was far from home and had limited numbers; their losses could not be made up. In his mind, however, he relived the two battles, the sudden ambush at Chenna field and then the long march to the Sow's Head and the fighting on that sunny morning. The chaos and noise, the crippling fear of making a mistake. It was a while this time before he was able to banish those images and put himself back to sleep.

The next day he was visited by the Meld. The little old aristocrat had a bandage around his head and another on his right hand and wrist, but the weight of responsibility had visibly lifted from his shoulders. He seemed ebullient, in fact.

"Thru Gillo, you are the hero of this fight. You saved the day. Turned the Sixth Regiment back in time, then rallied the rabble of the Ninth and stopped the enemy cold."

"Well, we managed to hit them at just the right moment. Stopped them gaining momentum."

"But you held a regiment back. I did not order that. You did."

"I had a premonition. I don't know why, but at the last moment I knew I had to."

"Well, thank the Spirit for that premonition, then."

"Yes, indeed, sir."

For a moment they were quiet together, giving thanks for the victory they'd eked out on the hill.

"What news have you from Ter-Saab, sir?"

"He has pursued the enemy to the shore. But they got away on their ships."

Thru groaned softly.

"You wanted more?"

"I wanted to see the enemy destroyed. That way they will never come back."

"Ter-Saab says the enemy were so afraid, they ran all the way. Our mots could not keep pace with them."

"I was afraid of that."

"But we won a victory!" and the Meld leaned over and squeezed his shoulder. The King is ecstatic."

And with that Thru had to be content. The next day the Meld traveled to Sulmo to report in person at a royal war conference. Thru was not yet fit to travel, so he spent a few more days recuperating in the tent. Then his clothes and other things were brought back, cleaned and pressed. His sword had been polished, too.

When he took a look at his helmet, he gave an involuntary whistle. Along the back was a neat-looking slice cut into the lacquered wicker. The helmet had saved his life all right, but only just. He saw the wisdom of having a steel helmet like the men. Alas, metal was too scarce in the Land to make helmets for soldiers. They needed what they had just for weapons.

His first unsteady steps took him around the village of Shimpli-Dindi, which was steadily getting back to normal. The people had come down from the hills and were hard at work repairing what had been damaged by the men of Shasht. Fortunately they hadn't had time to set the place on fire.

He was taking a mug of weak ale outside the village tavern when a child ran up shouting something incomprehensible and everyone nearby stood up and looked off down the road.

Then came a whistle and more shouts from the east. Now they heard something else, a steady tramping sound, and up the road from the coast came the first of the regiments of the army, back from chasing the men out of the Land.

They came with the tired tread of those who had been marching for days. But despite obvious fatigue, their eyes gleamed. They had discovered a new pride.

Their army had driven the men out of the Land once again. They'd held their own against the men and in the end they'd beaten them and forced them to retreat.

The villagers were pouring out of their houses, others were running up from the polder. Shouting and singing, they kept it up as regiment after regiment marched by, the bulk of the army in fact, heading down the road toward Chenna.

Thru watched them go and felt some of the same pride. They were all farmers, more or less, but they were learning how to be soldiers, and they'd met Man the Master, Man the Cruel himself, and come away with a victory.

Later Thru learned more about the chase from Ter-Saab by the campfire.

"They ran, they literally did not stop running until they reached the coast. We could not keep up."

"And when you got to the coast?"

"They were almost all off the shore in boats. We chased the last few hundred right into the waves. They chose to swim rather than stand and fight. We found a few hiding in the rocks and killed them. They would not surrender."

Thru shrugged. That was the way with the warriors of Shasht. Surrender was alien to their thinking.

"The ships turned away from the shore and were gone that same evening."

"Heading?"

"South, across to Fauste or Mauste I expect."

"You sent messengers?"

"To all the coastal cities, runners south to Glaine and north to Annion."

"And a bird took the news to Sulmo."

"Correct."

Thru raised his mug. Ter-Saab raised his.

"May they never come back!"

They drank to this, but neither believed in his heart that the war was over.

Thru's head was still wrapped in bandages, so it was too soon for him to resume active duty. Indeed, he was still suffering from headaches. But he was the nominal commander of the army at that moment. He made the decision to split the army. He sent the trained regiments back to their postings and the rest back to Sulmo. Ter-Saab and the Sixth Regiment headed back down the road to Glaine. Thru remained in Shimpli-Dindi.

He was still there three days later when a royal messenger found him and delivered a sealed packet. He opened it and found a letter from Toshak. He was summoned to Sulmo at once to share his opinions of the battle of Chenna/Sow's Head with the Royal Council. New training decisions needed to be made, and they wanted to hear from the veterans of the battle before they made them.

The following morning he set off, riding in a donkey cart, since he was still unsteady on his feet, and by noon he was far up the road to royal Sulmo, rolling through the lush landscape of the Sulo Valley.

Chapter 10

The great Shasht fleet rode at anchor in the bay. Thirty-three ships, most of them giants with three and four masts, were set in long lines across the water. Their names spoke of the civilization that had built them: "Sword," "Mace," "Axe," "Spear," and the mighty flagship, "Anvil."

Ashore, smoke rose from the chimneys of New Harbor, the town the men had built on the ruins of the monkey place they had conquered. Small boats plied back and forth between the ships and the shore, as they did every day. Inland the land rose up into a series of small mountains with sharp-edged peaks. This was the island of Mauste, the southernmost part of the Land.

Aboard the flagship, a tempestuous meeting in the admiral's grand salon was coming to a close.

General Dogvalth, still visibly shaken by the horrific events of the previous ten minutes, had just been promoted into the place of the disgraced General Hustertav. Filek Biswas, the chief surgeon of the fleet, was still chewing his lip in nervous reaction to those events. The smell was going away, thankfully, but the memory would linger. Hustertav's face contorted in that snarl of fear. His screams as he clung to the table, then to their legs. The horrific sound of his bones being broken by the Red Tops.

Admiral Heuze, who had ordered Hustertav to be taken from the room by the Red Tops, was rubbing his chin and staring out the window. Captain Pukh, Heuze's old naval crony, said something quietly to the admiral, and they both barked with harsh laughter. Filek shivered. There was something so cold in the admiral's good cheer. One moment he could be telling a joke and the next, signaling the Red Tops to take you away.

The slaves had finished mopping Hustertav's excrement from the deck, and they left with their buckets in their hands, their chains rattling faintly.

"Right," snapped Heuze. "Now that that disgusting little scene is finished, we can get on with the task at hand."

Everyone hunched forward under the lash of Heuze's scorn. To Filek's eyes, they looked like beaten slaves themselves. The generals, eyes downcast, manner hesitant, men uncertain of their position, were grouped together at the far end.

Filek exchanged a glance with Captain Rukil, now one of Heuze's favorites. The captain, a decent sort, was obviously shocked. He looked away, unwilling to share even that with Filek. The general had been removed with a complete lack of dignity, and Filek could tell that Rukil was a dignified man.

"So?" mused the admiral. "Tell me again, what were the total casualty figures?" Everyone looked to Filek, who for some reason was regarded as the source of such facts. Filek didn't want this position, but it had been thrust upon him. He had learned that it was best to please the admiral.

"One thousand and fifty-four dead, by the last count. Eight hundred ambulatory wounded, and one hundred and five non-ambulatory."

Heuze's eyes sparkled dangerously.

"That stupid fool Hustertav should be grateful I gave him to the priests. I wouldn't mind burning his legs off, very slowly."

Dogvalth, who had been a friend of Hustertav's, was still pale. Poor Hustertav was going to be tied over the altar come the morning sunrise. The priests would lift his heart, still beating, to the Great God.

"The question for you, General Dogvalth"—the admiral stared at the man like a hawk—"is simple enough. How are you going to turn this beaten army of ours around? This is the army of Shasht. This is the army of Aeswiren III. Where is the spirit of Kaggenbank? Why have we not had victory?"

"Well," began Dogvalth in earnest stupidity. "We had

them trapped against the river, but they were clever. They slipped away by swimming downstream. In the second battle we came so close to cutting them in two, and then they stopped the Blitzers. They are worthy opponents. We must give them that much respect."

"They're supposed to be nothing more than jumped-up monkeys of some kind. How can they defeat us! We are the spawn of the Great God, are we not?"

For a moment Dogvalth trembled. Was he about to be given to the priests as well?

"I forbade any frontal assaults!" boomed the admiral. "Hustertav then went and made two frontal assaults. Both cost us too many men."

"Yes, sir, but the truth of it is, we won't defeat the monkeys without taking them on toe to toe. We're better than they are anyway."

"By the purple ass of the Great God!" boomed the admiral slamming his hand on the table. Dogvalth fell silent. Heuze mastered his anger.

"My dear general, I know we can beat them. But, when we take them on toe to toe next time, we are going to do it on ground that suits us and assures us of a victory. Hustertav went to the priests because he was criminally stupid and wasteful of my soldiers. In the future, when we see the enemy perched on a hilltop with his army safely behind a ditch and rampart what are we going to do?"

"We will maneuver, we will entrench and starve him out."

"Exactly. We will not take our best troops and make them fight uphill into the teeth of the enemy's archery. This is my army now, and we will protect this army and use it to crush these insolent monkeys once and for all."

Filek noticed Captain Rukil's grimace.

No one dared to say that actually it was Nebbeggebben's army. Filek wondered whether the "Hand," the secret force that regularly pruned the ranks of those deemed troublesome to the imperial succession, had taken notice of Admiral Heuze's increasing signs of megalomania. Filek hoped not. He owed his position to the admiral's benevolence, ever since he'd removed Heuze's leg in a manner both painless and surgically perfect. If Heuze went, then Filek would probably go with him, such was the way of the Hand.

"He's cost me a thousand men, maybe more. How many of those wounded are going to die, Biswas?"

"Some, sir. There are many with infected, suppurating wounds. Gangrene will kill them."

"Exactly, see? That stupid Hustertav deserves what he's going to get. We're left with less than seven thousand soldiers in the whole fleet, and that is simply unacceptable, do you understand?"

Again, everyone hunched down, as if under the lash.

"Do you hear me, Dogvalth?"

"Yes, sir."

"I want those monkeys crushed, but I want it done without these long casualty lists. You are the men of Shasht. You will use your superior abilities of maneuver to get the monkeys into a tight spot, and then you will annihilate them, understood?"

"Yes, sir."

Filek wondered how poor Dogvalth was going to do this. The so-called monkeys had proved to be a tricky foe. They'd whipped the army of Shasht in the first campaign, the year before. Now they'd done it again.

"Now," said the admiral unrolling a large map of the southern territory, which had been chosen for this year's campaign. As with all the maps of the new world, the interior was largely a blank. "Where is the next attack going in? What are your plans?"

Filek noted with grim amusement that Dogvalth had obviously had the foresight to prepare a little speech in case he'd been asked that question. Dogvalth had obviously suspected that Hustertav was doomed.

"Well, sir, I recommend a landing on the western side of this peninsula. There's a good bay there, good landing sites along this river estuary."

"And why do you want to go ashore there?"

"Well, the land there is pretty flat and open. It ought to allow us plenty of room for maneuvers. And we have information that a major city of the monkeys lies up that river. So our presence there is sure to draw their forces into a battle."

The admiral nodded.

"At last"—he leaned over and patted Dogvalth's shoulder—"A general with some foresight. Good. Win me a battle, General, that's all I ask. We will put you ashore whenever you're ready."

"It will take us some time to prepare."

"Of course, after this last fiasco it will take at least a month. The men are in poor shape. You will have two months to get them fit and ready for action, understood."

"Uh, yes, sir."

Just two months? It might be possible, Filek thought.

After reviewing the potential of this campaign on the western edge of the peninsula, Heuze dismissed the soldiers and Rukil and sat there with Filek and Puhk, who formed the "inner cabinet."

"Well, what do you think, Filek? Be honest, do we still have a chance?" Heuze's disgust with the army was still evident.

"Dogvalth is a good officer. He will do his best. The men are still brave and strong, they will fight well."

"That has never been our problem. Arrogant leadership has been the problem."

Filek and the admiral looked each other in the eye. Both knew that the admiral had made that mistake himself.

"Dogvalth doesn't seem quite so arrogant as Uisbank or Hustertav. Maybe he has learned something."

The admiral shrugged and scratched his head.

"I just don't know. I thought Hustertav would bring us victory. He was intelligent, and a good leader of men. He saw the first battle, he understood the dangers. I don't understand what happened. Where did he go wrong?"

Filek had read the reports thoroughly, of course.

"He went by the book. He set up an excellent ambush, and it almost worked. But the enemy got away."

"He underestimated the fornicating monkeys again. So they got away and joined up with the other mass on that hill and that was enough to withstand our army in a frontal assault."

"Hustertav sent in a flanking force that almost won the battle. When you read this plan it makes good sense. It almost worked."

"Almost! Almost is not good enough." Heuze flicked his fingers, and Filek heard again those piercing wails of terror. "I'm afraid, 'almost' will just not do. Hustertav has to pay. The men have to see that their commanders will not get away with such a poor performance." The admiral hunched forward at the table.

"But, if we don't want to suffer the same fate as Hustertav, we must do our damnedest to make sure that Dogvalth wins the next battle."

And so for a while they calmly discussed ways of helping the army improve, as if a good man hadn't been dragged screaming from the room an hour before. Filek told himself that this was war. In war the craziest things became commonplace.

Heuze had the light of fanaticism in his eyes. The admiral was a fanatic in pursuit of one cause, his own survival. Whatever it took, he would find generals who would win.

"I will not allow us to fail again. We survived the winter. We conquered this island just in time. And so we recovered from last summer's disaster. Just as we will recover from this defeat and achieve victory. Remember, Aeswiren didn't win the throne in a day."

At last the meeting ended. Filek was released to deal with his own domain. In his cabin, which also served as his office, there was a small pile of notes and other papers for him to read. The fleet had thirty-three separate surgeries, and now in addition a small hospital was set up ashore. Filek was responsible for the provisioning and smooth operation of all of them. He went through the papers and signed those that required his signature. Other papers were filed away in wooden folders and pigeonholes. He had developed this system before, when he ran the hospital in the city of Shasht. In that other life, that warm life. But he quickly shut off those warm thoughts before they turned to memories of his dear departed wife. How lonely life was without her.

When the papers were finished he left the office, locking

the door carefully behind him, and went down the winding
stair to the lower decks of the ship. Down closer to the
waterline he came to the barred gate to the women's deck.
As a husband he had access, of course, and the eunuch
guards lifted the bar and waved him through.

He wound his way through the narrow passages to Simona's cabin door. At his knock he heard her rise from her
chair with a creak.

"Father? Is that you?"

"Yes, dear."

The door opened a moment later.

Simona was one of the few women who had elected to
stay aboard the ship rather than go to the new purdah
buildings ashore. Because she was the daughter of the powerful fleet surgeon, she had been able to have her way.
Now the women's deck was relatively uncrowded, and Simona had been able to have her cabin extended by removal
of a bulkhead. Now she had room for a table, a chair, and
a place to hang her hammock.

They embraced and she drew him inside. He sat on the
small chair, and she sat on the floor in front of him. He
stroked her hair. It was a comfort to still have his lovely
daughter, even if his wife had been snatched away by fate.

He observed a copy of Gallin's *Meditations* lying on the
table. He felt a surge of pride in his intelligent, well-read
daughter.

"Did you hear the screams earlier?" he asked her.

"Yes. We all wondered what was happening."

"They took General Hustertav away."

"The general?"

"Yes. They just dragged him out. The priests have him.
He will scream for the Great God tonight. They will kill
him in the morning."

"Oh, that is terrible, the poor man."

"Yes, it is, but the admiral had to do it. There were more
than a thousand dead, more are dying all the time from
their wounds. We cannot afford failure like that."

"Father, you sound like the admiral."

Filek nodded, accepting her words.

"Oh, my dear, my darling, sometimes I am afraid I am becoming like them. Am I just another insensitive brute?"

"No, Father, you are better than that. We both know it."

"Do we? Well, I hope so. But in this situation I can see the pressures that are building up on the admiral's head. He must have victory, or else he will pay with his own life. The generals are mostly stupid fellows, promoted because they are obedient. They cannot give him what he needs."

"So why doesn't the admiral go ashore and take command himself?"

"Hah!" Filek chuckled. "Trust my daughter to put her finger on the sensitive spot! After what happened in the north, the admiral swore never to put himself at risk again. He will not go ashore until the colony is established and the monkeys are destroyed."

"Father, they are not monkeys, they are mots, mors, brilbies. They are people like ourselves."

"So you have said, my dear, and I do not doubt you. But I cannot let myself believe it too much, or else I cannot go on with my duties. Do you see? I must blind myself to this, or else I must commit suicide."

"But, Father, you know it is the truth. You have said so yourself, their artwork, their houses, all are the work of civilized people. You met Thru Gillo. Did he seem like a stupid animal to you?"

"We must destroy them or be destroyed ourselves."

Simona sighed deeply, but made no reply. Filek would only get angry if she argued with him over this.

"You have been reading Gallin?"

"Yes, Father, he is so wise."

"Indeed. I wish the world could be ordered according to Gallin's teachings."

"Oh, so do I. There would be no purdah. Women would be allowed to go out without fear of men."

Filek chuckled again. As always, Simona found the one spot that was too sensitive to be touched.

"Well, my dear, for that we would need more than just the teachings of Gallin."

"Father, Gallin says that men do not need the protection of purdah to stem their lust."

"Yes, dear," Filek was feeling uncomfortable with this turn in the conversation.

"He says they can control themselves. He says the 'conscious man' is capable of great things, including the ability to restrain himself in the presence of women."

"Yes, dear, but Gallin wrote that many centuries ago, the men of Shasht are more potent now than they were then, perhaps."

"More potent than the men of Kadawak's time?"

"Well, I don't know about that, but the laws of purdah govern our lives now, and we must remember that. Or else the powers that be will notice us, and that will not be good."

Simona sensed that her father was eager to escape this topic. Since Chiknulba had died in the plague, Filek had been turning away slowly from some of the more daring and open-minded things that Chiknulba had taught him.

Simona was sensible enough to know when to change the subject, but not sensible enough to change it to something harmless.

"Father, have you asked about Rukkh for me, as you promised?"

Filek pursed his lips. From one area of discomfort to another. Ah, this daughter of his, he loved her, but sometimes she drove him to distraction.

"Rukkh has survived. He was involved in the battle, but he was not even wounded. He is now ashore."

"Father, did you think about the things I spoke of?"

"Yes, dear, but I do not want to talk of those things now."

"When, Father, when can we talk about them?"

"I do not know, but not now."

There was an edge to his voice, and Simona knew not to push any further. Her father was torn between the gentle, well-read medical man he had been and the new leading figure of the colony that he was becoming.

If she pushed he would get huffy and start talking about what a peasant Rukkh was, and how unsuitable he was as a match for the daughter of the colony's leading surgeon.

It was unacceptable in Shashti society for a woman to

remain unwed. Unwed women could only be slaves or whores. Simona had to be wed, and soon, for she was well into young womanhood.

But, alas for her, she had the strawberry birthmark on her left breast. No young man of her own social class would take her. It was seen as the mark of a witch.

"Red-mark girl . . ." Those were the cruel words she had heard all her life.

So the only "suitable" match that Filek could arrange for her would be with some withered old man who wanted a second, third, or even a fourth wife, and Simona thought she would rather die than submit to such a fate.

Rukkh was a peasant, but he was a good soldier in a crack regiment. He had looked at her with eyes burning with desire. This was the new world, a new social order was going to rise here.

She gave an inner shrug. None of these things counted with Filek, except the first. The Biswas clan had been a town family for centuries. Filek despised the peasantry for their ignorance and sloth.

"I have spoken to the builders," Filek had turned instead to a topic that pleased him, the construction of a shoreside hospital, along with a house for himself close by. "They assure me that the materials will be ready within a few more days. I have been over the drawings with the architect. The whole project has great potential."

Simona relaxed. She hated having to dissemble. She hated the gap that had opened between her and her father. But she knew that Filek, without Chiknulba at his side, was subjected to all the social pressures of his world. He wanted the intellectual intimacy that they had always enjoyed, but he himself was turning toward the more traditional views of Shasht society. Simona did not think that way. Her time among the mots of the Land had dissolved any remnants of belief in the official religion of He Who Eats. Thru Gillo had helped her see that there was another way.

Father did not believe in the Great God, either. Both of them knew that. Father was turning in this direction because it accorded with the views of his master, the admiral. Nor was the admiral a believer; but he was conservative in his social mores, and it was better for Filek if he became more conservative, too.

This was the same admiral who had ordered her to be tortured when she came back with the message of the Assenzi. Somehow, Filek had put this away out of his thoughts. He had hardly ever spoken to her about it, though he had heard her screams as the red tops beat on her hands and feet. Probably, she understood, he had to pretend it had never happened or he could not continue as fleet surgeon, working for the admiral. Part of her understood why he had done this, and part of her could never forgive him.

Out of the confusion of these thoughts and emotions, she recalled Thru Gillo's face. The wedge of the dark nose, the bushy eyebrows framing the eyes with their inhuman depth of color. Another being in the shape of a man. A man with grey fur covering him from head to toe. A man with an inhuman face.

They had learned each other's languages. The whole thing had taken a couple of weeks, an amazing, intoxicating process. She had learned so much from Thru. The experience had been both incredibly strange and still wonderfully familiar. She had forged a bond with Thru that was like none she had ever known.

She remembered the strange little city of the mots. The steeply tilted roofs and narrow windows, the winding little streets. Every building was unique. Compared to Shasht it was tiny, of course, but it remained exquisite.

And that was the world that her own people were determined to destroy.

Her father was happily talking about his new hospital. He had big plans.

"There will be three wings. I need an entire wing for the experimental work."

Chapter 11

"Cra-ack!" the sound of the wide bat on the white ball echoed back to the hundreds of spectators on the terraced seats behind the batting post in Sulmo's royal park.

The small white ball flew up, higher and higher, while underneath it the fielders scrambled to get back and make a catch. The crowd watching with bated breath, saw the ball reach its apogee and then fall, drifting a little in the clear air until it fell safely across the scoring line.

Another run for the Army team! Polite applause rippled from the stands, while some soldiers gathered in the tighter scrum right behind the batting post let out shouts of triumph. They were matched by the cries from the scrum of chooks gathered along the endline.

Army was on 66 runs and Thru Gillo had yet to bat!

The Academy team's throwers shrugged and looked to each other. The lead thrower took up another small white ball and then jogged toward the throwing line before hurling the ball with every ounce of energy he could muster toward the red-painted post.

The batter, wielding the wide-bladed bat, watched the ball, judged its flight, and swung hard. But instead of the hearty "crack" of the well struck ball there was only the "snick" of a deflection and the little ball whistled up and into the netting behind, only to be collected by the young mots who gathered up loose balls and returned them to the throwers.

The crowd chatter continued while the next thrower took a few practice moves before beginning his jog to the line.

Now came the delivery and the ball hurtled in. The batter swung, but missed completely, and the ball struck the red-painted post with a solid "thwack."

Now cheers rang out from the Academy supporters, who were sitting in a solid block on the left side of the seating. The soldiers gave a few groans and moans, but at 66 runs and with the famous Thru Gillo yet to bat, the Army team was still in control of the game.

Another mot was striding out to the batting post, ready to take up his position. Polite applause greeted his arrival.

Several rows above the tight mass of soldiers sat a small group of old friends, reunited that day for the first time in a year or more.

Nuza sat beside Toshak, now the overall commander of the armies of the Land, and gentle Hob, the brilby who had caught Nuza during her acrobatic performances, sat beside them.

Toshak and Hob were in Sulmo to assist with the training of the Sulmese army in the wake of the battles of Chenna and Sow's Head. The Sulmo army had won those battles, but it had come at great cost. Training continued and Toshak had brought with him some more northern veterans who were to assist in improving the Sulmo army's abilities to maneuver in the field.

Nuza looked at the scoreboard. The current batter was a brilby named Heplu. She squeezed Toshak's arm by the elbow.

"Thru will be batting next. I hope you can stay a little while."

"Well, I can certainly stay to see him start his innings. Whether I can be here 'til the end I don't know; his innings are sometimes very long."

They smiled together. Thru was famous in the circles that followed the ball game as "Seventy-Seven-Run Gillo" for a record he'd set in a village match years back.

Hob chuckled. "Thru Gillo is likely to stand at the batting tree all afternoon, win the game on his ownsome."

Nuza leaned her head on Hob's massive shoulder, so familiar to her from their years of working crowds together.

"It is so nice to be together again. I wish Gem and Serling were here, too."

"Nice thought, Nuza. Where are they anyway?" said the big brilby.

"Gem is in Lushtan, working with the bandage weavers. Serling left to go to his home village in Lunt. I haven't heard from him in a while."

"How is Gem these days?" wondered Toshak.

"Oh, he's like he always is. One week he's in love, the next week he's out of love. Then he's heartbroken."

"Ah, that again. His heart is a fragile piece, but he risks it constantly."

"That he does."

"And your family, Nuza. Are they happy in Lushtan?"

"Well, everyone's still crowded together, fur to fur as they say. My mother hates that. She's used to having her own house, but they've made the best of it and during the winter everyone worked very hard and got along well."

A loud crack! announced another good shot by Heplu. They watched the little white ball veer off into the sky and then curve down onto the distant green outfield.

"Heplu's getting his eye in all right," murmured Hob approvingly.

"Army's on 69 runs now . . ."

They watched another ball hurtle in, Heplu swung, but dug under the ball too much and skied it high.

The crowd gave a collective "ooh" as they watched the ball soar. Fielders bunched beneath it waiting. Down it came seeming to float at first then turning into a white streak. It was caught, and the Academy crowd gave another cheer.

Heplu had given up the first of his four "outs."

"What was that, Hob," said Toshak with a smirk, "something about his eye?"

"Well, I thought he had his eye in, but I guess I was wrong."

Heplu struck the next ball sharply and sent it skittering off toward the boundary, with fielders in pursuit.

"So tell me, dear Nuza, how is he?" said Toshak quietly.

"Nuza and Toshak exchanged a glance. How strangely entwined their lives had become, she thought. She and Toshak had been lovers once, and had parted just before Thru appeared in their lives. Then she and Thru had fallen very deeply in love, and great Toshak had somehow managed not to be so jealous that it poisoned things between them.

"He has headaches now, and there's a look in his eyes that I do not understand. He says that war is terrible, and I believe him."

Toshak was nodding. "It is."

"So he has another scar on his poor head, but he still smiles the same way he used to."

"I asked about him, because when I saw him after the battle, here in Sulmo, he was still not recovered from the wound."

"If you look at that scar you'll know that it's a miracle that he's alive. His helmet was cut clean through."

Toshak pursed his lips. "It's a pity we don't have enough resources to equip ourselves with metal helmets."

Another "crack" redirected their attention to the white ball now soaring toward the boundary with a fielder running hard beneath it. It might come down before the boundary line, and if the fielder was fast enough, he might make the catch.

He ran with all his might. The supporters of the Academy team were on their feet cheering him on.

They saw his arm outstretched just a few yards short of the boundary line. The ball was falling short. He threw himself forward and caught the ball. The crowd roared.

Heplu, now halfway out, grimaced while he took some practice swings.

The next ball went flying high right past the boundary. Seventy runs had been scored for the Army team.

"I think we better hope that Thru is still the same hitter that he used to be," grumbled big Hob.

A thwack announced another strike on the red pole, and a groan went up from the soldiers. Heplu had missed another accurate ball and was down to his final chance.

The next ball he drove to the boundary, but the one after that he knocked up in a soft curve that was easily caught. Heplu had added only five runs to the Army total, and he was obviously disappointed in his performance as he walked away from the pole. Still, the applause grew louder because now Thru Gillo came out with his bat under his arm.

As he took up his stance the crowd chanted his name, "Seventy-seven-Run Gillo!"

The throwers readied themselves. They had waited all afternoon for this moment. This was the real test of their power and skill. Some of them studied the figure of the mot at the batting crease making smooth practice swings. Then the first thrower jogged to the line and hurled in a fierce delivery. Thru eyed it and let it pass, as it was too high for a good shot and was heading wide of the red post.

A soft "ooh" came from the crowd, partly in disappointment.

The second ball was much too high as well. The third was in the dirt. Some of the soldiers behind him were calling out rude sallies to the throwers for the Academy, accusing them of being afraid to throw anything that Thru might hit.

Now the best of the Academic throwers ran to the line, and his ball hurtled in, on target and waist high, veering viciously in toward the batter.

Thru uncoiled with his smooth, deadly stroke, and a great "crack!" echoed around the game field as the ball was struck high and far, shooting out on a tremendous trajectory that took it over the boundary while it was still climbing.

Seventy-two runs for the Army team, and Thru Gillo was at bat.

The crowd watched in total absorption as Thru set about building his innings. He declined to swing at anything except balls that were certain to hit the red post, but even then he deflected away anything that wasn't in his best hitting range. Balls that dropped to the waist or below he pounced on and smashed them hard and far.

He reached 14 runs before a swerving throw got past him and thwacked off the red pole. He got to 30 before he gave up his first catch, a ball hit hard but not quite cleanly that corkscrewed up and off to one side and was caught after a thirty-yard run by a racing fielder.

Still, the Army team was over the 100, a crucial psychological test.

Thru continued his work from the batting crease and reached 39 before he was beaten again and a beautifully thrown ball dipped under his swing and snicked the red pole.

He took his time after that, deflecting balls away that were less than ideal and jumped on only those in his best hitting zone.

He reached 45, then 47 and then was caught out at last after getting a little too much under a ball and giving up a towering catch near the boundary. The Army had 118 runs now and still two more batters to take their stand.

Thru left the field with loud, prolonged applause ringing around the game field. Nuza was there to greet him with a huge hug. He exchanged hugs with Hob and Toshak, too.

"Well, well, just like old times," said Nuza. "All together again. Well, almost."

Thru nodded, just happy with having played well. The worries about lingering effects from his head injury were fading.

"How's the head?" said Toshak.

"Clear. No headaches now."

"Seventy-seven-Run Gillo came back today," said Hob happily.

The game continued. Toshak bade them farewell; he had appointments that could not be missed, but Hob elected to stay as did Nuza.

The Army team were finally all out at 131, an intimidating score. Now the Academics would bat while the Army mots would field and throw.

Thru was not a thrower, but he was quite good at catching long balls, so he was stationed way out on the boundary line.

The Academics had several good batters, and these mots soon made an impression on both throwers and fielders for the Army team.

Thru found himself pursuing well-hit balls that bounced over the boundary or flew high on their way to a score. He made one catch, when the Academics were at 76 runs. They continued to hit well, and when they reached 120 with one mot left to bat, there was growing concern in the mass of

Army supporters grouped tightly around the batting pole.
What had seemed like certain victory was now in doubt.
All their noise and smart remarks could not break the concentration of the last Academy hitter, though, and he struck
again and again, scoring 6 runs before giving up a catch.
Going on to 9 before letting a ball through to strike the
red post. He went past the Army score and then six more
before he was finally done in, and the game came to an end.

The Academic crowd was cheering wildly. The local
chooks were jumping up and down with loud whopping
cries. Most had thought their team was doomed once Thru
Gillo had hammered out his impressive score of 47.

The two teams shook hands on the open space by the
red post before leaving the field.

Afterward Thru met Nuza at the door to the Sulmo club-
house. He was cheerful despite the defeat. His skill with
the bat had not been lost. Nuza hung on his arm as they
walked up the broad avenue to the inner-city gate. The
Sulmo ball field was in the outer city, that part which had
been walled in during a brief boom era in the city's history.
The inner city remained the more densely populated, heavily built-up part, as it always had been.

The avenue was lined with graceful elm trees and stone
benches on which folk could sit and rest their limbs while
they watched others going to and fro. The avenue ran on
past the ball field to a large vegetable and grains market,
so there was quite a bit of foot traffic here throughout
the day.

Here and there, elder mots were playing the board game
called Chat, which was a popular pastime in Sulmo. On
either side of the avenue for much of its length lay parkland
with green lawns on which a few people strolled. Beyond
it were formal beds filled with southern flowers. It was a
peaceful scene, most pleasing to the eye.

"You can almost imagine that things are just the same.
That the men never came," said Nuza.

"Almost," he agreed.

Ahead of them rose the towers and spires of Old Sulmo,
the Fane of the Great Spirit, the Small Fane, the Royal

Palace, and the Corn Market, each very different, but each beautiful in its own way.

"If it hadn't happened, if they hadn't come, we would have been on the roads this summer."

"Yes, I know. But our lives will never be what they were. We have to make the best of what we have left."

"Someday," she said, leaning on his shoulder, "I hope we can have something of our old life."

Their hands interlocked, Thru prayed with all his heart that Nuza's hopes would not disappear. The future was clouded. Endless war, or else defeat and annihilation were the most likely prospects. The life they had once enjoyed seemed as far away as the moon.

Chapter 12

Harking back to an ancient tradition, the King of Sulmo, Gueillo X, had ordered a grand banquet in honor of the Meld of Daneep and the army of Sulmo. The city was abuzz with talk about this event from the moment the Royal Proclamation was read out on street corners. The next ten days were filled with public excitement. Almost as if everyone in the city had been invited personally.

Thru received his invitation under the Royal Seal. For a moment he caught himself as he opened it. A year before he had been no more than a traveling player. A wanderer, a roustabout, a weaver who couldn't get into the weavers' guild. Now he was invited as an honored guest to a royal banquet.

The war had produced so many strange occurrences that he supposed he shouldn't have been surprised by this one, either. Yet still, it felt strange to have been elevated like this so quickly at such a young age. He was barely a grown mot, and yet he was commanding a brigade on the battlefield. Sometimes it was all a little amazing to him, when he had the time to contemplate it.

When he found that Nuza was not invited, he wondered aloud about not going at all. Nuza would not hear of it.

"Of course you must go. It is you they want to honor. The people attending will be the wardens of each of Sulmo's counties. They will represent the people of their counties, and that means they must see you and all the other mots who won the battle. Of course, they can't meet the ordinary soldiers, but they can meet the officers. Then they will go home to the counties and spread their impressions of you and the others. So you will represent the army itself."

Thru understood. It was the way society worked. Everyone in the Land would eventually be touched by some report from this grand dinner. He was still left with a little dread concerning the heavy responsibility of representing the army in this manner. What if he made some social gaffe?

"What if I use the wrong fork for the shellfish?" he said plaintively.

"Bah, silly. You use the forks in order from the outside in. It's perfectly logical."

"It is?"

"And just don't drink too much wine. Keep a clear head and you'll be fine."

His coat and trousers were all repaired, and his boots were polished to a lovely shine. Thus he arrived at the Royal Palace among the throng of guests and was shown through the wide passageways of polished wood to the banquet hall, hung with red and gold in honor of the Royal Army of Sulmo.

A long table was laid with a scarlet cloth. Thru had never seen so much silver and gold. A hundred candles were lit in two lines down the length of the table. It was a vision of Old Sulmo, from her brief golden age.

The gathering was split into two noticeably different groups. The officers of the army, in their sober blue uniforms with the red-and-yellow pegs that denoted their rank, and surrounding them a more numerous mass of the cream of Sulmo society. Here were the Gryses of every province, the great Melds of the four Quarters and the shorelines, the Lady Mors dressed in grand finery, and many humbler folk, the squires of the shires and the constables of the larger towns.

Thru Gillo, wearing his simple blue outer coat with the red pin of his rank at the throat, felt the differences. He was but a humble mot of a Northern village. His accent betrayed that every time he spoke.

Still, the King had asked for Thru to sit by him. Nearby were the Melds of the South and the East and, of course, the Meld of Daneep. King Gueillo was a portly mot, with fine silvery fur and peculiarly large ears. Like most of the crowd the King was clearly enjoying the occasion. The wine had been flowing freely. Suddenly the King stood up.

"To you, Colonel Gillo," the King extended his goblet. Others were rising to do the same in a formal toast. Thru was half inclined to rise, too, but the King caught his eye and held it and thus he knew that he must remain seated.

"In the name of the throne of Sulmo and all the people of my realm, I dedicate this toast to Colonel Gillo, who was so instrumental in winning our victory."

Thru cast a look across the table. There was the Meld of Daneep, eyes smiling, raising a goblet to him.

Thru raised his own goblet, and toasted the Meld back.

There were loud murmurs among the gathered aristocrats who much approved of this public giving of respect to one of their own.

"To Thru Gillo," said the King again, and everyone raised their goblet and repeated his words.

The throng now sat down, and he saw by the King's glimpse that it was his turn to stand. He surveyed the table and the crowd of lesser folk gathered along the far wall of the huge room.

All eyes were on him.

He raised his goblet.

"I thank you for the honor you do me. I do not think I have ever felt a prouder moment, but I must pass on some of this honor, for it lies in truth with the mots and brilbies of the army that fought at Chenna and the Sow's Head.

"So, to the army!"

With a congratulatory roar the well-dressed folk rose up and toasted the army of the realm.

Then it was time to be seated for the first courses. Mots in livery brought in platters piled high with delicacies from the royal kitchen. There were wedges of lime and bewby pie, then fresh oysters in the shell, and crayfish cooked in the Sulmese way.

When the table was cleared once more, a round of introductions began. Thru was presented to the Melds of the Quarters and the other Melds of shoreline and hill. The

Meld of Daneep himself did the introductions, a singular honor.

Having met the Melds, he turned back to his seat at the table but was interrupted by a posse of Assenzi.

"Masters!" he said with astonishment as Utnapishtim and Graedon came forward.

"Hail to thee, young Thru Gillo," said Utnapishtim.

"Let me second that," said Graedon.

Thru grasped their thin, bony hands.

Behind them were another pair of Assenzi that Thru had never met. Utnapishtim turned to them.

"May we introduce you to our friends who guard the Southland?"

"Honored," said Thru with a bow.

"Culpura of Sulmo"—an especially wrinkled Assenzi—"Eisteed of Annion," Eisteed wore a small yellow cap with a white bobble on the end. Thru shook their bony hands.

The King, talking with the Meld of Daneep and the Meld of the North Quarter, now turned to the group of Assenzi. He had taken note of the warm greeting exchanged between Thru and the Assenzi.

"So, Utnapishtim, is my brigadier Gillo one of your Highnoth mots?"

"Oh, yes, Your Majesty," said the Assenzi.

"I see." The King smiled, and turned to Thru. There was something cool in his expression now. "So, Brigadier, is that where you learned to be such a good soldier?"

"No, Your Majesty, we did not learn about war at Highnoth. Master Graedon taught us engineering. Master Utnapishtim showed us the stars through his telescope."

"Oh-ho, so you have traveled to the stars!"

"Only in our imaginations, Your Majesty. We have merely seen the light of those stars thorough the telescope. They are bright, and the colors are strong."

A horn blared to announce the next course in the feast. They resumed their seats. The Assenzi squeezed into spaces up and down the table. Thru detected a certain unease, even distaste among some of the nobility when the ancient ones sat next to them.

In Sulmo the Assenzi were still not loved. For it was well

remembered that in the time of King Ueillim, the Assenzi had stifled the city's ambitions in the cloth trade. Just when Sulmo had taken a strong grip on the trade, the Assenzi had helped organize the weavers of the Braided Valley. Within a generation the Braided Valley had broken Sulmo's grip.

"So," the King returned his gaze to Thru. "Just where did you learn the arts of war so well?"

"In Dronned, Your Majesty, from General Toshak."

"Ah, from Toshak."

The King turned away to speak with the Meld of Daneep. Thru's sense of it was that the King was uncomfortable with the mention of Toshak's name. Something had come between the King and great Toshak, but it was hidden in the past.

A fine pie of savory bushpods and hammelbem was brought in and broken into. Plates loaded with stuffed vegetables and rich mussel stew came. More wine was poured, though Thru tried to keep his consumption to a minimum.

Then, to an outburst of applause, the cooks wheeled in an entire roast boar, its mouth stuffed with an apple. Truly this was a feast in the manner of the Land, and it was the first time in a long time that Thru had seen such a lavish display.

A conversation was underway to his right between the Grys Kreisa and several others. When a lull occured the Grys turned to Thru.

"Tell, us, Colonel Gillo, where do you think the next attack will come?"

"Well, Grys Kreisa, I would not claim any ability to read the enemy's mind. But he has many options."

"Meld Annion thinks it will be in Annion again. Now the enemy knows that country, they will return to it."

Another Grys, a heavyset fellow wearing a light blue jacket, leaned over to exclaim.

"I say they'll land in Annion."

"Do you now, Grys Capennion?"

"I do, and you know why? Because the Assenzi say they will not. I say the Assenzi are not to be trusted."

Thru looked up. "Why ever not, Grys Capennion?"

"Who knows the secrets in their dark hearts?" Capennion's face had screwed itself into a snarl. "They may sacrifice us to the men."

Thru was taken aback. "I find that remark astonishing."

"Ah, but you're a Northern mot, well liked by Highnoth."

"Indeed," said the Grys Kreisa, "he is a Highnoth welp."

"Ach!" Grys Capennion's face darkened even further. "Then, I shouldn't waste my breath speaking to you."

Thru was taken aback by such open prejudice. He bit back his first retort.

"Well, Grys, you can of course make that decision for yourself, but I grieve to hear such unjust accusations against the Assenzi. I know that in Sulmo you lament certain events from the past."

The Grys Capennion cut him off with a rush. "Listen to him! Lament? My family was stripped of its wealth, of its grandeur."

Thru nodded thoughtfully. "And yet, Grys, your coat is of high quality. You are not a beggar by any means."

"Bah, my forebears had a thousand looms working in this city. By now we would have had complete control of the cloth trade."

"The Assenzi built up the Braided Valley," said Grys Kreisa. "Our position was lost."

"And don't you think they still do?" sneered Capennion. "Believe me, these Assenzi are sly devils. They preach austerity while they invest in the Braided Valley and take the profits themselves."

Thru had to laugh. "Well, if that's the case then I don't know what they spend it on, because at Highnot they live very simply. They eat the same rations as the students, and they get no more heat for their rooms."

"Bah. Does not matter. It is what they did to us in Ueillim's time that counts. This city was rich with looms."

"But why should you have had a monopoly on cloth production? Why should all the wealth of the Land be handed to Sulmo?"

"Because we are the oldest city, the purest civilization. Because we inspired advances in technique."

Thru snorted. "I have relatives with family trees as long as your own. We may be just simple country mots, but we have lived in the Dristen Valley for just as long as your kin have lived here. And we may be farming folk, but that doesn't keep us from developing our senses. We can always tell when other folk are getting above themselves, that's for sure."

"So you come down here to preach to us, eh? What is this, a live-the-simple-life lecture? And meanwhile you exclude the Sulmese from the army's command."

Thru shook his head at these particular words. "That is a strange accusation to make. We came down here because we have experience of fighting the men. Do you?"

The Grys Capennion growled and looked away.

"We came down here," said Thru again, "because Sulmo desperately needed experienced officers for the army. I would be just as happy protecting my own valley as protecting your city, Grys."

"I'm sure you would. As you say, you're just a simple country mot. But the Assenzi don't want Sulmese running our own army. They know they must keep us docile and helpless. So they bring down you northerners and make you our army staff."

Thru felt the anger rising, he fought to keep it out of his voice.

"Both my regimental commanders are Sulmese. One of them is the Grys Glaine. The other is a hill kob from an ancient family of the hills of Glaine. My tour of duty here will end in the next year or so, and I will go back to the North. One of them will become brigadier. Within another year most of the Northerners will be gone, and your army will be staffed by Sulmese alone."

Grys Capennion was in no mood to hear this. "Bah, there's no point in talking to a Northerner. That's what my family says, and you know something? They're right."

Capennion withdrew into his chair across the table. The Grys Kreisa fell silent, embarrassed by the turn of the conversation.

Thru kept quiet thereafter, responding when asked questions, but concentrating on the excellent food, while his mind whirled over the words of the Sulmese nobles. For a moment he was reminded of Pern Treevi, his old enemy. Pern had developed that urge for great wealth, too, and Pern had expressed that same bitter contempt for others.

When the plates were finally cleared and carried away, there was a short speech from the Meld of Daneep and a longer one from the King.

Once again, the battles of Chenna and the Sow's Head were toasted, and then all the officers of the army were toasted, and toasted again. There was a strong feeling of Sulmo the Great in the air. Pride and patriotism of a kind that was hardly ever heard in the northern realms of the Land.

Now everyone stood to sing a verse or two of the Sulmo song, and then they turned away to mingle once more. The aristocrats gathered together at one end of the table, and the officers gathered at the other.

Thru found himself at the back of the crowd, unnoticed at last. There came a gentle tug on his arm. He looked around and found Master Graedon there. The eyes of the engineer studied him carefully.

"And how are you, Thru Gillo? How is your head now?"

Graedon had taken a strong interest in Thru's head injury from the day he'd returned from the battlefield to Sulmo.

"It is better now, Master Graedon."

"I have heard that you suffer from headaches."

"I have done, yes."

"And do these still continue?"

"Less frequently, but yes . . ."

"I would like to examine your wound."

"Here now?"

The Assenzi looked around. Utnapishtim was coming across to join them.

"I don't think anyone will notice."

Thru looked around the room, indeed no one was looking his way. For a moment he glimpsed the Meld of Daneep, still sitting by the King in the midst of some long explanation about the battle. They were moving the salt cellars around.

"Hail, young Thru Gillo," said Utnapishtim, coming up and putting a hand upon Thru's shoulder."

"Utnapishtim," said Thru with a small bow.

"So you have encountered the sour rage of the old nobility here?"

Nothing escaped those wise old eyes.

"Yes, Utnapishtim. Not for the first time."

"They will never stop harking back to that time. They cling to their wound and thereby water the seeds of their unhappiness."

"There's something very unreasonable about it."

"There is greed at the root of it. Some people are born with a hunger for more than they really need in life. Some people do not get enough love from mother and father and acquire this same hunger. If it is not controlled, it can be very damaging. The greed of nations and cities is a similar thing, and its evil effects are recorded in the histories of the ancient times."

Graedon tugged on Thru's arm again.

"Come into the light."

He had placed a chair beside a large floor lamp. Thru sat in the chair, and Graedon pulled out a magnifying glass and carefully inspected the back of Thru's head. He palpated the skull and asked Thru to add up some numbers and subtract others. Then he had Thru look close into a candle held up by Utnapishtim while Graedon examined his eyes with a magnifying glass.

After a couple of minutes he was done and put away his magnifying glass.

"No serious harm has been done. We have been fortunate. It would have been a sad thing to lose you, young Thru Gillo."

"Indeed," said Utnapishtim.

As mysterious as ever, thought Thru as the Assenzi bid him farewell and left the chamber.

He went across to join the other officers. Seeing him approach, some of the Sulmese officers turned their backs or walked away.

Downcast, Thru joined Briohj of Dronned, a colonel in

the Royal Military Staff, and Colonel Ibbert of the newly formed Fourteenth Regiment.

"Afraid the Southerners don't like to see the Assenzi."

"So, guilt by association, eh?" Thru took a goblet of wine and sipped it.

"You've run into it a thousand times, I bet. I know I have," said Ibbert, who'd been training his unit for several months. "The Sulmese think they were robbed of something very important to them. But when you find out what you think they were robbed of, you just feel glad that it happened. They wanted to make themselves the rulers of the Land."

"It's troubling to hear them speak like that," said Thru.

"What did the old ones want?" said Briohj.

"Wanted to be sure my head wasn't completely broken."

"It is an honor to be of such concern to them."

Thru looked over to the Sulmese officers, who were now grouped together, ignoring the Northerners. "'Tis an honor, but I wish they'd not done that in front of these Sulmo mots. It won't help in our dealings with them."

Chapter 13

The news flashed to the Shasht fleet first from the incoming frigate *Viper* as she hurried into the bay.

"More ships! More ships have come from Shasht!"

Admiral Heuze stumbled up onto the deck, eyes bleary, his stump itching and burning, as it often did first thing in the morning. He read the distant signal flags in an instant and felt a cold stab of fear in his heart.

Another fleet? So soon? Damn! Who commanded the newcomers?

"Signal!" he snapped. "How many ships?"

The signal boy hurriedly sent up a dozen fresh flags.

The suspense was agonizing. Furious calculations spun through Heuze's head. When the fleet had left Shasht, there had been no mention of any reinforcements. That didn't mean that the Emperor wouldn't include them; Aeswiren had long ago learned how to rule by keeping his secrets.

Filek Biswas appeared on the upper deck, blinking away sleep.

"Ah, Filek, good morning. We have reinforcements it seems."

Heuze was gratified by the shock and dismay that flashed over Biswas's face. Biswas knew he depended on the admiral for his very survival.

"What do you mean, Admiral?"

"See *Viper* over there? Captain Pukh reports sighting ships about to join us."

"More ships from Shasht?"

"Of course, where else would you expect them from?"

"I see." Biswas clearly was worried about this development.

You're not the only one, thought the admiral.

Heuze noticed message flags flickering on the mizzen mast of *Sword* and brought his telescope up to his eye.

"Eight ships!"

A reinforcement, but not necessarily a threat to his position. Heuze felt immediate reassurance. He commanded the larger force; that gave him a strong position.

Some hours later when the eight vessels entered the harbor, guided in by *Viper*, Heuze knew much more and was already planning for the upcoming political struggle. The eight new ships were under the command of Admiral Beshezz, who technically outranked Heuze by several years of seniority. This was a problem that Heuze would have to finesse.

Fortunately the new ships were crammed with three thousand troops. That restored their army to almost ten thousand effectives, which surely would give them sufficient margin to be sure of victory.

The new ships, lead by their flag *Arrow*, slid into the bay and took positions in a line, a quarter mile behind the line of Heuze's ships.

Admiral Beshezz fired the first volley in the struggle between the admirals. A set of signal flags few up requesting "commanding officers" to come aboard *Arrow* at once! Beshezz was announcing his seniority in the most public manner.

Heuze chuckled grimly to himself at the sight. He thought this display might not go down well with one important actor in the play. He swung his glass over to observe *Hammer*, the ship that carried the Scion of the Emperor, Nebbeggebben. He didn't have long to wait. The imperial banner broke from the masthead, and signal flags rose beside it.

Admirals Beshezz and Heuze were both to repair at once to the Scion's ship. Heuze couldn't keep an impish smile off his face. Nebbeggebben was a withered thing now, half dead as a result of the plague, but he and his advisors were still keen to show everyone that they were ultimately in charge.

Beshezz had certainly got off on the wrong foot here.

Heuze bellowed for his barge to be readied.

"Care to come with me, Biswas?"

"I'd be honored, Admiral."

Heuze continued his effort to persuade Nebbeggebben to accept medical advice and treatment from Biswas. Anything to get the heir out of the clutches of the witch doctors.

The barge was lowered with whistles piping and soon rowed across to the huge hulk of *Hammer*. They climbed, even Heuze with his peg leg.

Once ushered into the main stateroom, they knelt down and bent their foreheads to the polished decking while the withered form of Nebbeggebben was helped in and placed on his throne by the priests. Nebbeggebben had never recovered from the plague. He could hardly walk now, and spent most of his time dozing in a cot. But he had retained his grip on power, and Heuze had not attempted to remove the Scion. Heuze preferred to let the situation mature further before he risked any action. Failure, he knew, would mean death at the hands of the priests, his heart torn out and offered to the Great God.

Listening to the sounds of the priests helping the Scion into his seat, Heuze recalled another time he had come to this room. On that occasion he had been given the stark choice, either cut off his own little finger or have his heart torn from his chest by the priests. The feel of the knife resting on his finger would never leave his memory. But, following this most recent defeat he had not been made to expiate in such dramatic fashion. General Hustertav had paid the price instead. Nebbeggebben had deliberately not blamed the admiral, thus preserving his life.

Heuze had still heard nothing of Beshezz, which gave him some satisfaction. He hoped his new rival would take his sweet time about arriving on the scene.

"Admiral, welcome," said the whispery voice of the Scion of Aeswiren.

"Heuze raised his head, but remained kneeling, holding onto his crutch to stay upright. "Thank you, my lord."

"We appreciate your prompt response to our command."

Heuze bowed his head again but said nothing, enjoying the implied rebuke to the absent Beshezz.

"So," whispered Nebbeggebben. "What do you think I should do, Admiral?"

"Well, my lord, there are three thousand fresh troops. We have enough now to field two armies. I think we should accelerate our plans for a fresh campaign."

"You do? Though our previous campaigns have been anything but successful?"

"Yes, my lord. I have appointed General Dogvalth to command the army. He is aware of your concerns."

"Mmmm, and Dogvalth saw what happened to Hustertav, did he not?"

"He was in the front row, my lord. He was spattered with the holy drops of crimson."

"Ah, the rain of He Who Eats. Well, Admiral, I hope that General Dogvalth will do a better job. Because if we suffer a third defeat, then I will be forced to accede to the demands of the priests and you will go to He Who Eats yourself."

Heuze nodded. "Yes, my lord, of course. I would expect nothing else. Such failure cannot be tolerated."

There came a snort of amusement from the withered heir.

"Good, that's the spirit, Admiral. That's what the Emperor expects in those who serve him."

"Indeed, my lord." Heuze and Biswas were careful to press their foreheads to the floor again at the mention of the Emperor himself.

"As it happens, Admiral, I agree with your proposition. I think we should accelerate our attack plan. Perhaps we can catch the monkeys napping and destroy them. I would like to spend next winter in more comfortable surroundings than this ship. Which means we must take over one of the monkey cities."

Cities? Heuze was surprised, even shocked, to hear Nebbeggebben describe the monkey places as "cities." The priests were listening, and the priests had preached consistently that the monkeys were nothing but animals and therefore incapable of building cities. Any cities that actually existed, had been built by real men and usurped by the monkeys. It was implausible, but the priests were sticking to it. They didn't really have a choice. The worship of their Great God did not allow it.

Now they heard the whistles and drums as Admiral Beshezz was helped up the side of the ship from his barge.

"That sounds like a good plan, my lord."

The door opened and Beshezz was announced. Nebbeggebben waved languidly to the newcomer. Heuze and Filek remained on their knees with their gaze fixed on the Scion. They heard the new admiral enter with a heavy tread and then drop down for the ritual prostration.

"Welcome, Admiral Beshezz. You seem weary. You have been traveling for a long time?"

"Yes, my lord, our trip has been long and wearying."

"And you were slow to respond to my signal. More weariness?" There was an edge in Nebbeggebben's papery husk voice.

"I came as quickly as I could, my lord. There were matters that had to be attended to."

"Mmmm." Nebbeggebben left a long pregnant silence to hover over their heads. Heuze risked a glance to his side. Beshezz was a mountain of a man, wearing a red coat and white trousers.

"Tell me, when did you set out from Shasht?"

"One year ago, my lord. We put out from Shasht harbor with ten vessels."

"But now there are only eight?"

"Yes, my lord. We were caught in the father of all storms four months ago, and two ships were lost and never seen again."

"This is sad news. Truly our expeditions to this accursed place have not been blessed by He Who Eats. Since He Who Eats is beyond criticism, we must turn to the priests for an explanation. So far I have heard little that is convincing."

Heuze understood the remark about the monkeys' cities. Nebbeggebben was clearly blaming the priests for the calamities that had fallen on the expedition. Heuze filed that thought away. Perhaps they'd be able to get rid of the priests altogether someday soon.

"So, apart from losses, what else have you brought me?"

Nebbeggebben was also showing Beshezz who was in charge here.

"Well, my lord, we have almost three thousand soldiers aboard our ships. We are overloaded in fact."

"And no doubt you are hungry."

"Yes, my lord, we desperately need food. We have been getting by on thin gruel for the last month."

"Well, we have some food, but not that much. Our lives here in the new world have been harder than many would have ever imagined."

Heuze kept his eyes downcast. Old Nebbeggebben had certainly paid a price. The plague had left him as this broken husk. No wonder he was bitter. And from Chalmli, Nebbeggebben's chamberlain, Heuze knew that Nebbeggebben's life in Shasht had been one long debauch. In fact, his dissolute life was the reason that Aeswiren had turned against his heir and dispatched him halfway around the world to found the colony.

"Still, we can afford to feed the new soldiers. You will put the men ashore at once."

"Ur, thank you, my lord."

Heuze chuckled inwardly. Why did he think that this was the last thing Beshezz wanted to do? For a year now Admiral Beshezz had been the ruler of his own little world. Those three thousand soldiers were "his." And now he would have to give them up as well as any dream he might have had of a separate kingdom of his own.

But now came the real knife to the heart. Nebbeggebben's whispery voice lightened for a moment.

"Good. I want complete dossiers on all your officers. Send them to me at once."

Heuze knew that the papers would go to the agents of the Hand. Any officers with troublesome aspects to their careers might soon find themselves on the receiving end of a dagger in the night or a dose of poison in their grog. Beshezz would lose his most ardent followers, too.

"Now, the matter of command. Knowing military men as well as I do, I know that both of you admirals are fretting under the surface about who is to be my commander in chief."

Heuze sucked in a breath. Here it came. Sooner than expected.

Nebbeggebben paused for a long moment to let them suffer.

"I will keep Admiral Heuze, here, as the commander. Admiral Beshezz, you will accept a position as sub-admiral to Admiral Heuze, understood?"

There was a dead silence. Beshezz had seniority and besides, he came from the mighty Beshezz clan. This was a tremendous blow to his pride. Heuze was a relative nobody, a career officer and little more. Certainly he had little in the way of connections at court, whereas Beshezz had uncles who regularly prostrated at the feet of Aeswiren himself.

"Uh, yes, my lord. Uh, may I add something?"

"Yes, you may," said Nebbeggebben in a mildly threatening husk. Heuze wanted to giggle. Beshezz was clearly cutting his own throat.

"I have messages from your father and uncles, personal messages."

Heuze nodded to himself. Beshezz skirted the dangerous area of challenging Nebbeggebben, but announced his own connections to the high and mighty in the home country.

"Excellent, you will leave them with my chamberlain. I look forward to reading the words of my father."

"Yes, my lord." Beshezz was not stupid enough to say anything more directly. Pity. Heuze kept his eyes down and his face completely expressionless.

"Now, Admiral Heuze?"

"Yes, my lord." He dared to look up once more. Nebbeggebben's gaunt, wasted features had the look of a reptile, long dead, dried out and preserved.

"You will convene a War Council to be held here. General Dogvalth and his staff, yourself, the good surgeon Biswas will attend. We will go over our plans."

"Yes, my lord." Oh, wonderful, cutting the huge oaf Beshezz out of it completely.

"Beshezz, you will attend, but as an observer only, is that understood?"

"Yes, my lord." Beshezz obviously didn't know whether

to be grateful or outraged. Heuze kept any bitterness out of his face. What had been a complete victory was now a partial defeat. Nebbeggebben was staring at him with peculiar intensity. Heuze wondered briefly if any derogatory remarks he'd made about the Scion had been passed back to him. There had been times during the winter when, in his cups with Pukh, he might have said something dangerous. On many occasions during the difficult winter months, Heuze had wanted to simply put the Scion and all the fornicating priests to the sword and toss their bodies to the fish.

Now the situation had changed again. Heuze's position had weakened because of Hustertav's defeat. By not demanding that Heuze expiate on the altar of Orbazt Subuus, He Who Eats, Nebbeggebben had quietly placed him in his debt.

And now there was this Admiral Beshezz, ready to be appointed to fill Heuze's shoes whenever necessary.

Heuze hated the feel of these reins upon him, but he had to be grateful for the mercy shown him and for the chance to regain the upper hand. All that was needed was a damn good victory. Once they had that, everything would swing back into his favor again. They just had to get a foothold here in the new land and beat the fornicating, sodomistic monkeys!

Chapter 14

Weeks passed. The fleet bustled with preparations for the coming campaign. Whenever possible, about twice a week, Filek took the opportunity to dine in his daughter's cabin on the women's deck.

One evening in the fourth week following Admiral Beshezz's arrival, they were together for a pleasant dinner of fish stew and pastries stuffed with the sour sweet "newfruits" that grew in the new world.

After their meal they read poems from Banness, the poetess of Shasht. But after several of these amusing, witty poems, neatly skewering the overpaid and overblown characters of literary Shasht society one hundred years before, Filek reluctantly closed the slim book and wiped the tears of laughter from his eyes.

Simona had a fine color in her cheeks from the fun.

"That woman was such an astute observer of human beings!"

"Yes, my dear, a woman with a wonderful mind." Filek hunched closer and began to speak in a different tone, hurried, barely more than a whisper.

As Simona listened she felt the old dread returning. Their position was no longer invulnerable.

"The admiral, my dear, I think he is hanging on by his fingertips." There was a sound, Filek paused and both listened carefully. On the women's deck there was always the chance of someone trying to eavesdrop on a private conversation. The sound was not repeated, and Filek leaned even closer before continuing.

"The Scion is playing the two admirals against each other. Admiral Heuze feels his position weakening."

"How does Admiral Beshezz speak to you?"

"He doesn't. Admiral Beshezz appears inimical to the cause of science. He disdains any attempts to improve his ships' surgeries. That is one of the issues between him and Heuze. One of the issues that the Scion is using to keep them both off balance."

"What can we do?"

"Pray that General Dogvalth obtains victory over the monkeys, over the enemy if you prefer, dearest daughter. I know you are sensitive to the word 'monkeys'."

"They are people, not monkeys! They are just as civilized as we are, Father. Thru Gillo learned our language in a few weeks. They are not the illiterate apes that the priests tried to make us believe."

"My dear, always be sure to say things like that in a whisper. Don't let anyone hear you. The priests may yet regain their power."

"How can they do that?" Simona was a little surprised to hear that from Filek.

"I think Beshezz is trying to forge an alliance with the Gold Tops. They are eager for friends; Admiral Heuze has hurt them considerably."

"But the Scion would not prefer Beshezz over Heuze."

"Not yet, but if Dogvalth loses the next battle, then Heuze will go to the priests."

Fear crashed home like a huge wave in her heart. Without Heuze their position would be gone. Beshezz would either replace Filek or shunt him and his hospital plans aside. The priests would clamor for his heart. And then? The priests would come for her. Simona had already suffered a mild bout of interrogation at their hands, so she knew what that would mean.

"That is all that can save him?"

"We have suffered two defeats. The admiral cannot lose another battle."

Simona shook her head sadly. Her life was cut in half by this knife of war. Her people could only survive if they took the Land. She could only hope to stay a free woman if they conquered the mots and took the Land. And that meant the death of everything she'd seen in her short exile in the Land.

It was too horrible to bear.

"But, Father, Beshezz has a wife and two sons. Heuze's wife is dead, his sons were left in Shasht. He is no threat to Nebbeggebben."

"All true, my dear, darling daughter who knows so much and sees so far. But the admiral has been arrogant in his dealings with the Scion. The priests thirst for the opportunity to place him over the altar."

"So Nebbeggebben could gain considerable advantage with the priests if he gave him up."

"As always, my farseeing daughter has glimpsed the reality of the situation. But what you said earlier still remains. Heuze is no threat to the dynasty. Nebbeggebben has taken two young wives. He plans to have some more children for the new world."

"Are you sure he's capable of that? The plague marked him so, you said."

"That is a good question, but I've never been able to gain his confidence. He entrusts himself to the witch doctors not to me."

"But Admiral Beshezz has sons that are almost grown men."

"Which helps to stay Nebbeggebben's hand from Heuze. Also I think he enjoys the sense of power that it gives him to have two admirals fighting for his favor like this."

"But you have said before that Beshezz is an egomaniac who constantly creates difficulties."

"That is true. Today he refused to move some of his ships. He had to be ordered by Nebbeggebben to comply before he would do it."

"That will grow tiresome to the Scion, Father. I predict it."

Filek shifted back with a weary smile on his face.

"You know, my dear, I think you may be right."

"Yes, Father."

"But it won't be long before the next crisis. The fleet will move soon. The army is undergoing training now for the new campaign."

Dread rushed through Simona.

All this was not supposed to happen. The ancient Masters had given her the little scroll, and she had given it to the admiral, just as she had been told to do. But it had had little effect and had not stopped the war. Would the message ever be sent back to Shasht, as was supposed to happen?

Even if it was, it could be too late. The next battle would surely decide everything, and this time the mots would face ten thousand men. That could be enough to turn the tide.

"And then everything will be in the hands of General Dogvalth."

Simona prayed that General Dogvalth would be defeated. An easy defeat, though, with few casualties on either side. Something that would delay the campaign, and let the message from the Assenzi do its work.

Filek leaned forward again to whisper.

"I think Admiral Heuze is rethinking his determination not to set foot on land again. He may yet decide to take charge of the army. He has the authority. I don't think Nebbeggebben would try to stop him, either."

"Do you think he would be better than the general?"

"I don't know. The generals were selected for their obedience. A bunch of clods in my opinion. The admiral is certainly more intelligent, but he may not be any better at commanding an army in battle."

"And how is the dear admiral's health, Father?" she asked as he sat back again.

"Ah, well, it is not good. His nerves are bad, and he complains of being unable to sleep. He has bouts of headache."

"I am sorry to hear that."

"Well, my dear, direct your prayers to He Who Eats and ask him to be kind to our dear admiral."

Simona bit her lips. It was impossible for her to think so fondly of the admiral, who had cheerfully ordered her hands and feet pounded with mallets by the Red Tops. All she wanted was something that would delay the war. Something that would stop the killing.

She made herself listen patiently to the rest of her father's complaints. She understood that he needed someone to confide in. While he complained about the builders on the hospital project, she listened with one ear, plotting to turn the discussion to something more crucial to her than the hospital.

She knew that Filek was less and less likely to discuss Rukkh. And her dream of marriage to a soldier had in fact faded away. She understood now that she didn't really want the life of a colonist, living on the land that would be taken from the mots. Still, at times she liked to think of that young man, so hard-bodied and burning of eye when he had looked at her.

Unfortunately, none of her own thoughts on this issue had stopped Filek's schemes for marrying her to some old man for political advantage.

Filek had run out of complaints.

"Ah, well, listen to me ranting on. I have too much to do, that's the real problem."

"I'm sure you do, Father."

"Mustn't complain so much. It's hard sometimes, you understand I'm sure."

"Oh, of course, Father dear." Simona, who had nothing to do, dared not mention her own utter boredom.

"Now, let us turn to something else. Have you considered what I spoke to you about the last time I was here?"

Simona shuddered inwardly. He referred to Wurg Gembeth, a corpulent cousin of General Dogvalth.

"What was that, Father?" she said playing for time.

"Well, my dear, you're not getting any younger and now is the time to marry. I think you should consider marriage to Wurg Gembeth."

"He is thirty years older than me, Father. He is older than you."

"Yes, my dear, which is good news. He is also immensely fat. He will not last long. Once he's gone to join He Who Eats, you will be a wealthy widow."

Wurg Gembeth traveled aboard the Anvil and was wed to two other young women. He visited them regularly on the women's deck. Simona had heard too much of Wurg's excited bellows in the rut.

He was fat, he was coarse and repulsive, and he would live long enough to put a stain on Simona's soul that she would never wash out if she gave in to this. But, she could see that her father was increasingly desperate about his chances. If Heuze was taken by the priests, then they would need every ally they could keep. Wurg Gembeth might be that.

"Except that, dear father, what would happen if"—she leaned forward—"Wurg is Dogvalth's cousin, right? If Dogvalth loses the battle, won't Wurg be at risk as well?"

Filek stared at her, blinked a moment.

"Yes, to some extent, but Wurg is enormously wealthy, my dear. He has given Nebbeggebben gifts of gold and gemstones."

She stared back at Filek, sudden horror blossoming in her mind. Filek realized what she was thinking and clasped her hands in his.

"No, dearest, do not think that of me. I advocate this not for the gold alone. Gold is a good thing to have and I wish I had more of it, but gold is beside the point. Wurg has a strong position with Nebbeggeben. If General Dogvalth should fail, then Wurg could still protect you."

And by implication, protect Filek, too.

She stilled her anger. Filek was determined to use her to strengthen his position. It was useless to rail at him over this. He was afraid. And she realized that she should be afraid, too. There were real risks to their lives involved. If Filek lost his position, then Simona might end her days in the ranks of army whores. Simona would never forget the helpless agony she had suffered during a mild "questioning" by the Red Tops. When they slapped your hands with the mallets, it really hurt!

"I will think about it, dear father, but I would much rather be wed to someone my own age."

"Yes, dear, so would I. I wish you were marrying a Prince of the Realm. But circumstances may go against us." Filek leaned forward again.

"We may have to do things to survive that we would rather not do. But if there is another defeat, then we may have no choice."

"Yes, Father."

They embraced, and he kissed his marvelous daughter's forehead before exiting her tiny cabin.

Simona, left alone with these alarming strands of information, sat staring out the porthole. Away in the distance she could just see tiny gleams of light. The lamps burning on the shore, illuminating the new town the men had built. Rukkh was over there somewhere, she thought. And she thought about his hard, young body and the fire that had burned in his eyes when he'd come to look at her in the old days.

She knew she'd be bored by him. He was probably illiterate. But so was Wurg Gembeth—maybe death would be preferable after all.

Chapter 15

As she had in the old days in Tamf and Dronned, Nuza had sought out the local chapter of the Questioners in Sulmo. This was the group that met every week or every month in most towns and cities of the Land. At these meetings they voiced questions about the nature of society and the way things were. In the northern realms of the Land, they were regarded as slightly daring by the general public, but also important for allowing grievances to be aired.

The Sulmo group met in a room attached to a woodworker's shop inside the old walls. The woodworker, Sulp Emmers, was the group's leader. Nuza pressed Thru to accompany her for the evening session.

"Just because the war destroyed our old lives that doesn't mean we can't still ask questions."

"I have only three more days here. Then I must go back to Glais."

Where his brigade had reformed and was waiting for him. Let's not waste our time listening to questions about polder and land rights, he wanted to. Let's stay in your room and make love.

But Nuza wore him down, and so he found himself sitting beside her on a wooden bench that evening listening to the questions posed by the mots and brilbies drawn to the meeting.

Thru had learned that the Questioners were both discouraged more in Sulmo and yet at the same time more popular than in the North. In Sulmo certain kinds of questions were officially discouraged. Sulmo had too many memories of the city's brief time of glory, and at Questioners' meetings folk would harp on them.

That evening there were perhaps thirty folk in the room, the usual collection of the dour and the excitable that one found at Questioner's meerings all over the Land.

Sulp Emmers was a solidly constructed mot, his grey fur whitened by sixty years and his huge hands scarred by a lifetime of working with heavy tools. He introduced the questions and selected those who were to answer. A well-fed mot in the front row, name of Maskop, wearing the maroon shirt and hat of the royal service was the one usually chosen to reply.

Maskop's replies tended to accentuate conservative, un-challenging views of the various controversies that surfaced at the Questioners.

A young mor with fiery orange ribbons woven into the fur on the back of her head was the first to speak, and brought up a matter that was a perennial sore point in Sulmo. That being its downfall had been caused by the Assenzi.

"I am only a young mor, but I have read the Book and listened here to many questions. I want to know why we feel we must obey the Assenzi? Why do we allow so many of them to come and go from our city? When you remember what they did to us in the old days it seems wrong. Rumors say that they advise the King and speak to him of his dreams."

Her outburst caused a stir along the benches, because dream speaking was an ancient tradition in Sulmo and it was disturbing to imagine the King speaking of his dreams to the Assenzi.

The royal shirt arose. Sulp waved a hand.

"I think Maskop here is prepared to answer."

Maskop bowed. Thru observed that he was a singularly fat mot, something rather unusual in the Land.

"First of all I must say unequivocally that the King does not dream speak with the Assenzi. Our King is well aware of the feelings of the folk of Sulmo. He shares the beliefs of his people and knows that great wrong was done to our city. But he also knows that in this current emergency, we must set aside our differences and work together to win the war. Remember who our enemy is! Knowing that, you know that we must cooperate with the Assenzi. They can teach us much."

"Can they be trusted?" the mor with the fiery ribbons responded.

"Why should they not be trusted?" Maskop spread his hands out to either side. "Their lives are forfeit, too, if Man defeats us."

The mor sat down while a gentle murmur broke out along the benches.

Another hand was raised by a young brilba in an expensive black velvet robe. Receiving the nod from Sulp, she rose to put a very different kind of question.

"I have come to a few meetings here before, but I did not speak. Now I am troubled by a question, so I will put it before you.

"I have heard it said that what we read in the Book is not always true. There are those who believe that it was chooks who were created first by the Hand of Man. Man made the chooks and then later Man made the brilbies and finally he made the mots. I find this idea troubling, and I wonder if there is any evidence for it."

There was a stir on the benches again. This was an unusual question, far removed from the more common gripes about shortage of polder land.

Sulp chose to answer it himself.

"I have always been interested in the tale of our origins, too. I have studied the story of our birth. Assenzi writings and even some of the ancient records of that time still exist. Few know about them because they are kept under lock and key in Highnoth, the lair of the Assenzi."

Thru blinked at hearing Highnoth described as a "lair."

Sulp continued in his calm, measured voice. Thru could see that Sulp was an excellent host for a meeting of Questioners. He radiated a sense of calm as a lamp radiates light.

"That means it is impossible to have independent access to them. But the Assenzi themselves have written about them, and their works are available. I have read Cutshamakim on this subject. He quotes many diverse sources.

"In the last days of Man, when Highnoth was still a city

of power and light, there were great men who were skilled
in the highest arts of magic. They were men like Hargeevi
and Belnek. This was the time of the High Men. Men who
were skilled in the great arts and magic of the former
world. They were as different from the men of Shasht as
we are from the pyluk."

Thru was listening with full attention now. Thru had
spent more than two years living at Highnoth, learning at
the feet of the great Assenzi. But even there he had not
learned everything about the Origin.

Sulp went on as if reciting a well-learned screed.

"These men took the germ material of certain animals
and subjected it to arcane arts that have long since been
forgotten. They married the material they had made of animals to the germ of Man himself, and thus they brought
forth the peoples of the Land."

This much was widely known.

"It has been asked who was the mother of the folk? Was
it wo-man?"

Into Thru's head popped a memory of Simona. Wo-man
was like a mor, but perhaps a little heavier and taller. Both
were blessed with wide hips for mothering the young and
breasts for feeding them mother's milk.

"But the High Men did not use wo-man to be mother to
the new folk. By their magic they were able to bring forth
the folk from bowls of the purest glass. They brought us up,
but they used no mother's womb, just as the Book says."

There were appreciative murmurs along the benches. It
was good to know that the words in the Book were true,
for it was the central pillar of most people's beliefs.

From bowls of purest glass . . .

"First they brought forth the brilby and the brilba. And
they are called the longest lived of the folk."

With teeth of shining steel.

Some heads turned to look at the brilba Questioner.

"Then they brought forth the kobs and kobi. And it is
said by some that there is too much spirit of the antelope
in the kob and kobi, but they remain among us, the fewest
of our folk, but much loved by all the others."

Once again heads turned to a single kob in the audience,

and the big, brown-furred fellow blinked bashfully at the attention.

"Finally they made the mots and mors, and they went forth to populate the Land."

The mots nodded vigorously, for they were the humble farmers of the polder and the center piece of the society of the Land.

"But you have said nothing about the chooks," said the brilba.

"Correct, for little is known now about when chooks were first made. Some Assenzi claim that chooks existed before the Assenzi themselves were given life. One Assenzi, Histegrud, says that the magic that made the chooks was very very old and that chooks had been in existence for a long time before the great Hargeevi began his work. His magic took what had been done with chooks and extended it."

"Then it is true. The Book is wrong."

"It may be so. The Book was written by unknown authors. Their understanding of the ancient times may have been limited. Cutshamakim writes that he does not know whether chooks were truly the first, or the last. Chooks may have existed when the Assenzi first awoke, but the Assenzi are vague about that time. They worked in isolation upon the chores given them by the High Men; they knew little about the outside world."

Another Questioner had a hand raised, a mot in the third row.

"Whether chooks came first or not, if we can believe the Book and your evidence, then we were made by the Hand of Man. My question is why do we not worship Man instead of the Spirit?"

That produced another stir. Here was a truly heretical thought. Thru felt the fur stand up on his shoulders as he considered it.

Sulp was still ready to answer, though Maskop had risen to his feet, too.

"For that we can look to the Book. For the true face of ancient Man was not that of the High Men of Highnoth. It was Man the Cruel. And when we see the face of the men of Shasht, what do we see?"

"Man the Cruel" rose up in a whisper from the crowd.

"Yes, Man the Cruel with the whip and the knife and the tongs to castrate us. So although we were raised up by Man, we do not worship Man. We acknowledge the role of the High Men, but we know the truth of Man."

Now Maskop spoke. "In addition, we must remember that the Spirit was here before Man, before anything. The Spirit transcends all of the material world. In a sense, we might say that the Spirit is the world, for it informs it all with its ultimate purpose, which is hidden from us who labor within it."

Thru nodded at that. This was the wisdom of the Assenzi. Beneath the surface of the world and its creatures, there beat a hidden pulse of spiritual energy. It could only be sensed during the meditative state, and even then it was difficult to understand. Indeed it was only by giving up on understanding and accepting the chaos of the void that true understanding could come.

"So, although our Origin came from the Hand of the High Men, we must see that as an aberration in the general rule of Man. The High Men were not governed by the laws of Man the Cruel; they came at the end of Man's time. Much of what Man had wrought had already come to pass, for as it says in the Book:

"For poison in the waters had become poison in their seed . . ."

"The High Men were keepers of a dying flame and sought only to preserve that flame, the light of civilization here upon Arna. And so they made us."

Like everyone else Thru felt a sense of relief at hearing these words. Differentiating between Man the Cruel and the High Men was vital for them all in an age when Man the Cruel threatened once again.

Later, after the meeting, Thru and Nuza walked arm in arm along the avenue in the outer city. Thru had to admit that his imagination had been fired by the strange talk in the Questioners. Nuza had been aroused, too. An old concern of hers had reawoken.

"I think of this sometimes, and I can't quite believe it all happened. That there was a time when we did not exist. When only Man the Cruel lived and everything else suffered. I thought once that we could not think of it, because it was a shadow time, before our own memory. But now I know that it is just that I find it very uncomfortable to think like that."

"I know that feeling. It frightens me. But the Assenzi taught me that the world is older than Man. The reign of Man the Cruel was but a single night compared to the many years the world has existed."

"Did the Spirit exist then, before Man?"

"Yes, the Spirit has existed since the beginning of the universe. The Spirit is the universe, in a sense." Thru felt this with such conviction he had no doubts this was the truth.

"I do not understand that, either, exactly. How can the Spirit be both something of itself and at the same time part of everything else?"

"It is not easy to understand, it is something that you come to know when you follow the path of the Assenzi and learn their teachings."

"Then, I have more to learn." Nuza hugged his arm.

Rain began to spatter down while they were standing on the bridge over the Sulo with the spires of the palace looming to the west. The surface of the river reflected a million rain drops in a few moments.

"Uh-oh, this is going to be hard rain," said Nuza.

They ran for shelter.

On the south side of the bridge, they found a cookshop open selling pies and hammelbem cakes to a hungry throng.

They took seats at a table by the window. The rain was hammering down now, drumming on the tiled roofs. The gutters on the front of the cookshop were spilling into the street. There were no glass windows on this simple establishment, and the shutters were open so the wet smell of the rain in the street came in.

They ordered toasted hammelbem cakes and bushpod pies. With the cakes came a bowl of hot melted butter and a pot of tea. The pies were sweet and scented with cinnamon.

They ate quietly, listening to the violent rainfall, enjoying each other's company.

"We disposed of the past," said Nuza holding his hand. "What of the future?" Thru's eyebrows flashed as he shrugged. Dark clouds hung across the future.

"Well, I must go to Glais day after tomorrow. After that I don't know. Will the enemy attack again this year? We can't be sure, but we must be ready in case he does. We have no way to bring him to battle, we must wait for his attacks."

"Oh, I wish this war was over and we could have our real lives back."

Thru nodded as he finished his tea.

"I feel that way, too. Sometimes it seems like that life will never come back. That this will be the way we will live forever now. Always at war."

"Let us talk of other things," she said. Their time together was short, and she wanted to make it as pleasant as possible.

The rain had ended, and they walked back through the darkening streets of the city while lamplighters plied their rounds, lighting the large lamps on street corners that lit up most of the inner city after dark until the midnight hour. On Whiteflower Lane they caught the scent of summer flowers and heard the croaking of frogs in the pond. The small white houses glowed softly. For the moment they were left with their love and the light of the moon.

Chapter 16

Another long day in the camp of Sixth Brigade was coming to its end. Thru signed off on the last few bits of paperwork and noticed that the afternoon was verging into the warm evening of late summer. Thru got to his feet, stretched, pulled on the lightweight deep blue jacket that was the new summer-weight uniform, and made sure his red pin was clearly visible. He pulled on his blue cap, preferring it to the big hats worn by many other rank officers. The single glossy red button on the front was all the evidence of rank he needed.

He took a turn around the camp, observing the few formations of soldiers who were still drilling on the parade square. Sergeant Burrum bellowed orders in the near distance. Thru went the other way, walking down a lane between tents, acknowledging salutes from officers as he went. The mots, brilbies, and kobs of the brigade sat out around the tents; a few campfires burned to brew up tea. The camp had a good feeling to it. These last few weeks had seen a steady improvement in training levels. They'd recovered quickly from the mauling they'd taken at the Sow's Head and gone on from there.

He reached the orchard. Tents were set up among the trees. Thru strolled through the area looking for the plum trees that the Alvil claimed had been "mutilated." Down by the water's edge he found a stand of plums. Two tents were set up beneath them. No damage was visible, but there was a downed tree limb beside one of the tents. He strolled closer and discovered that it was oak, its few remaining leaves withered and brown.

He made a mental note to ask Major Ilb to investigate.

Someone had probably found the wood out in the forest and dragged it back here for the fire. But he wanted to be sure it hadn't been cut from any tree of the Alvil's. He turned at the edge of the orchards. Tents in more or less orderly lines were all he could see. Trees seemed undamaged. Typical. The Alvil had probably seen that oak branch pulled up by the tents and gone on to her own wild conclusions.

Back in the main part of the camp, he quickened his pace. After getting something to eat, he planned to write a letter to Nuza. Writing to her always improved his mood, and he gave thanks to the Spirit that she was part of his life.

Then a sudden shout interrupted his thoughts. Mots nearby pointed up, and he caught a flash in the golden light of a white pigeon, homing on the tower in the center of the village.

"Messenger bird!" was the word flashed around the camp. Thru watched it go on, over the trees, heading for the constable's tower.

Back at his command post Thru found Sergeant Burrum drinking a mug of cool tea.

"You heard?"

"Yes, sir. We're about to get some news. I expect everyone in camp knows that a pigeon went over."

Thru nodded. A pigeon meant news from Sulmo, or the coast. A pigeon meant war. Nor did they have long to wait before a young mot came running up, out of breath, having sprinted all the way from the constable's office. Thru broke the seal, read the contents, and turned to Ilb.

"The enemy has landed in force on the shore of Chenisee, near Farnem. We're to rendezvous with the Eighth Brigade at Telsher. The Meld is leaving Sulmo with four brigades. He marches toward the village of Chillum."

"Maps," said Thru. "What have we got of Chenisee? Where is Farnem, exactly?"

"There are good maps of the entire county, sir." Ilb motioned to the map rack. "Good, we'll take a look at them right away. Get orders out to every unit commander. I want everything ready to move at first light. Everyone should eat a hearty supper and get some sleep. Tomorrow we march."

"Right, sir."

"And what are the chances of sending a bird down to the coast tonight? I want Grys Glaine to move the twelfth regiment up to the Chenisee Gap at first light as well. He can't get there before us, but he can be close behind. I'd like for the entire brigade to be in one place by the time we reach Telsher. Understood?"

"Sir," snapped Major Ilb.

The regiments were filled with seasoned soldiers now. The next day they kept up a swift pace, and the columns left dust trails through the Chenisee Gap. The supply train was left far behind, plodding along at the pace of the oxen.

In the tiny hamlets they passed, the entire population came out to wave and cheer them on. Even up here in the wilds of the gap, the folk had heard the terrible news. The army of men was ashore down past Farnem and busy destroying everything in its path.

Through the hills they went and on down into the forest of Chenisee. The road dwindled to a trail through endless stands of oak, beech, chestnut, and pine. Where soils were sandy the pines predominated. The wet areas nurtured groves of mighty willows, their girths as much as those of houses.

Disturbed by their presence the animals of the wilderness had fled, though the wolves called out at their passing and the packs carried the news across the forest and into the hills of Glaine.

Off to their right lay Sulmo, perhaps forty miles over the hills. On their left, just ten miles separated them from the sea. Ahead, perhaps fifteen miles distant, was Farnem, a small town of fisherfolk and weavers.

The enemy was down there somewhere, near the coast.

A new determination filled the regiments. This time it would be different. This time they would do the job. They would take hold of the enemy and keep him fast while they pounded him to pieces. They would end the threat to the Land. They knew what they had to do. They had met Man on the battlefield, and they had beaten him. They knew they could do it now.

Morale was high; every single soldier was determined to

keep up the maximum pace. Complaints had dropped away to almost nothing. No one wanted to hear them anyway.

Thru saw the contrast with the march he'd made in the Meld's army on the way to the Sow's Head. Those had been green recruits, barely into the second month of their training. Those mots had spilled out of line every few miles, forced to rest a little by their sore feet and aching limbs. The soldiers around him this time were seasoned by battle, and hardened by months of marching.

Down the narrow trails they came, hurrying through the forests. Ahead, they could see out across the trees to the distant chalk bluffs of Norfarnem. They quickened the pace. The target for the day was to reach Telsher, a village several miles ahead. There they would hook up with the Eighth Brigade, which was marching up from Blana. Together they would proceed toward Farnem.

In command would be the Grys Blana, his rank confirmed by a message under the seal of the King of Sulmo. The King had been anxious from the beginning to maintain control of the army through the native nobility. Blana had a reputation for being "difficult." Thru hoped for the best, knowing that he had far more experience of war than the Grys. But the King always gave the nod to a Grys or Meld rather than a Northerner for such a command. And so it was the Grys who would have titular command of the two brigades when they came together.

A shout came from the head of the column.

"Smoke!"

Away to the north, across the forest green, a column of thick black smoke was rising into the warm afternoon air.

"Farnem?"

"Yes, sir. By our reckoning that's Farnem all right."

The smoke continued to billow up and then to slant inshore, caught by a breeze off the sea. As they watched it rise, cries of anger bubbled up from the ranks. Here was the Hand of Man again, invading their land, burning another ancient village.

Thru felt that anger, and also a renewed certainty. The enemy was here. They would have another chance to destroy him soon.

They followed the trail into a valley and could no longer see the distant smoke cloud. When they climbed the far side of the valley the smoke was still rising, and separate clouds had drifted farther inland. Farnem was burning to the ground.

Again they descended into a wooded valley, finding polder at the farther end, and soon after that entered the village of Telsher.

They were the first to arrive. Thru set about organizing the camp and set the Sixth and Twelfth regiments to camp in fields of stubble just outside the little town. Water was brought up on oxen carts, food was quickly prepared, and the mots ate a large meal and settled down to sleep. They'd covered twenty-five miles and climbed the Chenisee Gap into the bargain. They deserved a rest.

A messenger came in after an hour to say that the Grys and the Eighth Brigade were hurrying up the road from Blana and would be with them inside three hours.

Thru had a party fetch more water while others built cook fires in the fields across the road, where Thru assumed the Grys would want to camp. Thru met with his own regimental commanders, Ter-Saab and the Grys Glaine. The Grys had made up the extra miles from south Glaine. Thru made sure to praise him in front of Ter-Saab.

Ter-Saab smiled at Thru to let him know that he knew what Thru was up to. Thru gave him the merest raised eyebrow in return.

Later, Grys Glaine returned to his own command post. Thru and Ter-Saab took some tea, bread, and sour butter by the campfire while they discussed the coming campaign.

"Please excuse my presumption, sir, but I wonder what you know about the Grys Blana?"

"Very little. One of the Blana regiments is fully trained, the other is not. The Meld told me I could expect the Grys to be very enthusiastic, very driven to succeed."

"Ah." Ter-Saab sipped hot tea.

"Yes? Go on."

"Blana is a part of Sulmo that has often been independent, you understand."

"Mmm."

"Independent people with a certain arrogance is how most folk in south Sulmo think of the Blanans."

"You're suggesting that I'm going to have trouble with the Grys?"

"I would just like to suggest that you be prepared for those particular traits of personality. The Grys and his entire family are rather famous for them."

"Ah." Thru nodded thoughtfully. "Thank you for warning me."

Thru had reason to remember Ter-Saab's words, when the Grys Blana came marching up at the head of his regiments a scant two hours later.

The Grys was a full-fleshed mot of late middle age. His cheek fur had whitened early and his eye tufts, too. He came surrounded by banner holders with a drummer out in front. Thru was partly amused, partly concerned. Something about this little group—the Grys, his senior staff officers, three brilbies carrying banners, and a fat mot banging a drum—made Thru think of the army of Shasht.

"Welcome to Chenisee, Grys," said Thru after offering a salute.

The Grys returned the salute with a frown on his face, unhappy at being spoken to first by someone of lower social rank.

"I am disturbed to find your regiments in their tents. We must crack on at once and march through the night to Farnem."

Thru felt his eyebrows shoot up at hearing this. Farnem was nothing but smoldering ruins at this point.

"We're not sure yet of the exact location of the enemy army. I have reports from around Farnem, but they are inexact as yet. We will know much more in the morning when scouts return with some identifications of enemy units."

The Grys was dismissive. "Pah, this is much too cautious. We will march up the road, and if we find the enemy, we will get started on him right away. Let the Meld come and join the hardy mots of Blana, for we will be in the thick of it."

"I'm sure they will be. However, Grys, I would suggest

a little caution in attacking the entire enemy force with only four regiments."

"It is our responsibility to smash the enemy as soon as possible. Every moment that they stand on our sacred land is a horror to me and my soldiers."

"Yes, of course, I understand. But isn't it also our responsibility to hold this force together? The Meld will need our regiments."

"Bah, where is your courage, Colonel? If we surge to the attack at once, we will seize the initiative. That is all we'll need. When the Meld comes up to join us he can take care of mopping up."

Thru heard these words with mounting horror.

"Grys, if we attack the men with such a small force, they will counterattack very quickly. They are skilled at battlefield maneuver and quick to adjust to changing conditions."

"My regiments have trained intensively. Our morale is so great we are ready to take on twice our own numbers of these evil men."

"With all respect, Grys, you have not seen men in battle. They are more formidable than perhaps you imagine."

The Grys made a face. "Bah, I cannot understand such faintheartedness. Rouse your troops. I want to continue the march at once."

"At least inform the Meld of Daneep of your plan. He would expect you to notify him of our presence here. We should send messengers at once."

"We will send him a message from Farnem. That's if the sound of our swords beating on the enemy has not roused him already. I expect he will be in Chillum by then, so he'll hear us loud and clear."

With a sinking feeling in his gut, Thru sent the orders out to wake his regiments and put them on the road in the dark.

The fact that they were miles from Farnem and that the route there would pass mostly within the dense, dark forest of central Chenisee didn't seem to matter to the Grys. He was determined to find and attack the enemy at once. Alas, the Grys Blana had been given command because of his title not because of his brains.

Thru told Major Ilb to find a local messenger who could find a way to reach the Meld during the night. Thru was outranked by the Grys and could not disobey without serious consequences. But he was concerned that this ill-considered attack would put the entire army at risk.

Ilb proved once again that he was a master at anticipation. He produced a brilby from the nearest village who claimed to know a good route along the hill scarp to Chillum village. Thru sent him off with a message and a prayer.

Several hours later, in the depths of the night, the four regiments lost their way in the dark woods. They were on forest trails, barely able to see the back of the soldier in front of them. The wagons and carts could not be pulled through the thick forest so their supply was lost for the foreseeable future. Thru wondered if the Grys Blana had much experience of dealing with hungry soldiers.

Thru and Ilb worked their way through the gloomy woods until they found the Sixth Regiment gathered together in a glade. Ter-Saab, proudly in control.

"Well, Colonel, let me congratulate you first on keeping the Sixth in one piece."

"Thank you, sir, but I'm missing at least fifty stragglers."

"Well, the Grys is missing about half the Twelfth. Seems they took a right fork somewhere back there, and who knows where they are now."

"Poor old Pook, I know he'll be mortified."

"And I haven't heard from Blana in a while. I've sent scouts out to the left, looking for him, but still haven't heard anything positive."

"They're probably ahead of us. The stream crossing has tracks. Looks like a lot of them went over ahead of us."

"Major Ilb?" Thru turned back to his chief of staff. "Perhaps Blana is ahead of us. Have scouts sent forward right away. I want to send a message, too. We're getting hopelessly strung out in these woods."

Messages were sent to the Grys Blana and to the Grys Glaine. With mounting impatience and concern, Thru waited at the crossing of the stream while tea was brewed and dried bread handed around.

The sky had cleared, the crescent moon shone a wan light over the world. Thru thought back to the time just before the ambush at Chenna. Marching up the road straight into a trap. Poor Colss had paid for his mistake with his life. That ambush had happened fast, and the men had pressed their attack with their customary ferocity. If that ambush was repeated now, with Blana out in front with his two regiments and Thru strung out in the woods like this, they would face disaster.

Except that the enemy would be just as lost as they were in these dense thickets. Thru chewed his lips. The danger would come when they came out into open space closer to Farnem.

The message to the Grys Glaine brought a swift response, borne by the Grys himself who came hurrying up the trail. He reported that the missing companies of the Twelfth Regiment had realized they were going in the wrong direction, had backtracked, and were now following up at a trot. They would rejoin the rest of the command in less than an hour.

"Thanks be given for that."

Ter-Saab snorted. "Now if we just knew where the Grys Blana was."

The Grys Glaine blinked nervously. "I don't wish to criticize our commanding officer, but I do have questions about this advance in the dark."

"Well, I don't have questions," grumbled Ter-Saab. "I think this is plain crazy. The men are likely to be sitting in ambush up there at Farnem."

The Grys Glaine blinked again.

"How far to Farnem, anyway?" said Thru, peering at the map. It was hard to read in the faint light. On the map the trails were a morass of dotted lines.

"No more than four miles ahead, by our reckoning," said Ter-Saab.

"Listen," said Thru. "If my worst fears come true, then the enemy will be waiting for us at Farnem. They'll be hiding in the trees, and as soon as we move out into the open, they'll attack. That's what they did at Chenna. So I'm going to warn the Grys Blana, and we're going to hurry to catch up. As soon as we hit the open space, we must be ready to form a battle line."

"Understood," said the Grys Glaine. Ter-Saab merely nodded.

More scouts went out, and a messenger to Blana was sent forward with Thru's note outlining his concerns about an ambush at Farnem. The messenger returned down the trail after a while with only an oral command from the Grys Blana.

"Hurry forward!"

On they went. By dawn they were still a mile or so from Farnem, but Thru's front companies had made contact with the tail of the Blana regiments.

Scouting reports from Farnem painted a picture of a village burned to the ground; however, the folk had obviously escaped in time, for no bodies and no heads were found. The only sign of the enemy were their tracks. The men had been there but now they were gone.

The Grys Blana was obviously rankled by the lack of an enemy to attack. He sent the scouts out with orders to be more aggressive and vigorous. "Find the enemy!" were his words.

Messengers were also sent out with the scouts. They would seek the Meld a few miles farther north and east toward Chillum.

Thru prayed for the umpteenth time that his messenger had got through to the Meld during the night.

At the edge of the polder land of Farnem, a slash of bright green waterbush planted in neat rows down the river bottom, the army halted again. Smoke still rose from the embers of the village. The sight of the ruined village had rekindled the mots' anger, and cries for revenge riled the lines of regiments.

Blana called a conference with Thru and all the regimental commanders. Blana seemed wide awake. His eyes were preternaturally bright despite the long march without sleep.

"No signs of fighting here at Farnem, I'm told," he said

as they gathered around. "The village was burned, but the folk were gone and no resistance was given."

"Any report of the enemy's whereabouts yet?" said Kremen, commander of the Seventeenth Regiment.

"Not yet, scouts are working toward Chillum, but we still have no confirmed sightings of men."

"Should we deploy into line while we wait here," said Ter-Saab with a quick look to Thru, who nodded gratefully for not having to ask that question in front of the regimental commanders.

"No, I want to be ready to move out on a moment's notice."

Thru, still nervous about an ambush winced, but said nothing. He understood the Grys Blana's character a little now. If he pushed the fellow, it would only make him dig his heels in, even if he was obviously wrong.

After that it was only a matter of making reports about each regiment and being told to be ready to fight to the death. Then the meeting was dismissed. Thru pulled Ter-Saab and the Grys Glaine to walk with him.

"We have to be ready to march in column, but I want enough space in the column so we can deploy into a line at a moment's notice. We've practiced it often enough; now's the time to do it."

"Yes, sir," they chorused.

"Form up for the march. I don't want it to look as if we're openly disobeying the Grys."

Off they went. Thru waited at his command post, temporarily set up around the trunk of a huge fallen oak. Major Ilb and Sergeant Burrum handled the routine complaints and problems there—blisters, worn-out boots or sandals, lost equipment, and the few cases of mots and briblies who'd collapsed, too worn out to go on.

There were surprisingly few of those.

He closed his eyes for a few moments and thought about Nuza. He visualized her face, heard her voice, felt her lips against his.

He opened his eyes again. Before him stood the good Major Ilb, dealing with a case of a lost spontoon pike. The lacquer on the mot's helmets glittered in the torchlight.

By the fallen tree the brigade flag had been thrust into the ground.

They waited, growing more anxious with every minute.

Then at last three scouts returned at a run, hastening to the Grys Blana's standard. Within moments messengers were on their way, running full tilt along the columns to reach the regimental commanders.

The enemy was attacking the Meld's force, on the far side of the village of Chillum. The battle had already begun!

Chapter 17

They kept up a steady jog now, all fatigue forgotten as they ran between the famous orchards of the valley of Farnem. They forded the river and moved on across the strip of polder and into the village of Chillum. Now they caught the first sounds of the battle ahead: a dim, distant roaring with occasional high shrieks that cut through the rest.

Chillum was undamaged, though there were a few bodies, men with mot arrows in them. Here and there a door banged in the wind. The regiments deployed into a battle line, with the Eighth Brigade in front and the Sixth behind it. They moved out of the village in nice orderly lines, maintaining a steady pace.

Now upslope, across the trampled fields, they could see many more still forms. Sometimes the bodies were heaped up around a gate; mostly they were scattered across the wheat.

As they passed them, Thru saw men, mots, brilbies, even a kob, all sharing the same wild grimace in death. Some were pinned to the ground by spears, others lay facedown. There was a stink of blood and shit. A hedge had been broken and trampled to pieces, and bodies wedged into it, a pile of them on the far side. A lot of dead men lay here, mixed in with the mots and others. The only way forward was to climb over these bodies.

The sound of war grew louder. Bugles and drums, a sullen harsh chanting, it all wafted back to them as they hurried on. Thru felt a now familiar dread in his heart. War brought a terrible exhiliration and a burning fear that Thru hated.

And now they saw wounded men limping from the field

and others, clearly scouts, who were scurrying up through the wheat toward the crest.

Grys Blana came jogging by with his staff.

"I think we should attack immediately, don't you, Brigadier-Colonel?"

The Grys was literally rubbing his hands together, but whether in triumph or anxiety, Thru could not tell.

"I think we better hurry, sir," said Thru, thinking of the Meld's force trying to stave off six thousand men.

The Grys appeared to hardly hear him, and it didn't matter.

"Forward! Forward at the double!" shouted Grys Blana waving his sword toward the crest of the hill.

"Open out into line of battle immediately," Blana said to Thru before he turned to rejoin his own brigade.

Now the Twelfth Regiment dressed out to its left, formed into squads, and marched out to form a line. The Sixth Regiment hurried to form its own line. Soon all four regiments charged for the hilltop.

Wounded men, emerging from the trees, scrambled to get out of the way. Thru observed one man hopping frantically through the orchards, until the lines of the Sixth Regiment swallowed him up. He wasn't visible after their passage.

Chillum would suffer a poor harvest after this, Thru observed as they helped trample the grain. Wounded survivors struggled here and there. A brilby called out for aid, but all they could offer was a promise to come back for him.

"We'll be back soon for you, brother."

"Just have to sort out this trouble first," said another voice.

And then they came to the crest of the slope. Orchards grew here, and now they could see the enemy. A line hastily formed ahead of them as the enemy turned around to face this threat from the rear.

The fighting ahead was very loud. Screams, shouts, and the endless clanging of steel on iron, drums thundering, brass bugles braying, all boiled up from the orchards just ahead.

They kept moving, lifting the pace a little, losing cohesion around the trees, climbing a low rock wall. And then the lines joined in conflict.

The pikes lead the way, stabbing and thrusting, picking off men from the enemy front. But now the men hurled a volley of javelins and several pikebearers went down. Spontoon pikemots took their place, but more javelins came and more gaps appeared. The two sides were pushing closer as the men did their utmost to get under the pikes and close in on the mot front.

Swords and spears clanged while both lines pushed at each other, shield to shield. The pikes and spontoons struggled to keep the men back.

Thru noticed, though, that the momentum of the mots' charge had stopped abruptly. The lines were stabilized, shoving back and forth over a space of ten yards. He also observed that the mass of men facing them seemed to be growing stronger every moment. More and more arrows and javelins came flying over. Sergeant Burrum went down, skewered through the neck, dead before he hit the ground. Another javelin brushed past Thru's shoulder, missing by less than a finger's width.

The infernal drumming grew louder, and now a host of shrieking bugles gave Thru a sudden premonition of disaster.

They had come too late! The Meld of Daneep had been careless, and the enemy had caught up with him in time to destroy his army before the Grys Blana could join. The Meld's army had been defeated, and the entire enemy army now turned around on Thru's regiment.

He got up on a tree stump and looked up and down their line. The Sulmo regiments were still holding a good line. An arrow flashed past his nose, and he ducked down again.

The woods ahead of them were filled with men and their banners as far back as he could see.

Thru ran to the Grys Blana's position, visible beneath the banner of Blana.

"Sir, the enemy are coming on with their full strength. They must have driven the Meld from the field."

"Impossible," said the Grys, but in his eyes Thru saw

fear. The Grys had at least noticed that the charge had stopped, as if it had hit a brick wall.

"I don't think so, sir. I recommend strongly that we fall back in good order to the village and fortify it. We're going to have to hold off their entire army."

"I . . . How can you be so sure?" The brittle ebullience of the Grys had suddenly boiled away.

"Just get up somewhere and take a look over there. They'll be marching to outflank us on both sides in a few minutes."

The Grys glanced nervously left and right. A staffer pointed to a broken gate in a low wall.

When the Grys jumped down again, he had a new look in his eyes.

"Something is wrong. Perhaps the Meld has withdrawn." He swallowed. "You are right, we must move back to the village."

"Quickly, sir. No time to waste."

But a withdrawal while under full engagement was a difficult maneuver even for highly trained troops. The young regiments of the Grys Blana were not ready. Their line broke up as they tried to pull back. More and more men came swarming forward. Men broke out onto the open field to their right now, lapping around the flank of the Blana regiments.

On Thru's side of the line, the Sixth Regiment held fast while the Twelfth retired in an oblique line, refusing its flank to the enemy. When the Twelfth had gone a hundred paces back, they halted, and the Sixth began to retire in order, trying to keep a crescent-shaped front to the enemy.

On their right the Blana regiments teetered on the brink of collapse, then pulled themselves together with great effort and threw back the men. The fight hung in the balance, but the mots and brilbies had seen total disaster staring them in the face and this gave them a desperation that momentarily overwhelmed the men in front of them.

Their power did not last for long, though, because the Blana mots were outflanked and forced to move farther down slope as their left moved forward.

Thru pulled a company away from the Sixth Regiment and sent it at a run to help the Blanans.

The little army was now halfway back to the village. But the men poured down on them and soon surrounded them completely. On the front line the fighting continued, but less intensely. The men could only muster spasmodic bouts of fury.

A flurry of bugle notes confirmed this fact, and the men on their front pulled back ten yards, retiring to the ranks behind them. The second and third lines also pulled back and retired, but immediately a horde of fresh men came through to fill the front rank. A forty-yard gap opened up between the lines.

It was the last chance for the mot regiments.

"Now!" Thru said to Ter-Saab. "We have to get back to the village. Run for it." Ter-Saab screamed the order himself, running along the back of the Sixth Regiment. The Grys Glaine followed suit, and the two Glaine regiments began to back away as quickly as they dared from the line of battle. They ran back a few paces then stopped and turned, then ran some more as they found the gap widening between the two forces.

On their right the Blana regiments were still in place, beset on the far flank.

The Shasht bugles wailed. The enemy realized what the mots were up to, but the men's ranks were still in transition. They could not pursue for a few more seconds.

Finally they began to advance, but their line was ragged, and harsh voices could be heard raging at them about that. Correcting the problem didn't take long, with well trained Shasht soldiery though and they soon charged forward with a roar.

"Hurry!" Thru ran among the retreating troops. "Back to the village, we have to try and fortify it."

The men were coming at a run now, more regiments of them pouring over the crest of the hill.

The Blanans suddenly turned and ran, their units breaking up entirely as the mots and brilbies bounded down the slope and into the village. When they reached the village, they bunched around the pump in a mob, panicked and became helpless. Men stabbed and hacked at the hindmost, since the mots were so jammed up they could hardly swing their swords.

Thru and his officers tried desperately to shape the retreat of his own brigade and form barricades in the streets to hold the village, but the men pressed the Blanans into a hopeless mob right in the center.

More men came forward on the far left and threatened to surround the village entirely. In fact, Thru could see, this was inevitable; there were just too many men.

The Sixth Regiment had managed to build loose barricades in the two main roads leading into the village from the north. They had filled the houses, occupied the roofs, and were breaking up stone walls for rocks to throw. The men of Shasht now pulled up to the barricades, and both sides traded arrows and javelins.

To the left, the Twelfth Regiment had not had time to build any barricades, so they fought in the streets, in the houses, and in the courtyards.

The flank company from the Sixth fought a cohesive retreat in a square across the field and rejoined the northernmost barricade force.

The Blanans continued to mill, while being hacked and stabbed from behind. Thru saw the Grys Blana, with other officers, trying to pull the mots out of the central square of the village and push them down the narrow street running south.

But time ran out. Men filtered in rapidly on the south side to fully encircle the village.

A fight began on the southern road and rapidly advanced into the heart of the village. Men savagely carved through the Blanans.

In desperation Thru lead a company of the Sixth Regiment in an attack on the seam between the enemy units facing their front and those pressing the Blanans. They got over a wall into the street and through a courtyard, but then ran into a granary occupied by men. From its roof men hurled down rocks and javelins. More men pressed in on either side of the yard.

The space in front of the granary was a killing ground,

and reluctantly, Thru signaled a retreat. They had to run back across the street and climb the wall the other way. But the men closed in behind and the last mots to climb were pulled down and killed.

There was no longer room for maneuver. The regiments from Glaine and Blana were surrounded. The fighting raged through the morning hours, eventually dwindling into small unit combats. Mots and brilbies fought to the end inside kitchens, narrow alleys, grain silos, and the like.

Thru had lost his sword somewhere along the way. It had stuck fast in a man's shield and been torn from his grasp. For a while he fought with a broken spontoon, using the last four feet of it as a club. Then he took up a farmer's woodchopper and buried it in a man's shoulder and took his sword.

The Shasht-made blade was heavy and clumsy in his hand, but it served anyway. He'd been cut and hit hard. His left arm had taken a couple of very hard blows and felt numb, almost useless.

For a while he was with a group of mots from the Sixth Regiment, fighting in a large house close to the center of the village. Men came over the wall into the yard, but the Sixth pitched into them and killed them, driving the few survivors back. Then more men broke down the gate and flowed into the front. The mots fought them all through the front rooms of the house. Windows were broken, doors torn off their hinges, but in the end the mots were all slain except for a couple who escaped by jumping out of the second-floor windows.

At the end Thru ran down an alley all alone. He stopped, for there was no visible pursuit, so he turned into a pigsty and pulled himself up on the beams and wedged himself under the narrow eave. Hauling himself up with his left arm was agonizing, but the place was quiet. The pigs were gone, but it still stank. His arm throbbed.

Two men looked in, missed him up in the eave above their heads, and ran on. He scrunched back into the narrow space, but couldn't get both legs inside. His left arm turned numb once more.

His mind was awhirl. Disaster had befallen the Land.

The army of Sulmo had been defeated. Thru had no idea how badly the rest of the battle had gone, but he was certain that the Meld must have been driven from the field. Now four regiments were gone, slaughtered to the last mot.

Suddenly his exposed foot was seized, and he was pulled down into the mud below and struck repeatedly with heavy objects. He was still trying to get to his feet, and fight on when he lost consciousness.

Chapter 18

He awoke to a sharp jab in his side and rolled over. The sun was directly overhead; he squinted, trying to focus.

Men stood around him. A spear was pointed at his chest.

"Alive," said one of them. Thru understood the Shashti word clearly. For a moment Simona flashed through his mind.

"Think he's good enough? He's kind of bloody and all."

"See if he can walk."

They scourged him up onto his feet with blows and jabs from spear and sword. Trembling, he stood, nauseous from the pain. His shoulder and arm felt broken. His head throbbed and momentarily blanked out, as he came close to falling on his face.

They shoved him ahead of them through the battered village. He saw a pitiful huddle of a dozen other wretches, all cut and bloody, pushed together in the center of a ring of men with spears. After another heave on his unsteady legs, he joined this group. They were mots of the Sixth Regiment. They recognized him, nodded, one or two tried to salute, then thought better of it.

Around them the village echoed with the victory shouts and whoops of the men. There was no doubting who had won the victory. The mots of Glaine kept their eyes downcast. One, badly wounded in the chest, collapsed suddenly, twitched a couple of times, and died.

Two men pushed into the group, shoving them all back with their spears, and dragged the dead mot away by his heels.

Other survivors were shoved into the group. Among them Thru noticed Ter-Saab. And then he gave an involuntary shudder as he saw the hill brilby's full face. Ter-Saab's left eye was gone, broken from a terrible cut that had placed a dark, straight line from his temple to the far side of his nose. All was ruined. Thru wondered that Ter-Saab was still alive.

They found each other, gripped hands with terrible strength.

"Can you see?" whispered Thru, wanting to say, how are you managing to stand up?

"Still have one eye. How about you?"

"All right, I think. Keep blacking out."

"What will they do now?"

"Kill us," said Thru tonelessly.

A few more survivors were pushed into the group, and then orders were bellowed. Thru understood some of the words, his Shashti came back to mind with a sudden clarity.

"Move, the 'somethings' down along the south road" was what he heard.

"What are they doing?" Ter-Saab was looking around himself with anxiety. Was this the signal for the killing?

"They want us to move somewhere," said Thru, feeling puzzled by this development. Indeed, the men did not kill them; instead they were herded out of the village.

Soon they were standing along the road, between small fields surrounded by stone walls. More survivors, from the Blanans and the Twelfth Regiment, were added to their group. The back of Thru's neck and his entire shoulder were stiff and swollen. Moving either was extremely painful. His left arm still numb, with a deep pain in the upper part, convinced him it was broken.

But compared to most of the others standing with him, he was in good shape. Despite everything, despite the imminence of death, Thru felt a little tremor of pride. The mots and brilbies had fought until they could no longer lift their weapons. They were all walking wounded, many of them staggering like himself, but they were still walking.

His head cleared somewhat, though it still hurt. They headed away from the village into the forest on a road that he could have sworn lead to the sea. He checked the sun's position, which he judged to be well nigh at the apex. The fighting had been in the early morning. He must have been unconscious for several hours.

Under the eaves of the forest, they escaped the heat of the day. It was dark and cool as they shuffled along, with men in front and behind them. Surprised at first that the men didn't bind their captives, Thru realized that none of the fifty or so survivors was capable of running ten steps, let alone trying to escape.

They stayed on that road all afternoon. One or two mots collapsed along the way and were speared and left for the scavengers. Once they paused by a stream, and the men made them drink from the stream on all fours, with spears pressed into their backs.

After being watered like this they were broken into smaller groups, ten mots apiece, with guards in front and behind. Now they were spurred on again with jabs and blows. Thru heard the curses, but did not understand them.

They were urged on to a faster pace until darkness when they halted for the night in a small clearing by a stream. Once again they were made to drink, then they were bound together in threes, roped at ankles and wrists.

Ter-Saab was still alive. His terrible wound had scabbed over and was no longer bleeding. He sank down beside Thru, and they were bound together with a skinny youngster that neither of them recognized. None of them had any energy left for conversation, and all were asleep in moments after being allowed to lie down.

The men posted a three-man watch while they ate some way bread and dried curd and went to sleep themselves. In truth, they hardly needed a watch. Their captives were so exhausted that none stirred until kicked awake at dawn.

There were no dreams for Thru, only the renewal of the nightmare the next morning when he was awoken with a blow from a spear butt on his agonizingly sore shoulder. With the rest he was hurried onto his feet after his bonds were loosed. A handful of mush, some kind of paste of beans and water, was thrust into his mouth from a spoon, and then a man with a whip started cracking it above their heads. The mots bristled at the crack of the whip. But it was a sound they would soon grow used to.

Thru and Ter-Saab walked beside each other. It appeared that as long as they were furtive and spoke in whispers they could converse.

"We are heading west, toward the sea," said Thru.

"Yes. I have heard that they kill their victims on the shore, then take their bodies out to their ships as meat."

Thru swallowed hard. "Yes, that is what I have seen."

Piles of heads left on jetties and headlands along the coast of the Land had become the calling cards of Shasht.

"What will happen now? To the Land I mean," said Ter-Saab.

"I don't know. There will be more battles. Our armies will improve. The Meld was not the best general we have."

"We should not have attacked so hastily," said Ter-Saab.

"We were just a little too late. The Meld's army withdrew too soon."

"Disaster."

"That is war, my friend. Triumph and disaster, so the Assenzi warned us. We have tasted triumph, it is sweet. Now we taste disaster. I would have preferred to have neither."

Ter-Saab straightened his shoulders and got a grip on his emotions.

"Until they do kill us, we must fight to stay alive. We may have a chance to escape."

The march went on to the noon hour when they were allowed to drink again, on their knees from a stream. Some of the men amused themselves by urinating in the stream at the same time.

An officer saw them and berated them angrily. Another man, heavyset, clearly a sergeant type, came up and threatened the men with whippings that would peel the hide off their backs.

"These is special!" snarled the sergeant, turning on his heel.

The guards made jokes after that about the "special" animals in their care, but they refrained from damaging blows or sharp jabs with their spears. After being allowed to drink the captives ate another handful of mush from a communal bowl and then staggered on the trail through the forest that ran past Farnem to the sea.

In the late afternoon they glimpsed the blue water for the first time, a little later they came down by the sea on the fishermot's road. Men had been building a fort there. Thru expected the axe, but instead boats waited on the shore. The captives were pushed into the boats and then rowed out, ten at a time to the ships.

The mots knelt in the center of the boat, while men with spears kept a close watch. Other men, in front and behind, heaved on the oars and made good speed through the chop to the huge ships anchored farther out.

The huge Shasht ships awed the mots and brilbies. Thru had been on one of these ships before, and he knew something of their huge size, but now contemplating them as they approached he was struck again by the might of the enemy. Such ships were far beyond the power of the folk of the Land to build. Simona's descriptions of her homeland returned to him. A harshly lit, brilliant city of stone, much larger than any place in the Land.

And then they were under the side of the huge ship, and netting was being lowered over the side for them to climb up.

Now was the moment, if they were ever to try and make a break for it. Thru looked at Ter-Saab, but both saw the defeat in the other's eyes. They had no weapons. The other mots were just as badly hurt. The men had taken up spears and swords.

Spears jabbed at them. They climbed up the heavy netting. For Thru that climb was an agony of grinding bone endings in his arm. Somehow he managed it, knowing that the alternative was to be left to drown. For some reason the will to live was too strong.

He lay on the deck for a while recovering. Then with the others he was driven below decks to a dark, narrow room. They had to remove their clothes and boots. Their clothes were taken away by the men with the scarlet paint on their shaved heads.

Now, Thru thought, came the killing.

But instead they were taken one by one through a door to another room.

There Thru was examined by a man wearing a white canvas apron. He recalled the other man, Simona's father, who had examined him in this manner. That man had given Thru a razor blade. This time there was no such assistance.

Thru's broken arm was set and bound in a splint. The shoulder was palpated, but apparently it was not broken, just severely bruised. His cuts were cleaned and treated with a sharp smelling liquid that stung furiously. Thru's curiosity was piqued. Clearly they were not going to be summarily executed.

Then he was placed with another dozen captives in a dark place, deep inside the ship. Their clothes and boots were returned to them, and they were left unbound. The air was hot and close, but to the exhausted captives that hardly mattered. They slept as if they were dead.

Chapter 19

Victory was sweet. Admiral Heuze rested his stump in his private tent, set up behind the command post. The walls of the monkey city had finally been breached. His army was busy looting.

With military matters taken care of for the moment, the admiral summoned Biswas, his favorite confidant. When Filek appeared, now wearing his new uniform, the black tunic with the yellow stripe down the center that marked him as the army's chief surgeon, the admiral's good spirits were in full flow.

"Well, well, Filek, come in and take some of this ale. We found it in a monkey shebeen. There are lots of them inside the walls. The men are enjoying the fruits of conquest."

"Actually, sir, I will take a little. I'm not sure if we can trust the water here. And I have to say I'm very concerned about looting the city."

"Ach, by the Purple Ass of the Great God, the men need some fun."

"You recall the plague of last summer?"

"Who could forget? Killed a third of our army." Heuze shrugged. That was in the past. Victory was in the present.

"That began soon after we looted that first city of their's. I think the two events were connected."

"Ach!" Heuze downed a gulp of the beer. It was excellent stuff, full-bodied with a nice bitterness to it as well as a hint of sweetness.

"The men have been stuck in this pestilential hole for almost three months. It was time we let them loose. Besides, you can forbid looting, but the men will loot anyway. It's their nature."

"It's a risk. That plague came from the native people somehow."

"Bah, stop calling them 'native people.' They are not people. They are nothing but sodomistic monkeys, and we are going to kill every last single one of them."

"You have that woven piece, some carvings of theirs. We're even drinking this beer they made. You know that they aren't just monkeys."

"Well, of course not, but we have to believe that so we can do what we have to do."

"It isn't essential to exterminate the natives."

"According to the orders from Aeswiren himself, it is essential. The Emperor's advisors have delved deeply into the histories of ancient times. They say that in the event that we meet a native folk, of whatever kind they may be, we must exterminate them. Any fragment that we leave to survive, will revive in time and threaten our hold on the new lands."

"They were peaceful folk until our arrival."

"Well, they haven't been very peaceful since," snapped Heuze. He wanted to bask in his triumph, not worry about the fornicating monkeys. Or even a renewed outbreak of plague.

Filek shut up, thirstily drained his beer, and called for another. He had more surgery ahead of him that day, two leg amputations, and a spearhead removal from a chest, but his tolerance for beer had increased markedly since the beginning of this campaign.

Indeed, he was fit, tanned, and far tougher physically then he'd been on the day they'd come ashore four months earlier. Every day of that time had been filled with a crisis of some kind and the challenge had done him good. Filek had taken to the life of an army on the move. He hadn't expected to like camping, but he had, and the country they'd marched through had been extraordinary.

Forest covered the terrain, like nothing any of them had ever seen before. Sometimes the roads gave out and became mere trails in dark woodland. The trees were enormous, far larger than any he had seen in Shasht. At other times they overlooked great sweeping vistas of wooded hills and vales. And almost everywhere the land was virgin, untouched except in the river bottoms, where the natives made their dwellings among a multitude of ponds. It was exhilarating to march through this bountiful land and breathe in the scents of forest and meadow.

"This was a splendid victory," said Heuze, since Filek didn't seem to appreciate what he was supposed to say.

"Indeed, sir. A very clean one, few casualties, until today."

"Well, it's not possible to storm a walled city without suffering some casualties."

"No, of course not. I understand that, sir, but you see, as a surgeon, busy sewing up our wounded men, I see it all from the point of view of the casualties."

"Of course, of course, perfectly understandable. That's why I enjoy your company, Filek. You're not like the rest of these butchers."

Filek knew well why the admiral liked his company. The army was headed by dolts, since all the brighter officers had long been weeded out by the secret killers of the Hand of Aeswiren. So Filek offered the only chance for good conversation that Heuze was going to get.

"Well, sir, have we taken the entire city now?"

"No, not yet. The pestilential enemy have retreated into a kind of fortress sector of the inner city."

"Monkeys that build fortresses?"

"Shut up, Biswas. They're monkeys and that's that."

"If you say so, sir."

"I do. And we're going to loot this place of theirs and then burn it. Just like we did with the one we took last year. We'll send up a pall of smoke to terrify the fucking monkeys."

"Yes, sir, if we must."

"But first we'll help ourselves to their finery. There are some amazing things to be had."

Filek heard the greed in Heuze's voice. Filek had seen the shimmering woven mats, the carvings in wood and stone, and the paintings of country landscapes that decorated the homes of the natives. Beautiful work, of a quality beyond anything he'd ever seen before. He knew the market in these goods was already strong, just within the fleet. Once these things could be auctioned in Shasht, their value would grow exponentially. The admiral's liberality in regard to loot was sure to be popular with both men and officers.

"Stay and dine with me, Filek. I want to show you something. Going to be an excellent dinner. My hunters have brought in a dozen deer. The game in these hills is absolutely breathtaking. Our hunters can barely contain themselves. Two hundred ducks were taken the other day, from a single lake."

"Thank you, sir, I will. It's been warm work today, and I have a few more operations to undertake later. A good meal would set me up properly."

Soon afterward the slaves brought in the first course. Grilled breasts of duck, sauced with fresh-squeezed blood and served with wild mushrooms.

It was delicious. That was another thing about this expedition, thought Filek as he chewed. The food had been wonderful. After years of getting by on mush and fish, they were eating well on the bounteous game of this new land.

The admiral was still caught up in his plans for the army.

"Now that we've taken this place, I intend to burn it and turn back to the coast. I prefer that we operate in reach of the fleet."

"Wisdom, sir, if you don't mind my saying so."

Heuze nodded, smiling. "These duck breasts are sensational, aren't they?"

"Wonderful."

"And I've got something to show you afterward that will astonish you. Yes, even you, the connoisseur from old Shasht."

They gulped down beer and duck breasts.

"What news is there from the fleet?" asked Filek. "I forgot to ask."

"Not much. The monkeys have not troubled them in the slightest. No fire ships this time."

Filek felt a twinge at the mere mention of those things. The thought of his daughter left behind on the ship, alone, troubled him enough. He had appointed his young deputy Tomak to become fleet surgeon in his absence. But Tomak could not protect her from fire ships.

"Has the post packet come yet today?"

"Yes, there are some letters for you."

Filek always enjoyed receiving letters from his intelligent daughter even if she was also rebellious and wicked for not obeying him and agreeing to wed Wurg Gembeth. She wrote every day and always found something witty and up-lifting to say.

"Anyway, the timetable I'm thinking of is to spend the next couple of days here, letting the men loot while we see if we can reduce this fortress. Then we'll burn the place down and march to the sea. Along the way we'll burn all their places that we find. We'll make them remember us, by God."

Filek heard the admiral's thirst for vindication in the history books. He knew that historians would not treat him well for the conduct of the first campaign the previous year. Or for the earlier campaign this summer. But now Heuze had taken a more active role in command, and victory had followed victory. Now the army was ready to follow up with a great raid to the sea, burning villages and cutting down the enemy and piling their heads in the ruins.

"You know, Filek, when the historians come to write of this campaign, your exploits will be mentioned, too." Now Heuze was being generous, in his way, incorporating Filek into his grandiose projection of the future.

"Thank you, sir. I merely serve to the best of my ability . . ."

"You have improved the survival rate among our wounded enormously. With your techniques, your 'science' as you call it, we will . . . Ah! Take a look at that!"

The slaves had brought in a haunch of roasted venison. With great gusto Heuze carved slices of the meat for them. It was sauced with fat and juices and eaten with some sauteed greenstuffs.

"Excellent, what, Filek?"

"Excellent, sir."

"You shall establish a great hospital, Filek. Generations

of future colonists here will revere your name. Whereas I, I will fade slowly into obscurity. Just a famous general who won some crucial battles."

"Surely not, sir?"

"Well, not unless I take some steps that I'm not sure I should take."

"You mean?" Filek's eyebrows shot up. Heuze was planning a takeover again, he was sure. With some solid success under his belt, Heuze was in a much stronger position now.

Instinctively they leaned close together so they could whisper. Any listeners to their conversation outside the tent would hear nothing.

"I think the time may be coming when we must unseat the priests. Perhaps even Nebbeggebben."

Filek leaned back, not particularly surprised. He knew Heuze had been thinking along these lines for a while.

"Wonderful meal, sir."

"Yes, indeed. And your hospital will extoll your virtues, Filek. Your dedication to science and medicine and so on . . ."

"Our hospital will have your name carved on the lintel, Admiral. I promise you that."

"Why, that's very noble of you, Biswas. A very noble offer, your health, sir!"

They drank and returned to their meat. When they'd finally finished, Heuze pushed his plate away and clapped his hands.

"Bring in my special find."

Two men returned shortly, dragging a small figure behind them on the end of a chain.

They shoved it into the center of the tent and held it fast between them.

Filek gasped, it was a female of the monkeys, a "mor" as Simona insisted they be called. Filek had seen very few of the females, since they were not usually captured, and when they were, they were killed for meat. He'd dissected one female corpse. The reproductive tissues were very similar to those of women.

But his reaction now was to more than simple femaleness, for this "mor" had an entrancing beauty that struck

him at once. And even more intriguing was how similar to
a young woman she was. She had the same weight to the
hips, the curve of the thigh and breast. The same swell in
her movements that spoke of fecundity and sexual attraction. The face was inhuman, of course, the nose much
too small, the eyes too far apart, the lips too thin, the eyebrows much too large, but still there was beauty. She had
a regal poise and a profile that reminded him for a moment
of a female cat. Indeed she moved her lean muscles like a
cat, too.

"Extraordinary, sir. I've never seen anything quite so
wonderful, so strange . . ."

"It's not just her looks, man, which I'll grant you are
astonishing. This one was seen doing acrobatic tricks. We
think she's some kind of trained monkey!" Heuze dissolved
into mirth at his own, weak humor. Filek smiled, truckling
unashamedly. But at the same time he had other thoughts.

If the young mor were presented without the soft grey
fur that covered her from head to toe, except for an area
around her face and the palms and soles of her hands and
feet, he would have had to accept that her body was that
of a woman. Include the strange face, and he would say
she was a woman with a tiny nose and overlarge eyebrows,
but still a woman of a sort.

"Isn't she amazing?" gloated Heuze. "She has such a
strange, devastating beauty. Don't you think, Filek?"

"I do, Admiral, I really do."

"I have tried to force her to do her tricks, but she will
not. Only when we put her in the pen with the others and
she thinks we're not watching. Then she does the most
amazing things."

"She seems like a woman to me, sir."

"Ho-ho, better not let the ladies hear you say that, my
friend. This is just a monkey, Filek. No woman of Shasht
would perform these acrobatic exercises; it would be too
undignified."

"Yes, sir, but still, her hips, her breasts . . ."

"Yes, indeed, there is the very obvious, femaleness of
her body. Rather sexy really, sort of like a cross between
an alley cat and a ripe young whore. I wonder if the impe-

rial family will decide to use her. The sexual characteristics are very similar to our own. You know their reputation. That Aurook is said to be a cocksman of epic proportions with endless lust. And then there's Aeswiren himself. His legend is equally well marked."

Filek blanched. Aeswiren was a man of propriety, it was said. He had three wives, but treated all well and equally. But his sons, particularly the sons of his second wife, Alchia, were the rotten fruit of the dynasty. First Nebbeggebben and then Aurook, had won reputations for evil behavior.

Looking at the beautiful creature, Filek felt his heart torn by pity, but he kept his feelings to himself.

"Yes, sir, of course. Our Emperor is first in all things."

Heuze chuckled. "Well said, Biswas, well said. But I think I will send this one to the Emperor. After our great victories it is time we sent back another ship with some more trophies and a full report. And this particular creature will be among them.

"Astonishing. The Emperor will revere you for it, sir."

"Yes, I rather think he will be amazed by the things we will send him."

Filek understood at once that the admiral referred to the mysterious little scroll that Simona had brought back from her sojourn among the monkey folk. That scroll was a message to the Emperor. Filek knew that Heuze had read the thing, and that it had produced some kind of dramatic effect, but the admiral had been closemouthed about it ever since.

"Amazing things," murmured Heuze, lost in reverie.

"As I've said, sir, I find it hard to think that 'monkeys' could produce such things."

"Stow it, Filek, they're monkeys. Man is the spawn of the Great God. That's the official line, and that's what we're sticking with. These creatures are just chaff, trifles, animals of no more consequence than pigs or chickens."

"If you say so, sir."

"But there's no doubting her appeal, eh? Look at the insolence in her. She won't meet my eyes. If I didn't want her unmarked and fresh for the Emperor, I'd have her whipped for that."

Heuze was obviously excited by that thought. Filek shuddered. The admiral was his protector but he had a few too many rough edges for Filek Biswas's liking.

"Another thing, Filek? I've been thinking that we need to send someone back who can describe the land here in the proper way. Your daughter has seen much of it. She could tell the Emperor her tales of life among the monkeys. That would amuse him, I'm sure."

Filek's heart leaped. Going back to Shasht? Simona would give up her right arm for that opportunity. And part of Filek was overjoyed at the thought. Another part was not, since if she went back she would never be wed to his advantage.

Simona had told him many times that if she ever returned home, she would go up to their country house, or "Zob" in Shesh and stay there for the rest of her life.

Conflicted, a part of him wanted nothing more than to go back to Shasht and resume his old duties at the hospital. But another, newer part wanted to make something in this colony they were going to found.

"Thank you, Admiral, that would be very kind of you. My daughter would love to go back."

"Who knows? Perhaps the Emperor will find her suitable for his bed. Your daughter as concubine to Aeswiren, Biswas?"

"Oh, sir, that is too flattering . . ."

A slave brought news that dessert was ready. Heuze sent the men with the chained mor away.

A rich pudding fried in fat and sugar was brought in, and they ate it with beakers of hot tea while the admiral described some of the gorgeous loot he had seen brought in from the city.

And then their cheerful meal was interrupted by a frantic, disheveled messenger brought in by the sergeant of the Guard.

"From Captain Karby, sir, the patrol on the north approach."

"Yes, I know where Karby's located. What is it?"

"Sir, an enemy army is approaching. Coming down the road that runs north into those hills."

"Another army?" Heuze set down his hot beaker. A new force had entered the equations. Heuze had not expected anything like this so soon.

Chapter 20

The fourth day of the retreat saw the army of Shasht retire over the battlefields where they'd won their great victory. They moved back over the exact spot. Broken spears and shields were still scattered about. Ordinarily the men would have taken souvenirs, but now their reduced spirits made them weary of the soaring landscapes around them.

They had no idea which side in these impenetrable woods the stinking monkeys would attack. Now they had to fight an enemy with huge numbers, who constantly came up with a fresh surprise for them.

From the first contact outside the monkey city, this had been the pattern. There would come a short clash of arms, the discharge of clouds of arrows, and then the enemy would pull back with magical precision and fade into the forests. Then a savage assault followed on the flank of the Shasht army.

Heuze would be forced to shift positions, strengthen the flank, and prepare to retreat again. The other flank would be tested, and the fight would shift back across the battle-field. Clouds of skirmishers hung around the Shasht army, curtailing scouting and keeping Heuze uncertain. Scouting patrols now had to go out in full company strength, which limited them to the most essential task: scouting the route back to the sea.

Heuze's plan to burn villages was set aside. The villages were out of reach now, and there had been no time to damage the city. The enemy's direct attacks had been much too powerful to ignore from the outset.

Heuze would never forget the sight of those disciplined regiments marching out to confront him on that first day.

They had looked almost like regiments of crack Shashti troops. Before Heuze could pull his army out of the city and face them, the enemy had attacked in three places. When Heuze finally had his men in some sort of formation, his right flank was attacked by a powerful hidden force.

Since then constant attacks by archers and even occasional raids on their lines kept the men from properly organizing.

Heuze had a terrible urge to get back to the sea and the waiting fleet. Convinced that the enemy had twenty to thirty thousand fighters, he could not figure out a way to make a stand.

Back at the coast they had erected a small fort. With ten thousand men backed up by the fleet, he was confident he could hold that fort for years, but out here in these trackless forests he had nothing but high anxiety. One crucial mistake, and he could lose everything.

The men sensed the officers' fears, so when they trampled over the old battlefields, they openly made signs to ward off evil. The priests screamed at them for these forbidden pagan practices, but to no avail. Many men intoned the ancient prayers to the older gods, begging for protection. Some said that the army was in the grip of disaster and they were marching into the jaws of death. Nothing could match retreating over an old battlefield for bringing on bad luck, everyone knew that.

As he was carried across in his litter, Admiral Heuze noticed with a chill that the bodies of the fallen were gone, all of them. Those of the monkeys and those of the men. They had removed all the dead, and all the metal. Simona Biswas had sworn that the monkeys did not eat the bodies of the enemy, but Heuze really didn't want to believe that. For some reason it was important to him that the monkeys ate the flesh of men. Especially since he knew no other reason why the monkeys would take the bodies of the fallen men. The idea that the mots would bury the bodies of their enemy with respect and proper ceremony was too appalling to even entertain.

On the far side of the old battlefield, Heuze met his chief of scouts. The flank patrols reported quiet conditions on both sides of the position that faced north and east. One flank backed up to an area of crags and naked rock. It was unusual in the landscape of the new world and had been nicknamed "Old Shasht" by some of the men. The other flank pushed out among the trees, using a deep stream gulley for cover.

The center of the army was drawn up on a flat meadow just south of where they'd defeated the second monkey army. On their front the trees began a hundred yards distant. A stream bisected the position, but it was no more than a few inches deep and ran between flat stones.

The enemy had broken off contact, except for occasional arrows from the trees in front.

General Dogvalth brought the latest reports from the flanks to Heuze, while the admiral sat on a rock by a pond. His bearers, four strapping fellows from the Third Regiment, eagerly plunged their heads in the pool.

While they refreshed themselves, Heuze huddled with his officers and then with Filek Biswas. A stale lunch was hurriedly broken out and distributed. Some hard biscuit, some pressed cheese, and a little sour wine mixed with water. While they ate Heuze studied the reports, looked at the crude map, and tried to think like his opponent.

"He's up to something, Filek. I can smell it."

By now everyone in the army could smell trouble. They were all hanging on the enemy's next move. The initiative had been in his hands for days.

"We're up against a master tactician, Admiral. I think that's clear. It is just the latest in our misfortunes."

Heuze spat and cursed. Even Filek had become a defeatist. How bitter, how galling. Everything had been going so well! They had won two quick victories and then taken the accursed monkey city, too. But then everything changed. Like that plague the previous summer, it was a curse.

"He's backed off. We don't have contact on either flank. Why is he leaving us alone? Normally he is always engaged on one or the other flank. We can count on it, just as we can count on being attacked at first light every day."

"Well, he knows where we are."

"Oh, yes, he knows that. And he knows he's got me at a serious disadvantage on this ground."

"He has kept the initiative by working on that disadvantage."

"Oh, damn me, do you think he could be marching his whole damned army onto our rear?"

"It would fit the pattern, certainly. He's always threatening to cut around us."

For the bountiful land was now a treacherous trap, and every mile that separated them from the coast was one too many.

"Any messengers from the fort get through today?"

"No, Dogvalth says the woods are filled with ambushes."

"We must get back to the coast." Filek's anxiety was showing, but Heuze gave a chuckle, then a guffaw.

"Softly, softly," murmured the admiral gloatingly.

"I'm sorry, what did you say?"

"We must catch this monkey. You know the old saying?"

"No."

"Softly, softly, catchee monkey . . ."

"Mmm, how do you plan to catch this particular monkey? He seems more likely to catch us."

But Heuze was thumping the map.

"He's trying to march his army around us and attack us from the rear. That means his force is somewhere out there, marching fast along narrow trails. Maybe he's even split his force. Maybe we can pick off the two pieces just as we did before. Whatever he's up to, I intend to take our whole army and turn it about and attack."

"What if we don't find him?"

"Then we'll be leaving him behind. For the first time we'll have a real separation of our forces. So we'll just march on to the coast and get behind the walls of the fort."

"I see."

"Either way a thrust to our right is the proper way to go."

Heuze turned to an aide. "Get Dogvalth."

General Dogvalth came running. He had learned to run in response to the admiral's summons.

"General, I think I've rumbled him this time. He's trying to get behind us."

Dogvalth blinked in stupid surprise.

"Behind us?"

"Yes, probably planning a double envelopment from ambush, knowing him. So we're going to do something about it. Do you think the men would like to take a crack at the enemy?"

"By the Great God's hot blood, they would like nothing more, Admiral."

"Good! I want to take the whole army and push straight south from here. There's a river down there somewhere, and we'll have to cross it when we reach it."

"You think the enemy could be out there?"

"He's either down there or out on the other side. If we can catch him in transition, we can hurt him badly."

Dogvalth nodded. "Yes, of course."

"And if we miss him, then we can disengage completely."

Heuze's hand brushed this way and that on the map while Dogvalth watched and nodded.

"Yes, Admiral, a good move. I will see to it."

Soon the men were roused from their meager lunch, and the regiments were reoriented to the south in two assault columns separated by a hundred yards.

If an attack now came from the old left wing then the Blitzers and the Fourth would form the new front line. The army of Shasht was well drilled. They performed the maneuver flawlessly despite the difficulties of the terrain. The men wanted to find the fornicating monkeys and hammer them hard. They were tired of being forced to retreat for days at a time, constantly harried about the flanks.

They filed into the trees on their front, leaving the open space of the meadow behind. Good formations became more difficult, but they continued the march.

But then suddenly a rush of monkeys attacked from the trees to their left, hitting them along the axis of the old front line.

The Second Regiment was taken by surprise and broke up into a series of groups, some of company size, some smaller, all surrounded by the enemy. The racket soon brought the Blitzers up to help. With their aid the Second managed to break up the enemy concentrations and regain its own cohesion, but there were casualties and a loss of confidence among the men.

Meanwhile Heuze had been apprised that the enemy had attacked where the army's old right wing had been set. Heuze instantly ordered his leftward line of regiments to face the source of that attack. Unfortunately, they were now stretched out on narrow deer trails. This was a reason Shasht commanders avoided battles in the forest.

Heuze wanted to get away from this position, and move southward, but now another enemy assault was launched, straight onto the southern front of his regiments. Thousands of monkeys flooded forward under the trees in an unstoppable tide.

With a roar the battle caught fire up and down the line and became a long solid line of stabbing, hacking warriors, digging and gouging with shield and spear, while swords rang and drew sparks under the dry trees.

"Damn!" Heuze cursed again. The enemy had been a step ahead of him once more. He'd played right into this attack. Now he'd have to fight his way through to get the men to the roads that lead to the sea. He unrolled the maps once more, and studied them while he chewed anxiously on his fingernails.

Chapter 21

Filek Biswas turned away from the small hospital cot. The man lying in it was dead. Like so many others in the other cots that lined the dark room.

He gave a sigh. So many dead, so little that he could do for them.

The plague had struck again, just as he'd predicted, igniting among the men who'd come with Admiral Beshezz. Just as it had done the previous year, it killed about one in three and left many others severely weakened.

Also affected were men who'd survived it the previous year. They came down with the same fevers, and were incapacitated for a day or two, but then it passed and within another day or two these men were back on their feet. Weak as kittens, but alive.

Although the fort was besieged the entire time by a large enemy army, it was not a catastrophe. Luckily, only a quarter of the previously infected men came down with the fever again, so there were enough soldiers to keep the monkeys out. Also food supplies came in from the sea.

He pulled off the hat, tunic, and gloves he always wore on his ward visits. Outside the ward he washed his hands and face from the tub he'd ordered set up there. He even changed out of the clogs worn in the wards and his ordinary sandals.

Filek's strict quarantine had worked. Imposed from the moment the first case had been reported. From then on no one had gone to the ships, and no direct contact with anyone aboard the ships had been allowed. So far, it had worked. The men aboard the ships had yet to report any outbreak of fevers, even the newcomers among them.

Filek had a theory that diseases spread by some kind of invisible form of life. Perhaps simply too small to see. Filek had been introduced to the telescope in his youth and understood that there was a scale of things that went beyond that of the normal world. So, he reasoned, maybe a miniature world existed that was invisible to human eyes.

If the plague was caused by a minute life-form, then his quarantine kept it from reaching the fleet. His theory was reinforced by every day that passed without any plague reports.

As a scientist he was elated. He was onto something, something big, but the outlines were still fuzzy. And thinking that the plague was a small life-form made Filek wonder if he could find some substance that could be fed or injected into men that would destroy it. Or at least prevent it from killing them. Such research would require infecting many men, then giving them a drug to kill the infecting life-form. By trial and error they might discover something that would save millions.

Filek was also intrigued by the fact that men who'd already had the plague once could have it again, but not nearly as seriously and with no mortality. That seemed to indicate that suffering through one bout of the disease hardened a man to the next bout. Surviving a single infection left men changed in some way. They could then resist the plague life-form. Here was a profound mystery that Filek wished to study carefully. He would need men as experimental subjects.

In the new world this would be hard to achieve, for men would be at a premium. He would have to go back to Shasht for this type of experiment. Perhaps a message to the Emperor with the news of his discovery, along with a dedication to Aeswiren, would lure the Emperor to summon him home and allow him to begin the project.

This insight of his could change the world forever.

Outside a cold wind had sprung up, coming off the sea. Low grey clouds covered the sky, making the fleet invisible as it moved out to sea.

The fort was a simple palisade with four stout towers at the corners. One of the towers doubled as the main gate.

Inside were eight large sheds and several small structures. Filek headed for one of these, where he was billeted with three good-sized rooms on the second floor. Since Dogvalth had fallen sick, Filek had become the virtual commandant of the camp.

He reached his rooms and closed the door behind him, to be left alone. They were the first private place he'd had since he'd been forced to leave Shasht, which he had come to relish after such a long period aboard the crowded ships.

He examined the stack of papers on his desk. Nine more death notices, all soldiers, so the proper forms had to be filled out. But it would wait until the morning. He sat in his favorite chair, a rough-hewn construct of wood that still had the bark on it, and picked up a notebook.

A knock at the door was followed by Hottom, his personal aide, bringing up some soup and mealie biscuits for his supper.

He propped the book open before him and ate his meal while studying the figures the new bout of plague had generated. He barely tasted the food, so intent was he on the page in front of him. The twelve men in ward three, who were survivors of last summer's plague had all recovered within three days. More confirmation of his theory. That meant a total of 348 survivors of the old plague had come down with the new, and all had survived. Among the newcomers there were three more deaths. He entered the names of the latest victims on this tally and finished the soup.

After ruminating on the way the plague was progressing, he picked up Retuloge's *Pharmacy of the known Toxins,* a reference tome that Filek had been investigating as his new ideas took shape. Old Retuloge had spent his long life on this masterwork. Filek opened to the letter "T," and ran his finger down to the entry for Tars. A solid, substantial piece of work.

"These noxious black substances are to be derived from oily plants and oily tissues or organs," he read. Many interesting forms existed. "Tar of Whale was highly greasy while Tar of Vegetable smoke was like wax. There was even a Tar rendered from the livers of Eagles. The toxic effects of these substances varied. Some, perhaps most, had no effect at all. Others produced acute effects, including death.

Another knock at the door broke his concentration.

"Come in," said Filek wearily. Probably just another breach of camp rules. Most involved drunken fights ending in injuries.

The door opened, and two men shrouded in cloaks and black velvet hats entered. Alarmed, Filek jumped to his feet. Was this a visit from the Hand? Had they finally decided to put him to death?

"What is the meaning of this intrusion?" he began.

And then he realized that one of the men walked with a strange gait. The cloaks were pulled back.

"Admiral?"

"Sssshhhh!" said Heuze raising a finger to his lips. The other man shut the door and stood guard.

Filek had not seen the admiral since the quarantine began.

"What is it?" Filek dropped his voice to a whisper. "Why are you here?"

"The time has come for us to make a move. We are about to take certain, actions."

"Actions?"

Heuze looked around, stepped closer, and whispered in Filek's ear.

"We have to kill the Gold Tops. We must also kill Beshezz and maybe Nebbeggebben, too."

"Oh, I see." Filek's pulse raced. He realized he was in great danger.

"No you probably don't see. Because I need you to do it with me. I cannot trust many men at this juncture."

Filek immediately saw that he would be fatally implicated in what was certain to be an offense to Aeswiren. The Hand would want his head.

Filek also knew that he could not turn the admiral down. He owed the man his life. Moreover Heuze would never forgive such a rejection.

Helplessly, Filek saw himself dragged into this dangerous operation.

"What do you need me to do?" Filek still hoped he could get away with just some medical help.

"You will come with me to see Nebbeggebben. He is feeling poorly again, and he has finally decided to let you examine him. We will take him hostage to neutralize the Hand."

Filek felt a shiver run through him.

"But I cannot break the quarantine," he said weakly.

"Believe me, Filek, if we don't get them, they are going to kill us, very shortly. Don't think you will be spared. You are much too closely identified with me for that."

"They're going to kill us?"

"Yes. That's why I have to move. It is too soon for my plans, but it can be done. Once we have Nebbeggebben, we will use him to summon the Gold Tops one by one. We will kill them as they arrive and throw them to the fishes. When the Gold Tops are dead the Red Tops will be a leaderless mob. We will dispose of them quite easily."

"If we fail . . ."

"Oh, if we fail then they'll have our guts for garters. The priests will work hard to purify our flesh before they grant our pleas for death. But they're going to do that anyway if we don't stop them."

"How do you know?" whispered Filek.

"I have my sources. They're planning my demise for the end of this week. Beshezz has been to see the Gold Tops several times in the past ten days. Now, when that happens they aren't gathering together to pray for my soul, that I can assure you."

"What are the chances that Nebbeggebben will see it your way and go along with this?"

"Slim, to start with, but later I think I can reconcile him to it. As long as he has nubile girls to play with, he's happy."

Filek's face must have betrayed his agitation.

"When this is done with," said the admiral, putting a hand on Filek's shoulder, "and we have Nebbeggebben's cooperation, I will send a ship back to Shasht. You will go on that ship as my personal envoy to the Emperor. I will also promote your ideas about medical practice and beg him to set you up with the resources you need for your research."

Filek's eyes lit up. Heuze smiled, knowing he had Biswas hooked.

"You would do that?"

"Of course."

He might even return to the hospital and do his research there. They would resume their old lives, except of course there'd be no Chiknulba. His darling wife had died in the plague the previous year.

Of course they wouldn't want to live at West Court. The place was too big and held too many memories of Chiknulba and their old life together. Filek thought he would apply for an apartment in the Bronkolo tower, an elegant building quite close to the hospital.

"So you're with me, Biswas?"

Filek came down from the clouds with a jerk.

"Yes, of course, sir."

It was odd how ambition came in so many different flavors, he thought.

Chapter 22

Filek had taken a few drops of opium oil and a shot of brandy before setting out on this mad mission. It had made him quite calm for the first few minutes, but once they'd set out, with twelve handpicked seamen rowing the barge, his nerves returned. His hands shook, he was dry-mouthed and he was terrified.

He was not a man of action. But now he was going to have to be. In his traveling kit bag was the long needle that he was going to use to take control of Nebbeggebben.

Filek had never been in a fight in his life. In his school days he had avoided fights. He was mild-mannered, more comfortable in the company of women than with rough-hewn men. But now fate had thrust him into this position, and he would have to threaten another Man with death, to save his own life.

They reached the ominous black hull of *Hammer*, Nebbeggebben's ship. The net was already hanging over the side to greet them. They scrambled up to the deck, the admiral hauling himself up with his strong arms, and were met by a party of officers with an honor guard for the admiral.

While Filek looked around with anxious eyes, the drums banged and whistles blew as Heuze inspected the line of soldiers turned out to greet him.

When it was done, the captain of the ship came forward.

"Come this way, Lord Admiral," he said, and then ushered them through several doors and into Nebbeggebben's presence.

Filek remembered the room. Very spacious, well-polished floors and pillars. The uncomfortable throne chair for the heir.

Tall, withered Nebbeggebben sat on the throne looking out of sorts. In one hand he held his cane, a heavy ebony rod capped with a silver death's head.

A wide couch crowded one side of the room, with a table beside it cluttered with objects. Clearly, Nebbeggebben spent most of his time lying down.

Heuze and Filek knelt and knocked their heads on the floor. He let a second or two pass before speaking. Just to let them know who was in charge.

"You have come promptly, I thank you for that."

Heuze spoke while lifting his head a few inches from the floor.

"I am most concerned about Your Revered Majesty's health. It is time you listened to the good surgeon Filek Biswas. He is bringing about a revolution in how we treat our wounded and sick. Our losses are far less than all of our predictions. I can say with all honesty, Your Revered Majesty, that this is going to change many things."

"Hah," snorted the heir. "And one-third of the entire expedition died last summer. And I was left like this. Weak, barely able to sit up."

"Yes, Your Revered Majesty, that is sadly true, but the good Filek Biswas was not responsible for that plague. He has a theory concerning such illnesses. He will be happy to tell you of his ideas, if you wish."

"Bah, I hear enough mad ideas from the priests. They are always at me, worrying away with their suspicions. Oh, yes, you should hear what they say about you, Admiral."

Heuze kept his gaze rooted on the floor in front of Nebbeggebben's platform-soled shoes.

The heir snapped his fingers.

"Oh, damn it, look up, stop groveling. I do so hate it when it goes on too long."

"My apologies, Revered Majesty."

"And stop apologizing all the time. Anyway, the priests think I should order you lopped and pressed down to the slave deck. They say you threw away a great victory and put my army at risk by going too far inland. They say you hunger for glory and that you desire to take my head."

"Lord, the priests speak with twisted tongues. You know

that. I am no threat to you. I wish merely to serve my master and bring about the safe implantation of our colony on this new world."

Heuze did not bother to defend his record. Nebbeggebben knew perfectly well that the generals were politically acceptable nincompoops and only Heuze could be trusted with the army. Hadn't the admiral beaten one enemy army ashore and then fought a rousing retreat to the sea pursued by a much larger horde of the monkeys?

"Yes, yes, yes, of course. Well, I think you can still be trusted. I read your reports. You caught the enemy while his force was separated, and you destroyed them. All reports concur. Very good work. Our spirits were greatly lifted at the time. And I admit that I agreed with your plan to push on into the interior in pursuit of the broken enemy. When you found their infernal anthill, I think you were right to invest it and put it to the torch."

Listening to this favorable treatment, Filek wondered if the admiral had miscalculated. Perhaps Nebbeggebben really did want to keep Heuze alive. Perhaps he was not going along with what the priests wanted.

"But then you became careless. Then you were caught in a perilous situation by a sudden attack." Nebbeggebben's voice had grown harsh. "They caught you napping!"

Filek and Heuze stared down at the floor again.

"Your men were inexcusably absent, looting the infernal monkey hill. For that alone they should be decimated!"

And if this army was in Shasht, they would have been. But they were in the new land, and every man was vital.

"And from that moment on you were on the defensive. You never regained the initiative."

The silence was awful. Once again, Filek feared they were about to be sentenced to death. Heuze, he knew, had a smuggled knife hidden in his shirt, but Filek didn't think he could bring himself to resist. Then, suddenly, Nebbeggebben's voice changed pitch. The tirade turned off.

"However, you were outnumbered. I understand how difficult it can be. The enemy are not the stupid animals that the priests would have us believe."

Filek took a breath, the sweat congealed on his brow.

They would live, for now. Nebbeggebben had turned to more interesting topics, like his health.

"All right, enough. It is time for more important matters. Attend me, physician."

Heuze knocked his head again and withdrew to the middle of the room. The guards retreated with him. One on either side, armed with spear and sword. Heuze had to kneel but could raise his body upright leaning on his crutch. A slave stood behind him and stroked a cymbal to make a constant sound so that Heuze would hear none of what transpired between Nebbeggebben and Filek.

On the dais, Filek asked the usual questions while taking the pulse, examining the eyes and ears, smelling the breath and palpating the belly of the patient.

Nebbeggebben said he had pains in his digestive tract, irregular stool, and many other things. His toes hurt, so did his fingers sometimes. He had headaches frequently. Indeed the litany of woes was long.

Perhaps this was the time to kill him. But Filek could feel the nerve draining out of him.

Filek continued the examination. He lifted the Scion's shirt, and tapped the back of the chest, and listened through his listening tube. He heard some rasping in the breathing. Then he lifted the front of the shirt and palpated the belly of the heir in sitting position, then again while he lay down.

The flesh was slack, the skin sallow, obvious evidence of malady. There was soreness in the liver, soreness in the colon, and general discomfort from the entire region of the belly. Any of these things might be fatal or chronic or inclined to clear up under the right circumstances.

Filek asked what the heir had been eating.

He paled as he heard the list of powerful purgatives and toxins that the witch doctor had been prescribing. Red Dust, a pernicious poison, and the Powder of Ground Entrallium, that was guaranteed to cause tumors in the liver. It might already be too late for the heir. A pity, thought Filek the doctor.

"Your Revered Majesty, I must tell you some important facts. The red powder is a most pernicious substance. First they ground up sulfur with a rock rich in iron. Then they

add arsenic and cantharides beetle extracts. My own research has shown that a spoonful will kill a sheep, a pinch
will finish a rat."

He had Nebbeggebben's attention.

"So how much do they put in the medicine?"

"A pinch usually, but if it becomes ineffective they add
a second."

"What's it supposed to do, kill me?"

"It will cause you to purge your bowels, but it will
weaken you and harm your liver."

"Hmmmph." The heir was displeased.

"The use of metal powders is an equally pernicious mistake. These metals are almost all toxic. But the powders
glitter so, and that makes the ignorant vulnerable to their
prescription. Also they are expensive; metals are rare. And
so the expense is part of the lure of them. However, only
the most costly of all is harmless. Ground gold seems to be
relatively nontoxic. All others kill rats and rabbits quickly.

Nebbeggebben was wide-eyed and angry.

"They've been poisoning me, haven't they? The foul un-
grateful swine. By the Balls of the Great God, I'll have
them split open and roasted from the liver out."

As Nebbeggebben grew more heated, he waved his cane
around and promised the most hideous tortures to his
witch doctors.

The mere mention of the rack and the hot irons caused
Filek's nerve to fail completely. He started thinking that it
was an awful pity to threaten old Nebbe. Why risk it all
like that? Nebbeggebben was going to go after the witch
doctors. He seemed to be converting to Filek's own way
of thinking.

Steadying his voice, Filek prescribed a healthy diet. Fresh
green vegetables, oatmeal, and small oily fishes. To be followed with fruit and tea. There was to be no alcohol, no
meat, and very little fat, except from the fishes.

"My research on the inmates in the mental asylum back
home showed that on this diet elderly sufferers from many
diseases grew healthy and survived several more years."

The heir was not enthusiastic. "I hate oatmeal."

"Yes, Your Revered Majesty, but it will help your bowels. You see, we need to clean out as much of the toxins as we can. The fibers in these foods can help in that way. The oils in small fish appear to be very beneficial to health and can help to regulate the heart in some way that we do not understand."

Nebbeggebben quickly grew bored with details. He waved Filek to silence.

"Don't bore me with it, just do it. I have decided that you shall care for my health from now on. You will live just as long as I do."

The audience was over. Filek stood there for a moment completely nonplussed. He didn't have to go through with the stupid plan. He could just step away. He would be safe here, on Nebbeggebben's ship. There was no need to risk his life at all.

The moment was passing, he started to turn away, abandoning the opportunity.

"Noooo!"

A sudden whirl of motion broke the tableau.

The admiral had surged up on his one and a half legs and cut the nearest guard open from belly to neck. Now he whirled, knocking away the other guard's spear with his crutch and swept the knife across the other guard's front, intersecting his right wrist. The poor man's hand was severed in a moment, and his sword never left the scabbard.

Blood squirted in the air, and the guard spiraled to the floor while Heuze lurched toward the heir.

Nebbeggebben was too surprised to scream, but the admiral's open rebellion enraged him, so he stood on his wobbly legs and met Heuze with a great swing of the heavy black cane.

To Filek's horror, the cane struck Heuze on the side of the head, and he went down with a thud. Knocked cold.

Filek realized they were undone. Heuze would be taken, and under torture he would implicate Filek. Under torture himself, Filek would confess to anything and then his fate would be sealed. The tortures would be slow and terrible and then there would be death. All his work would be undone, all his hopes lost forever.

Filek opened the kit bag and pulled out the long needle.

He jumped forward and seized Nebbeggebben around the shoulders. Nebbeggebben elbowed him in the mouth. The heir was a big man, albeit withered by the plague.

"Leave me alone, you fool!" snarled the heir, still thinking that Filek was trying to help him.

Filek, stunned by the pain, saw his moment and lodged the needle firmly into Nebbeggebben's neck behind the ear. A trickle of blood ran down the heir's skin. Filek angled the needle perfectly for a death stroke. With a single thrust he could drive that needle under the edge of the skull. So he had dispatched many poor sick people, in agony from terminal illnesses. Nebbeggebben would be dead before he hit the floor.

"Don't move," hissed Filek Biswas harshly in the heir's ear. "This is a trephination needle. It is a foot long. If you don't do what I say, I will drive it into your brain. In case you were wondering, I've performed this act many times, to put patients out of their misery."

Nebbeggebben went rigid. He could feel the sharp prick of metal in his skin. Sweat beaded his forehead. Filek had amazed himself. He had taken charge of the situation.

The outer guards had entered the room but were halted ten feet away, swords drawn. They could see that shiny silver of steel in Filek's hand.

"Tell them to keep back and to close the doors."

Nebbeggebben did as he was told.

"Now, move back here and sit on your chair. Move very slowly, or I'll kill you."

The heir shifted back to his throne. Filek moved behind the throne, getting Nebbeggebben squarely in front of him, still with the needle jabbed securely into the scrawny neck.

"What do you want?" said Nebbeggebben in a harsh whisper.

Filek struggled for a moment to speak. Now his terror returned.

What was he doing? They would feed him to the eels for this.

"The admiral will tell you. It is not my place."

"Hah! The precious, sodomistic admiral won't be awake

any time soon. That was a good blow I caught him with. If only I'd had a sword in my hand. I'd have taken his head."

But Heuze's head was a hard one, and now to their surprise he stirred, and made swimming motions with his arms and legs. They could see the straps of his stump as his short trouser leg rode up.

"We will wait and see if he recovers . . ."

"And what if he doesn't recover? Had you thought through that part of this madness?"

"Please don't say anything. I feel shame for my embarrassing attack upon Your Revered Majesty. I am not disloyal . . ."

"If you're not disloyal, then why are you holding a knife to my neck."

"I cannot answer that question at this time, Your Revered Majesty."

"Well, you'd better be thinking of a good answer, because the priests will want to hear it. They'll make you wish you'd never been born."

"I already do, Your Revered Majesty."

"You have no idea, you stupid peasant."

Filek colored. "I am no peasant, Your Revered Majesty. I am of good family. Biswas has been a name in the dyes and paints trade for a hundred years in the city of Shasht."

Nebbeggebben laughed sourly.

But then the admiral stirred again, and sat up. He shook his head and looked up at the figure of the heir, seated in his throne. Then his vision sharpened, and he saw Filek crouched behind the heir with a hand on his shoulder.

The guards were back against the walls.

Hope bloomed anew.

Heuze got back to his feet a little unsteadily, shook his head, and picked up the heir's heavy cane. He swung it sharply against Nebbeggebben's shins.

"Ow!" shrieked the heir, who jerked and almost shed the needle.

But Heuze pressed his sharp knife against the withered neck of the Scion of Aeswiren.

"I ought to cut your throat, you old gander . . ."

Nebbeggebben stared back at him, unable to speak.

"But I won't." Heuze had a nasty smile on his face. "Because we can do business. I don't want your position. I want to be safe while I do my job."

"Traitor . . ."

"Shut up!" Heuze raised a hand. Nebbeggebben stifled his angry response.

"Tell the guards to put their weapons down."

The guards disarmed and stood in one corner of the room. Filek went out to pass the message to the men in the barge.

They swarmed up the side of the ship and hurried to take control of the throne room. Now events were swinging their way.

Soon the first Gold Tops were summoned from other ships. Each for an audience with the heir. Each to lose his head.

Chapter 23

Filek stood on the after deck of the frigate *Cloud* and watched the land falling away to a grey smudge on the horizon. It was done. He would never have to see that world again.

He put his arm around his daughter, wrapped in the hooded robe and veil. They were going home. And with them they carried the best protection possible, good news. In addition there were the scrolls, a royal one from Nebbeggebben, reporting favorably on the state of the expedition and the other, that mysterious little scroll from the rulers of the aborigines that his daughter insisted on calling the "mots."

After long and earnest negotiations with the Scion, Nebbeggebben had been won round to their point of view. The admiral and Filek had begged forgiveness and accepted floggings, twenty lashes apiece, and then been forgiven.

The choices were stark for all of them. Either Nebbeggebben forgave them, or they had to kill him. But they all knew that then they would live under the shadow of Aeswiren's wrath, and inevitably another fleet would appear with another army. So each side had cards to play. The bargaining consumed the first night of their rebellion—even while they killed the Gold Tops. One by one their bodies were stuffed into Nebbeggebben's changing room. At one point they had to soak up blood leaking from under the door with heavy velvet torn from the windows so as not to alert the unsuspecting Gold Tops as they were brought in.

What brought the breakthrough in the end was the realization that once they'd killed most of the Gold Tops they'd taken away Nebbeggebben's strongest support. The Scion needed the admiral, after that, because the admiral held the loyalty of the fleet commanders and of the army.

Filek winced as he shifted position. His back was healing well, but it was still a mess of cuts and bruises. By the Great God, Nebbeggebben had demanded fifty lashes, but was persuaded to lessen the sentence. Filek didn't think he could have survived fifty. By the third he was howling, and he lost consciousness twice after the fifteenth.

"Oh, Father," said his wonderful, intelligent daughter, "we are going home."

"Yes, darling."

"I never thought we would. I thought we would have to live there for the rest of our lives."

"We have been retrieved by a miracle."

"Father, you were very brave, you know."

"I wish I could agree with you, my dear."

"No, you were. You are not a soldier, not accustomed to pain like that. You cried out, but then you were silent."

"Because my throat seized up."

"What do you think will happen to us now?"

"We will go to Aeswiren. If he chooses, we will live. If not, then we will be given to the Great God."

"But before that we will give him the scroll?"

"Yes. He will look at your precious scroll first."

Simona smiled behind the dark veil. The admiral had said the scroll was powerful, and from the look on his face, she knew it had worked magic on him. Simona had renewed her faith in the powers of the Assenzi.

"And if we live, Father?"

"Then I will go back to the hospital. I have an enormous amount of research to do."

"Yes, Father, I know. I think I would like to go to Shesh Zob. I would like to spend the rest of my life there."

"I know you would, dear. And I agree that you will spend most of your time there, but there will be social occasions in the city when you will need to be seen by my side."

"Oh, I will come to the city whenever you want me to, dear father, but the rest of the time, even the winters, I will be in the country."

Filek shrugged to himself. His daughter had been exposed to privations and terrors in these last few years that he had never dreamed would come her way. If she needed a year or two to recuperate in the country, then she would get them. But, eventually she would have to be wed. The family would need an heir.

"It is good that I am going back. My work needs the resources of the city. But I'm sorry in some ways that I won't see this lovely land ever again. It was beautiful there, wasn't it?"

For a moment both of them recalled the soaring trees, the rushing torrents, the boundless life of the land.

"I never imagined the world could be so beautiful."

"Nor did I, Father. Or that our people could be so wrong."

Filek frowned. "You must keep those opinions to yourself, my dear. Remember that the Hand will be listening to you. If they can find the slightest thing, they will put you to the questioning."

How brutal of him to remind her like this. His darling daughter who had already endured one questioning, when she'd returned from her sojourn among the aborigines. But, he was concerned that she didn't take this danger seriously enough.

"I know, Father," she said after a moment.

Filek turned away and looked past the sails, stretched taut by a good wind out of the north. Away there, ten months' sailing, according to the captain, lay the great city. They would be so surprised to see him again at the hospital! Old Klegg was in for a shock! Poor old man had been crying when Filek had last seen him. Klegg hadn't relished the thought of having to take up the administrative burden that Filek had carried.

For a moment he wondered again if Nebbeggebben hadn't sent another message, secretly, that would expose the admiral's mutiny and seizure of power. Heuze had expressed confidence that Nebbeggebben wasn't double-dealing and that he had truly forgiven them. Heuze claimed that the Scion was happy to be rid of the Gold Tops anyway. Now Nebbeggebben ruled the Red Tops more directly, through his own appointed high priests. But it was always possible that the Scion was merely biding his time before killing Heuze and Filek.

Again he shrugged. If his fate was to die on the temple pyramid, then so be it. He could only do his best. He had a serious goal: to find a cure for the plague. The machinations of Emperors were beyond his powers, as inscrutable as the wind and the rain.

Becalmed for days, the ship was surrounded by stinking water. The heat pervaded the closeness of the hold like a physical thing. Like some huge animal with fetid breath it crowded their space, sitting on their chests, cutting off the very air they struggled to breathe.

Thru Gillo awoke with a gasp. The dream faded, but the images it had brought did not.

"What did you see, Thru Gillo?" asked a voice at his side, Ter-Saab.

Thru looked at the ruined face in the dark.

"I saw a small boat carried across a great sea of darkness, and in the boat were the seeds of light and life eternal . . ."

The others had roused themselves to listen. They had all had such dreams, and in the darkness of their prison they clung to these shafts of light, insubstantial as they were, for in truth they had nothing else to give them hope.

Chapter 24

"We will never return to our homeland," said Pern Glazen in his usual gloomy way.

"You cannot know that for certain." As ever Juf Goost stood up to him. They had been opponents on this issue since the beginning of their captivity aboard the *Biter*.

Bodies shifted in the fetid darkness. It was cold again. More evidence that they had gone a long way south of the equator now.

"How many new moons have we counted, twelve? We have been on this ship for a year. How do you think you would ever find your way back? The men will not take you back."

"We will find a way. Remember we have the great secret."

"Bah, so we know some of their language? So Thru Gillo taught us the meaning? It is good that we have that power and that we keep it hidden from them. Maybe it will help us escape somehow, but how will we sail a ship like this halfway around the world? There are only eleven of us."

"It doesn't matter, anyway," said Pern Glazen. "When we reach the city of men, they will kill us. They will sacrifice us to their dark God."

"Damn their God, if he exists," swore Juf Goost.

"He doesn't," said Juf Nolo. "They delude themselves with their vicious God. It gives them permission to kill and destroy."

"The great secret will come to our aid at the right time."

"So you say, Juf Goost. But we may not live to see that time. They may march us straight from the ship to the temple and kill us on the spot."

Pern Glazen had an unerring eye for the bleakest scenario . . .

"The men say their God gave them dominion over the world," said Jev Turn, who was much taken with questions of god and spirit. "They say that gives them their right to do whatever they want with us."

"God didn't give them the right," griped Juf Nolo. "Their strength in battle gave it to them."

"What if their God is really stronger than our Spirit?" said another voice.

"Uh-oh, there goes Jevvi again," chuckled Pern Glazen.

Jevvi Panst was not deterred. "You don't like to think about it, but it's like I've always said, what if their God is real? Then maybe this is the way God really wants it? How are we, who are only God's creatures, able to know what God wants?"

"Bah, there is no such God. The Spirit is all, unseen but felt, singing in all the corners of the world. We know the Spirit. Their God is but an illusion." Juf Nolo was a firm adherent to the orthodox position of the Land.

Thru Gillo stirred at last, and the others fell silent. With his Assenzi training, Thru was wise beyond his years.

"Juf Nolo always speaks for the true heart of our beliefs, does he not?"

No one disagreed with that.

"Our beliefs teach us to glorify the world, to accept its beauty as it is, and to reflect it in our craft. We live beside the stream, sharing it with others."

Again there was no disagreement.

"But that is not the way of Man. For Man, there is only desire and hunger. Man is a hungry ghost, who can never be filled."

He paused again.

"The men of Shasht claim their God is the Great One. They claim that he killed and ate the other gods. Do you see what this is? They give unto their God the very hunger that eats at their own hearts.

"We see the world as a treasure. They see the world as something to loot and burn. How can a God, who would be responsible for creating this very world upon which we live, how can such a God accept its destruction by his worshipers? If the world was made by their God, then he would want it to be cherished. Instead, they think of the world as something to conquer, something to kill.

"We have always been taught to treasure the world that gave birth to us, to care for it. That is the way of the Spirit. Man chooses the opposite way. He takes everything and leaves nothing in his wake. This is not the way of the Spirit. If this God of their's exists at all, then it is nothing but some fell demon, for its works are marked only in blood and terror."

Thru paused a moment. When he spoke like this, they seemed to be lifted to a higher plane.

"For we know that the world is a gift to us. That it has taken vast aeons of time to prepare it. Out of that enormity, rising from the most humble beginnings, it has grown, turn upon turn, filling with life and the bounty of its beauty. It is our place to use that bounty and to use it wisely."

He sighed.

"But Man chooses not to follow the path of wisdom. The nature of Man is always to take, always to kill. For Man can accept no restrictions on his rule. In truth, Man is his own God.

"At Highnoth we were taught that it was greed, simple greed that destroyed the world of Man the Cruel in the long ago. Each Man wanted the whole world for himself. Each Man wanted to rule over all other men. In the end they consumed everything and poisoned the waters and then themselves."

Among the others arose a murmur, a scrap from the Book . . .

And the day came when no sound of Man stirred in the world . . . For I am the broken pig and I bear witness to those days. . . .

Thru had fallen silent now and lay back in the darkness, listening to the sounds of the ship as it rode the waves.

"We will see their land today, that much we do know for certain," said Ter-Saab after a while.

Indeed they'd been awoken by the glad shouting of the men on deck above, some hours earlier when the first hail had come. Land had been sighted at last, the land of Shasht.

"Then, we may not live to sleep again."

"Oh, give it a rest, Pern," said Thru Bush, an older mot, who was never at the battle of Chillum but was captured from the woods outside Farnem.

"We must face whatever lies in front of us," said Pern Glazen.

"We will when we have to, until then I'm going to sing the 'Jolly Beekeeper,'" said Juf Nolo.

"That's the spirit!" rumbled Juf Goost. The two of them lifted their voices again.

"Once there was a beekeeper,
forty hives had he
and honey flowed from all the hives
and riches made for he . . ."

Oh, I'd be a beekeeper
If only, but for stings
Oh, I'd be a beekeeper
If only for one thing . . ."

After a while even Pern Glazen joined in.

They sang, even when the guards banged on the door with their spear butts and growled at them to be quiet.

But they kept singing, in quieter voices, refusing to be cowed by the proximity of death. If they were going to be sacrificed on the altars of the evil God of Shasht, then they would go proudly to their deaths, ready to spit into the faces of the priests even as they raised the knives above their chests.

Later, they were roused by the guards and driven up to the open deck for their daily ablutions. When they came on deck, they found the land of Shasht waiting for them, clear and precise in the cold, dry air.

Ocher yellow cliffs rose from the sea. A white line of foam broke along their base. They saw distant mountains, brown and grey, a world of brown rock, bare ground. A few evergreens broke the arid vista, but seemed alien to it, unwanted.

"Look," said Ter-Saab. Thru turned and saw off to the right, far away across the water another brown blur, marking the far side of the wide bay they were entering.

"This is Shasht," said Thru.

"May the Spirit protect us."

When the Master awoke, he summoned Basth as usual to help him rise from his couch.

Basth saw that the Chest of Skulls was open, and one skull, marked with a splash of red ocher, was sitting out on the table.

The Old One saw Basth glance at the skull.

"D'you know who that one was?"

"No Master."

"That was Kadawak. Sometimes I commune with his spirit."

Basth could see the ghostly outlines of a smile on the Master's lips.

"Men are blinded by their short spans, you see. For all their glory they cannot see what I see. D'you understand, Basth?"

"No, Master."

"Good. Now, help me with these slippers."

Chapter 25

As she climbed out of the carriage, Simona shivered from the cold wind and glanced up at the awesome facade of Aeswiren Ill's palace. The pediment rose almost two hundred feet above her head. The pillars supporting it were twenty feet across. The steps, banked in tiers of forty, led to the great dark entrance.

Simona wore a full-length hooded black cloak and under it a double veil to ensure that her face would not be glimpsed by any man not of her family. She walked carefully up the stairs with her head bowed. To expose even a female ankle would be a grave breach of etiquette. The cold wind whipped across the staircases and tore at her cloak. Was it her imagination, or did she hear the voices of dead soldiers, calling from long-ago battlefields.

The great doors were shut against the cold. Huge men, clad in black and gold, stood on either side of a small door inset in one of the large ones. They studied her as she came close, then one of them rapped on the small door with his spear butt and it opened. Looking at the guard's brutal features for a moment, she thought of Rukkh, left behind in the new world. She supposed Rukkh would find some other woman. Probably one of a lower caste than she. They would have many children to populate the colony.

The air inside the great hall was warm and enveloped in hush. A massive black throne stood on a pedestal ten feet high, dominating the place.

During an imperial audience the Emperor sat on the black throne encased in a bulky suit of gold cloth. On his head he wore a blue turban, the color signifying Aeswiren's identification with the great Norgeeben.

The New Empire dynasty had been enormously popular because it brought to an end the ghastly madness of the final years of the previous dynasty. Norgeeben had ended the chaos, eliminated the corruption and brought back order and prosperity. However, though his successor Shmeg was a reasonable Emperor, unimaginative but steady, Shmeg's son was an idiot with a sadistic streak. Aeswiren's revolt and subsequent rise to the throne had been received with joy by the masses. Aeswiren had stood for unfettered markets in corn and wood, plus a reduction in subsidies to the priesthood. Aeswiren had brought stability and economic growth. No one had bothered raising a rebellion for more than eight years now.

Passing through the great hall again on her way to an appointment in the Emperor's private quarters, Simona recalled her first imperial audience very well. It had taken place very soon after they'd returned to Shasht, about three months before.

Then she'd trembled here on her knees beside her father while the Emperor took the message she'd delivered from the Assenzi and broke the admiral's seal.

She'd waited for the angry order to take her away and kill her. Instead there had occurred the strange miracle of the message, as Simona had thought of it ever since.

For a long time there'd been nothing but silence. The Emperor had peered at the scroll with puzzled eyes. Then the Emperor gave a strange cry and beat his hand in the air. The guards looked up at once. But there had been only that one cry, the movement of the hand, and then silence. The Emperor continued to peer at the little scroll in his hand. The guards remained immobile.

The silence lengthened. The Emperor appeared frozen. No one dared to move. After perhaps an hour the mood broke suddenly. The Emperor gave a heavy sigh, rolled the scroll up, and put it aside.

Simona had braced herself again for the death sentence. But the words she actually heard took her by surprise.

"I will see the girl in my chamber. Alone. Now."

The glittering gold suit had risen from the throne, taken a slightly unsteady step or two, and then disappeared down the stairs behind the throne that lead to the Emperor's private office.

Trembling she had risen to her feet and followed a soldier in full-battle armor around the throne and into a small passage leading to a plain wooden door.

Inside, in a room furnished with chairs, desk, and a lovely Nisjani rug, she found the Emperor waiting for her. She had not expected such civilized treatment.

He grilled her, of course, but it was not the terrifying experience she might have imagined. In person the Emperor was nothing like his image from afar. He was not huge, merely sturdily built. His black beard was trimmed short, his hair, now grey was cut short as well. He was a kindly person, obviously intelligent, with careful, crafty eyes. They frequently crinkled to show that he was amused.

Rather than terrifying her, he behaved like a friendly parent. The whole experience astonished her.

"Do you know what was in the message?" was his first question as soon as they were together.

"No, Your Majesty, I have no idea."

"Good," he said, and ordered hot tea.

She discovered she liked the Emperor enormously. Aeswiren had been such a successful ruler because he could charm a lion out of its skin. The palace eunuchs said of him that he could catch trout just by talking with them for a little while in that special "gentle" voice of his.

She told him everything she could think of about the Land and the folk who dwelled in it. He listened and asked more questions, and in the end sent her away with words of affection.

Since that fateful day she'd come several times to see him, always in his private apartments.

The Emperor was fond of expensive rugs and furnishings, but beyond that he was not a greedy or ostentatious man. His private office boasted a different rug every time she visited.

Aeswiren was solidly built, a former soldier who fought to keep the flab off his body. Once he'd been a brutal man, and cruel to his enemies. But for more than twenty years he'd simply tried to govern his huge, polyglot empire. The job was too big for any one man, but he had to try. He was fortunate that his sense of humor had survived the transition from warlord to Emperor.

Now when she came to see him, she found him dressed in casual cotton pants and vest, usually with a black silk jacket. She was expected to bow deeply, but not to kneel. He would offer her tea from the tray kept constantly resupplied in the corner. Sometimes they would eat while they talked, but mostly they just talked. The foods they ate were very simple, for Aeswiren had plain tastes. Apart from his appetite for women and new rugs, Aeswiren had little interest in hedonism.

"Welcome, Simona of the Gsekk. Have some tea, it is freshly brewed."

"Thank you, Your Majesty, I would be honored."

"Good, good, tell me, how are your new quarters?"

The Emperor poured tea with a spirited expertise, keeping the pot a foot from the tiny cup and yet never missing or losing a splash.

"Wonderful, Your Majesty. My father asked me to express his boundless thanks for your kindness."

As indeed both Filek and Simona should, for they now inhabited a wonderful apartment on the upper floor of a three-story house in the imperial city. Being under the Emperor's favor had brought them a vast increase in status.

"Your father has an original mind, Simona. His work may outshine my own in the end."

"Surely not, Your Majesty?" The tea was hot and strong, as she'd expected. "Without tea," he had said to her on her first private audience, "I would have been overthrown many years ago. This empire runs on tea."

"Yes, dear, there have been twenty-three emperors, but there will only be one discoverer of medical science. My work will mostly die with me. But your father's work will inspire the world. Others will build on his discoveries. It may be the beginning of the climb back to the stars for our race."

"The stars, Your Majesty?"

"Yes, child, you heard me. There is nothing to limit our race now. We can attain the glories of the ancient time.

Not overnight, not in our lifetimes, not even for hundreds of years, but your father is helping us put our feet back on that path."

"I know nothing of these things, Your Majesty."

"Yes, yes, of course, you say that, but I know you now, miss penny bright eyes. You understand me most of the time."

He rubbed his hands together and smiled.

"But now, to work. We talked last about the manner of their agriculture in the Land. I had many questions."

"Yes, Your Majesty, you always have many questions."

They both chuckled, enjoying the intimacy they had achieved despite the vast difference in their status.

"You described the land there as having abundant water. Pools, ponds, and fields deliberately flooded and then drained again."

"Yes, Your Majesty. They are called the 'watermots' because they work so much in water. They build weirs and dams to deepen the rivers and lakes. They channel the water wherever they want it."

"The principles of this way of farming are well understood. We have similar powers, and there are places in our own territories that employ the water in the same way. No, the difference lies elsewhere." Aeswiren sipped from his small white porcelain cup.

"They farm only in a small area, they leave much of the rest to wilderness?"

"Yes, Your Majesty. They farm on the bottomlands of the rivers, but not on the higher land, not at all."

"You say they have cities, that says they have a certain level of population. How do they feed themselves from so little arable land?"

"I asked a very similar question. They said they simply worked very hard. And the wild lands provided them with game all year-round."

"Hah, if only we could have the same." The Emperor put aside his cup and stood up and stretched. Now he paced up and down in bare feet on the lovely new Nisjani rug that had been put down this week. It had a delightfully firm but silky feel.

Simona had seen the Emperor pace like this on every visit. It was his way of marshaling his thoughts.

"You also mentioned a plant that is unknown to us in Shasht."

"There are many plants like that there. The forests are enormous."

"Yes, but they grow this plant for food."

"Oh, yes, Your Majesty, that is the plant they call 'waterbush.' "

"Waterbush, yes, and that is very productive, too."

"They revere the waterbush, Your Majesty."

"It tastes like toasted wheat bread you said."

"Sometimes, but other times it has no taste. They flavor it with eggs and fish and other things."

"And they grow the waterbush everywhere?"

"On the bottomlands. It needs a lot of water."

"Yes. And what else do they grow?"

"While I was living among the mots, I saw fields of oats and wheat. Their fields are small."

"Yes, you mentioned that before as well. So they restrain their use of the land. And no one objects?"

"According to those I spoke with it seemed that all accepted the need for this way of doing things. They all share the bounty of game from the land, but they carefully manage their hunting to preserve the stock of game. They have seasons to hunt for the deer and the wildfowl, and everyone partakes of the feasts. Among the worst crimes, I was told, is that of the poacher."

"Yes, this is extraordinary. We have all the same rules and dreams, but in practice they have all failed us. Their culture seems built on the same foundations but to have become very different from our own."

"Yes, Your Majesty, it is."

He placed his hands together, palm to palm.

"And now that culture is being crushed and extirpated by my armies."

Simona could only bow and fight off a sob.

Aeswiren turned again and walked on the Nisjani rug.

"Well, I will have to do something to try and stop it, won't I?"

Simona fell on her knees in front of him.

"Oh, Your Majesty, I thank you with all my heart . . ."

"Yes, yes, child, get up now. I don't like that kind of thing in my private quarters." She rose up once more.

He was studying her with those careful, dark eyes. She saw him make a decision. The sight frightened her a little, as if she had glimpsed a place where enormity ruled and mere human beings were like ants.

"Come, I want to show you something. I'm going to ask you to take on a most formidable task."

Simona put on veil and hooded robe and followed the Emperor out of his private suite, down a public stair past guards on every landing and then to the ground floor of the palace. He turned to her and gave her that deep look again.

"Now prepare yourself for something quite remarkable."

A door opened before them, and they entered a cool, stone corridor. Another door lead to a narrow room and a stair that took them to a darkened gallery overlooking a large room below.

In that room sat a single figure. Wearing dun-brown trousers and a loose shirt of similar tone. At first Simona thought it was a woman with a shaved head. Then with a little shock she saw that it was a mor.

"Be very quiet," whispered Aeswiren. "She does not like to be watched." The Emperor motioned for them to take seats in the gallery. The stone felt cool to her body.

As they watched, the figure in the room down below stood up and began to move around.

Her movements were initially slow and graceful, and obviously part of a long practiced program of maneuvers that went from arm circles and leg raises to a kind of stately slow dance on the spot, the arms sweeping out and back and around behind. And then to Simona's amazement the figure bounced forward on her feet and did a perfect forward somersault hands tucked in, legs straight, head over heels and back on her feet again with her arms outstretched.

Simona felt her heart skip a beat at the indescribably fluent nature of the move. She looked to the Emperor and saw him watching intently, blind to all else.

The show continued as the mor down below performed somersaults in both directions, plus other tumbles and rolls that took her back and forth across the stone floor at a dizzying pace. Then finally she tired, drew herself up with her arms raised above her head, and came down to a resting position. A moment later she had left the room through a narrow door.

The Emperor turned to Simona.

"Well, child, what do you think?"

In the darkness Simona could not see his eyes, but his voice was husked by something akin to desire. The mor acrobat had an astonishing grace and beauty, something quite transcendent, and he had responded.

"She is amazing to see, Your Majesty."

"Isn't she? Well, here's what I want you to do. Either way it's going to be very hard. You can speak their language, can't you?"

"Yes, Your Majesty."

"Exactly. So I want you to teach this divinely beautiful creature to speak Shashti."

Simona felt her jaw drop for a moment, but he had not noticed.

"Otherwise," he went on, "you'll have to teach me the monkey talk."

Chapter 26

The door to the cell opened again. They never knocked, of course. Nuza looked up but remained sitting and fought to maintain a calm appearance. She succeeded. She looked away from the door and calmed her breathing and slowed her pulse. Thru would be proud of her, she was keeping an iron grip on her emotions, no longer jumping at every sound.

On the voyage it had been easier. She hadn't been alone for one thing. And for another the stone walls of this place unnerved her. Harsh sounds echoed in the passages outside the door and the armed men terrified her.

Someone came through the door. When Nuza turned to look, her eyebrows flashed up and down involuntarily. Instead of the huge, heavily armed guards a single figure, wrapped in black cloth entered. When the door shut, the figure bowed to her. The person in the black robe was scarcely any bigger than Nuza herself.

Nuza rose slowly to her feet, pushing back the wooden chair, struggling to keep her composure. What did this sinister figure portend? Was this to be her death? She wondered for the hundredth time whether they were finally going to kill her and get it over with.

To tell the truth she was tired of waiting. Death would be a release.

The black robe was pulled open, then removed, and Nuza felt her jaw drop. The figure revealed was not a man, it was undoubtedly female from the hips to the breasts, but it was no mor. It was "wo-man," as Thru had named it, or rather, her.

It was the first woman that Nuza had ever seen.

Nuza studied her carefully. The wo-man was a little taller than herself, but was not as muscular. It was strange to see a face so naked, so exposed without beard or helmet. The pale colored hair was pulled back behind the head exposing the pale skin of the forehead. The lips were thick, heavier even than those of men, and similarly reddish. The eyes seemed set too close together, the characteristic of men.

No fur. That was the thing that stood out the most in her mind. Were the full young breasts of wo-man as naked as the rest of her? Nuza felt a twinge of something like competitiveness for a moment. Then she felt chagrin at such pettiness.

The wo-man was smiling, she carried no weapon. Nuza concluded that she was not about to die.

"D'thaam," said the wo-man quite clearly. "Greetings, my name is Simona," she continued in a slightly halting speech, the tongue of the Land.

Nuza had to sit down again to absorb this. Not since she had been torn from her companions on the ship had she heard the sweet sounds of the tongue of the Land. All around her had been nothing but the harsh babble of Shasht.

The wo-man came closer and reached out. Nuza gave a little shriek and sat farther back.

"I will not hurt you," said the wo-man.

Nuza knew that either she was hearing this for real or she was losing her mind at last. This was an incredible hallucination if that's what it was.

At times during the lonely days of the long voyage, she had thought she was falling into insanity, but nothing had been quite so "real" as this.

"No, really, do not be afraid. I am a friend. Listen."

It was astonishing. Nuza had her hands over her mouth. A friend? What could this mean?

The woman came closer.

"Listen to me please, I speak some of your language. You understand me, yes?"

Nuza could not immediately formulate a response to this. She still wondered if she was hallucinating, or dreaming, and might soon wake up. Since that dread moment when she'd first been taken captive, all she had known was the harsh terror of men. And now this wo-man spoke the sweet language of the Land. The accent was strange, but the meanings could be heard clearly. "You understand me? I think you understand. I know I speak the right words. I know because I was taught by a mot who befriended me. His name was Thru Gillo."

Nuza jerked up with a start. "Thru?" she whispered.

"Yes, Thru Gillo. Who has scars on face."

Nuza felt a little scream escape her lips.

"You know Thru?"

Simona's face shook.

"Yes, indeed. Thru Gillo saved my life. He came to rescue me when I first landed."

Nuza's eyes widened again. "Thru told me about you. You are Sim-o-na. I am Nuza."

Simona shook her head in amazement. By some inexplicable twist of fate, she had found Nuza, lost in Shasht, just as Thru had found her, when she was lost in the Land.

"By the Pure Skin of God, this is amazing . . ." she whispered in Shashti. Nuza's big bushy eyebrows rose up and down.

"You are Nuza?" She went back to the tongue of the Land. It was coming back to her, but there were still lapses and things she'd forgotten.

"Thru told me that he loved you."

"I love Thru. We met before . . ." Nuza fell silent. How could she tell wo-man what she had seen? How could she describe the horror perpetrated by Man? She hesitated, then said simply, "Thru may be dead. He did not come back from battle. But his body was never found, so it is also possible he was captured. We will probably never know."

Both of them knew the likely fate of prisoners in the hands of men. Simona pressed her hands to her mouth and sobbed.

"They call this war a holy war," she ground out. "They fight for the Great God. But I cannot imagine any true god wanting the death of Thru Gillo."

Nuza's gaze had hardened. "I have seen the works of your Great God."

The piles of skulls left on the dock at Bilauk would never leave her. She still woke up screaming.

Simona could not meet the mor's eyes.

"I hate what my people have done. I feel shame every time I think of it. I hate the Great God, and I give him no worship."

Nuza's gaze softened slightly.

"You are not like Man."

"I belong to them, but I do not think like them."

"Yes, I think I understand. You are wo-man, Thru told me."

Simona tried not to cringe as memories arose. The horrible memory of those platters of meat was hard to dismiss. How could she confess to Nuza, that her first introduction to the folk of the Land was when she ate rib chops cut from their flesh.

"I have been sent by our . . ." Simona searched her memory, there was no word for Emperor in the language Thru had taught her. "Our Great King," she concluded. "He wants me to speak with you."

"Why is this?"

"Well, let me explain. The Emperor rules by the terror his reputation inspires, do you understand?"

"Everyone fears him."

"But he is more than that. I have spoken many times with him. He is wise, and he wants to end the war in the Land."

Nuza's eyebrows flashed up and down again. "Thanks to the Spirit for this! When?"

"It is not quite as simple as that. The Emperor is not the sole power here. And the colony is far away. It will take time for him to bring it under control. The priests will oppose him when they discover his plans, and the priests have great power still. Indeed I would hardly dare say these words to you in my own tongue in case they were heard by an agent of the priests."

Nuza's quick mind had jumped ahead.

"What do they want of me? How can I help?"

"They want you to learn the language of Men."

Nuza was shocked.

"After killing my people, after burning our cities, after burning my family's home, after killing my love, my Thru. Now one of them wants me to learn their harsh, bullying tongue?"

"Yes."

"I will not."

"The Emperor has fallen in love with your beauty, Nuza. I have seen him. He comes to watch you when you exercise. I think he is obsessed."

"Watched me?" Nuza was angered further. "Ah, in the dark space, where there is a gallery. I thought I saw a face there once."

"It would have been him."

"Why does he not show himself? Why does he hide in the shadow?"

"He does not want anyone to know what he does. The priests would kill you if they could."

"Why should I entertain him?"

"Because he will help your people."

"Then, I will continue. But were it not for that, I would not."

Across the great city, down near the harbor, Filek Biswas opened the door of the carriage as it came to a halt at the hospital gate. It was cold, the fifth day of Ribrack. He wore his winter cloak and stout boots. Living way out in the imperial city had lengthened his trip to the hospital enormously. His walk from West Court had only been a few blocks; now he had to ride four miles down the long avenue.

He knocked and the doors opened. He was ushered in by Spinx. Removing his cloak in the sudden warmth Filek enjoyed the familiar smells of alcohol spirit, of turpentine and hot brine, the sounds of distant trolleys thundering along stone corridors. It was all like home to him. His spirits rose at once. He who had been cast into exile had returned in triumph to resume his life here.

He hurried up the broad stone staircase, accepting greetings from surgeons and administrators as he passed. On the third floor he entered his own realm. He had taken over one whole end of the building. He nodded to an assistant in the outer office, waved to Balbu, who was overseeing the carpenters working on the project, and slid into his private office then closed the door.

This was not his old office, all cramped and filled with boxes of papers. He'd left that and his old position in the hands of Mushuq Balembo, a young relative of Klegg's. This new office was twice the size and had a desk and a wide table with a built-in drain for autopsies and dissections.

Old Klegg had been overjoyed that Filek had left Mushuq in charge, and Filek had made sure that no corruption was going on with the hospital accounts. Mushuq, it turned out, was a scrupulous young man.

Filek hung his cloak on a hook, put on a jacket he kept for indoor wear, and sat down at the desk to look at the new drawings. New lenses were arriving every day from the grinders. Once polished, they were being tested by Balbu and his crew.

Together they were exploring Filek's first great idea, the micro-scope. Two or even three lenses of just the right focal point and magnifying power were being combined in a tube a foot long. The lenses had to be adjustable, but when tuned correctly and looked at through one end of the tube, they produced an enormous magnification of anything placed under the lens. Already they'd made astonishing progress. They saw things now that were completely invisible to the naked eye. Hints of tiny life-forms could be seen.

Someone knocked on the door.

It was Mushuq.

"Ah, Mushuq, how are things?"

"Very good, Surgeon Biswas. I just wanted to let you know that I have received an imperial drawdown of four thousand silver pieces."

"Excellent news. Come in, come in. I want to show you this."

Filek indicated the drawings.

"See, we are going to use two different lenses to make a superior lens, and with that we will be able to see very small things. Very small."

Mushuq understood. Although he knew the priests opposed the research, he understood that Filek was doing something very important—and with the Emperor's support.

"Have you seen the 'small seed' that you spoke of?"

"Not yet, but we have seen things that are not ordinarily visible. It is a fantastically complicated world, the world of the very small. I think we are on the verge of great discoveries."

Chapter 27

Within moments of the ship coming to rest, their peaceful, if tedious, existence came to an end. The doors were flung open, and the men with shaved heads painted red cracked whips and screamed at the top of their lungs.

Thru got to his feet without his coat and had to reach down at the last moment to pick it up. A Red Top seized his arm, jerking him forward.

"Move, animal!" He brandished a short whip.

Thru held his ground and pulled his arm free with a stare into the man's eyes. The Red Top looked down, then screamed again and cracked his whip on the wall. Thru shrugged and turned to follow the others out of the hold.

Blinking against the bright sun, shivering in the cold air he came up on deck.

"What?" muttered Juf Goost, "they're calling us, 'animals'?"

Thru patted Juf on the shoulder. Good old Goost, always seeing the absurd in the presence of the terrifying.

The scene before them both amazed and appalled them. A great cityscape of stone was filled with tens of thousands of people. The docks, the streets behind were jammed solid. Every rooftop, every window, every balcony was packed. Apparently there was enormous curiosity about this ship's cargo.

At the sight of the captive monkeys on the deck, the huge crowd broke into a roar that broke over them like surf. Fanatic groups began chanting short slogans over and over. For the small group of captives, the prospect was dismal.

"By the Spirit, they make a lot of noise," said Juf.

"And I'm cold," muttered Ter-Saab.

No one else could even speak. The dense hatred roared unceasingly. Thru heard a group to their left chanting simply "Kill them, kill them, kill them, kill them," over and over.

And above it all loomed the immense buildings of white stone. Thru had never seen structures so huge. Pillars as tall as trees held up vast pediments. Walls of white stone rose on every side. Every window was crammed with black gesticulating figures.

Then the whips cracked over them again, and the Red Tops screamed threats and insults. Thru heard the words clearly. The mots were the damned, the condemned, the abomination, the thing that could not be allowed to exist. The Great God would eat them. On the morrow he would eat their hearts!

Thru shivered inside. It was hard to be the focus of such hate. He stared at the huge throngs and realized that the population of all Dronned would be lost in this great mass like a drop in a barrel.

The Red Tops drove them onto the ramp leading down to the dockside. Now the noise reached a new crescendo.

The hordes surged forward and had to be held back by the Black Tops, enormous men who usually guarded the high priests. The movement forward of thousands of men with hate in their eyes was terrifying. The mots quailed, hesitant to move. Red Tops cursed and struck them with whips. Still they stood there, frozen.

And then Thru broke the spell by walking down the lane opened in the mob by the bullnecked Red Tops. A squad of drummers fell in behind them and began to hammer out a steady roar of noise. The crowds redoubled their screaming. Only men, nothing but men; no females existed in the world of Shasht, or so it seemed.

They walked beneath the giant buildings while the crowds chanted phrases about blood and hate over and over. Again and again Thru heard the phrase "He will eat your heart!"

They turned past a ten-story building and entered a wider space. At the far end it opened onto an avenue that ran straight out to a vast shape, a hulking pyramid that loomed above the city like a great spider of stone.

Step by step they walked closer to the pyramid, a line of small figures bent before a frenzied gale of insults. Thundering drummers followed and behind them a wedge of Red Tops lead the huge crowd from the dockside.

As they drew closer, the sheer bulk of the pyramid weakened their spirits. It was enormous, dominating even the great buildings of the city itself. Every step forward was a step toward certain death, for the pyramid held the altar where their hearts would be torn from their bodies.

As they approached the steps leading up to the pyramid the pressure became too much for Jev Turn and Jev Ummim, who both suddenly dropped to their hands and knees and rolled over on the stone, weeping.

The line was forced to halt. The Red Tops shrieked invective and cracked their whips.

The roaring crowds worked to unman the victims, to lead them to beg for life as castrates, anything but death on the altar. By the time they were killed, the captives were supposed to have lost their own will. By becoming unmanned they would thus leave their very souls behind in the hands of the priests of Shasht.

The two Jevs were pulled back to their feet and beaten some more. They were lost to the terror, their brains fogged by the overpowering fear, their eyes rolling up into their heads. Thru pushed aside the Red Tops and leaned forward to embrace them.

For this he was struck with the whips, too. Juf Goost looked around with defiance in his eyes.

"Now would be a good time to sing, I think," said Thru.

Juf was quick to try a note. It could barely be heard above the snarl of the mob. Ter-Saab came in, then Thru and the rest of them.

"Who'd be a jolly beekeeper
and always suffer stings?
When you could be a slee—ee-per
And never mind those things.
A jo-o-o-o-olly beekeeper

whose always getting stung. . . .
That's me and we, and you and he, and we are all just
one. . . ."

The silly, cheerful lines of the old song came up from
their hearts and the strange sound made the crowd fall
silent. Suddenly the mots felt the strength in those faltering
phrases and were heartened and they sang the next verse
with everything they had.

"A jo-o-o-o-lly beekeeper . . ."

And it resounded from the awe-inspiring mass of the
great pyramid of Shasht.

The crowd erupted and a great howl of anger echoed off
the walls of stone. But the ten mots standing before the
monstrous pyramid continued singing, though they could
barely hear themselves at all.

The Red Tops, goaded beyond endurance, kicked and
whipped them forward to end the singing.

The crowd's rage continued as they climbed the wide
span of stone steps toward the base of the pyramid itself.

The short line of mots fell into the great doorway, pushed
into the dark maw of the pyramid. Now the huge doors
closed behind them, and the crowd's noise was abruptly
shut off. The executions would be in a few days' time. Many
rituals of purification would be performed before then.
Slaves would scrub the entire pyramid from top to bottom.

It took a few seconds for their eyes to adjust. The corridor was on the same grandiose scale as the exterior of the
pyramid. Huge bas reliefs snaked along the walls. A man-
like figure, but with eight arms, danced in these carvings.
He gripped the severed heads of victims, he cut other heads
from bodies; he was the All Powerful One, He Who Eats.
The Red Tops tugged and swung their whips, but their
incessant shouting and cursing had stopped.

The darkness was eery. Their ears still rang from the
roar of the crowd, but now only the sounds of their feet
on stone and the harsh breathing of the young Red Tops
could be heard.

On they were driven, along a wide passage and then into
a narrow corridor leading off at right angles. A small door

opened and they were herded into a narrow room, with only a slit window at the far end. The room was barely big enough for them to stand.

"They got enough space in this damned thing to let us all have our own room. And they have to stick us in a closet?" said Juf Goost.

Few chuckled, for they were too drained by the procession to the temple to speak. Most simply stared at the floor.

"How about a round of the Green Linnet, then?"

"This is not the place for us to sing," said Pern Glazen.

"Oh, you're always feeling oppressed. I'm for singing. Who's for a round of the 'Jolly Beekeeper?'"

But this time no one joined in. Still, Juf couldn't give up. To cope with the horror, he had to deny that it had any power over him.

"How about a 'Brilby goes a Courting?'" Juf dropped his voice for the opening lines.

"Away, he goes, away he goes, a Brilby goes a courting. . . ."

No one else joined him. Ter-Saab put a restraining hand on his shoulder.

"It's all right, it's better to be quiet now."

Juf shuddered and seemed to shrink a little.

"Thru?" He looked to Gillo, but Thru merely shook his head. Not even Thru could sing in this tiny room, trapped inside this huge machine of death.

Juf sniffed, wiped his nose with the back of his hand, and was silent. With death imminent, each of them wanted to make his peace with his ancestors and the Spirit. They were all young, except for Thru Bush. They all had hopes and dreams, and now they reconciled themselves to the fact that they would never be wed, never work their own polder, and never have children.

Thru thought about the insanity of this. He and the others had been plucked from the Land, halfway around the world, and brought here just so they could be slaughtered in front of a crowd. And all this was being done in the name of the Great God.

Time passed, they remained trapped in the narrow room. The air grew close, then fetid.

Abruptly, the door burst open and burly Red Tops dragged them out one at a time, lined them up, and drove them down the passage to another room, a huge place, with high galleries lining the walls above and a central dais raised up in the center. In the center of the main gallery, a closed door stood behind a small box containing a single seat. Below the box hung an immense gong.

They were urged onto the dais. The great room filled with a buzz of conversation from the crowd of Gold Tops seated in front of them. Figures in the galleries, hidden beneath black robes were engaged in fervent conversation.

All came to an abrupt end as a Black Top struck the gong. The deep sound throbbed in the air for many seconds. When it faded, the high door opened and a slim figure emerged to stand in that box, above their heads. The figure remained hidden in the shadows. It did not sit down.

There was absolute silence now. The Gold Tops stared up at the box. Thru looked around himself carefully while questions pounded in his brain. Was that the Emperor up there? The great Aeswiren that Simona had spoken of? If it was, then why did it remain hidden like that?

The moment lengthened. And a feeling of oppressive power filled the room. A magical essence took hold. Little sparkles and shimmers of light appeared in the air as if it was charged with electricity. The mots were awed. Some gasped and hid their faces in their hands.

It was getting hard to breathe. A force flowed from the hidden figure, a force that was determined to press them down on their knees.

And Thru knew, somehow, beyond all shadow of doubt that this was the source of all the evil that had ruined his life and shattered the peace of the Land. He stared up at it, refusing to be cowed.

The others quailed, even Ter-Saab crouched, raising a hand as if to ward off a gale as the unseen force beat down. Thru stared and fancied after a while that he caught the glitter of two red eyes, hot and feral staring back down at him.

Thru tilted his head back and broke into song.

"Who'd be a jolly beekeeper
and always suffer stings
when you could be a slee—ee-per
and never mind those things!"

His own voice amazed him in that place. Driving into the dark blanket of magic like a shining knife.

"A jo-o-o-o-olly beekeeper
whose always getting stung
That's me and we and you and he, and we are all just one."

And now Ter-Saab straightened up and joined him along with Juf Goost. And then the others lifted their heads and sank loudly, proudly, and clear.

The little winks and gleams of light vanished. The heavy sensation of oppression disappeared.

The figure motioned sharply with one hand in obvious irritation. The Red Tops struck with their whips. One or two mots went down on one knee, but none stopped singing.

"Who'd be a jo-o-o-o-olly beekeeper. . ."

The Red Tops grew frenzied. Juf Nolan was knocked off the dais and crashed down among the Gold Tops in the nearest seats. They reacted with cries of horror and outrage. Thru was struck, slapped, and then thrown down to the floor. He got back to his hands and knees and kept singing.

"And we are all just one . . ."

The figure in the private box had gone away, the door closed behind it.

Chapter 28

A day passed, and they received only a couple of cups of water and no food. They moved to a larger cell, with a barred window that let in a little air. The window opened onto a narrow courtyard with an alley behind it that went out toward the light. They were in the back of the pyramid, in a part where people lived. The door was stoutly built, wood lapped with narrow bands of iron. The iron bars in the window were well seated and unlikely to give way no matter how hard they tried them. Escape seemed unlikely.

The next morning they discovered that the water had contained a powerful purgative. To humiliate them further the Red Tops gave them only a single bucket. The cramps were severe for several hours, a wretched feeling.

"Why do they do this to us?" said Juf Goost. "Isn't killing us enough for them?"

"You don't understand," said Pern Glazen. "They want to be sure our guts are empty so we don't desecrate their altar when they rip us open."

Juf Goost responded to that idea by emptying the bucket out the window through the bars, which caused a furious outcry in the yard beneath.

A minute later the Red Tops stormed into the cell, and Juf threw the bucket at them. For which they were all beaten. But during the whipping they exchanged furious looks. Something flew between them like sparks in a forest fire, and suddenly all had changed. They were no longer bound at neck and wrist. The men had forgotten that. Suddenly they rose up and attacked their tormentors. The mots and brilbies had nothing to lose, but plenty to say with their fists and feet.

Thru ducked under the arm of an oncoming priest. He tucked his shoulder in hard against the man's chest and felt the fellow rock with the impact. Thru's first punch was to the man's throat, and he felt it crumple under his fist.

That man would give them no more trouble.

Master Sassadzu would not have approved of all the kyo that followed. During the voyage Thru had taught the others kyo, and they were keen students. But they were too eager, too angry, and too desperate perhaps for Sassadzu's level of perfection.

The Red Tops were taken by surprise, however. Then they were taken. In less than a minute four were stretched out on the floor of the cell and the rest had flung themselves back out the door to raise the alarm. Soon dozens of them jammed in the passage outside the cell. Strangely, however, they stayed there.

The impasse could only be broken by the Red Tops flooding inside and overpowering the mots, who were now armed with four clubs and four knives. The Red Tops halted and were shoved aside by a party of Black Tops, wearing battle armor and carrying small shields.

The Black Tops were huge men. They burst in and began wielding their clubs. The captives fought back with everything they had, but they could not prevail against these giants. The struggle was terrible and brutal, and was over in a few minutes. Three of the Black Tops were dead, and so were Juf Nolo, the steady mot of the Spirit, and Raan Oner, a quiet son of the Sulo Valley.

The survivors were beaten black-and-blue. Juf Goost had lost his front teeth, his nose had been mashed flat, and one of his ears was partly torn off. Old Thru Bush could barely move, and soon lapsed into unconsciousness.

Thru Gillo was left with sore ribs, sore arms, and sore shins. When he'd finally been knocked down he'd managed to stay rolled up in a ball while they beat and kicked him. He counted himself among the fortunate as he tried to staunch the bleeding on poor Juf Goost's battered nose.

The Black Tops bound them all at wrist and ankle and left them on the stone floor for the rest of the day.

The oldest mot, Thru Bush had been silent for several hours when Jevvi wriggled over to put his ear to his chest.

"He's not breathing," Jevvi announced.

Another of their small group had passed on.

"At least they won't get to kill him on their damned altar," said Ter-Saab.

Things faded in and out after that for Thru. Exhaustion overcame the tension, and he slept, but fitfully with sudden starts to wakefulness, cold and afraid.

At some point Thru saw the door open, and a group of Gold Tops came in. They wandered around the cell looking at the bound and beaten captives. They prodded Thru Bush's corpse and then ordered the Red Tops to drag the body away. Then the Gold Tops left.

Slaves entered and washed down the walls and floors. When they finished, they threw buckets of cold water over the mots and left them shivering on the stone floor.

Red Tops entered and performed a ritual cleansing of the window that had been defiled by the captives. They lit incense and intoned prayers before scattering purified bones and ashes over the windowsill. Before leaving they scattered more ashes over the prone bodies of the mots. A mad kind of glee shone in their eyes.

The door slammed again. Cold, wet, aching, the captives lay there as the dim light of day faded and their final night on the world began.

Thru had long since resigned himself to dying far from home and family. But he thought it especially cruel that he might never see his darling Nuza again. He visualized her back in the Farblow Hills, with the wind on her fur, her eyes alive to the beauty around her, walking in the hills.

May she have a good life, he prayed. May she wed a good mot and have a fine family. When the peace came. When their lives could return to the old ways. Thru told himself that Toshak would win. Thru was sure. Toshak would have come south after the disaster in Sulmo. Toshak would have brought the army of the North. And when Toshak got to grips with them, the army of Shasht would have found itself facing a much more serious task. Toshak would win, the Land would survive. Peace would come eventually when the men of Shasht finally abandoned their attempt to plant a colony on the Land. Nuza would live through it, and her life would be a good one. All of this had become a kind of truth to him during the months they'd been at sea.

But still, it was bitter to have had so much promise in his life and then to have lost everything. Thru recalled Cutshamakim's words concerning existence,

Hark! For ye listen now
Ye taste now
Ye breathe now
But ye have no peace
Later . . . there is peace.

The bittersweet irony of life, and for every living thing there comes the time when life cannot go on. He commended his soul to the Spirit, whispered a prayer for his mother, and fell back to sleep.

He next awoke to a loud thump against the door. It was followed by a barrage of more blows. There was a faint ring of steel on steel.

The mots stirred, some propped themselves up on their elbows. A fight was in progress just outside the door!

It was a hell of a fight too, by the sound of it, but it didn't last very long and when it stopped there was a silence. Then there came quiet voices talking to each other, and a key scraped in the lock. The mots looked to each other with eyebrows lofted quizzically.

The lock turned, the door opened, and a lantern lit the dark room. A single figure entered, holding the light.

Thru was surprised to see that the man's head was not shaved and daubed with thick paint. It was not a Red Top or a Gold Top, nor even a giant Black Top. Instead a slender man of smaller stature, edged into the cell. He was a nervous-looking fellow, dressed in velvet with puffed shoulders and sleeves and a matching square-cut hat, bearing a fancy red tassel.

The Man's clothes might be those of a fop, but he also carried a sword in his hand, a sword with blood on it. Every mot saw that sword, and a stir went through the cell.

Thru glimpsed a clean-shaven face, thin, with anxious-looking eyes that darted around the interior. The man seemed to be counting the mots, then he whistled. Other men, dressed in simple white linen came in and began to cut the ropes that bound them. When they were freed, they got slowly to their feet. A few, like Jevvi, could barely move. Poor Juf Goost's face had been destroyed, the blackened blood crusted all over the fur on his head and shoulders. He needed a little help to get to his feet.

The Man with the black jacket pointed to the door and made a gesture to encourage them to go through. Thru heard him say "come with me" several times.

The others looked to Thru, even Ter-Saab. This was the strangest thing they had yet seen in the land of Shasht. A man who seemed peaceful toward them. A man who didn't bluster or curse.

Even with the bloody sword in the man's hand, it was an easy decision. The door opened and to wait in that room was to wait for death. Even though it hurt just about everywhere when he moved, Thru headed for the door. The others came right behind. Outside, in the narrow passage leading to the cell, they found other men, three wearing velvet jackets of green and dark brown, and then farther along five more wearing plain linen shirts and breeches. The Red Tops were gone. More lanterns were held aloft to guide their path. Everywhere the men lead them on with smiles and hand gestures and the mots followed, having no other choice.

Instead of returning to the wide corridors they had walked before, they entered a narrow door to a much smaller passage. The only light was that of the lanterns carried by the men. They walked in this dank adit before reaching a heavy wooden door that jerked open onto a loading dock under the stars. They were outside the pyramid once more. The smell of jacaranda trees was strong in the soft night air.

They faced the walls of a narrow courtyard with a wide passage leading to the far side. Through the passage came a wagon pulled by amazing animals, horses, the like of which the mots had never seen. Horses like these had been extinct for a long time in the Land. In fact, in the Northern Hemisphere only wild ponies, no bigger than donkeys, survived, and only in an area of grassland far to the east of the Drakensberg mountains that hemmed in the Land.

They gaped at these beautiful animals, who were seemingly quite domesticated, since they pulled the covered wagon at a good pace. Some of the mots stood dumbfounded, but the men pushed them inside the wagon, where they sat on benches along the sides. Once aboard, the wagon pulled away into the night, rattling down the passage to a gate manned by a small group of men wearing black cloaks and hats similar to the first man into the cell. These men were actually riding on the beautiful animals. Again the mots marveled at the sight. The wagons rolled out the gate and turned onto a curving road, which then passed between bulky tombs and mausoleums erected to honor great dignitaries of the past. Herculean masonry lofted orbs, finials, and pinnacles toward the dark sky. Here were represented the great figures of the courts of the First Dynasty, the time of Kadawak and his successors. The tombs threw up fantastic shadows into the night, while behind them the pyramid's vast bulk seemed to blot out the sky.

"Where are they taking us?" Pern Glazen wondered aloud, looking out the back of the wagon.

"Depends on who they are, I'd say." Ter-Saab grinned through bloodied lips.

"That's a good point," said Pern. "Who are they? Not at all like the usual uglies."

"They're not priests, they don't paint their heads."

"They don't hit us with those damned whips, either," said Juf Goost thickly.

"I don't think these men mean us any harm," said Thru.

"It could be a trick of some kind," said Pern Glazen.

"Hard to imagine why it would be a trick. They killed the Red Tops at the door. We all heard it."

"Maybe they just do this to raise our hopes, so as to crush them completely later when they kill us."

"Maybe," said Ter-Saab, obviously disagreeing.

Thru was as puzzled as the others, but nursed a wild

hope that perhaps these men were an opposition force to the temple and all it stood for.

The wagon rolled on, turning every so often, still passing between great bulky structures of stone. They crossed a river as wide as the Dron. On the other side the character of the buildings changed. Now they went on cobbles through streets of tall stone houses. Lanterns were lit at every intersection, though they saw no one out on the streets.

After another turn they saw larger houses, grand enough to have gates and staircases. A light ahead drew their attention. Two men were waiting beside an open gate.

The wagon entered and the gate closed behind them. They came to a halt, and the mots were urged in whispers to climb down and follow the men in the black velvet jackets.

The men urged them to hurry with tense gestures.

The mots struggled to walk, and some had to be half carried. They passed through a door that led to a dark hallway with a brick floor. A door opened ahead throwing red light into the passage. The walls were covered in painted figures. Thru glimpsed stylized figures of men, and beautiful horses. Then they passed through the door and stepped down into a dimly lit wine cellar. In an alcove among the wine barrels they found bedding laid out, with water and some rough, dark bread. It was the first food they'd seen for two days, and they were ravenous. Even Juf Goost, who couldn't chew with his battered mouth. Thru helped Juf soften bread in the palm of his hand by pouring on the water very carefully. Then Juf shoved some down past his broken teeth.

It was all consumed in a few moments and merely left them feeling hungrier than ever. The men had gone, the door had shut, they were left with the single lantern burning above the door.

They sat there feeling the tension and excitement of the escape drain slowly away. They were definitely not in the hands of the priests of the Great God, He Who Eats. Beyond that they could only guess who their saviors were.

They didn't have long to wait. The door opened again,

and a group of men came into the cellar, lead by the one they'd first seen with the bloody sword. He now wore a linen shirt and knee breaches in black velvet. His companions were more sumptuously garbed. White stockings to the knee, velvet breeches, silk and velvet garments, and square-cut hats with plumes and tassels.

These five men gazed down at the battered captives. Thru could sense a common excitement among them. Their eyes flashed in triumph. When they spoke Thru understood them easily, their words were almost without accent. They were very pleased with themselves.

"I have to say, they are magnificent."

"A little bruised, perhaps."

"They staged a revolt apparently. Killed some Red Tops."

"Well-done, I wish we could kill all the goddamn Red Tops."

"So they had to be taught a lesson. Black Tops were used of course."

"Damn the priests, sodomistic peasants, all of them."

"No breeding, they behave like the filth they spring from."

Thru wondered what he was hearing, for some of it made sense and other parts did not.

"Anyway, well-done you fellows."

"I say, a big hand for Janbur, it was his idea."

"We were all in it together," said the one in black, Janbur of the Gsekk. "I could not have done it without you."

"We're all in it together all right, and we'll die on the altar together if the priests track us down."

"We have sprinkled gold enough to hide our tracks. This is a good place to hide. In a day or so we will move them into the Shalba."

"Why the Shalba? Why not out to the country?"

"They will be guarding all the roads. We have thrown down a gauntlet to the priests. Later I will send word to the Emperor that the creatures are safe. The Emperor will have to make his decision."

"And whatever his decision is, we will obey it," said the

thin one who had worn black and carried that bloody sword.

"Who among us would betray our oath to the Emperor? But we know he does not really want these creatures to be killed."

"The Emperor must rule. Out with the priests."

"Out with them," said the others.

"Indeed, damn the sodomistic priests, all of them."

"And what of our new friends here? That one looks as if he might not last long." The speaker pointed out Juf Goost.

Juf's eyes were wide with alarm at being selected. Thru whispered reassurance. The men didn't appear to notice.

"Yes, he does seem rather poorly. Well, you've still got seven if that one goes."

"Damned priests, what did they do to the poor creatures?"

"Look at all those eyebrows going up and down. Damn me if they don't look like a lot of big monkeys!"

"That's why they call them monkeys."

"I can see why, but they're obviously much more intelligent than monkeys."

"Of course. You've seen the objects brought back?"

"Incredible work. The rug things with the bright colors. The pottery and wood carvings, too."

"They are an artistic bunch of monkeys if that's all they are."

"Bah, they're obviously intelligent. Perhaps not as intelligent as men, but more intelligent than anything else. . . ."

"I've heard they're offering two hundred in gold for some of that pottery. Beautiful work."

Thru had heard enough. Slowly, painfully, he pulled himself to his feet. They stared at him.

"Excuse me," Thru said in good Shashti. "Could we have more water? More bread? We are very hungry."

The men stared at him with open mouths.

"It spoke to us?" Gasped the one called Janbur.

Chapter 29

"We have been lied to about this colony from the beginning. It is not Aeswiren's wish. Aeswiren obeys some other force, perhaps the priests, perhaps the Hidden One."

"Why do you raise that name here, Janbur, under my roof."

"Because, dear mother, the time has come when we must confront this thing and remove its fangs, whatever it is."

"Bah, it's all a silly fantasy. Spooks and bog-sprites! You'll be worried about ghosts next."

"Whatever you say, you have to admit that this mot is not at all like a 'monkey.' Isn't that so?"

Behind the screen the hidden figure of Janbur's mother, Tekwen Gsekk, sniffed, but said nothing. In truth, she was stunned by the appearance of this talking animal that Janbur had hidden in her house.

"You know the emperor is searching high and low for these creatures of yours."

"Of course."

"The priests would love to use this as an excuse to destroy our family."

"Don't worry, the mots will be moved tonight."

Thru, who was sitting in the elegantly furnished room, looked up at this.

"Where will we go?" he said.

The woman behind the screen shifted. She was not yet comfortable with this creature being able to speak Shashti like a citizen.

Janbur, however, answered with hardly any hesitation. He was used to speaking with Thru.

"We plan to move you out of the inner city to an estate

in the suburbs. You will be hidden there for a few days, and then we will move you again. That way we can be sure to keep ahead of the Hand. They will be searching for rumors among the city's serving classes. It's hard to keep the servants from learning about something like this, and such knowledge is worth gold."

Thru nodded. He and Janbur had discussed this eventuality. In the three days since he had broken the silence and spoken to the men, they had undergone a sea change in relations. Great new vistas of understanding had opened up for both of them.

"So, dearest mother, you can see why it is important that we stop this horrible colony. Why must we destroy this other people? They have done us no harm. They have much they could teach us about preserving the fertility of our land."

"Mmmm," Tekwen had been wavering. This idea sparked her interest. As the owner of more than ten square miles of grazing land worn down to stubble and dust, she was perennially concerned with such ideas.

"So, tell me again, where did they originate? They are not men. What are they?"

Janbur shot Thru a look to say "forgive her, she doesn't understand yet."

Thru shrugged slightly. He had grown used to it. Humans had a hard time accepting the idea that any other creature might be able to talk to them. Thru thought it pretty understandable. Men would probably not want to hear what the animals might say.

Speaking in a patient voice, Janbur repeated the story.

"They say they were raised up by the High Men. Long ago, in the time of the ice."

"Who were these High Men? Why have we never heard of them?"

"We don't know. I have asked the scholar, Petazm, but he says that there are no records of the older time. We know only of the Old Kingdom and the Empire."

"Stuff and nonsense, how do you know it wasn't all begun by the Great God, just the way the priests say? The world began when Kadawak built the Empire."

"But we know that's silly. The world had existed for a long time before any priest shaved his head and painted it red. There were other gods for thousands of years."

"The priests would break you for that thought."

"Of course, they keep the people ignorant on purpose. They rule the nobility with intimidation and occasional brutality. But it is still true. We had other gods before the coming of this one, this He Who Eats."

Again Tekwen lapsed into silence. This was an uncomfortable area of thought. Getting in the way of the priests could only cause trouble.

"And for a start the priests have obviously lied to us about these creatures. Our guest here has told me things that changed my ideas about the world."

"Impossible."

"Not at all. Mother, please accept this. I am introducing you to Thru Gillo. He holds the equivalent rank of a colonel in his own army, and in his civilian life he aspired to become a weaver of fine rugs."

"A weaver, well, he's not very big so that's more believable than his being a soldier." She gave a snort, then realized that Thru understood her word for word. She took a breath.

"I apologize, Master, uh, Gillo. This has all been a terrible shock to me."

Thru looked to Janbur, unsure how to respond. Janbur raised a hand and spoke instead.

"Thank you, Mother. When I talked with Thru Gillo, I learned that he already knew something about our world, we know nothing of his."

Silently Tekwen Gsekk sized up the situation.

"All right. I will spread the word among my friends. I will tell them that the creatures are intelligent enough to speak Shashti and that the policy of exterminating them is surely immoral and must be halted."

"Thank you, dear mother, I will repay this favor, I promise. And you are doing the right thing. We are doing what Aeswiren would want, I assure you."

"So you say, but how can you be sure that your friend the Erv is telling the truth about the Emperor's wishes?"

"The Erv of Blanteer can be counted on, Mother. He is the soul of honor."

"He had better be, or we'll all wind up with our tongues tied to some red hot steel."

With that the meeting was ended. Tekwen Gsekk withdrew, and Janbur and Thru prepared to return in secret to the cellar. Thru donned a cloak with a hood and covered his face with a veil. If they were seen, he would hope to be taken for nothing more than a woman outside of the purdah line in the house.

From Tekwen's private rooms on the first floor, they negotiated their way through the bulk of the big house. The wine cellar lay two floors down, accessible only by a stair in the butler's quarters.

They used the lady's gallery on the west side of the house. Only Lady Tekwen used these rooms, so they were safe from prying servants' eyes. Furnished with the treasures of centuries, the rooms contained polished wood furniture, walls painted with scenes of natural beauty, and large rugs with complex patterns. Through the windows along the western side, Thru could see the ominous hulk of the pyramid, where it dominated the skyline.

"The pyramid has not always been there, then?"

"No, my friend, it was built by Kadawak. He announced the coming of the Great God. It changed everything here. Before then the old country, old Shashta, was a different land. Very poor, of course, our Empire was only a quarter of the size of what it is now. We were constantly at war with our neighbors, and that was expensive, too. But we never won the wars, nobody really ever won, and that was both a curse and a blessing."

Janbur sighed. "But Kadawak was unstoppable, and he conquered all our rivals and crowned himself Emperor."

"So then there was peace?"

"No. There has always been war. We are a warlike people. Rebellions are frequent. Our armies themselves sometimes try to install a new Emperor, usually their own commanding officer. So there have been wars in every reign, for five hundred years."

He recalled something Janbur had said to his mother.

"You have mentioned a 'shadow.' I think you called it the Hidden One."

Janbur gazed at him for a long moment, as if trying to decide whether to speak or not.

"Yes, that began with Kadawak, it is said. Though others say that the Hidden One was already at work in the days of the Old Kingdom. Some believe that the Hidden One is the curse our people will always bear, but come, we must not speak of this here."

For a moment longer Thru stared thoughtfully over the rooftops to the pyramid. The hulking mass seemed to brood in the middle of the great city.

They descended the stairs with great caution. The servants had been kept in the dark about the visitors to the wine cellar. Only the house butler knew, since the wine cellar was part of his purview. But old Guyad, the butler, was trustworthy. He would not even tell his wife. Of course, you couldn't keep anything a complete secret from servants, but Janbur had taken precautions to minimize the effect of the mots' presence. Their food, for instance, was all brought in on wagons that went to the butler's yard and was unloaded by his warehouse slaves. These slaves were blind and mute, quite common in warehouses and treasure vaults. They sensed only that there was a strange smell in the wine cellar.

Janbur's friend Chemli of Weald supplied the food from his own kitchens, at Weald House, which lay just on the other side of Shalba Park. The extra rations were not enough to draw any questions.

Having goods unloaded into the cellars, either that of wine or dry goods, was a very common thing, and so the extra cart carrying bread and water did not cause rumors. The servants knew something was amiss, but since none had entered the wine cellar, they had no suspicions as to what was down there.

Better yet, of course, the priests had kept the loss of the "monkeys" a complete secret. Such a loss of prestige could not be borne. So while they mounted a furious search of the city, they claimed that it was to find a renegade priest, wanted for seditious preaching of the Old Gods. Thus, even while gangs of Red Tops turned over the hovels of the poor from Zufa to Kashank, the abduction of the captives was not revealed.

The priests had long been aware of the seditious nobility, so they turned to the wilder young nobles. They investigated, but found nothing. A few rumors floated. Arrests were made, and wellborn youngsters were tortured with the rack, the screws and the wooden boot, but they knew nothing of any real substance.

Fortunately, no one in Janbur's group of friends was taken. Janbur and his group worked quietly in the background, helping refugees escape persecution, rather than writing seditious samizdat. They were careful and kept their activities secret from even their closest friends. And so they were invisible to the Red Tops scouring the city.

Meanwhile the news spread that the Gold Tops had delayed the sacrifice of the "monkeys" because of a bad alignment between the moon, the Red Star, and the planet Zanth.

And yet, despite the success of their venture, Janbur would not leave the mots in his mother's cellar for even one more night. The Hand of Aeswiren was also searching for them, and the Hand was skilled in finding those it wanted. Even the mention of a wagon leaving the temple in the night at an odd hour could lead the Hand to the mots. So that night the mots would be moved. Out of the Shalba, across the park, and into a suburban estate.

They tiptoed down the back stairs to the ground floor, where they faced the greatest danger of exposure to the servants. To reach the butler's back door, they would have to pass close to the kitchen. They took the passageway that ran past the pantries and the granary. Two muscular young black cats got up and sauntered away as they approached.

At the end of the passage a stair led to an outside gate and other passages to the right and left. They turned right and entered a passage frequently used by slaves coming up from the kitchen garden.

At the far end was the back door to the butler's quarters, and Janbur had the key. Halfway along they heard figures moving behind a door to their right. The door handle turned.

Frantically Janbur pulled open another door and pushed Thru inside a narrow room with large windows and good light. Astonished, Thru saw three looms set up with work on them. A man bent over the nearest loom, working on a red rug.

"Is that you, Ijji?" said the man, without turning around. "Time for some tea, I'd say."

Janbur went up to his shoulder and spoke quietly.

"It is I, Janbur. How goes your weaving, Old Meethiwat?"

Old Meethiwat was a little surprised by Janbur's presence, and when he looked up Janbur stepped close to him so that he would not see Thru.

"Oh, it goes well enough, lord. Thank you for visiting."

Janbur studied the completed part of the rug for a moment.

"An old Shashta pattern?"

"Aye, young master, it's called 'Birdsong.' "

Behind him Thru heard the receding footsteps of the men. He took a step forward and peered at the finished part of the rug, an interesting geometric pattern of colors ranging from deep red through orange to ocher and dusky yellow. But it was the process that really drew his eye. The looms, with heddle and shedding rods, were the same used in the Land. The sight of these looms filled him with amazement, and then sorrow for the work he had been forced to abandon.

Janbur patted the weaver's shoulder.

"I know that my mother is looking forward to seeing this carpet when it is done."

"Oh, that means so much to an old weaver. Thank you, young master Janbur."

Old Meethiwat went back to his work without appearing to notice Thru's existence. More footsteps went past outside in the hallway and diminished in the opposite direction.

Now Janbur put his head out, listened carefully, and signaled Thru to follow while closing the door quietly behind them. They hurried down the passage to the butler's door.

The skeleton key went in without difficulty, but it would not turn easily. Janbur struggled.

Now they heard a door slam and footsteps in the hallway. Janbur tried to force the key, but it would not budge.

"Let me try," whispered Thru.

Janbur hesitated for a moment then took his hands off the key. Thru took hold, tried the lock, pulled the key back a little, and tried again.

The footsteps were almost on them.

The lock turned, the door opened, Janbur pushed him inside, and they almost fell over in the entrance. Janbur whirled around, closed the door, and leaned against it while sweat ran from his brow.

They heard footsteps pass the door and recede into the distance.

"That was too close, my friend," said Janbur in a whisper.

They were in a small, dark hallway. Two more doors lay before them. They tried one, it opened after a struggle, but the passage beyond was blocked with sacks of roots. The other door opened onto a room where cooking oils were stored. Moving very quietly, they reached the stair leading down to the wine cellar. The door opened more easily to the keys, and they were safe once more.

"What do you mean when you say 'the Hidden One'?"

Janbur hesitated again before speaking, and then whispered.

"It is not known what it is, but 'tis said there lies a shadow on the pyramid, and a fell demon from ancient times dwells there unseen."

Thru recounted what he had seen inside the pyramid. The room full of Gold Tops, the sudden hush, and the opened door above. The solitary figure hidden in the shadows.

Janbur was awed.

"Long have we suspected something like this. The Gold Tops keep this secret from the world, but from what you say, this being rules them from its hiding place!"

"And the ordinary people do not know?"

"It is no more than legend. And I think what you saw shows that this is the force behind the war against your people. I think it began in Norgeeben's time, a hundred years ago."

"How could it have happened?" Thru wondered how this calamity had occurred without anyone in the land ever knowing.

"I have heard it said that a ship called the *Goodventure* returned with claims of finding a lush land on the far side of the great ocean. The crew died on the altars for blasphemy, and the ship was broken up. The whole story was suppressed, but not completely."

Thru nodded to himself. A ship had scouted the Land and not been seen. It could happen. The men were great sailors, and their ships were far superior to those of the mots. But he also knew something else. This being in the pyramid was known to the Assenzi. They had mentioned some hidden hand behind the war. Utnapishtim had a name for it, but Thru had forgotten what it was. This was the being that the Assenzi had fashioned their message for.

Had he not received it yet?

Janbur clapped him on the shoulder.

"My friend, you have brought us great news. If you will repeat what you have told me, then it could help our cause enormously."

"I would be glad to."

"Good, then I will gather a group of influential men to hear you speak of this being in the pyramid."

They entered the cellar to join the other mots. Thru recounted what he'd seen in the upper house and the conversation with the Lady Tekwen.

Rueful chuckles erupted from some of them when he described the lady's insulting words.

"But she apologized. That shows they can learn," said Ter-Saab with a sardonic grin.

Chapter 30

"Thank you, my dear," said the Emperor as the lesson came to an end. "I think I have a better idea now of these irregular verbs."

"If you remember that the 'dolo' suffix often changes to the 'lolo' suffix in the plurals, then you'll usually be safe."

"Indeed! Tricky those little endings, eh? I wonder if I'll ever be good enough to speak it."

"Oh, yes, I think you will. You have worked very hard, Your Majesty. I can see how it is when you make an effort. Your intensity is tremendous, even frightening."

He smiled. "If they came from anyone else, I would take such words as flattery and be offended, but with you, my dear, I know they are meant sincerely."

He had encouraged her, from the beginning, to be open and frank with him in all things.

"No deceits with me, dear, d'you understand? You do not serve me by lying to me."

She had taken him at his word, and they had become good friends.

"I am having a small meal of figs and cheese. Would you like to join me?"

As always he held to the smallest courtesies. He was like this with his guards, with soldiers, with everyone, even his enemies. No wonder so many would willingly die for him.

"I would be honored, Your Majesty."

"Yes, yes, but are you hungry? Would you like something more substantial?"

"Oh, no, Your Majesty, whatever you are having will be more than adequate."

The small eunuch, who served as Aeswiren's personal

slave, brought in a tray of figs, cheese, flat bread, olive oil, sesame paste, and a pitcher of weak beer.

While they ate they discussed Filek's plans.

"This 'micro-scope' that your father is working on has tremendous potential. He sent me a copy of the plans, and I studied them last night. Wonderful work, I am more convinced than ever that I did the right thing by sending him back to the hospital."

"My father is absolutely in love with his work. It is all that he has dreamed of. He prays for your health every morning, Your Majesty."

"That is good of him. Well, he has already gone far beyond what I might have expected. Apparently this microscope is a success. He sees a world at the level of the very, very small, which he says is far more complicated than anything he had ever imagined."

"Oh, Your Majesty, he came home a week ago singing about the 'small seed' that he has imagined as the source of infection. He had finally seen them. I have seen them. It is a wonderful sight."

"Good, I had hoped for this. Tell me more. I have arranged for a demonstration of the device, but it will not be until tomorrow. I have unavoidable engagements until then."

"The tube is as thick as this," she held up her finger and thumb an inch apart. "And it is a foot long, and held in place in a kind of cradle. A sliver of glass is set at the bottom, on which he places a drop of dirty water. A lantern's light is directed under the glass by use of a mirror, and it illuminates the drop of water."

"Mmmm, yes, yes, I see. Go on."

"Then you place your eye to the top of the tube and look down it. The lenses inside the tube magnify the drop of water enormously."

"Ah, yes, exactly as I'd imagined from the drawings he sent."

"And in the water are all these things, well, they must be little animals. They spin and writhe and eat each other, and yet they are invisible unless you look through the lenses in the tube."

"Wonderful. You see, my dear, I was right. Your father is a genius."

Simona did not disagree.

"And now he wants to expand the hospital and open a new building devoted entirely to research."

"Oh, my father's plans grow quite giddy. He wants to examine every plant, every kind of fruit and insect, and see if they contain substances that might be useful for healing."

"A visionary, no doubt of it, but of course, it is expensive. The hospital sits in the middle of the Old City. Everyone has claims to every scrap of ground around it." Aeswiren sighed, they would need forty thousand pieces at least, and he would have a battle squeezing it out of next year's budget. Especially now that a dozen new ships were to be built and sent to reinforce the colony expedition.

And that was another problem that Aeswiren intended to tackle very shortly, but he knew he must move carefully. He would have to show the message to the Old One soon, and he knew it would displease him. Emperors who ignored the Old One's wishes had a way of dying suddenly, of inexplicable causes.

"But we will find the money, from somewhere. I have in mind some demonstrations of your father's micro-scope. Perhaps some of the wealthy merchants will show a little foresight and invest in our project."

Simona nodded enthusiastically, seeing the sense of this idea.

The figs were gone. The Emperor poured more tea and settled back in his chair. Simona noted again that despite his advanced years Aeswiren had kept his shape. He lived simply and drank little wine.

"And now, my dear, tell me of yourself. Have you thought again of what you wish to do?"

Simona bit her lip. Previously she had told him everything about her life while he listened patiently. He knew of the witch mark on her left breast that would forever keep her from a good marriage, and he had expressed his sympathy for her situation.

"I think I could best serve by writing of my father's work

and publishing the accounts. That will spread his ideas across the whole Empire."

"That is an excellent idea. I had already thought to offer you a position as my scribe. I want you to write a detailed account of the Land and all its peoples."

"Oh, Your Majesty, I would love to do that."

"Good. You shall. I can set aside 600 pieces for the work, enough to see you comfortably set up in your own household. Then your father can stop harassing you with his dreams of dynastic developments."

Aeswiren was smiling, but Simona had tears running down her cheeks. The Emperor's generosity eliminated her need to constantly fend off her father's attempts to marry her to some wealthy old man. She would have her own earnings, and therefore be able to set up her own household.

"How can I thank you, Your Majesty?"

"You can thank me by writing as well as you are capable, understand?"

He allowed her to kiss his ring and then poured them both more tea.

"Now, to the matter of the captive mots."

"Oh, yes, Your Majesty. What news do we have of them?"

"Nothing. Which surprises me a little. I have my sources in the pyramid, but they say they hear nothing on this subject. Although the priests are looking high and low for a subversive preacher, or so they say."

"What could it mean? Your Majesty?"

"It could mean several things. My sources inside the priesthood are limited, you understand. Not even the Emperor can overrule the temple. It may simply be that the mots are dead and all the fuss is devoted to covering this up. The priests are a cruel lot, they may not have restrained themselves during the torture. If they are dead, then the pyramid will be embarrassed on the day of their sacrifice, for they will not have hearts to give to the Great God."

Simona made a face. Between them there were no secrets. Both despised the cult of Orbazt Subuus, He Who Eats.

"On the other hand, it could be very good news. It may be that they have been rescued."

"But how? By whom?"

"That is the mystery of the moment. Believe me when I tell you that my operatives are working very hard on that subject right now."

Simona nodded, she could just imagine. Visiting with the Emperor in private, teaching him another language, she had glimpsed some of the workings of his realm and she understood that as Master of the Hand of Aeswiren, he was a different person from the gentle grey grizzled man she dealt with.

"May I tell Nuza of this?"

"You may. And I hope I will be able to tell her myself, very soon. Well"—he grinned faintly—"I will try and tell her myself. I think you will have to be on hand during my first attempts."

"Nuza has said that she would like to meet you in person. She has performed for you so many times and yet only glimpsed your silhouette in the gallery above."

"Well, I want to make a good impression when we meet."

Simona smiled now. Aeswiren's constant wry self-deprecation was so at odds with the official face of the Emperor that it still amazed her sometimes.

"Nuza has also said that she will try and learn some Shashti soon. When I told her how well you were doing at learning the language of the Land, she changed her mind about things. She wants to understand us better."

"Ah, well, she will have her work cut out for her there, because we don't understand ourselves very well and we've been at it for thousands of years."

Chapter 31

A dozen men from the noblest families of Shasht were present in the gloomy space for the most extraordinary meeting they had ever attended. Crammed at the back of the Blanteer family mortuary and sworn to secrecy by Janbur Gsekk, they stared at the slim figure they had come to meet.

Naked to the waist, the figure stood before them, exhibiting soft fur from skull to navel, except for a small region around the mouth, nose, and eyes. It was an astonishing mixture for the nobles to absorb—soft grey fur and huge white eyebrows, a muscular body and a quiet voice speaking good Shashti!

"My name is Thru Gillo. I come from a land on the other side of the world. I was brought here as a captive. I come to you for your help in stopping a grave injustice."

Their jaws dropped at the sound of Shashti from the creature's mouth. The Erv of Dinak had slipped off the stone he'd been sitting on and landed on his behind with a thump and a cry.

"I have fought the army of Shasht many times. I have seen the men of Shasht defeated in battle, and I have seen them victorious. I saw this at the battle of Dronned, where we slew more than a thousand men. I saw the men beaten again at the Sow's Head Hill. We made them run that day, although it was a close thing. The men have taught us well. Now we, too, can make war."

The nobles simply stared at him. All of this had been kept secret. What battles had been lost? Until the frigate *Cloud* arrived back with the first load of captives, there had been little news about the expedition since the day, years before, when the great fleet had sailed away from Shasht.

"Your priests declare my people are an 'abomination.' They say we must be destroyed. They say that we are no more than animals and that we are incapable of speech. They say that only men, your kind, is given the benediction of the heavens. Only your kind are loved by your God. As you can tell, your priests are wrong about one thing at least. I speak your language. If we had the time, I would try and teach you mine."

He paused. The nobles stirred after a moment.

"Upon my soul, the creature speaks very well!" murmured Rotty Uspich.

"Extraordinary. For a moment I thought it was a trained animal. But it isn't?" The Baron of Chelo was struggling to accept what he'd just heard.

"Whoever would've dreamed this was possible," said someone else.

"Well, I don't see how the priests can justify what they've been saying. They're clearly lying about these, uh, people."

"Are you sure they're people? I mean . . ."

Janbur stood and raised his hands. "My friends, let our visitor speak. You will learn everything you need to know. The most important truth is that the priests have lied outright about many things."

With some nervous snorts and grimaces, the nobles resumed their earlier attitudes.

Janbur turned to Thru. Now for the second revelation.

"My friend, we will return to the question of your people's identity in a moment. But I wonder if you would tell the assembled company what you saw inside the pyramid of the Great God."

Thru described the scene: he and the other mots brought into the great hall by the Gold Tops, then the gong and the appearance of the mysterious figure in the high box.

"Did you see his face?" said the Erv of Blanteer when he had finished.

"No. It was hidden in shadow."

The nobles looked to one another. So it had been described before. " 'Tis the Hidden One," muttered the Erv of Dinak.

"The shadow lies across the pyramid," said Kelim Meliba. "We must trust in Aeswiren. He is our champion."

"Indeed," Janbur was up, addressing them all. "The Emperor hates the priests. Once he knows what we know, he will withdraw his backing from the colony expedition. He will seek peace with the mots of the Land."

"But what of the Hidden One? If it is true that he exists in the temple, then he is the real ruler. How many times have Emperors died suddenly? Or been deposed in mysterious circumstances. How much power does Aeswiren really have?"

"They are all dead, those who disparaged Aeswiren the Third."

"Aye, a mighty man is Aeswiren," said Krito of the Aveniba. "But also a clever one. He will find a way."

"So the priests have lied to us for centuries," grumbled the Erv of Dinak.

"The sodomistic priests are controlled by this thing, this struldbug that we harbor in the temple," said Janbur with some heat.

"Brave words, my friends," said Kelim. "But caution must be our guardian in these circumstances."

Everyone nodded.

Janbur raised his hands again to gain everybody's attention.

"I think we are all loyal men to Aeswiren. I would give my life for the Emperor gladly. He has brought peace and prosperity to the Empire for twenty years or more. But we know that there is something rotten in the heart of the pyramid. Long has it been suspected. Long have there been rumors, but the Gold Tops never speak and so the secret was kept.

"Now we know. Now we must find a way of helping the Emperor."

"One moment, dear Janbur," said the Erv of Dinak. "You must allow us to hear more from your guest. We have many questions, I am sure."

"Ask them, then. Thru Gillo will answer."

The young nobles peppered Thru with questions. Some

demanded that he add numbers in his head and then subtract others, to prove his intelligence. Others asked about the Land, and he described it as he knew it, rivers and forests, mountains and meadows. Still others asked more detailed questions about the campaigns and the military situation. Thru described the mustering of the Land, the raising of the regiments, and the training they had gone through.

"And your homegrown army has defeated the colony expedition twice?"

"Yes. Before they won the battle in which we were captured."

"But after that battle, how well could your people have resisted?"

"The army of the North would have come."

"Ah, so you claim to have more than a single army?"

"There are other armies being raised. All of my people know that we face extermination if we do not defeat the men of Shasht."

"Ah, yes, that would rather stir one up, wouldn't it?" rumbled Rotty Uspich.

"What would, Rotty?" muttered the Erv of Dinak.

"Extermination, my dear Erv, what else?"

Chapter 32

These visits to the pyramid were nerve-racking for Aeswiren. Not only did Aeswiren feel naked in public without a dagger in his belt, the Old One was chilling to meet with.

Twelve times he had come to see the Old One in this room. Always he had come by the same method. A plain carriage to the back entrance of the pyramid. A tense meeting in the courtyard, where he bid his bodyguards to wait. Not even Klek was allowed to accompany him. Then, blindfolded, he was lead by Gold Tops through a maze of passages and stairs until they reached this room. He knew the smell of it well, stale incense and floor polish. The blindfold was removed, and the Gold Tops backed out of the room and closed the door. A few seconds later he heard the outer door to the suite close. He was alone in the simple room.

The rug on the floor was a handsome Nisjani rug. The "four flowers" pattern was distinctive, a style that Aeswiren personally liked. A simple bench and a small chair of polished wood were the only furnishings.

Aeswiren had yet to sit down in this room.

He hated being without a dagger, it left him feeling naked. But there was nothing to be done about it, so he simply set his face like iron and stood there, poised for instant movement, waiting. Then . . .

"Greetings, Emperor Aeswiren," said the curious flat voice with its usual overtones of condescension.

He turned, willing himself to move slowly and keep all expression out of his face. He never heard the Old One come in, not even the faintest scuff of a slipper. Perhaps it floated in, perhaps it simply materialized out of thin air. The thing was a spook, no doubt about it.

As always the Old One wore a suit of brown wool, thick felt boots and gloves, a silk choker around its neck. It felt the cold, apparently, even in the summer months.

The face was dead-looking as ever, as if the flesh was frozen. The color was that of a sick old man, yellowed by age and decorated with wens and blemishes. When it spoke, the skin barely seemed to move—although the lips did. The eyes were blank, devoid of interest.

Aeswiren felt that familiar anger. How long had this ancient thing tormented Shasht? Feeding on the wars, building up the insane cult of He Who Eats?

"Greetings," he said in a quiet level voice.

That was another thing that irked him. It had no name. It was just "the Old One."

Aeswiren noted that the hairless head was reddened with cracks and peeling skin. The condition had grown steadily worse in the last three meetings. Perhaps this was a sign for hope.

"Welcome to the temple of the Great God, Aeswiren, Emperor of all Shasht for twenty-three years. Welcome to my abode. You have not requested a meeting in many years. Nor have we seen you in the temple giving worship to the Great God."

Aeswiren's eyes narrowed at the tone of voice. The Old One tried to provoke him and was amused by the Emperor's reaction.

"I pay my respects to the Great God elsewhere."

"Yes, of course you do. Anything else would be blasphemy." The Old One sat down in the small chair, as it customarily did. Aeswiren remained standing. He was the Emperor of Shasht, victor of two dozen battles, and bent the knee to no man. Indeed in his heart he did not bend before the Great God, either, if that God even existed, which he doubted. Aeswiren had fought his way to the throne and had ruled the land with benevolent strength for more than two decades; he felt he'd earned the respect of the old thing. He hated this jousting over the cult of He Who Eats.

"Your note mentioned a scroll that you think I should look at."

"Yes." Aeswiren produced the little scroll with its antique handles and placed it on the outstretched palm of the thing. The hand withdrew. After a long hesitation, the Old One examined the scroll, but did not open it.

"It has been opened and resealed. What does this mean?"

"Yes. I have read it. So apparently did the commanding fleet officer in the expeditionary force."

"Then, if it has already been read, if it is not private correspondence meant for my eyes only, why do you want me to read it? Why can't you simply tell me what it says."

"Because I do not understand what it says. The message is imbued with a powerful magic. A voice calls for 'Karnemin' to listen. I believe it is meant for you."

Another long silence. Aeswiren would've sworn he saw the thing's eyebrows rise slightly at the mention of that name.

"Oh, so there is magic in it is there?" For a moment Aeswiren saw the withered face break into an evil little smile.

"So tell me, Aeswiren, Emperor for twenty-three years, what did you think of the message in the scroll?"

"I am not equipped to understand it. I think maybe it refers to another time, possibly another world."

"And it was brought to you by this girl you have been seeing."

With another smile the Old One let him know that it understood that the Emperor was debauching the girl as a matter of course. Randy as goats were all Aeswiren's clan, after all. Aeswiren would have gladly driven a sword into its guts at that very moment.

"That is correct."

The Old One fell silent, and for a long moment it seemed to regard the scroll in its hand, as if weighing the danger it contained.

Then with a slight grunt, it broke the seal and flipped the scroll open. It read for a few moments and then gave a much heavier grunt. Aeswiren knew why. He'd seen that sudden panorama of the ancient city, the enormous towers thrusting into the sky. He'd felt the huge power unleashed by the magical writing. One moment the strange characters had been still, scratched in ink on the oddly soft parchment, and then in an eery transformation the writing had begun to move, flowing as if floating in a stream, and then everything had opened to a vast view of some enormous, ancient place.

The Old One's eyes were locked on the vision for a long ten seconds, and then it tore its gaze away with a couple of strange jerks of the head. It rolled the scroll up with trembling hands.

"So," it said with a little hiss, "this was what they sent you."

"The girl said they were ancient beings of great wisdom."

"This girl, this Simona of Gsekk, she is the daughter of Filek Biswas, who has returned to work in the hospital?"

"Yes."

"The priests tell me this man has a mark beside his name. They say he is not a devout believer."

"I know nothing of his beliefs or lack of them." Aeswiren lied. "He is doing great work that will advance our understanding of the world. He is breaking down the curtain that has separated us from the deeper arts of science."

"And you consider that to be a good thing?"

"Yes. Why not?"

Again, there was that tiny smile. Aeswiren shivered with the pure hatred he felt.

"For men to grasp the levers of science is to risk much, for Man is irresponsible, little more than a cultured ape. I am not sure that those levers should ever be grasped by human hand again."

Aeswiren was baffled. Like everyone else in his era, he knew very little of the world before the ice, and even the Ice Age, some twenty thousand years before was a thing of religious myth more than understanding. The history of the world as he knew it began with the ancient kingdom of Shasht.

"The man promises to bring about a revolution in medicine."

"I know, I know, and one consequence will be a vast increase in the birth rate. The population will soar, and it is already too great for the land. Indeed the land of Shasht is already overcrowded. The soil is exhausted."

"There are possible remedies. We could change land-holding laws. Give the peasants their own fields. They will be more productive and take better care of the land. Another useful remedy would be to govern the corn markets to eliminate price fixing."

The Old One shook its head slowly and decisively.

"And risk instability? You do not know what men are capable of, good Emperor Aeswiren the Third. But I know and I forbid such forms of progress. Men need strong hierarchies, powerful gods that keep them on their knees. Men become too haughty, too given to chaotic impulses if you remove the yoke."

Aeswiren heard the insolence and deep-seated contempt behind these words. He frowned, pursed his lips, and returned the stare of the dead eyes.

He could not accept that there was no chance of improving the economy of the Empire. But suddenly he felt caution muffle his response. He was Emperor, but he did not want to challenge the ancient thing. His own plans were in the making. Hesh and the Hand would do the job, but he must not betray his intentions too soon.

"The land needs water, it needs rest. Too much grain is grown to fatten meats for the wealthy."

"So what would you do? Confiscate land and give it over to communal ownership? Fool! When men have no personal, private stake in the land, they will always cheat the group. Starvation and corruption follow inevitably. So, would you instead take the land into state holdings? A terrible mistake, because then the entire covetous instinct of your society becomes aimed at the state, and in short order it is entirely corrupted and all authority rots away. Chaos or barbarian invasion invariably follows."

Aeswiren stared back, unsure how to respond. To this old thing all men were like rabbits, short-lived, stupid, unable to control their basic urge to overbreed and fill the land with their flesh.

"Does any solution have to be so extreme?"

"Of course. The land is exhausted, the fields worked to the bone. Food costs have been growing for generations. Despite Norgeeben's efforts, hunger has become widespread among the lower orders. Soon there will be social unrest. Half measures will do nothing but slow the slide into disorder."

"And yet we have great areas that are kept just for the comforts of the rich."

"A drop in the bucket. Norgeeben stripped the great families of all the lands they'd stolen during the final reigns of the second dynasty. Compared to that, you'd not get much good farmland now."

Aeswiren suppressed his next thought. Cut the number of priests and reduce the need to feed them.

The thing knew what he was thinking, though.

"I know what you're thinking, Aeswiren, Emperor for twenty-three years. And I can tell you that such a solution will not be allowed. There will be no reduction in the burden imposed by the priesthood. Don't you understand that we are taking on society's unwanted children by making them Red Tops? If they weren't priests, they'd be criminal elements."

"They could be put to more productive uses."

"Hah, now there's a thought!" The Old One had that evil smile again. "Well, don't worry, they soon will be put to work. But not in your lifetime, eh?"

Aeswiren wasn't sure what that remark meant. Would they try to kill him right here and now? He was unprotected. But his popularity still protected him from summary murder, he thought. Or did it? Would this old horror feel any compunction about killing him in an instant?

"And as for this Filek Biswas, well, the priests have marked his name. If they mark him again, then his heart must go to the Great God."

Aeswiren frowned. This sounded almost like a challenge to him. His voice steadied as he returned the fire.

"I am sure the priests will restrain themselves and leave Filek to his work. Meanwhile I will see that the man is urged to show more piety."

A long pregnant silence ensued. Then the Old One spoke again, but in a new tone, a voice filled with more emotion than Aeswiren had ever heard from it before.

"Let us move to another, more important subject. You

are aware, I'm sure that the captive creatures that were to have been sacrificed have escaped. They were given assistance by powerful forces in this escape. They are being sought now."

Aeswiren suppressed any surprise he might have shown at hearing this news in this way. He and his operatives had indeed been wondering what might have happened to the captive mots.

"I see," he said quietly.

"These vermin will soon be retaken, and this time they will be given to the God at once. I wish no further contaminations from them."

Aeswiren wondered at the vehemence in the ancient being. He'd never seen it get this excited about anything before.

"What is this 'contamination' that you fear?"

"They carry deadly diseases. You have read the report."

"Yes, the expedition was hit hard by a plague. You say they carry it and can infect us?"

"We must annihilate this filth. All of them must go to the altars, all!"

Aeswiren flushed involuntarily. Did this creature refer to his Nuza?

"Ahem, I must admit that I have wondered about this course of action. Why is it so important that we kill them all?"

"You do not know enough to understand. These vermin are the creations of the demons that rule that faraway land. Those demons will not stop until they can destroy our world. If we do not strike now and expunge them from existence, they will swarm across the world and overwhelm us eventually. It is us or them, literally."

Aeswiren could not square this view of the mots with what he knew from Nuza and Simona. The thing spoke with a lying tongue, it was clear. But he knew better than to challenge it. The vehemence, the passion of the Old One was fixed on this object.

Aeswiren left the meeting deeply concerned.

Chapter 33

"My fault, I insisted that we stay together," said Thru. "The men wanted to break us up. I told them not to."

Ter-Saab grinned back at him. "So that's why we've been living in cellars the past month."

Juf Goost, spirit unbroken despite his smashed mouth, chuckled. "You mean if we'd been broken up, we'd have been sleeping on feather beds?"

"And eating something other than stale bread, too," replied Ter-Saab, easing himself back against the damp stone of their present hiding place.

Thru understood their feelings. None of them would complain, but all were as weary of this frightening life as mice, hiding in holes in the ground. Most of their wounds had healed, but poor Juf had lost most of his teeth and was left with a hideous face, his nose all smashed and flat.

"I'm glad you didn't let them break us up," said Jevvi Panst, voicing what they all felt.

"Me, too," said Juf.

"Oh, I don't know," groused Ter-Saab playfully, "I wouldn't have minded a feather bed."

"Listen to him," said Pern Glazen. Someone tossed a wet sponge at Ter-Saab, who ducked too late.

"Well, at least we're all still alive, even if we've had to sleep on stone."

As usual it was Thru, who addressed the essentials.

Indeed, Janbur Gsekk's strategy had worked well. They'd survived several weeks of the most intense search of the city, and the priests were burning with rage as a result.

However, during the second week, some servants had stumbled on them in a wine cellar under a great house in the outer Shalba. After a frantic afternoon Janbur of the Gsekk pulled them out. First they'd shaved the fur off their faces and necks. Then dressed in rags like slaves, they rode out on a wagon with a few real slaves openly through the streets.

Not a single Red Top noticed them. The priests and the guards were too busy looking at covered wagons and carts to bother with a wagon of slaves uncovered and open to view. The servants who had seen them were sworn to silence, given gold to seal their lips and threatened with death if they spoke. None did.

The captives were alive, and rumors had spread in the city, the most popular being that the captives had disappeared. As the priests hadn't sacrificed the captive monkeys to the Great God, the rumor made sense. Among a certain class of people this was cause for great merriment. Among the priests there was nothing but rage.

They were going to be moved again soon. So they shaved. The strangest feeling the first time. Some never got used to the wetness, the cold steel drawn across the skin, the sudden change of color in the face.

"I feel like a naked baby every time I do this," said Ter-Saab.

"Don't worry, my friend," muttered Thru, wielding a razor on the back of Ter-Saab's neck. "You don't look like one." Indeed, kob skin was anything but baby-like.

The loss of their soft grey fur had revealed a band of skin tones among them. The Northerners were very pale, the Southerners were darker, and the kob was light brown. These tones were new to their eyes, because before, all had been covered in the common grey fur of the folk of the Land, all except kobs, of course.

But without their big eyebrows, with their faces shaved and dressed in slave rags, the mots and brilbies could become almost invisible in the world of men. They wore caps or rags tied around their heads and worked a certain amount of dirt and grease into their skins. Free men didn't really "see" slaves. And even on the few occasions when they'd traveled in a group with slave men, the slaves themselves didn't seem to notice.

They were moved again that very evening.

Until then, they'd been lodged in the unused cellar beneath an old palace in the Outer Shalba. Back on the wagon, they were taken down the lanes that wound between the palaces and streets of grand houses in the Outer Shalba. They passed across one of the grand ceremonial avenues, which were restricted to the carriages of the finest.

At the bridge over the Cho River, they passed close to a post filled with Red Tops. At this point Thru looked up and saw one of the young priests looking at him. The Red Top blinked. Thru looked down immediately and then they were past, just another wagon of slaves on its way to a field of vegetables somewhere.

Except that the Red Top had seen something.

The wagon rolled on. Thru dared not look back, even to warn the men on the back board. Janbur of the Gsekk was driving the wagon, and two friends of Janbur's, not afraid to risk their lives, were riding on the rear of the wagon, looking back. If someone were to stare at the wagon from that angle they would see these true men first, then behind them the mots and brilbies, all hidden variously under hats, caps, and rags. So far it had worked.

They came through the river park and onto a service road for a great house. The young lords on the back shifted uneasily. Down the road behind them they could see a group of Red Tops following at a trot.

"Janbur," called the pale young Erv of Grezack, I think they've spotted us." Janbur looked back, then whipped up the horse to increase its pace. They rounded the curve in the road at a trot, and the road sank down between stone walls.

Janbur looked around himself with a frantic eye. There were tall walls on either side of the service road. Begham house loomed over the trees on their right. To the left somewhere was the river, and the canal beside it.

A gate appeared in the wall on the left. Janbur jumped down and ran ahead. The gate opened at once, and Janbur ran back, got back on the wagon, brought the horse to a halt, and then turned it into the gate. The Erv of Grezack closed the gate behind them.

Ahead of them a straight brick road ran between two

fields of vegetables, alternating rows of lettuce, cabbage, and cucumbers.

"Quickly," said Janbur. "Get down and pretend to work."

The young lordlings were transfixed with terror.

"I cannot be caught here," said the Erv of Grezack. "My family would lose everything. . . . " The Erv had completely lost his nerve.

Janbur himself was undecided. Then they heard fists on the outside of the gate. The two young Ervs broke and ran for the far wall. Janbur stared at the gate with his hands balled into fists.

The mots looked down and found the rows filled with weeds. They started weeding, something that came naturally to mots of the Land.

The Red Tops pushed the door open and began berating Janbur.

"Slave! Why did you not halt when we called?"

"Called? I did not hear your call, master priests."

"Bah, you heard us and you whipped your horse on. We saw your wagon increase speed."

"Well, the truth is we are behind schedule, master priests. We should have finished in this garden yesterday. We have much to do by the end of the day."

Janbur put on an excellent performance. The Red Tops muttered and poked around the wagon.

Others, though, studied the mots and brilbies bent over the rows of cabbages, lifting out weeds with nimble fingers.

"Mushrat," snapped the leader, "which one did you see that you thought looked odd?"

The Red Top called Mushrat pushed into the rows of broccoli.

"This one, I think," he said, seizing poor Jev Turn by the sleeve and pulling him out.

"Look at him closely, he's odd-looking."

"You, slave, what's your name?"

Poor Jev Turn was plainly terrified. He could barely speak.

"I sorry, master," he said in broken Shashti after an embarrassing pause.

Thru tensed.

"What did you say, you pig?" The Red Top slapped Jev Turn across the face. Jev spun away from the blow.

Another Red Top kicked him and shoved him to the ground. "There's something strange-looking about this fellow. Let us take a look at him more closely."

Thru edged closer. He noticed Janbur staring at the Red Tops with a peculiar intensity.

Three Red Tops now pulled at poor Jev Turn. They would have his shirt open in moments to expose a body covered in fur. Thru moved. Out of the corner of his eye he saw Janbur in motion, too.

Thru caught hold of the nearest Red Top's shoulder and spun the man around. The astonished face that looked into his had barely accepted that a slave had grabbed hold of a priest when Thru's fist smashed into the man's throat, crushing his Adam's apple and dropping him to his knees.

Red Top rage exploded. A stave swished past Thru's ear as he whirled away in a tight kyo curve.

The other mots were coming. A moment later there was a whirling little fight in progress. Fists, feet, and staves were the only weapons and the sounds of thudding blows and heavy exhalations of breath were the only noise. The country kyo of the Land proved effective against the boxing style taught to Red Tops.

Meanwhile Janbur had slammed the gate shut and put a brick against the bottom. Ter-Saab leveled another Red Top and took a staff from the man. With that in his hands the old kob was too much for any of these Red Tops.

Outnumbered and bewildered by this turn of events, the Red Tops tried to flee. But they rebounded off the gate and were run down in the vegetable rows, beaten to the ground. The captives were not gentle with these men, caring little if they lived or died.

But other Red Tops had arrived outside the gate.

"No time," said Janbur in sick despair.

"Move the wagon in front of the gate," called Thru.

Janbur saw the need, slapped the reins, and the horse responded. Two seconds later the wagon was parked right up against the gate, just as the brick gave way and the gate started to open. Now the Red Tops were stymied.

The mots ran down the field and clambered over the wall at the far end. Ahead was another field, very similar to the first, but with a gate at the far end. They ran for it. Beyond the gate was a narrow cart track and then an open stretch of bare ground that flanked a canal. Across the canal lay more fields. All in all the scene was very familiar to mots who lived in a land of polders, ponds, and canals very much like this.

But this was not safe land for them. A couple of men, fishing from a bridge over the canal, saw them and hearing the hue and cry behind them started shouting and pointing at them.

They hurried along the side of the canal, with Janbur ranging ahead, seeking some escape route. Behind them they could hear the angry cries of the Red Tops, who had pushed into the field by now.

Looking back, Thru saw the first Red Tops climb over onto the canal path. Their shouts increased in volume.

"Here," said Janbur, pulling open another gate, leading into a narrow lane running between high wicker walls. They left the canal and went down this lane, with wicker walls on either side, screening off the garden plots of middle-class houses from the Outer Shalba. Behind them they heard the priests.

Quite suddenly they came to a fork. Janbur took the left side, the mots followed. Thru had fallen behind slightly and sensed the Red Tops closeness. Looking back he saw the first of them coming into view around the curve of the lane. The man gave an exultant yell.

Thru took the right fork, heading back toward the canal. He ran, but not to outdistance the oncoming priests, just to keep them following himself. Meanwhile he looked anxiously ahead for some way of escape. The gates of the maze were as high as the walls for some reason of tradition or security. There seemed no way out. The path forked again, and once more he headed right. Now a number of Red Tops followed him, and he let the leaders see just enough of his heels to keep them coming.

The game could only last for so long, though. Suddenly he was back on the canal path. A long narrow boat passed just twenty feet away. It was drawn by a horse lead by a child. The boat was painted a dull green, and was partly open at either end, with a closed in section in the middle. Since this was a long straight stretch of the canal, no one manned the tiller.

The child studied him as he drove the horse up the bank. Thru noticed the steam rising from the horse's massive hindquarters.

To either side the canal path stretched away. The Red Tops were coming, but they hadn't seen him yet. Thru didn't hesitate, but dove neatly into the canal and struck down through the cold water to the depths. The cold was shocking, just like the sea in winter. He swam under the looming mass of the canal boat and then up to the surface on the other side. The water was so cold it seemed to burn the skin. Then he broke surface and took a breath. The boat was only a few feet from the side of the canal here, but he could cling to a heavy hawser that was wrapped around the boat's side to protect it from the edge of the canal.

No one aboard the boat appeared to have seen him.

Then he heard the Red Tops burst out onto the canal path on the other side of the canal. Only a few fading ripples from his dive could be seen. The child and the horse never broke stride, and the boy didn't look at Thru now.

The Red Tops called to the boy. Some ran along the canal, seeking Thru under the water.

The boy slipped Thru a furtive glance, then looked past him.

"No, masterful priest, I see nothing."

"Well, do you see anything now?"

"No, master," said the boy.

Chapter 34

"Seems a useful sort of fellow" was fat Gevuv's comment when he finally noticed that the crew of his canal boat, the *Euchre* had gained a new member.

Along with little Riro and big Delp, there was now Thru, a middling sort, well-built and active. Had a strange sort of face, eyes too far apart, nose too small, but good looks weren't important in boat crew on the old Shasht canal. And since they'd lost Huppy in an accident at Guvnor's Lock, they'd been shorthanded. Riro had to do way too much, and Riro was only eight years old.

Gevuv, who had inherited the boat when his father died, was one of those owners who did no physical work. A conservative type, he stuck with the trade in general goods that he'd inherited. This involved taking cargoes of spices, salt, spirits, and housewares up the canal to inland parts like Shesh and the Trov Valley, then returning to the great city with tea, yeast, dried herbs, and country textiles.

"We need him, honorable master," said Riro, hands twisting a length of rope.

"I know," Gev said with a shrug. "I know, Delp is strong, but . . ."

Useless was a word Gevuv avoided, since he had paid fifteen pieces for Delp at the slave market. Huppy had always complained about it, but Huppy was dead, crushed by a lock gate when he slid off the side of the boat at the wrong moment. Huppy was one of those unfortunates who couldn't stay away from the spirits of alcohol. Riro didn't miss Huppy.

The new fellow, with the unusual name of Thru, was indeed useful. Very good with his hands, he was, and had soon repaired all the boat's ropes and lines. Also he sewed up some rents in the canvas covers that went over the open ends when it rained. Gevuv was pleased, for it was the month of Ribrack and soon there'd be ice on the canal. So Gevuv forbore to ask any difficult questions. This Thru must be a runaway slave, perhaps running to avoid castration. Gevuv would take care of all these matters at a more appropriate time.

Thru also improved the diet of the *Euchre* owner when he turned his hand to catching fish in the canal. Big bream and carp began to appear regularly on the dinner table, and Gevuv loved that. It saved more silver and was a break from oats and beans. Thru even took over the cooking, which was a vast improvement on Delp's efforts.

In just a week of moving through the crowded valleys, Thru became a favorite of Gevuv, who even indulged the new slave in a few coins to buy some warmer clothes, a thick homespun shirt, and an oilskin coat and hat.

Together with Riro, Thru worked the horse, a stout, uncomplaining animal called Deji (barley bread). Deji was not difficult at all. Nor were the other tasks of managing the boat. The only hard work was maneuvering through tunnels and locks.

But in the smallest, oldest tunnels there was often no tow path, and they had to work the boat through by pushing with their feet on the ceiling of the tunnel above. Delp was good at this, of course, though he was hopeless at everything else. Riro sometimes joked that that Deji was smarter than Delp. Certainly Delp could not be trusted to lead Deji, who would always find a way to slow down and eventually come to a halt if Delp was leading him.

Thru slept in Huppy's old bunk and used the communal razor and strop to keep his face and neck free of fur. Indeed he increased the area he shaved and made sure to do this when he wasn't being observed.

Taking over as cook also put Thru at the center of things. He began to copy the hard regional accent he heard from Riro and did his best to learn things without seeming to ask too many questions. He understood that, at least for now, he was cut off from his companions, essentially alone in an alien land.

Fortunately, Delp and Gevuv were incurious, to say the least. Riro though, missed very little. This became apparent one day, after a meal of Thru's roast fish with corn bread and sour vegetables. Thru had discovered that cornmeal behaved very much like bushpod meal and could be used in all the same ways. Riro was helping clean up after the meal while Delp went ashore to buy the master a pitcher of ale from a nearby tavern. They'd washed everything and were drying the pans before hanging them back over the little stove.

Suddenly Riro turned to him.

"So, tell me, were you cursed by a witch or something? Is that why you're covered in hair? Or are you a werewolf?"

Thru almost dropped the ladle he was drying. So much for thinking that he'd fooled young Riro.

"No," he said. There was no point in denying it. "I wasn't cursed. What is a werewolf?"

"Oh, you don't know? They are terrible things: men who turn into wolves and eat their neighbors. Everyone is afraid of them."

Thru had never heard of such a thing, but he kept his disbelief to himself.

"No, I am not a werewolf."

"Then, where did you grow the fur?"

"I've just always had it." Thru struggled to explain. How could he tell the youngster that all mots and brilbies were covered in fur? And how could he tell him that the bare skin of humans was a little disgusting to a mot?

Riro's face showed that he was trying to absorb this odd information.

"I have never heard of that before. Are you sure you're not a werewolf? They are said to be covered in fur. But they are also said to have red eyes, offensive breath, and long claws."

"Indeed."

Clearly, Thru did not fit the bill exactly.

"Still, your accent is strange, and you say little of where

you come from. You're not a Shashti, that's for sure. All Shashti like to boast about their hometowns."

"True. I am not from Shasht."

"Are there others like yourself in the land you come from?"

"Yes." Thru did not elaborate.

"Perhaps it is very cold there? So this helps to keep you warm?"

"Perhaps, but no one is sure."

"Is this place you come from part of the Empire?"

"No."

"Then, it must be far away indeed."

"Is it against the law for me to work on the boat?" said Thru to steer the conversation away from his homeland.

"No. Gevuv assumed you were a runaway slave. He won't tell the slave catchers, though. But when we reach Shesh he will have new papers written on you. You'll be Gevuv's slave after that. He will also have you castrated."

Thru's eyebrows rose for a moment. He would have to disappear before they reached Shesh, then.

"How long does it take to reach Shesh?"

"About twelve days, depending on the traffic at the lock ladder at Grand Junction."

"And we will reach the locks tomorrow?"

"Yes."

Thru hung up the ladle and put up the knives. When he left he would take the smaller of the kitchen knives. It could be hidden in his coat, yet it was large enough to serve as a weapon in a pinch.

"The truth is that I come from a far distant land. Very different from this one." He didn't have to glance out at the endless vista of two- and three-story houses that covered the treeless plain to know how alien this place was to a mot of the Land.

"The Red Tops were chasing you, but I didn't tell. I hate the Red Tops."

"Yes, I hate them, too."

That night they tied up in the dock at Evkun, another huge village of brown brick that stretched for several miles along the canal.

Other boats lined the wharves. Barrels, crates, and a dozen bales of hay were set along the dock. Carts and wagons took on their final loads and departed. The dockmaster blew the whistle for the end of the day. Men set down tools, locked stalls and warehouse doors.

Riro joined a group of other wharf kids, all slaves to various boat owners. They were rolling dice, and a couple of youths from the boat *Wiggen* had stolen some alcohol and passed the fiery potion around.

Riro didn't care for spirits, but he had a fatal attraction to games of chance. Luck often came his way, and he seemed to know when to bet a few coins.

Thru spent this quiet time working on the old pair of boots Gevuv had given him. They almost fit, and they helped keep his feet warm. Thru had cannibalized some leather from an old piece of hose and sewed it over the broken toe of the right boot.

As he worked, he contemplated his position. Lost in the heart of Shasht as a slave, he was invisible. For a few days he was safe. But he had no way of knowing what had happened to the other mots. He prayed that they had escaped the Red Tops and that Janbur had been able to hide them.

And for himself? He was simply lost in a desert of dusty towns of brick filling the flatland on either side of the canal. When he thought about his predicament, the sense of isolation was oppressive. So he did his best to put that aside and simply survive day by day. He worked hard on making himself useful, yet invisible. He had been able to pass as a human, at least to the insensitive. As long as he didn't spend too much time around anyone, they didn't seem to see through his disguise. Gevuv and Delp had never said a thing. Of course, Delp never said much of anything anyway.

And now he saw the world of Man from a fresh perspective. Before, he had seen it only from the other side of their battle lines, and then in chains from the hold of a ship. Now he saw the rude life of the canal, the villages of the plain, and he felt the desperation of these populations. From the cruel God to whom they sacrificed their captives to the harsh hierarchy that governed their affairs, the men of Shasht were ruled by fear and punishment. When their armies flowed out around the world, they took their fear, their hatred with them.

The starkness and sheer alien quality of these mud-brick towns hit him every day. Endless squalid streets, clouds of dust, swarms of flies, no trees. To Thru it was a landscape from hell.

It brought on a sense of desolation, a withering of hope. No wonder the men drank the fiery spirits of alcohol and fought each other in senseless rage outside the grogshops. Their's was a life of toil and hunger, deprivation and grief.

At this level of life one never saw the rulers, the wealthy in the carriages and covered wagons. At this level, even the meanest servants of Janbur Gsekk were regarded as lordlings in their own right.

But amid the violence and desolate loneliness, he had one fragile hope to cling to. The *Euchre* rode the canal and they were going all the way to Shesh, which was Gevuv's home. Shesh was the name of both a town and a region known for beautiful countryside. This information he had gleaned from Gevuv one evening. And he immediately put it together with another word that he had learned by accident from Janbur Gsekk. The Shashti word "Zob" was often used for a small country estate. Nobles went to their "zobbi" for periods of relaxation. They usually contained a game park for hunting and a stream for trout fishing. According to Riro, Shesh was surrounded by forest. It was a special place. Riro liked it.

Obviously there would be many zobbi around Shesh, but he knew that Simona of the Gsekk had often mentioned that she had loved to ride in Shesh Zob, a country place belonging to her family with an enclosed parkland where a woman could ride a horse in private, and thus escape the rules of purdah. Simona had often said that if she could she would withdraw to Shesh Zob and stay there forever.

Thru had decided to find Simona's Shesh Zob. Perhaps she would be there. Or possibly he could devise some way of sending her a message. She was the only person that he knew in this hostile land who might befriend him.

Not much of a plan, but it was better than sitting on the

Euchre until he was taken to be castrated. Then he would be exposed and soon placed in the hands of the priests.

Of course, running off was not without dangers. Riro had told him that Gevuv would notify the authorities, and the slave catchers would take him in time. Slave catchers roamed the cities constantly. Runaways were often blinded and sold down as animal-slaves. Thru had seen plenty of animal-slaves, too. They often worked in the locks, chained to the capstans used to raise the doors of the lock. Their faces were usually broken by a brand.

Although this was a terrible fate, if he was captured he would be sacrificed on the altar of the Great God.

So he had to run, and stay in hiding in the woods around Shesh until he could identify Simona's Zob. Not an easy task, for a strange slave could not just walk into a fine house and ask questions. He'd be lucky not to be whipped for his insolence.

He needed to plan carefully.

Suddenly an eruption of loud noise came from the wharf. Thru looked out and saw a circle of youths had gathered around a fight.

The smaller of the two in the fight was Riro. Riro was too good at dice. It often got him into trouble. The bigger boy he was fighting had lost his temper at losing so much.

Thru watched carefully. Riro fought with energy but no skill. The bigger boy had no skill either so the fight was a windmill of punches that mostly missed or banged off the backs of heads. They clutched at each other. Riro was thrown and the bigger boy was on him and it was quickly getting ugly for Riro.

Thru stepped ashore, turned an empty barrel on its side, and set it rolling across the wharf, right into the fight. The boys scattered, the boy punching Riro jumped back, and Riro rolled out of the way.

But he wasn't quick enough, and two other boys grabbed Riro and held him while the bigger boy came forward ready to punch his victim some more.

Thru materialized out of the dusk.

"Do you really need three to fight this little fellow?"

The bigger boy was a burly youth, he didn't back down.

"Why don't you take your nose out of this? This is between the short stuff and me."

"Well, it was, but now you've got two friends holding him."

"So? What do you care, you weirdo?"

"I guess I just like to see things fought fair. So let him go."

The bigger boy unshipped a clasp knife that opened with a smooth snap. "Go fuck your mother!" he snarled.

Surprised a little by such bravado in a boy of no more than twelve years, Thru took up the stance of kyo, hands extended, relaxed, knees slightly bent.

The boy slashed at him, but Thru did not remain in place to be cut. He shimmied away from the steel, and the boy turned in the air, thrown over a hip while the knife hand was held, bent, and the knife fell free.

Thru caught the blade and spun around with the knife in his hand.

The boy on the deck got back to his feet a little slowly. He'd landed hard, and he'd never seen such speed in a fighter. Worse, his knife was now in his opponent's hand. The two behind Riro moved away as if he was a source of contagion.

"That's better," said Thru. "There's no need for fighting. What was it about anyway?"

"The short stuff was cheating!"

"I was not," said Riro, enraged by this unjust charge. "I didn't bring the dice. They're not weighted. We tried them."

"Nobody wins all the time like you do. You must be cheating."

"You just don't watch me. I don't bet all the time like you. I wait until I feel the luck. I know what I am doing, you drink spirit, you don't know what you're doing."

"Hey, shut up, you little piece of . . . "

"Enough!" said Thru. "Does anyone else here back up your claim that Riro cheated?"

The other boys and youths shuffled their feet. Riro was well liked among the canal kin but the smaller boys were too afraid of big Hen and his friends to speak. Then one of them found his courage.

"Riro speaks the truth. He doesn't cheat."

The others nodded and mumbled agreement.

Hen snarled at them, but they took no notice.

"Seems like you were wrong, then. Unless you've got proof that the dice were weighted or that Riro was cheating, you've got no right to go after him."

Hen and his friends withdrew. Thru watched them leave. The party was over, the game finished. The boys drifted back to the canal boats, warehouses, and dock buildings where they worked.

"Thank you, Thru," said Riro as they walked back toward *Euchre*.

"You weren't really cheating were you?"

"No, I don't cheat. They were just sore losers."

Later, before turning in, Thru looked back across the dock, the warehouses, and the dusty, endless streets beyond. Everyone in this sad place was a loser as far as he could see, and what they had lost was the world itself.

Chapter 35

After Aeswiren returned from his disturbing visit with the Old One, Nuza was moved to new rooms, a suite on the far side of the palace. Her security guards were increased and monitored by operatives of the Hand. The rooms were warm and blessed with a grand view to the west. Each day they were lit spectacularly by the setting sun. They looked out across the Shalba and the parklands of the Outer Shalba, and she amused herself by counting the spires and turrets of the great houses there.

In the afternoon of the second day, the Emperor came to visit her. He greeted her in the language of the Land, his usage was often clumsy, but steadily improving. Her heart had been touched by the effort she could see that he was making.

"I hope you like rooms. They are safer for you now."

"They are nice rooms, but I don't quite understand. You are Emperor, correct?"

"Yes."

"But you cannot keep me safe."

"It is"—he groped for the words—"explain, hard." Indeed, he thought, no Emperor had been freed from the curse of the priesthood. "Powerful are priests."

"But you rule?"

"I rule, but I must my back watch."

Aeswiren did not fear rebellion among the people. His policies had encouraged trade among the cities and growth in skilled crafts and industries. Even the old nobility had given up their rebellious ways. Aeswiren had brought more of the stability that they'd enjoyed under Norgeeben. The terrible chaos of the previous dynasty still haunted many great families. No, it was not rebellion among his fractious people that he feared, Aeswiren feared murder. That was the way the Gold Tops would choose.

Nuza struggled to comprehend the idea that the priests might wish to kill the Emperor. In the Land, Kings ruled by custom and tradition and with reference to the wisdom of the Assenzi. There were no priests, though mots in search of holiness would remove to the fanes of the spirit. They would dedicate their lives to the quiet pursuit of meditation, and work to keep the fanes and temples in good repair. To imagine such mots and mors attempting to kill the King of Tamf was very difficult.

Moreover she understood how great Aeswiren's power was. She had lived within this vast structure for months. He was the man in whose name the whole huge machine of the empire churned onwards.

"Nice rooms," said Aeswiren, trying to turn the conversation to a more cheerful concern. "I hope you will be able to practice here."

Out the window the trees of the Shalba glittered bare and cold in the morning sun. On the right was the graceful vault of the tomb of Norgeeben. The gallery was a long space, ten feet wide, that ran along the side of the palace windows. The floor was smooth white marble.

"Thank you for your kindness."

Aeswiren stayed, drank tea with her, and did his best to converse. She peppered him with questions about his empire and its ways. She found slavery very difficult to understand. The many grades of slavery were confusing: house servants and noble eunuchs at the top of the chain, animal-slaves who scrubbed the public places at the bottom.

"But how can a person 'own' another person. It seems completely against the teachings of the spirit. We learn that each person is a unique being. Each person has a spirit that sanctifies him or her. Nobody can belong to another individual; although it can be argued that everyone should belong to everyone else, but only in the way of love and the spirit."

Alas, shrugged Aeswiren. If only such a thing could be

true. "Our God is different. There have always been slaves."

Nuza shook her head after a moment. "Then they cannot be Gods. No god would sanction such a thing."

The mor had a way of driving straight to a point that no subject of Aeswiren would have considered. Men had always owned other men, men had always owned women. Thus it was in Shasht and always had been. The Gods had nothing to do with it. The Gods of Shasht had once been a cryptic crew, fond of festivals and sacrificial lamb. But that was long ago, before the coming of He Who Eats, the Great God.

Later, as the afternoon light turned golden, Nuza practiced in the gallery and Aeswiren watched, entranced. As he watched, his mind tore at the knotty questions that obsessed him.

This creature with its unhuman face, had yet beguiled him with grace of movement and then with its serious, sweet intelligence. He felt as if he were in the presence of an angel. No woman had so touched him, at least not since his second wife, the mother of Nebbeggebben, that evil child turned monstrous man.

No, he had not been lucky in his choice of women.

But this was not a woman, this was a mor, a being of another race, though female enough in her breasts and buttocks to stir the strangest erotic thoughts. The alien angles to her face, the soft grey fur, they might have put him off once, but now only attracted him even more. He was not a man of sentiment, nor in recent years had he been a man of passion, but this creature stirred him.

She finished her exercises and turned back to him.

"When I was brought here, there were seven other mots on the ship. I have not seen them since I arrived. Could I see them?"

Aeswiren bit his lip for a moment. "No. I am afraid they were killed by the priests."

Nuza closed her eyes for a moment and took a deep breath.

"You could not prevent this?"

"No. Nor did I know what I know now."

"So, I am alone in this city?"

"Well, actually, no. There are some other mots, but they escaped the priests."

Her eyebrows shot up and down.

"Where are they?"

"I don't know. My agents are trying to find them now. We want to take them to a place of safety."

"You don't know?"

"Not yet, but soon, I think. We had some word the other day. They were alive, safe so far."

"I want to see them!"

"You will, just as soon as I find them."

Chapter 36

When they moored in Embun, the last stop before Shesh, Thru waited until the early hours of morning and then he rose and slipped over the side. Red Kemm was in the northern sky, the moon was rising in the east and looked enormous. He wore his boots, coat, and hat and carried a piece of cheese, some dried apples, and a chunk of bread left over from the evening meal. He also took the kitchen knife and a roll of twine.

Thru couldn't bring himself to say good-bye to little Riro, not because he feared Riro would betray him, but because he and the boy had become good friends and he knew that Riro would grieve over his going. Alas, there was no choice in the matter for Thru.

Alone in the dark muddy streets of the village, he felt acutely vulnerable. He kept to the shadows and back streets, avoiding the lanterns hung at the major intersections. All the time he kept a wary eye for the slave takers, who he knew roamed the night with their dogs and nets, hunting for slaves out of their homes after curfew.

After a couple of miles of dodging, he had a stroke of luck on a broad avenue, heading east. A large drive train of forty wagons and dozens of smaller carts headed for the zobbi hills. The entire road was dominated by drovers and drovers' boys whipping the animals to get the wagons rolling. Merchants and peddlers of every description filled the wagon train.

Thru simply joined the throng, and ran alongside the ox teams as if he were just another slave getting the oxen up to speed. No one appeared to notice him.

And so he walked right out of the village, even going

directly past one gang of slave takers, with fierce man-hounds straining on the leash. These grizzled men, who scanned the wagon train for runaways, missed him completely, since he blended in among the ragged boys who scurried up and down the flanks of the train.

The moon rose ahead of them, and the houses gave way at last to open fields. It was a cheerless view, however, for the landscape was flat and empty of cover with no trees. Several miles away the mountains were dim masses of darkness against the sky.

The caravan trundled onward, the drovers talking to each other in the softer cadences of hill country Shashti, with a distinctive burr in the accent. Thru took up a position behind a wagon, walking with his bundle on his back just like many other slaves up and down the train. The road ran straight toward the hills. The drovers talked about a big festival that would be held the following week. Most of the wagons took provisions up to the zobbi of Cashu. Wealthy families would arrive shortly for the early winter festival of "First Snow." And of course everyone was betting on whether there'd be snow by then. Usually there was, but not always, which was good for the Almanac industry. It was also beneficial to the bookmakers. Gambling was endemic in Shasht.

"We be taking the festival at Heemp's House, over in the Gelmen Valley," said one drover behind him.

"A good board they set by all accounts," said another voice.

"That they do," said the first.

"Haw!" said a ragged slave passing Thru. "Lucky for those who get to eat in Heemp's kitchens."

The slave gave Thru a nudge. Thru looked sidelong at the grinning face.

"Be lucky if we even see some scraps!" said the man in a cheerful tone. Thru shrugged, the slave hurried on.

"You'll see no scraps from me, you scurvy dog!" called the drover.

The slave had seen nothing overtly strange about Thru in the dark. But dawn would bring a much greater risk of discovery. He had to sneak away before the light grew strong.

An hour went by and another. Still, they passed nothing but endless flat fields, bare of anything but stubble. It would be difficult to run without being seen. He began to despair when at last the road curved to the right of the valley and soon climbed into the hills.

After another mile the road grew steep, then began to curve back on itself as it climbed. Above them loomed dark crags.

Suddenly, picked out in a moonbeam, Thru saw a single tree, standing out of a crag. He took a breath, feeling just a little better for it.

A little later there were more trees mostly scattered on the ridgelines. The land by the road was given over to grass and sheep. Shepherd dogs barked back and forth. There was no likelihood of escape in such a bare setting. Thru began to grow concerned again.

Now the road turned about the base of a great crag. On top of the crag Thru saw a tower silhouetted against the light of the moon. The solitary structure was stark and forbidding. Thru wondered if it was a beacon for times of danger, or a military outpost against bandits that Riro had spoken of, who were said to terrorize the hills. Behind the crag a narrow bridge of rock and trees connected to the hills.

The road wound down into a narrow valley, where trees at last turned into a forest. But dawn could not be long in coming.

The road ran beside an unchanneled stream, its bed filled with great rocks. On the other side, the pines stood twenty steps from the road. Thru drifted over to the edge of the paved road. Ahead were stacked boulders and beside them a group of young trees. Fighting the urge to turn around and look to see if anyone was watching him, he stepped off the road and knelt down behind the trees as if to tie a boot lace. The wagons rumbled by on his left; no voice called to him; no one seemed to have noticed.

A cart pulled by a pair of donkeys rumbled by while two sleepy voices continued to argue about whether there'd be snow for the festival or not. Thru heard a reference to the *Old Style Almanac,* which predicted little snow for the coming winter. The crop of mulberries had failed, which meant no snowfall until well past the beginning of the month of Ribrack.

Thru took a breath and then crawled farther into the trees. Every moment he expected the shout from behind him, but it never came, and after a few seconds he was hidden in the pines. He halted, barely daring to breathe. Peering back through the branches, he watched the wagons roll along. No one had called an alarm.

Now he turned and ran, moving as quickly as he dared through the little forest of pines and birch. The trees thickened after a while and progress slowed. He searched for a game trail, but the ones he found ran parallel to the road and he wanted to climb the ridge. The going became difficult, pushing through tangles of branches and dead trees.

Then he came upon a place where bare rock rose in a staggered cliff, much collapsed with piles of huge boulders resting on one another like a child's discarded blocks.

Thru hid himself in the recesses, and listened for any sound of pursuit. Reassured after a full minute, he began his climb.

After an hour he reached a ledge, and dawn broke, offering him a view of the valley below. He could see the wagon train quite clearly, a line of brown and white, some miles to the north.

He sat on the ledge and ate some of the bread and cheese, plus a dried apple. He climbed farther, reached the top of the ridge, and examined the world below once more.

He was free. He sucked in a breath of clean air. He had taken another step toward the uncertain future. He resolved to die rather than allow himself to be taken captive again.

Chapter 37

A week of living in the wintry hills had brought Thru to a fine understanding of hunger and cold. It was reminiscent of his days at Highnoth, only colder. But he had employed all the woodcraft he'd ever learned from his father, and with the stolen knife and the twine he'd staved off starvation with a few lean rabbits taken in his snares.

In the interim he scavenged for acorns and chestnuts, and even tried chewing bark and twigs. The country was bare. For a while he wandered east as far as the hills that looked down upon a near circular lake. Houses and fields were visible around the water and along the river valley that ran off to the south. He went back to the west and roamed across another range of hills until he could see a reek of smoke ahead. He crossed a road to get closer. From the next ridge he saw a large village in the valley below. He retreated back into the deeper hills.

Fortunately, he'd found a tight little cave, in a stratum of grey rock beneath a hill with a curious sharp tip, like a hook. He lined the narrow space with brush and dry leaves and wove it into a nest in which his body heat kept him from freezing to death at night.

The land was bare, though. He wandered the hills in search of food, but animals were scarce. Only a distant pack of wolves to the north howled. Once he saw a deer and it bounded away the moment it caught his scent. Not that it mattered, he had no means of killing a deer, except through a snare. At home any mot with a bow could find meat for his family's table on any day, within an hour or two in the woods. Here, in bony, picked-over Shasht, there was nothing.

The lake in the east drew him back. In the evening he saw lights in the great houses. Those houses had to be the zobbi. Somewhere in these hills lay the zob of Simona's family.

Inevitably hunger drove him back to the southern edge of the wilderness, where he gazed longingly on the flocks of well-guarded sheep on the hillsides. Large dogs guarded these sheep, and the smoke of the shepherds' fires a little farther off assured him of a hot pursuit if he dared to take a lamb.

He moved on, working his way cautiously across the bare hills toward the settlements. Nothing but scrub pine and saplings grew here, and these only in isolated places. Every other tree had been harvested for firewood, long before.

At an outlying farm he noticed poultry pecking in the yard. The smell of roasting meat and bread came from the ramshackle farmhouse. He closed in as carefully as he dared. A dog slept on the back porch, but Thru was safely downwind of the dog. The cooking smells were maddening. He got as close as he dared, without being seen by either the chickens or anyone in the house. Now he waited, hidden behind an old broken cart, watching the chickens and the house.

After a while the door of the house opened and two men came out, picked up tools from a chest on the porch, and strode out of the yard and down the lane toward the fields. The dog merely rolled over and went back to sleep. A little later a woman wearing a heavy cloak of homespun came out and threw crumbs to the chickens, who descended on them with much clucking and flapping of wings.

Thru was struck by the parallel with giving out to the chooks in his home village. There was the same wild excitement in the birds.

The woman went back inside, and the dog, taking advantage of the opportunity, slipped in behind her, determined to scrounge some scraps.

By that point Thru would have been happy to eat the bones set aside for the dog, or even the crumbs the chickens were eating, but instead he went for a chicken, an older bird, a rooster, with his comb dulled by the years.

The chicken was so involved in the pecking of crumbs

that he failed to notice Thru's swift, but silent rush across the yard. Then Thru caught the bird around the neck and swung it up in a smooth motion while turning and racing back for cover. The woman returned, scolding the dog as she came.

The old rooster flapped furiously, shedding a feather or two, but could not get a squawk past the hand that gripped its throat.

Behind the shed Thru killed the bird with a single stab from the kitchen knife. He listened carefully. The door banged again. He dared to sneak a peek backward. The dog was busy with a bone, the chickens continued to peck over the crumbs; only a single feather fluttering across the yard betrayed the disappearance of the old rooster.

Thru went back into the hills and ate the stringy old bird that night.

Every two or three days after that he made his way down into the settlements to steal food, a few handfuls of grain here, a chicken there. His depredations were noticed in time, and the farm folk became more watchful. The dogs were deliberately starved to sharpen their wits and children were driven out to scour the lanes in case a runaway slave was on the loose.

Thru noticed the new state of awareness when he came down for his sixth raid on the farms. He saw a pack of children searching the hedgerows and heard dogs barking back and forth between the farms.

He kept his distance from the farm buildings therefore and gave up any thoughts of taking another chicken. Instead he broke into a locked turnip shed set on a muddy lane far back from any farmhouse.

He took a few turnips, pushed them into his coat, and slipped out again, but was seen by a yellow dog as he climbed over the back fence. The dog began a frenzied yipping and howling that soon set other dogs barking.

Thru hastened up a lane between low-set stone walls. The village behind him had come to life. Men were hallooing to one another amid a general uproar from the dogs. All around him were open fields, filled with stubble and no cover except for the stone walls. Off to his right, after a mile the fields gave out on sandy soil, where a few pines and scrub birch struggled to make a living.

He ran along crouched down behind the stone wall and hoped he could remain unobserved.

At one point he had to pass quite close to a flock of goats, working over the stubble in the field. The goats sensed his passing and moved over to investigate. Their movements aroused interest in other eyes, and soon after he heard a fierce shout behind him and knew he'd been spotted.

Thru legged it for the sandy barrens ahead. The sound behind him rose up in volume, topped by a crescendo of barks and yips from the dogs of the village now in hot pursuit up the lane.

He had a good lead, perhaps half a mile, and that was just enough to allow him to reach the end of the lane, run up a rubble-strewn slope, and vanish into the bracken.

He ran on, not daring to waste a moment looking back. The trees grew widely spaced, the brush was broken up by many small trails. He ran at a steady lope now, his breath coming relatively easily. Thru was not the speediest of runners, but he had endurance.

The slope tended upward, and further off he saw a ridgeline and a mighty crag. The crag was familiar. He remembered that it stood near the road up from Shesh and was crowned by a grim tower. He kept on running hard, and the sound of the dogs behind him grew fainter. Now they searched for his scent in the trees, but being simple village dogs first they ran off one way, then another, while cursing men tried to organize them and get the dogs with the best noses on the track.

He climbed a bank of scree, then some sand dunes and broke out onto an upland meadow. Across this he ran at full tilt, his breathing now labored. The crag loomed above the meadow.

Far behind him he heard a new, chilling sound, the call of the man hounds. The slave takers had joined the hunt. The pursuit was coming on quickly. Looking back he could see small dots, hurrying onto the meadow.

He tore through trees and brush, heading downslope for

a hundred feet until he emerged at the edge of a thirty-foot drop, falling precipitously to a mountain stream in a canyon. He ran along the edge, downstream, hoping to find a place he could get down the side and up the other, but nothing presented itself. Then he spotted a pine that had toppled and bridged the canyon. Quickly he walked out onto the pine.

A young tree when it toppled, it was no thicker than Thru's leg. It bent beneath his weight, and he wobbled for a moment in the middle. Thirty feet below the rocks and boulders of the canyon were waiting if he slipped. Another step, the whole tree sagged beneath him and he rushed his next, got a foot on the tree, and wobbled there for a long moment while he waved his arms around and somehow kept his balance.

His next step caught a broken stub of a branch and set him lurching, once, twice, and on the third the tree was gone, falling into the canyon and he was launched, but only weakly, toward the far side. He landed hard, with his chest and shoulders alone above the cliff top. It knocked the wind out of him and for a moment he started sliding backward. At the last moment his outflung arm caught a handhold, and he broke his descent. He hung there suspended for a few seconds with his legs milling in the air until his foot found a crack below and gave him something to lever up from.

Now he pressed his free hand down, heaved himself up, and in a few moments rolled onto his back on top of the cliff.

Barely on his feet, he heard the hounds break free of the trees just across the canyon. They halted at the edge of the canyon and bayed in frustration.

He staggered on into the trees. The hounds bayed endlessly, but their barks faded as the distance grew.

He climbed upward along the spine of land between two stream gorges. The ground was increasingly rocky, and the tree cover had thinned out. By this point he was breathing hard and needed a rest. When he emerged onto a flat rock ledge with a good view of the ground behind and below, he paused to look back.

Beneath him lay a view all the way back to the villages. The scrub of sand barrens fell away to the brown fields of stubble and houses, wreathed in smoke. Farther away the land was hidden in a haze of smoke from other villages.

And then the hounds broke into view about a half mile behind, climbing up a switchback trail between clay-colored boulders. Even farther back he caught sight of men, in red hats carrying spears with bright banners.

He whirled and ran on up the narrow deer trail. After a hundred paces it turned back on itself as it wound up the steep slope. Dense brush covered the draws on either side, but Thru knew that the hounds would smell him if he hid there.

He kept on the trail, toiling back and forth as it mounted up the ridgeline through patches of rock and boulder, climbing steadily. At length he crested the ridge and ran on down the farther side.

But now he heard dogs below on his right. The pursuers had taken a shortcut and were much closer than he'd thought. He tried to redouble his speed, but he was too worn out, and could only maintain his steady pace. At least downhill it was less taxing than before.

He worked through an area of berry bushes, then passed through some dwarf pines clinging to bare rock. Here there was no grass, only patches of leprous-colored moss and lichen. Thru had no time to contemplate the strange beauty of the lichens as he scrambled along the rock ledges and down the gorse-lined draws.

And then there came a sudden scrabbling of paws behind him, and he turned to find three village dogs closing in. By chance they'd outrun the rest. They saw him, dropped down into the draw, and came for him.

Thru turned to fight, crouching, pulling out the kitchen knife in a smooth, fluid move.

The dogs rushed in. One tried to bite his ankle; he pivoted away and kicked it in the ribs as it passed.

The others dove in. He kicked a second, but felt the third rip into his right ankle. He shook it off, but the first dog was back and jumped at his crotch. He got his knee up and it bounced off, but the small yellow one had hold of his other ankle and he stumbled. At the same moment the biggest dog leaped at him. They collided heavily, and Thru landed atop the dog. He finished it with the knife in a moment.

The other two retreated, barking furiously. Thru ran. Both ankles were bruised and bleeding. Shortly, more dogs followed, and now he could hear the hounds getting closer. Once the hounds caught up he'd be done for, because they'd hold him until the men came.

He turned and ran on. They followed.

Up the steepest slope he went, and the dogs closed in again and charged him in a tiny hollow where a pine tree had grown up with three separate trunks. Thru was below them, and thus they launched themselves straight at his throat and shoulders.

He caught the first with a fist, then the knife and whirled it away to bounce off the tree and fall under their feet.

The second tore the side of his neck and chewed on his shoulder before he hit it hard enough in the belly to loosen its grip. The third came straight on into his chest, and he fell backward, toppling as he went. His head struck the tree trunk and momentarily dazed him. The animal snaked its head toward his throat. He held a hand up, there was a burst of pain as the dog bit his hand, then shoved its snout under his arm, going for the throat again.

He struggled and clubbed it clumsily with the good hand. Again, it bit him but he hammered it so hard with his right hand that it went down and he stabbed it with the knife.

The remaining dog scrambled out of the hole behind the big pine tree, yowling. Thru got to his feet and drove himself up the little slope to get away. His hand hurt, but he could not stop. With only this single yellow village dog left, he had to push on.

Other dogs were calling, and getting much closer, but there was still just the one that was close. It called and followed him, but kept its distance.

Thru's only chance to evade the rest of the dogs closing in was to kill this one. He picked up a rock the size of a small white ball and slowed his step, luring the dog closer. It was incautious and kept coming, only turning away when it was just out of reach. He threw the rock with all his might and was rewarded with a strike that clipped the dog on the side of its head and flung it headlong.

He continued to run, but it was getting hard to keep moving in his semi-starved condition.

The dogs behind had found the bodies around the pine tree. Their calls took on a slightly different tone for a moment. But they didn't linger for long.

Then he saw salvation. Ahead lay a sharply defined spur of rock with a vertical cliff face about twelve feet high. Beyond the spur lay an area elevated above similar cliffs, and beyond that the upper part of the crag loomed.

He reached the bottom of the cliff, cut from resistant limestone. Lots of chinks made good handholds. But his hand hurt badly, and he had to grit his teeth and bite his tongue not to cry out as he climbed the cliff.

By dint of giving it his last, he reached the top before the dogs reached the bottom. They barked below in fury while he lay there sobbing for breath.

The hounds were coming, and with them would be men. He rolled over, got to his feet, and lurched on through scrub and dwarf pines growing from the rocky surface.

Suddenly he came upon a low stone wall that cut across the surface. A wooden gate lay to one side.

Thru paused for a moment to take in his surroundings. Beyond the gate the track he'd been following joined a road. The road curved around the top of the crag out of sight.

He approached the gate with caution. The wall was well made, squared and mortared. The arch of the gate bore an inscription in Shasht characters that he could not read. Beyond lay the road, laid in brick and well maintained.

The gate was locked, but he climbed over and passed inside. Trees lined the road. He even saw squirrels. The road made progress a little easier, and he climbed around the crag once more and then came out onto a paved space beneath the massive stump of the tower.

The great door of the tower suddenly swung open. Thru halted in his tracks. A man emerged. He was a tall man, thin, gaunt-faced, wearing a wide-brimmed white hat. He carried a cudgel in one hand, and Thru made ready to defend himself . . .

But the man only smiled at him and indicated the open door.

"Go on in, friend. I can see you are a victim of persecution, as I am myself. You are welcome at the Tower of Quarantine."

Then the man trotted away. "I have to be sure the gate is locked. There are dogs out in the forest. I won't have them coming in here."

Thru spent a few moments staring after the fellow, digesting these extraordinary words. The man had been friendly. He spoke accent-free Shasht, and he had gone down to the gate to keep the hounds out.

Thru knew he had little choice except to trust the man. He went up the steps and into the tower.

Inside, in the dim light he found a series of doors and rooms, and at one end the stone steps that rose to the second floor. He climbed. The second floor was considerably more refined, with painted walls and rugs on every floor. A fire burned in the grate in one room, and Thru was drawn to the warmth it gave off. He had been cold for many days.

He must have dozed while standing there, for the next thing he knew the door closed and the tall man entered the room. He removed his hat and cloak, revealing a heavy tunic and loose wool trousers. On his feet were clogs.

"Well, are you a little warmer now?" The man smiled, rubbed his hands and warmed them by the fire. Thru could only manage a nod.

"Welcome to the Tower of Quarantine, friend," said the man. "You have the look of a worn-out fugitive about you. I assume you were being hunted?"

Thru nodded.

"Well, they won't come in here. They're all afraid of this place."

Thru found his voice. "What is this place?"

"A prison cell!" The man threw his hands out around him dramatically. "No, listen to me, I do not jest. For all the luxury of the place, it is a prison and I am its only prisoner. I am kept here in case someday my talents are needed."

"Who keeps you here, the priests?"

The man chuckled. "You must be from a far-off country. The priests would never keep a prisoner like myself for very long. The altar of the temple calls out for too many hearts for that."

The man's forehead suddenly wrinkled as he stared at Thru.

"I say, you are an odd-looking fellow. Very hairy, aren't you? You poor fellow, what was it, an accident of birth?"

Thru didn't know how to respond.

"Well," he began, but the man spoke again quickly.

"Doesn't matter to me, friend. I don't care if your mother or your father was a donkey, you can speak decent Shashti and that's enough for this old patriot." Thru stared at the man, completely uncertain as to how to reply. Unsure if he was understanding what he was hearing. Still, the man didn't seem to need much of a response. He was glad to do all the talking.

"So you are welcome to my prison cell. There's plenty of room here."

"Who keeps you here? If you don't mind me asking."

"Mind? No I don't mind. It was my good friend Aeswiren who put me here. He keeps me safe here, see. In case they ever need me again."

"Aeswiren the Emperor?"

"That's right, friend, and he was my good friend long before he became the Emperor. Known him all my life."

The man straightened up having noticed that Thru was holding his wounded hand.

"That's my misfortune. But hold on, you're hurt. Why didn't you say something? What happened? Did those wretched dogs . . . ?"

Thru nodded and the man turned about at once.

"I've got to get some water and bandages. We need to clean the wound, dog bite can turn nasty if left untreated."

In a few minutes the man reappeared from another room carrying a kettle, which he set on the rack and swung into the fire. He produced a bottle of green lotion.

"This stuff was recommended to me by a field surgeon once. He said he'd learned about it from a hospital in the city. You put this on wounds, and it stops the rot from beginning."

Thru allowed the man to examine his hand, then to clean it with hot water before applying the green liquid, which had a strong smell and stung when it touched the open cuts.

"Do you feel it stinging?" said the man.

"Yes, why does it do that?"

"That shows that it's working. I don't know why it works, but it does."

The man was friendly, welcoming. Thru's understanding of the alien world of Shasht had become considerably more complex during the last few weeks. He knew that the men were not of a single opinion. But a few were willing to risk their own lives to help fugitives such as himself. He gave thanks to the Spirit for guiding his feet to this tower.

"Tell me, my fur-covered friend, what are you called? Do you have a name?"

Thru looked up. "Yes, I am Thru Gillo."

"Thru Gillo, eh? An unusual name for these parts. You're not from around here, though, are you?"

"No, sir. I am from a land that is far away. Across the ocean."

"By the winds of Lady Canilass, that is extraordinary news. And how did you come to reach my lonely crag?"

"I was taken from my home by the army of the Emperor. They sent me to this land with others of my people. We escaped, I became separated from the others. I left the city and traveled on the canal. I ran away from the boat before we reached Shesh."

"Oh-ho, so you're a runaway on top of everything else! That is a saga worthy of the old heroes. I am honored to make your acquaintance my fur-covered friend. Well, what's to do, eh? The priests must be after you, eh?"

"Yes." There seemed to be no point in lying about that.

"Well, they won't get any help from me. I detest them and their horrible God. They preach the false prophecy, the evil that came in with Kadawak, may his name be cursed forever."

"I know nothing of these things. But I thank you. Will you tell me your name?"

"Ah, no, that I cannot do. Ask anything else of me, but not that. I have no name. By order of the Emperor himself, I can only be called the Eccentric."

"The Eccentric?"

"Yes, I am the Eccentric in the Tower of Quarantine."

Chapter 38

The tower was huge, and drafty, but as far as Thru was concerned it was warm and comfortable. He slept for the rest of that day and the night and then woke to eat a huge breakfast. As he was to learn from the man, who called himself "the Eccentric," the food was plentiful, but plain. It consisted of army biscuit, dried beans, and sea vegetable. This was flavored with hot pepper sauce and sour salt. To Thru, half-starved, it was simply wonderful and he ate it three times a day with no complaint.

The bad hand healed quickly. The stinging green juice had had a good effect. No rot set in. The Eccentric examined it every morning and treated it with more of the stinging fluid. The man asked many questions at these times, and they would talk for an hour or more. The rest of the day Thru was left alone, for the Eccentric disappeared into a room several floors above, where he remained at his desk, writing an endless screed of which he would say only that "it provides some of the answers for the troubles of the world."

On the afternoon of the first day, Thru explored the tower from top to bottom. Indeed, the Eccentric had encouraged him to do so. "Oh, yes, that'll get your blood going again. Eight floors to the top, my friend, eight floors. And two floors down below the ground, too. And who knows what might be living in the bottom cellar; no one's been down there in years, heh heh." The man's laugh was desolate. Still, Thru was eager to explore.

For more than an hour Thru wandered through rooms of former grandeur on the lower floors. Dust and cobwebs hung from the tapestries in the empty salons. Grand tables had broken legs in the dust among ruined chairs. The windows had been boarded up and shuttered, but a few beams of light came through anyway to illuminate the faded glories. A few walls were covered in great murals, executed with a fine hand, though the colors were muted by age.

He discovered that the place was a warren. There were narrow passageways as well as the grand halls, small hidden rooms as well as the salons. Besides the main staircase, there were at least two smaller ones, and Thru even discovered a vertical shaft running between the three lower floors, where the largest rooms were situated. Inside the shaft were hooks and pulleys so Thru deduced that some kind of weight had been lowered up and down. Above the three grand floors there were floors of smaller rooms, some of which might have been offices once. Some had desks and chairs, while some had nothing. Some contained rotted bedding and forgotten supplies, such as large clay pots and rolls of old cloth.

At the top was a single round room with eight narrow windows. The roof had been leaking in one corner for quite some time. From the narrow windows it was possible to see in all directions for many miles. Hills, ridges, and more hills mainly, though to the west beyond the hills there was a reek of smokes.

"Shesh town," said the Eccentric when asked about this. "Due west of here about six miles."

To the northeast, just over the nearest hills, the circular lake was visible. Indeed, it formed a shimmering disk in the late afternoon sun.

"Lake of the Woods. It borders one of the Gsekk Zobbi up there."

When he heard those words, Thru felt his eyebrows shoot up on their own accord. He tried not to let his excitement enter his voice. Simona was of that family.

"What are the Gsekk Zobbi?"

The Eccentric gave him another questioning look.

"You really aren't from around these parts, that's for sure. These are the zobbi hills of Shesh. Around here there are lots of country zobbi, you understand? Zobbi are country houses for the better sort of people. They come up here in the hot summer months. Zobbi, yes?"

"Yes, I've heard that word."

"Yes, well some of the zobbi here are famous. There are zobbi big enough to be counties of their own, but most are much smaller than that. They contain a forest and some riding trails, some fields, maybe a couple of farms. The Gsekk are a big family with many branches, they have been spending their summers in Shesh since the time of Shalmaagen the First. They have many zobbi over there."

"The Shesh Zob lies up there by that lake?"

"On the northern side there is a Gsekk Zob, a big one. It runs all the way up into the purple hill country. There are zobbi up that way for the Fauniku, the Saup and the Honn clans. All the best noble families have zobbi around Shesh, but the best of all are up here in the hills."

"Excuse me for asking, but how do you know all this, if you are a prisoner here on this hill?"

"Oh, I knew the great zobbi before I was made a prisoner. I was often invited up to one of the Saup Zobbi. It belonged to Palian Saup, may the Gods take care of his soul, who was such a benefactor to me once upon a time. Beautiful countryside up here, wouldn't you say?"

"Yes, I would."

"And now, even though I'm confined here, I'm not completely ignored by people. There are some who write to tell me what's going on in the city and even in the zobbi in the summer."

Thru filed all this information carefully away for further consideration. He didn't know how long he'd be able to stay in the tower. If he had to move on, at least he now knew where the Shesh Zob of Simona Gsekk must lie. He'd seen the houses around that lake, just off to the west of the hills. He could find it again, he had no doubt of that.

Thru turned to another subject, something that had troubled him since he'd discovered it during his explorations of the tower.

"In the first cellar you have a lot of roofing materials cached away."

"Yes."

"But the roof of the tower is leaking."

"Yes. A beam has rotted out, too."

"I do not understand." Thru was from a village where no one left the roof leaking for very long.

"They sent the thatch and the new beam, but they never sent anyone to do the work. It's been sitting down there for more than a month. And the winter rains and snow are coming soon."

"Well, would you object if I did the work?"

The Eccentric stared at him for a long moment. "My fur-covered friend, would I object? By the sweet dust of Cani-lass, I would not. I would welcome it. It is difficult, even dangerous work."

"I have often worked with my father to repair roofs in our village."

"Ah, well, from all you've said I understand that you come from a place much industriousness. What you told me about the manufacture of thread and yarn in your home made me yearn for the return of our old crafts. The people of Shasht have no skills anymore. Quality craftsmanship has disappeared, everything is purely brummagem."

"I am sorry to hear that. It must be difficult to be useless," said Thru innocently.

The Eccentric eyed him a moment.

"Aye, but sadder still are the awful conditions in which they live. So many are poor and hungry."

Thru nodded. "I have seen much poverty in your land. I came here on the canal, from the city. I see houses everywhere. There is nothing left to the wild, barely a tree grows."

" 'Tis true, unfortunately."

"We believe that you must leave the land as wild as possible. That way it will always support you. When you grow so large upon the world like this, you drain its soul."

"Ah, you are a naturist of some kind! You think the world has a soul? That it is conscious? That is very different from the beliefs in Shasht. We believe souls must be earned in this life. Only men are conscious, therefore only men can earn a soul."

Thru had heard this concept before, from Simona. To

him it was another aspect of the harshness of life in Shasht behind the magnificent marble facades. Life, soul, freedom, these were all things denied in varying degrees to the Shashti. The root cause was always the same, over-population.

"We think everything in the world has a degree of soul to it. It is more realized, more discernible, perhaps, in the higher animals than in the tree, but it is no greater for that."

"Hah! You think a tree is important?"

"Yes!" Thru's eyebrows jumped and his eyes flashed. "Without the trees the land dies. The water fails, the soil withers. Without good land your people go hungry."

"Ah, but you speak only of the poor." The man grunted bitterly. "They are but shadows. Rather than have a multitude of men live small lives, we give huge lives to a few men and then watch them from afar."

"And the rest live brutal, boring lives." Thru recalled the dreary canal cities of the plain.

"They do, but they also attend the ceremonies so they can glimpse some of the glory."

"I have seen them. They seem filled with hate. To escape their misery they drink the burning water. They gamble and fight."

"Ah, yes, the human tragedy. Much of our literature, our opera, and our art concerns itself with the tragic aspects of the lives of men."

Thru blinked, not sure he had heard this right. "But surely the problem is that there are just too many people."

"You have an unerring eye for the tragic truth, my fur-covered friend. Once, it is true, all men lived in something like equality. There was enough to go around. But the superior blood soon showed itself. Some men became the rulers, others the ruled. Over time we have separated to a degree. Only the rulers will ever be remembered. We concentrate on them and ignore the rest."

"But why must there be so many people?"

"Another good question. Our rulers say we must supply the Gods with worship. And they are hungry, our Gods, especially He Who Eats. The people must be numerous to sustain him."

"But when they are so numerous, they must also go hungry."

"Well, such is the fate of the world."

"It does not have to be that way. In my homeland starvation was unknown before the men brought war. Even in the coldest winters, after the worst of harvests, we made our way, because we could work harder in the sea pond despite the cold and we could hunt in the forests. Our numbers never overwhelmed our land."

"Ha!" the man laughed and slapped his thigh. "You breed slowly, then. That is not the case with hot-blooded Man. The rabbit is our God of breeding. Every man wants children to remember him. But children die so often that every woman must bear six, seven, or eight to keep two or three."

"That means your numbers will grow without restraint."

"Well, yes, but when they can't feed 'em the poor sell the children. That keeps the slave takers happy."

"Slavery," murmured Thru, "we do not have slaves in my homeland."

"By Kipchaki's dusty feet! What an incredible thing . . . "

"No one, not even a chook can be owned by another. They have the right of contracts, the right of law to exist as free beings."

"Who would've imagined? Never in my wildest dreams did I think I would live to hear that. No slaves. Then, how does anything get done?"

"We have no need for slaves."

"Then, you must live like savages, half naked in the wilderness."

"Not so. We have many of the same arts. My father carves wood. I am a weaver."

"Gracious. That means you must work with your own hands! No one will do that. That is for slaves. I'm afraid your ways would not work well in Shasht."

Thru felt his eyebrows loft at the thought of men who did nothing for themselves, generation after generation. They had to become soft, dependent, weak.

"No, no, no, my dear fur-covered friend. You see, the free man is the superior being. He stands above all women, and above all slave men. The man who falleth into slavery belongs in that position and must be treated as no longer human. That is our way, it made us strong."

"But your land is worn-out. Your numbers have drained it of life."

"True, but that is our way. Now will come our downfall. Already we have turns of starvation. The poor suffer terribly in the droughts and floods. The catastrophe comes, but not yet. So it is written, so it will be."

The man seemed to accept this disastrous future. He shrugged after a moment and spoke again.

"And your home is so different then?"

"Your land is but a desert in comparison."

"Well! Your land sounds like it comes from the Appian Age, when Shasht was young and the Old Gods ruled. Ah, but I wish I could go hunting in this land of yours. It must teem with game."

"Our land is rich in life. We hunt for rabbit and wood turkey within a few miles of the village. We take deer in the winter within a day's walk."

"By the Gods, what our hunters would do on such lands! I'd like to see this land of yours. There weren't many deer when I was young. Probably aren't any now."

Thru wore a sad smile. "There's no game in these hills. That's why I had to raid the farms."

"Yes, far too many hunters here, heh heh. So you had to raid the farms, understandable, of course, but caused a problem didn't it? Actually, that reminds me, I have something to tell you that may be important. I received a message today from the village. They claim that a fugitive slave savaged their dogs. They claim the said fugitive then took shelter in this tower. They have asked for my report."

The Eccentric paused, grimaced.

"Of course, I told them I knew nothing of the matter. They may send someone to investigate, but on the other hand they may not. It's a long hike up here from the village, and the fat, perfumed officials of the county aren't known for their eagerness to hike up hills. I never see them."

Thru nodded. He would have expected no less, and it was good to hear that the officials were lazy. But clearly, he would have to be ready to leave in a hurry. The safety of the great tower was an illusion. Certain preparations would be necessary.

"I see. Thank you for warning me, and again, many thanks for your aid. I owe you my life."

"My friend, I sense that you would have done the same thing for me, were I to show myself at your door, exhausted with hunters on my trail."

"If I ever return to my own land, I will tell everyone about the kind Eccentric who helped me survive."

"That's very good of you, very good."

"And I wonder if I could have the use of a razor?"

The man stared at him for a moment before understanding came into his eyes.

"Oh, why, yes, of course, of course. And if they do actually show up you'll just slip away, will you?"

"Well, it would be best if they did not find me here."

"Yes, probably right about that. Well, they probably won't bother. But if they do, let me say that it's been a pleasure to have you stay here. Truth to tell, I see nobody at all to talk to, and you've been a patient listener." The man grinned, Thru was impelled to reach out, and they clasped hands warmly.

The next day Thru opened up the roof, removed the rotten patches of thatch, and cut out the beam that had rotted underneath. A good selection of tools were kept in the cellar. Axes, adzes of various sizes, good saws and hammers, drills. There were also supplies of wooden pegs and rope, pitch and gum. Metal, of course, was too scarce in the world of Arna to be used for nails.

Before nightfall, he had rigged up a frame to support a cover of canvas for the night. The Eccentric climbed the tower the next morning to inspect the work. He found Thru replacing the beam.

"You have great skill in this kind of work."

"Thank you, but I am not so skilled. I learned it all from my father, who is indeed skilled, and that helps a lot."

"Well, you've done more in a day than I would have expected in three from the workmen they usually send up here."

"Thank you, but aren't those workers slaves?"

"Yes, of course. Free men don't work in this way, not here."

"So they are not working for their own gain in any way?"

"Well, if they don't work they'll be whipped!"

"So they have to work, but I expect they work very slowly."

"Yes, that is the usual complaint." And suddenly the man gave a vigorous nod as if this simple realization had never crossed his mind before.

"Yes," he said. "You are right. They don't work hard because they are slaves."

Perhaps it hadn't, thought Thru, so blind was Shasht to such aspects of its own culture.

In the afternoon Thru put up fresh roofing boards and replaced the canvas cover. Working in that high, lonely spot, with the bare world spread out below him, Thru felt a strange sense of exaltation. He was alone, deep in an alien world, and he was not exactly free from danger. For the moment he felt alive and imbued with purpose. He would survive. He would go home. He would not die in this alien land. Somehow he would get to the sea and steal a boat.

That evening they dined on the usual fare, the hard biscuit, the looga beans, and the hot red paste. As always the Eccentric grumbled to himself as he ate. Thru ignored the Eccentric and thought about the thatching of the roof. He had worked with reed stems before, though his father preferred to thatch with bush stalk. He would need to carefully recall the techniques for stemming and bunching. A different pattern was required than one would use for bush stalk.

Suddenly the Eccentric broke into these thoughts with a question.

"I have been thinking about what you told me about

your religion, my fur-covered friend. You said you have no Gods, no Goddesses either."

"We do not have such things. We speak to the Spirit only."

"But how can you speak to something that is only a spirit. If it has no personality."

" 'Personality' is only something you invent. The Spirit is everywhere, in everything. It is subtle, but huge. It rules the universe, but we cannot normally sense its presence."

"Hmmmm. The 'Spirit' sounds very vague to my ears. There's nothing to get hold of, no image, no figure of the God."

"It is not necessary to give an image to the spirit."

"Well, I might agree with you. I was never the most religious of men. But our religious thinkers say that men are special, that we are only temporarily part of the world. Free men, that is, not slaves or women. Free men when they die are supposed to go to heaven and sit with the Great God."

Thru shook his head in dismay.

"I do not understand such things. You were born into this world, and you have lived all your life within it. How can you be beyond it?"

"Well, because I am Man and I am blessed by the Gods. The Gods created Man in their image. The Gods look after men and are worshiped in return."

Thru did not tell the man that the mots of the Land had been created by the High Men.

"I have seen your temple in the city. I know what they do there."

After a moment or two of silence, the man shifted, embarrassed, perhaps.

"Ah, yes, well, then you know how it is with us. The cult of He Who Eats fulfills something in the people's heart. The folk love the rituals of the temple. All the seats are always filled."

"You admit then that men enjoy the spectacle of such slaughter?"

"Yes. It is true, there are many who do. But that is not all there is to us. The human spirit is capable of much more. We have advanced all the arts to the highest levels. Can your people match our sculptors? Our painters? Our embroiderers? You should see the great Chorales, when thousands of singers gather to sing the hymns of the Great God. And then there are the theaters! Such comedy, such tragedy, all enacted on the stage."

Thru nodded as he heard this passionate defense of Shashti society.

"We have artists, too. We are not so different in that regard."

"Well, well, well." The Eccentric took another look at Thru. "Well, of course, you are men of a sort, different from us, but still men."

Thru felt his eyes bulge, but he controlled his anger.

"We are not men," he said firmly. "We live within the world, we tend to it and water it, men destroy it."

"Yes, yes, but you produce art. You can speak good Shashti, all of these things indicate that you really are men."

"No, we are not men."

And on this point, Thru would not be swayed.

The next day Thru completed the thatching and was collecting the tools when he heard a noise down below. He looked out the window and saw a group of men at the gate, arguing with the Eccentric.

Thru left the tools where they were and sped down the stairs to the ground floor. He took down the emergency pack he had prepared and slipped out the door.

Chapter 39

The message had come an hour before dusk. A soldier knocking at the door of the house, the whispers in the hallway, and the feet hurrying to her room. Simona was already awake and ready when the serving girl handed the envelope through the door. Everything then took on enormous significance: the huge seal bearing the letter "A," the knife to break the wax, a candle to read by. And Simona already knew what the message must mean.

Aeswiren warned her to leave the city at once. The time of danger that he had spoken of had come. She sensed that it had come sooner than the Emperor had planned. He fought powerful enemies within his own administration and inside the temple. He expected that all would end well enough, but in the meantime he wanted Simona far from the city.

After sending a message up to Shalee, the butler of the house at Shesh, to tell him she was coming, Simona left the city in a plain purdah wagon. She rode with four other women of good family, heading up to the mountains with their maids. The women rode in the main booth, on well-padded seats. The maids were crammed in the back section, sitting on the luggage. Everyone was going up-country for the coming Festival of First Snow and, of course, the big topic of conversation was whether there would be snow or not. The Almanacs did not agree this year, and that was a big source of comment, even passionate argument, for some of the women were advocates of one or the other Almanac.

Simona tried to pay attention and to keep up her end of this conversation, but she found it hard not to think about more important matters.

First was her overpowering concern for Nuza. She assumed that the Emperor had already taken steps to move Nuza to safety, because Simona understood that Nuza was a target for the ire of the priests. The Emperor had intimated as much, the last time they had met, a few days before.

"Nuza does not sleep here anymore" was all he had said.

Once, Simona would have offered up a prayer to the Great God. But she had lost all her faith in him, if indeed she had really ever had any. She knew of the Older Gods and she thought of them fondly, but she could not believe in them, either. When it came to the Gods, she was lost.

And so she thought of Nuza's face and hoped that she would see her again someday, when the danger was over and the Emperor was triumphant. Simona was certain that the Emperor would triumph. The power of Aeswiren III had always resonated in her life. Even now he retained that aura of strength.

But during the struggle poor Nuza would be alone, without anyone who could speak her language properly. This made Simona feel miserable.

However, she was thankful for her wonderful father. With the dawn light breaking over the city, he had struggled to wake up at her sudden appearance in his room and then had immediately granted her her wish to go up to Shesh Zob. He'd gotten up and embraced his wonderful daughter and told her that he was happy for her to get out of the city for the festival season.

"I cannot go myself, but if you go then it will serve to show that we have not forgotten our friends and relatives. It has been weighing on my conscience. For really we should go this year. Haven't been up to the Zob in years. Many old friends of Chiknulba will be there, they will want to know what happened. But, I cannot leave my work. We have designed the larger instrument, and it is now being built. I have to be there. It will be three times more powerful than the first one. We have done a great deal of work on lenses. There are strange qualities to light, properties that I cannot understand." He tapered off into silence, and she sensed that he was straining against the limits of his time. Never before had she seen the faraway look that his eyes held now.

"I understand, Papa."

"Yes, hmmm. And while you're there, you can visit the elder aunts. In particular, I mean old Lady Piggili. She was Chiknulba's favorite."

"Oh, of course, Papa, I will visit Aunt Piggili. And I will speak to the others and tell them that Mother died bravely in the distant land."

Simona bent and kissed him on the cheek, something that pressed against the line of permissible behavior in the world of Shashti purdah.

"And remember to behave with modesty, darling daughter of mine. Even in Shesh Zob we must keep up the front that we are just as traditional as the next family. We don't want to be singled out by the priests. We certainly don't want any raids by the morality squads. So remember that and be a good girl. No swimming without clothes on."

"Father! It is midwinter. I will be wearing plenty of clothes, and I certainly won't be swimming."

"Yes, yes, of course. I'm sorry, but that last incident caused us trouble in Shesh. The magistrate even sent a note of inquiry."

"Oh, Daddy, those awful people."

"They may be awful, my dear, but they have power. They can order fifty Red Tops into the Zob with the power to search every crevice to root out vice or immorality. We don't want that."

Filek's eyebrows had taken on a paternal frown for a moment.

"Of course not, Daddy."

"Good, now travel safely, offer prayers at the shrines for your mother. And write to me, tell me how everyone is. I want to know everything."

Simona left him then. In truth, she looked forward to seeing Shesh Zob. Four years had passed since she had last taken the purdah wagon to Shesh. The journey took eight or nine days, depending on the weather, even with fresh horses at every stop. And along the way the traveler would encounter a lot of big, cold inns. The worst was at Evkun, which was smoky and had the most awful food.

But, she consoled herself, at the end of the journey she would be in the country, and during the winter festival as well. It had been years since she'd had First Snow at Shesh Zob. She had such warm memories of it when she was a little girl. She remembered her mother during an intimate, mixed-sex family gathering. Because everyone was related, the women wore light veils only for covering their faces. The feasting, the singing, and the dancing! It was marvelous, and all just within the Gsekk clan. Her wonderful uncles and aunts, her favorite, Aunt Piggili, who was closely related to Mother. Aunt Piggili's wonderful high-pitched cackle and her apple pie, they were unforgettable.

And as soon as she was settled in, she was going for a ride. She hadn't ridden a horse in four years. She hoped that Silvery, her favorite mare, was still alive. Silvery had been eleven when last she'd seen her. And she wasn't going to ride sidesaddle, not Simona Gsekk. She would have her legs wrapped around the horse.

Indeed, despite the seriousness of the situation, she wanted to jump up and sing aloud. All the terrors of the tense politics of Shasht seemed left behind in the city.

Her thoughts were interrupted. One of the women was speaking to her. Simona stopped thinking of riding her horse and concentrated.

"Will you be staying in Shesh, then?" said the woman.

Simona was about to answer honestly and then checked herself. Be discreet, the Emperor had said.

"Ah, no, I will go on to the Ramp Valley. I am staying with relatives there."

"Ah, the Ramp," said the woman, dismissively. "Well, I'm afraid I shan't see you during the festival. We will be entirely taken up with festivities in the purple hills."

"Oh, the purple hills are so beautiful. How fortunate you are."

"Yes," said the woman, adjusting her ample flesh. Completely satisfied with the superior accident of her birth.

The wagon rattled on. Simona prepared herself for what she feared would be something of an ordeal.

The first night was at the Old Halt in Shojin, a dilapidated structure, with purdah quarters that were barely habitable. The bare floors had gaps, the wind whistled through the windows, barely slowed by the worn-out shutters. Dinner consisted of a weak broth, some mushrooms, and hot loaves of bread. Simona was cold all night.

In the succeeding days they rattled over the cobbles of the imperial highway. To either side stretched the grim little towns of the valley, an endless expanse of mud-brick houses. Dust rose above the plain, grey clouds swept in, and a cold rain lashed the road.

That night they stayed in much better conditions at Tencourt. The inn was warm and served an excellent farmer's pie for dinner, with good ale and a roaring fire. Simona slept much better that night, though she woke in the morning from a dream about Nuza. Nuza had been waving goodbye, as if she were never coming back. Simona did not know what the dream meant and was afraid to think about the possibilities. But worries about Nuza kept returning.

That day, the third, the ladies in the carriage were quiet. They'd exhausted the conversation in the first two days. Now everyone knew who everyone was and had compared family trees. The hierarchy had been established. For the moment this knowledge inhibited conversation.

The journey continued thus. Most halts were in old pensions where the shutters banged in the wind and rain leaked through the worn-out roofing. Three days in a row it rained, which caused a day of delay at Trelsay, where the road crossed the river and the canal.

Then things improved, until Evkun. Looking out on the bleak rows of ocher brick housing, Simona felt a familiar desolation in her soul. The hinterland was crowded with people, and most of them lived in squalor. In Simona's world these people hardly existed. They were not involved in the chorales, they did not attend the theaters, they were not part of the society of Shasht. They were but a step away from slavery, ekeing out their existence in these wretched alleys, swarming with their children.

That night she heard the sounds of distant struggles. Men fighting in small groups after drinking fiery bashool. Shouts, cries, sometimes running feet, followed the sounds of beatings. Howls of agony rent the sky, sobbing away to nothing.

Simona slept poorly again and slept sitting up much of the next day.

And then, at last, they were in Shesh, and the lovely spires of the temple rose above the valley in which the town reposed. They crossed the canal again and entered the town proper. The stone buildings with their white plaster facade were an immediate contrast to the mud brick of the river towns below.

They lodged that night at the Oak Tree Inn, a building boasting beams several hundred years old. Fortunately, it was a prosperous place and in good repair. Simona slept well and was up early. She left her companions of the journey behind. They would scarcely miss her, she hadn't said much to anyone for most of the trip. But having said she was going to the Ramp Valley, she had to take a different wagon from theirs to get to the purple hills. So she ordered a two-person carriage, made purdah proper by being completely enclosed with a single door that was easily bolted shut. Lake of the Woods was fifteen miles away, and it would take much of the day to make the trip.

From the narrow window slits she watched the pretty hills of Shesh passing by. Long stone walls flanked the roads, boasting gracious gates. They were in the zobbi countryside now. There was traffic, supply wagons for the most part, and the road was in excellent condition. Indeed, they passed slave gangs working on the roads in several locations. The county administrators were well aware of the high priority required for the roads leading to the grand zobbi and so kept them in good condition.

Bare trees covered the hills, except for the conifers that began to proliferate in the higher elevations. After the treeless plain these were a pleasant sight. Her spirits improved continuously. Simona now trembled with excitement. At Shesh Zob she could stand outside in the open air, under the sun, and twirl and shout and be alive. The whole suffocating burden of purdah would be removed. She could barely restrain her eagerness to be outside and free.

It was a long day, and she slept for part of it, but with

the light fading behind them, she glimpsed the north wing of the house through the trees. Her heart soared. Here was sanctuary, here she could at last feel like herself again.

The carriage clopped up the driveway toward the west-facing main facade of the house. The pale orange walls, topped by red tile work, brought back wonderful memories.

She heard the slaves knocking on the carriage door, and she drew back the bolts.

Shalee was there, his narrow face split by a huge smile.

"Welcome, Mistress Simona, welcome back to Shesh Zob."

Chapter 40

The hour before cocks crow, the great city was asleep. Scarcely a light showed at this hour, except at the palace. There, within the very heart of the Empire, panic ruled.

The Emperor's throne had suddenly begun to wobble. The priests had spoken against Aeswiren, so it was said. Armed guards stood alert at every doorway. Men with lamps searched the passageways and halls for assassins.

The day before had been the festival of the Blood of Bulls. At the great sacrifice of the white bull, a strange travesty had occurred that set every tongue to wagging. When the Red Tops pried open the chest of the bull to release the Nymph of the New Blood, they found an old hag, toothless, one eye missing, instead of the lovely young girl that was expected. The ceremony had ended abruptly.

Then had come the more telling blow, at least as far as Aeswiren was concerned. Before the old hag could be questioned, she was killed, in mysterious circumstances while within the protection of the Hand. Her body showed no marks.

We had her, and yet she was killed? This spoke of a penetration of the Hand.

Aeswiren was pressing very hard for answers. He had demanded that the temple hand over the priests responsible for organizing the ceremony of the Blood of Bulls. Aeswiren knew perfectly well that the "nymph" did not come from the innards of the bull, but was introduced in a skillful maneuver when the Red Tops tore the bull apart with crowbars. The temple had refused to hand over the priests to the Hand. They claimed that important spiritual matters were at stake. The Great God had obviously expressed his displeasure about something, and the priests had to decide what it was. Something had gone awry within the very heart of the empire, that was the only possible explanation.

This was dangerously close to a treasonous statement. When the priests spoke out against Emperors in the past, those Emperors fell. Perhaps not immediately, but soon the authority of the Emperor would weaken if the priesthood of the Great God turned against him. It had happened many times.

And even more important than this looming problem was the mysterious disappearance of Hesh, the First Finger of the Hand. Hesh was a closely guarded individual, but his guards had been slain outside his door and Hesh was missing. No trace had been found in two days' frantic search of the city.

Aeswiren had been Emperor for twenty-three years. He had come up the hard way. He knew to keep his own counsel in a time like this. No one could be trusted, although he would have to rely on the officers of the Hand. Hesh's deputies knew too much not to be involved in his efforts to turn the situation around.

One thing he was certain of, all this trouble came from the Old One. All due to Aeswiren's refusal to hand Nuza over to the knife.

At the thought of the Old One, Aeswiren's lip curled into an involuntary snarl. Aeswiren had his sword on his hip now, with helmet and chain mail, too. The Old One had ruled a long time, removing weak Emperors when necessary. Aeswiren would show him that he was made of different material. Nuza was safe and would stay hidden. Unless they could rip it from his own lips, they would not find her.

But Hesh's disappearance was about more than Nuza. For Aeswiren had been working along the same lines as the Old One, only his trap was planned to shut in three more days. A picked force of five hundred men waited for the order, then they were to clean out the temple. All the Gold Tops were to lose their heads, and the Old One was to be eradicated. His remains were to be burned in a large, hot fire, just to be sure they could never be resurrected.

But the enemy had moved first. Possibly the enemy had known of his plans. A chilling thought, because it meant the organization he had built, with the help of Hesh, had been penetrated. How much did his enemy know? Where was Hesh?

Aeswiren had reviewed the structure of the Hand and the chief officers. The other Fingers were located in Hadda, Yerumala, and Bajj, the leading provinces of the Empire. Yet they were irrelevant in this struggle. Aeswiren sensed this would all be over within a few days.

For local control, the Hand relied on the Fierce Fists, a cadre of a hundred picked men. Aeswiren knew most of these men, had read all of their files. He had selected six of these men to give his special trust. Aeswiren had sat with these young men, eaten meals with them, worked to instill loyalty into them. But now he knew that one of that cadre had to be the traitor.

The immediate task was to replace Hesh. The Hand needed a First Finger. Either Grimes or Chenko could do the job; they had been Hesh's deputies for many years, though neither exhibited quite the same degree of chilly resolve as Hesh.

Aeswiren never lingered anywhere for more than an hour. Accompanied by three guards and Klek, he shifted his location about the palace. Strangely, he found himself happier than he'd been in years.

Grimes accompanied him to a small room on the fourth floor of the west wing. They discussed the qualities of the Six, the young men Aeswiren had groomed for the highest levels.

"Bayrid and Chebble have always seemed very solid to me," said Grimes.

"And to me. I find it close to inconceivable that one of them could be the traitor." And then Chenko hurried in with the strangest look on his face.

"What?" snapped Aeswiren.

"We have found him, we have found Hesh."

Aeswiren's heart leaped.

"Good. Give thanks to the Gods for that. Where?"

"In the gardens of Lakank House. He was found by a bed of zajola flowers, just standing there."

"Is he sane?"

"I don't know."

"Let us see him."

"It makes me uneasy, my lord."

"Yes, but you have searched him thoroughly by now. He is only a man. I fear no man, not with Klek here and my own sword on my hip."

"This is magic, my lord. The First Finger says he remembers nothing. He feels well, he commends himself and his health to you, my lord. There are no visible marks on his body."

"What did he say, exactly?"

"What did he say, oh, many, many things, my lord. I could not remember them all. He babbled like a madman at times, but then he calmed and became perfectly normal."

Aeswiren's eyes tightened momentarily. He hated this evil magic and knew its source. He itched to bury his sword in the Old One before another day was gone.

"Bring him to me." Aeswiren looked around at the room. "Not here. Take him to the Library of Euphasian."

"Yes, my lord."

Chenko left them.

"What do you make of that?" Aeswiren asked Grimes.

"Magic, my lord. You mentioned the Old One. That must be the source."

"Aye, it must be. It is time to rid Shasht of this malign presence."

"Yes, my lord."

Aeswiren looked at Grimes for a moment. The response had been lacking ever so slightly in enthusiasm. A tiny thing, but in this situation Aeswiren knew he could afford no mistakes.

He moved to the Library of Euphasian, a long, gallery of shelves and windows on a high floor of the east wing. It was one of the better libraries, established by Norgeeben's personal secretary, the learned Euphasian.

Hesh was brought in. As Chenko had said, Hesh appeared quite normal, from his flat-top, iron-grey hair through the flinty eyes and level mouth.

"My lord, forgive me." Hesh dropped to his knees and lowered his head.

"Hesh, please get up."

Hesh got to his feet, stood before Aeswiren.

Aeswiren searched in the man's eyes. "What the hell happened to you, Hesh?"

"I do not know, my lord. I was in my bed, asleep, and then I awoke in the gardens, under a linden tree."

"I do not like such mysteries."

"No, my lord. Nor do I."

"You were in bed and you remember nothing, not a single thing?"

"Nothing, my lord."

"This must have been magic of a most fell and powerful kind."

"Yes, my lord, my conclusion, too."

"Both of your guards were killed."

"Yes, my lord, I heard that. I grieve for them, they were good men."

Aeswiren paced up and down. He wished he could kick off his boots and walk barefoot on a nice Nisjani rug. It always soothed him to walk on a fine rug.

"This is the work of the Old One."

At the mention of the name, Hesh nodded, but his eyes widened momentarily. Grimes and Chenko, too, rose up on the balls of their feet. All three were aware that this was the gravest of the Secrets of the State.

"Hesh, you remember my plan?"

Hesh's eyes widened further.

"Yes, my lord."

"It will be put into operation at once. Do you understand?"

Hesh's face had changed color, flushing a wild red. His eyes bulged in his face, his mouth worked.

Suddenly, with no further warning, he leaped at Aeswiren with arms outstretched. Aeswiren was taken by surprise by Hesh's speed. Hesh's hands closed on the Emperor's throat. The fingers dug in like talons. Aeswiren thrust up with his knee, hit Hesh across the side of the head with either hand. The fingers still closed on his throat, still tore at the skin.

Aeswiren heard a voice bellow; hands gripped Hesh by the shoulders and tried to pull him away. Someone screamed. The door to the library burst open, and the guards came in. Klek was already there.

Aeswiren drove his knee into Hesh's belly again and finally broke the man's grip. Aeswiren's right hand came over and smashed Hesh on the side of the face, spinning him around. Aeswiren's left hand came in at the solar plexus as Hesh spun, and the man was driven back a step.

By then many more details of the scene were horrifyingly obvious. Chenko was down, Grimes stood with a sword dripping blood. The Hand had been thoroughly penetrated.

But before Grimes could finish the job and kill him, Klek was there. He engaged Grimes, sword to sword. The pair of guards surged toward Hesh.

Unfortunately Hesh came back up onto his feet with insectal rapidity and met the guards head on. His high kick knocked one guard down, and then Hesh tore the other guard's sword from his hand. That guard fell a moment later as the sword ripped out his throat. Then Hesh turned back to Aeswiren.

It had taken but a few seconds, but that had been enough for Aeswiren to ready himself. The Emperor met the onrush with his sword, and though Hesh's blow was powerful Aeswiren parried it with a smooth stroke. He handled the next cut as well, but then Hesh whipped a quick backhand too low for Aeswiren to counter. The sword slid by and struck Aeswiren across the chest. The mail held, but the force of the blow drove the Emperor to his knees.

Hesh came on and Aeswiren could only block the next blow. Hesh landed astride him, and drove his sword down two-handed at his chest.

Instinctively, Aeswiren's sword deflected the stroke a few degrees, just enough to have it slice wide of his body and bury itself in the wooden floor of the library. It stuck fast there.

Aeswiren sucked in air that felt red hot in his lungs and punched Hesh in the face with every ounce of strength he could muster. Hesh fell backward, and Aeswiren heaved himself clear and started back onto his feet.

Hesh sprang up with an eery, inhuman speed again and tackled him around the legs. Aeswiren went down once more, but wriggled around just in time to block the dagger in Hesh's hand. Aeswiren had Hesh's wrist and Hesh had Aeswiren's. The struggle swayed there for a moment, but Hesh's terrible strength was beginning to tell.

And then Klek drove his sword into Hesh's back while wrapping an arm around his neck and hauling him back from the Emperor.

Aeswiren got to his feet, shaken. Grimes was dead. One of the guards was dead, the other was back on his feet, also looking shaken.

Hesh was arched over on his back, his face rigid in death. Except that Hesh was not yet dead. With a strange squeal he sprang back to life and came back onto his feet as if he were made of rubber. Then he reached over and tore his sword free from the floor.

The guard was the first to reach Hesh. Their swords rang as they clashed. The guard shoved Hesh with his shield, and then Hesh stabbed over the shield with the rapidity of a striking snake and the guard collapsed. The next moment Klek smashed into Hesh, but slipped on the bloody floor and fell heavily. Hesh ignored him and came straight back at the Emperor. Aeswiren met the sword, turned it, went chest to chest with Hesh. The man's eyes were focused on eternity, there was a strange gasping sound coming from his throat.

Aeswiren shoved with his free hand, turning Hesh slightly, an ancient trick of the swordsman. Hesh's thrust missed, but Aeswiren felt his own blade slide deep into Hesh's belly. He ripped upward and dumped the man's guts on the floor. Aeswiren stood back thinking it was over.

It was not. Hesh kept fighting, the strange gasping sound never stopped. Aeswiren felt his helmet fly from his head as Hesh hammered him with the sword. His head was ringing, he came close to blacking out.

Again, Klek saved him. This time he struck at the base of the neck, and Hesh's head was half severed from his body. Blood fountained over them, and the head of the thing flopped over grotesquely.

And still Hesh lived, for he spun around and drove again at Aeswiren. Horrified, almost unnerved, the Emperor barely parried the first blow, felt the second break the chain mail and cut into his ribs. Aeswiren stumbled, the killing blow missed him by a hairbreadth and then Klek caught the thing around its chest and pulled it aside while working his own sword into its chest cavity. Hesh's guts were all over the floor. The room was a charnel house. Hesh hammered Klek in the face and knocked him aside. It turned back to the Emperor. Aeswiren dug deep for his last bit of strength and swung again two-handed. Hesh's head flew across the library and struck a bust of Norgeeben in the far window.

Hesh's body fell headlong and lay still.

Aeswiren looked into Klek's face and saw his own astonishment and dread reflected there. The air carried a stench of blood and shit. Blood was running from Klek's battered nose.

"We must hurry, my lord, your enemies are on the move."

Chapter 41

Through the lamp-lit corridors of the east wing, the Emperor staggered, with faithful Klek at his side. Treachery was abroad, assassins were at work.

On the floor just below the library of Euphasian, they found twenty of the Fierce Fists bodies. From blood trails in the hall, it was clear the young men had been killed in various places and then brought there.

Apparently Grimes had not been the only traitor in the Fists.

On the ground floor near the east gate, a half dozen officers, stood in a group, looking lost. The ranker was Colonel Culchep. The sight of the Emperor, covered in blood, limping, shook these men.

"Where are the five hundred men I ordered stationed here?" wondered Aeswiren.

"Back in the barracks, my lord. We received orders, under your seal, to return to barracks while officers waited here."

Aeswiren sucked in a breath.

"And who delivered those orders to you?"

"Grimes, my lord. I did not question them. Are you saying they were not your orders?"

"Yes, Colonel, that is what I am saying. There is treachery at work here. You had best look to your men. I imagine that if you stay here, you will be killed."

The colonel blanched. Aeswiren looked up. Klek was signaling urgently from the doorway. Aeswiren lurched over to take a look.

A battalion of Red Tops entered the east gate. More Red Tops were visible on the battlements above.

"The fornicating sons of dogs," muttered Aeswiren, feeling the layers of civilization sloughing away from him like dead skin. The old Aeswiren, the man of war was reawakening.

"I know a way out," Aeswiren murmured quietly to Klek.

His mind raced ahead. Obviously the priests had moved to take control of the city. Other packets of forged orders would have been used to move the guards regiment to barracks. Red Tops would be everywhere, guarding the gates, monitoring whoever entered or left the city.

When they knew he had escaped, they would redouble the search. The Old One would not rest until Aeswiren was dead.

In his stead they would crown Aurook. Aeswiren had often wondered if the Old One had done something to his sons. Aurook had been a worthwhile person until a few years back. Then came the darkness that turned the boy into a vicious sadist. Aeswiren had fought to save him, but in the end he had lost. Nebbeggebben had been lost, too, exactly five years before. So it went. As the Emperor's heirs approached their majority, they became corrupted. The story was as old as the Empire. He had rid himself, and Shasht, of Nebbeggebben by sending him off on the expedition. Aurook was still here, and now he would be the imperial puppet of the Old One.

Aeswiren felt cold fury burning in his heart. He had waited too long. He had underestimated the Old One. He would not do that again, but he would survive, and someday he would kill the Old One himself. Nothing else would ever banish the sight of Hesh at his end. No man should die like that.

"Colonel, I think you should all go to the barracks at once. There appears to be a regiment of Red Tops entering the palace compound."

Culchep was stunned.

"By the Great God's purple ass! That is unforgivable."

Aeswiren laughed at such military frankness. Culchep had blushed red to his helmet line. At least, Aeswiren, thought, he knew he could trust Culchep!

"Beg pardon, my lord, I . . ."

Aeswiren stopped him with a hand and a craggy smile.
"I want you to get your men into arms and readiness for
action, understood? We have to stop this, and stop it now!"

Culchep and the others clattered off. The swarm of Red
Tops in the distance was heading their way.

"Come," said Aeswiren, and he hurried back up the passage, toward the southern end of the palace. The men
would put up a fight, he was sure, but the Red Tops would
overwhelm them in the end. The Old One would have mo-
bilized several battalions for the job, just in case.

They entered the sinostile, crossed the gallery above the
indoor gardens, and ran down a staircase that lead to a
secret door.

On the landing above the hidden door, they found Bayrid
and Chebble, high-ranking members of the Fierce Fists, accompanied by a pair of puzzled-looking guards.

"Your Majesty," said Bayrid, bowing low. The others
bowed deeply.

"My lord, you have been hurt. Come, let us escort you
to a place of safety."

Chebble stepped forward, his hand moving back toward
the hilt of his sword.

Despite his wounds, Aeswiren didn't hesitate, nor did
Klek. Their swords flashed first, and they drove forward,
spitted Bayrid and Chebble, and dropped them to the cold
stone floor.

The guards stared at the Emperor, perplexed by this unimaginable violence.

"These men were traitors," said Aeswiren. "There has
been an attempt on the Emperor's life. Do you understand?"

"Yes, my lord." The men went down on one knee.

"Are you loyal to your Emperor?"

"Yes, my lord."

"Then, come with me and be prepared to sell your lives
dearly. Bring those torches from the torchère."

There was a sharp twinge from the wound along his rib
cage. The blood had crusted and matted his shirt to his
skin, and when he lifted his shoulder it pulled the wound

apart painfully. Damn! He'd almost paid with his life back there. He cursed himself. How could he have been so blind?

They went down another floor and lit one of the torches. The walls were of brick and mortar, a passage led off to the right, another to the left. Aeswiren stepped across to the far wall and counted the layers of bricks up from the stone-flagged floor. At the ninth brick he felt along until his fingers ran across a sharp line in the surface. He pressed hard and felt something resist, then slowly give way. With a loud click a section of the wall, from the ninth brick down, swung open. A dark passage, smelling of damp, was revealed at the bottom of the wall.

To enter, one had to wriggle under on one's back. Once inside, there was room to stand up in a passage that one could easily reach across with one arm. They lit another torch that highlighted brick walls dwindling to nothingness in the distant murk.

Aeswiren led the way, moving as quickly as he could manage, though it cost him. He prayed his ribs weren't broken. The passage would take them into the city. But getting out of the city would not be so easy. Shasht's defensive walls, which only enclosed the central part of the sprawling metropolis, were tight. Aeswiren had bricked up three secret adits himself.

After a few minutes walking down the damp passageway, they came to a heavy brick grating. They pushed on the inside of the disk, and after an initial effort they were able to swing the grating open and step outside. They found themselves in a marble-lined trench that ran behind the great fountain of Pelas in the plaza of Norgeeben.

They peered out from behind the fountain. The city seemed quiet, but watchful. Hidden in a crack behind the bulk of the fountain they were safely out of view, but once they crossed the street they would risk detection.

They had no choice. They slipped across, torches doused, hurrying for the safety of the shadows on the far side. No cry of alarm came. The Red Tops were elsewhere for that moment.

They hurried down the street. A few faces looked out from behind shuttered windows. The word was out that

Red Tops were in the palace. The Emperor had fallen. Few folk were brave enough to be out on the streets. To be taken by the Red Tops now would guarantee a quick trip to the altar of the Great God.

By happenstance they took the right fork at Nebo's Column and found themselves on Harbor Street. But Red Tops were patrolling and spotted them.

Now they had to run for it, since about five or six Red Tops were heading their way at a brisk trot.

"Hurry," snarled Aeswiren, legging it painfully back to the circle of Nebo's Column. They ran on, taking a smaller street past humble warehouses and factories. Red Tops came from behind. They took another turn, and slipped through a narrow alley into an old part of the city that was a warren of small streets and yellow brick houses.

They took lefts and rights at random, and soon lost the Red Tops. Purple in the face, Aeswiren paused for breath, but they could hear the Red Tops bellowing back and forth several streets away. After catching their breath, they moved on quietly, the two guards at front and rear and the Emperor and Klek in the middle.

At the end of a narrow street filled with two-story brick houses, they came out on a plaza in front of the old Mission Hospital. The hospital was set back behind a walled yard and lit up by a series of big oil lamps placed along the front. A few people were gathered outside the gate, ragged beggars primarily. The gate was open and inside were gathered a hundred or more wretches, from lepers to amputees.

The Emperor didn't miss the irony that he was now hiding among the lowest strata of society. Well, he hadn't been born to noble status, and he didn't share the common snobbery of Shasht.

Still, they obviously couldn't hide in the courtyard. They stood out simply because they were well fed, let alone wearing blood-covered armor. So they pushed through to the main door. Four stout young men stood guard with staves, under the direction of an older eunuch.

The sight of these guards and men covered in blood brought the young men to attention. They were ready to repel looters no matter who they were.

Fortunately the old eunuch, Penukles, recognized the Emperor at once. Penukles had heard the rumors. He also knew that Filek Biswas was a favorite of Aeswiren. He motioned for the guards to let the Emperor and his retinue through without further ado. Secrecy was certain to be vital.

A pervasive smell of alcohol and hot water wafted through the hospital's broad corridors. They turned a corner into a large hallway surfaced in white plaster. A group of slaves scrubbed the floor.

Penukles ran ahead of them, opening doors and calling up the stairs.

A young man named Mushuq, the director met them at the next landing.

"Your Majesty, can we assist you? It seems that you are wounded."

"Thank you. Where is Biswas?"

"I think he slept in the laboratory again. I tell him to go home, but he says it's too far and he sleeps on a cot in there."

"That sounds like Biswas. A hard worker, I like that in a man. Bring him to me now."

"Ah, yes, Your Majesty." Director Mushuq bowed low. Penukles and another eunuch were sent scurrying away to fetch Biswas.

Aeswiren and Klek stood there, the two guards facing the door, while Director Mushuq bobbed up and down in embarrassment. He, too, had heard the rumors. He knew he might be endangering his own life by allowing the Emperor to remain here unchallenged. Once a purge began, it could become very widespread.

Aeswiren paid little attention. His side hurt, his legs ached, and he was bone-tired from the aftereffects of the fight with Hesh, the lack of sleep, and the flight through the city.

A cry from the floor above broke the tableau.

"Here I am, Your Majesty." Filek appeared, running down the steps with Penukles behind him.

"Good to see you, Biswas. We have some cuts to be seen to. You know Klek."

Filek nodded to the formidably muscled Klek. He had

hardly ever spoken to him before, but he knew of his reputation. Looking back to Aeswiren, he saw that the chain mail hung off the Emperor's torso. There was blood everywhere.

"My lord?"

"Aye, there has been treachery. It's failed so far, though."

"Treachery? May all the traitors die a horrible death! Come, we must go to the surgery at once."

Turning to Mushuq, Filek assumed control of the situation. He could see that Mushuq was nervous, obviously calculating his chances of staying off the altar of He Who Eats.

"Director, I will see to the Emperor's wound. I think we should post the guards and tell no one that the Emperor is here."

"No one," said Mushuq.

"Absolutely no one," repeated Filek.

Mushuq's eyes betrayed his panic. He leaned toward Filek. "But what if the priests come?"

"Not very likely. There are only poor people here. But if they come, send them away again. They have no business here."

Mushuq blanched, but bit his lip.

Filek looked up, Klek had noticed the director's ambivalence. Mushuq saw the look in Klek's eye and became even more frightened.

"No one," repeated Mushuq in a whisper.

Filek leaned close. "Remember, the Emperor was beaten three times before he became Emperor. Aeswiren will come back."

Mushuq nodded. He had decided to keep silent about all this, it was the safest policy. Opening your mouth to the priests could send you to the altar. It was far better not to earn their attention in the first place.

Moments later in the surgery, Filek helped Aeswiren remove the mail shirt.

"Thankfully you were wearing this mail, otherwise you would be dead."

"Thankfully, Klek was there. In truth, without him I

would be lying on the floor back there. Klek, old friend, you saved your Emperor's life today."

Klek grinned.

"Not for the first time, eh?"

Aeswiren laughed, then gave a hiss as Filek went to work.

"Damn the priests," said Filek as he used tweezers to pull rings of mail out of the wound where they'd been driven in by the blow. Aeswiren gave small grunts every so often during this process.

"Red Tops are running wild in the palace at this very moment."

Filek shivered. He understood what that meant. His comfortable life here was over. Filek gave an inner sigh. Once again his work would be delayed. But, he swore to himself, he would survive. And thank the Gods he had made copies of all the important diagrams. He would take them with him.

"I have to leave the city at once."

Filek nodded. "I know of a way."

"How?"

"We are loading a wagon with the recently deceased patients. They go to the mortuary in the morning."

The first light of day was just beginning to color the sky in the east. A few cocks started to crow in the old quarter.

A drum thundered briefly from the temple, welcoming the gift of another day of life. Filek cleaned the Emperor's wounds and sewed them up as quickly as possible. Aeswiren bit down on the leather during the needle work. Filek was quick and efficient. It was done in less than two minutes, but it was long enough for the Emperor to sweat profusely as he struggled not to scream.

When it was over he looked Filek in the eye, while he sobbed for breath.

"Thank you, my friend. You understand that you no longer have protection from the priests."

"I understand, Your Majesty. I cannot stay here. The first micro-scope has been hidden. The second one is too big to hide and will be destroyed. We are resigned to this, but I have already sent one of my assistants away into hiding. He will know everything that I know. If conditions improve, he may be able to complete the work himself."

Aeswiren nodded. "You have shown foresight, perhaps better than my own." Filek knew not to answer that as he turned to Klek's wounds, which were more numerous, but less serious.

"And your daughter, I warned her to leave the city."

"She did, my lord. I have a message readied for her. It is in code so that if it is intercepted no one will know my real words."

"Biswas, perhaps you should have entered the service of the Hand." Filek smiled and bowed at such a compliment from the Emperor. His thoughts went with young Per, who was heading north at that very moment with Filek's message to Simona.

A eunuch knocked to interrupt. There came a hurried whisper to Filek.

"Red Tops have been in the yard, but no one told them that the Emperor was here. The poor folk love you, my lord."

"I wish they had better reason. Damn . . ."

Aeswiren thought of all the ideals he had brought with him when he took the throne. Precious little had survived the rough-and-tumble of real political life.

Klek gave a small grunt of pain, then fell silent as Filek sewed a cut on Klek's thigh. Klek was as tough as old leather. Aeswiren wished he was, too. Filek finished the sewing, applied bandages, and then packed away his tools.

"We must put our plan into operation quickly, Your Majesty. There's considerable traffic out of the city at first light. We must be among it."

"You wish to come?"

"If Your Majesty will allow it. I thought I would ride beside the driver. Yourself and Klek would be hidden among the bodies."

Within a few minutes all had been arranged. The Emperor and Klek were buried so deeply under the layers of dead patients, they could scarcely breathe. The two guards remained behind, with orders to return to barracks unob-

trusively and await developments. If all went well, they
would be handsomely rewarded when Aeswiren returned.

The mortuary wagon started up at the crack of the whip,
and pulled by a pair of horses it rolled out of the hospital
side gate and into the street. Ten minutes later it was
wedged in a solid mass of traffic that slowly inched its way
out of the gate past a mixture of guards and Red Tops,
who scrutinized every passing vehicle.

Filek watched the Red Tops with mounting tension. The
driver seemed unconcerned. The Red Tops searched every
wagon, even pulled chests down from carriages and forced
them open.

The mortuary wagon finally drew abreast of the pack of
Red Tops. Filek and the driver kept their heads low while
the Red Tops asked who they were and where they were
going. Red Tops jumped up onto the wagon and poked
among the bodies. Here and there they stabbed down with
spear points, to be sure that all were truly dead. One thrust
into Aeswiren's calf. Aeswiren was taken by surprise by
the sudden pain, and gave a tiny squeak before he cut off
his response.

Filek gave a quick cough to cover the sound. The Red
Top cursed him loudly and stabbed down again, this time
digging into Aeswiren's groin. The squeak was not repeated. The Red Top stabbed down in a couple of other
places, but only struck the dead. Finally he gave up and
jumped down. Filek released his breath and felt the blood
return to his face. He didn't dare move in case he trembled
too much.

The wagon was finally passed by the Red Tops. The whip
cracked, and they rumbled on through the gate and into
Outer Shalba.

Chapter 42

Four days later, the Emperor stood in the well of the fishing smack *Zuppe* as she sailed into the hidden harbor on Rat Island. Eighty miles off the coast from Fishguard, the Noh Islands were mostly uninhabitable crags, home to vast colonies of seabirds. A few tiny fishing hamlets existed on the largest isles, further north. It was a cold day, grey and overcast, with a useful breeze from the west, which the *Zuppe* rode in before on a single small sail.

Rat Island had no population, but it did have a small patch of level ground, set between two sharp crags. A harbor with a fishing station had long served the cod fishermen who worked the southern banks. The station looked deceptively ramshackle. In fact the interior was in good repair. Aeswiren had bought the island early in his reign. It was a very well-kept secret.

From the window of the station, Nuza watched him step out of the boat. She knew him at once, despite the shabby bulk of homespun he wore. He had a certain bearing that gave him away. It was part of the man, part of some inner force that shone out of him.

Two other men, very different men, climbed out of the boat onto the narrow dock and walked ashore behind the Emperor. One was short and wide shouldered and had a brutal air about him. Nuza had seen him before; he was the Emperor's bodyguard. The other was the tall doctor, who she knew was Simona's father.

Nuza understood that if Aeswiren had come here himself, it meant he had lost the struggle in the capital. What that might mean for her, as well as for him, she was less sure of. It could mean further flight, more hiding. It could mean an early death. Nuza had sworn to kill herself rather than let herself be taken alive by the priests. But at least the waiting was over. She would soon know the worst.

He came in with a gust of wind, smelling of fish. With obvious relief he shed his grubby outer cloak and the waterproof hat the fishermen had forced on him. Nuza noted the glitter of chain mail under the wool jerkin. On his hip he carried sword and dagger. This was the Aeswiren she had never seen, the man of war.

"Lord Emperor, I am glad to see you alive and well." Nuza bowed. She had spoken in Shashti, which she had begun to understand. She had had to communicate with the guards and the young men who looked after her, as well as the fishing station, and that had increased her vocabulary enormously.

Aeswiren lit up as he realized what she'd said. He took her hand in his. Her heart went out to this rugged monster of a man as his eyes peered into hers. She observed that he had massive bandages under his shirt of mail.

"You are well?" he wanted to know. "They have treated you properly?" His eyes showed a tender concern. Nuza felt a slight flush in her skin. It was almost the look one expected in a lover.

"Oh, yes, my lord. They have been very good to me."

Aeswiren looked on into the room, and his eyes glittered. Two young operatives of the Hand waited there, kneeling, heads bowed.

"Good. You two, see to Klek and the doctor."

He looked back to her.

"By the grace of the Gods, we have been brought together again. I am thankful for that." He pulled her closer, and she reached out and put her hands on his upper arms and kissed him on the cheek.

This was not as strange as it had been the first time. The hairless skin, the heavy beard that was so alien to her were not as repulsive as they'd been. She'd grown used to seeing such things on men.

He held her at arm's length for a long moment. A strange light glittered in his eyes betraying some inner torment.

"No, I could never have done it," he said suddenly, and he turned away with eyes suddenly hard with anger.

They went into the inner room, where a fire in the grate was putting out some warmth to cut the damp chill. Aeswiren stood in front of the fire and held his hands up to warm them.

"Ah, that's good. There's nothing like the cold of the sea in winter. Gets right through to the bone, eh?"

Nuza had to agree. Rat Island was hardly cosy. "But this room is always warm," she said, taking a seat near the fire.

"Well, you wouldn't have liked it the way it was before I had it repaired." He chuckled to himself. Above their heads the wind howled through the rafters.

"I have been pleased well enough here. I like it better than the rooms in the city."

"Yes, I expected you would like it here after being cooped up there."

"I have run to the top of both crags."

He laughed. "And I should have expected you'd do that. I bet that surprised young Galluk and Kimil."

"Kimil said that I should not go outside because I am female. He said I should wear a long black cloak down to the ground at all times for the same reason."

"Ah, yes, well, my dear, you do not yet understand the way our culture works. Kimil meant no harm, he thought he was protecting you. Women are not meant to go outside. They have no reason to go there. Woman's world is within the house of men. Men deal with the outside world, and when they go to their homes their women serve them. That is the way we are in Shasht."

"That is not the way we are in my homeland." In her anger Nuza had reverted to her own language.

"Yes, I understand that. I find it very hard to accept, but Simona said it was that way and I believe her."

"No mor alive would consent to be shut up in her home like a prisoner!" Nuza's eyes flashed and Aeswiren marveled at the beauty of her anger.

A head poked around the door. Klek.

"Lord, there is hot porridge and butter."

"Good, Klek, I will have some of that and some salt fish, too. And bring me a cup of ale if there is any."

Klek disappeared again.

Aeswiren, warmth returned, undid the straps that secured his jerkin and let it fall open. It was good to get out from under all those heavy clothes. He pulled off the kerchief he'd tied around his neck to keep out the wind on the *Zuppe*.

Nuza saw the top of the bandages that were wrapped around his chest.

"My lord, you have been hurt!"

"Aye." There was no point denying it. He was touched by her concern.

"What happened?"

"Well, we've had a little bit of treachery. For the moment I am on the defensive."

"The wounds?"

"Are healing. The good doctor Biswas took care of them."

"He is a great man, I think."

"You are correct. He will bring about a revolution in the history of the world, but only if I live and triumph over my enemy."

Nuza looked down into the fire for a moment.

"What will happen?" she said in a quieter voice.

"In the city I imagine they are anointing my son, Aurook, to take my place. My enemy found ways to corrupt him years ago. Aurook will do my enemy's bidding. The Empire will not suffer that much—Aurook's cruelty will only be felt by a few—but the changes that I had hoped to bring about will not take place."

Aeswiren had dropped his head almost to his massive chest while he spoke. Suddenly he shook himself free of the despondent fog.

"But the game is not over. Nor have I played all my cards." He turned to her, he realized he'd been speaking to himself in Shashti, her eyes were filled with questions. He returned to the pidgin between Shashti and the tongue of the Land that they had evolved between them.

"We will be safe here, but my enemy will pick up my trail eventually. Before then, we'll be gone from here. Captain

Moorsh should be here tomorrow sometime. He commands the *Duster*. Very fast ship. We will be in Gzia Gi in a week, and there I will see about turning this situation around."

Klek reappeared with a tray. Aeswiren lit up as he contemplated the hot food and a hefty mug of red ale.

"Another thing this sea air does is stir up a man's appetite."

"A good thing because the food is very plain."

"Hah, plain you call it? It's perfectly horrible, but it is food."

"Yes, it is better than to go hungry."

"And after I've eaten some perhaps we shall go and walk up one of these hills, eh, and you can tell me more about your homeland. I have missed our talks."

"Yes, my lord, I will be happy to do so."

Chapter 43

The Festival of First Snow was going very well, although snow seemed quite unlikely. Simona had received seven invitations, one for every important day of the festival. In addition, she was going to host a small dinner party for several close relatives on the Gsekk side. The party would be held on the third night of the festival, traditionally a quiet night, the least important of the seven nights of the main festival. So it was the perfect time for her own small affair, held in part to commemorate her mother, poor Chiknulba, who had died of the plague in a far-off land.

Fortunately, her haughty relatives had accepted her invitations, which had been a great relief, though she suspected that Aunt Piggili might have applied a little pressure in that regard. Simona knew that her status as a girl with a strawberry birthmark on her breast was decidedly low among the Gsekk clan. The consensus was that Chiknulba had married beneath herself socially. Her husband was a sawbones of some sort, who had some kind of naval connection, and the Gsekk were not much involved in the navy, which was felt to have much less glamour than the army. Aunt Piggili was a great ally, however, and her opinion had high status.

But all that was still days away. First there was The Last Night of the Year, which was always the time for the grandest events of all. Lord Iblesse of Fex held a huge party. Simona had been invited and on entering had been embraced by Lady Yeleema, hostess of Fex. Such marks of social favor had been rare and far between in Simona's life. A part of her treasured them, while another part despised them.

The party was held in a great room divided into two

sections by a gauze curtain hung down the middle of the
ceiling. The men were on one side, the women on the other.
The filmy gauze made it impossible for a man to clearly
see the face of any of the women present. They could converse freely through the screen, of course, and even pass
written notes to each other, but the rules of purdah were
enforced.

At such festival gatherings among the elite, it was customary for young men to pass notes to the most desired
young women, begging for the chance to view their bodies
with an eye to marriage. Young women expected to be
so courted and were ready to reply, often with withering
contempt. Of course, Simona knew that she would not receive such notes of desire. She had been viewed by eleven
men already and was unwed. The strawberry mark was a
well-known mark of witchery. No man of her own class
would want her.

She found it galling that sitting just on the other side of
the gauze were several young men who had examined her
body, the precursor to a marriage bid, but had refused to
bid afterward. "Nibbling the apple" it was called and was
a mark of shame. These young men had enjoyed seeing
her naked body and then had refused her because of the
strawberry mark.

They took no notice of the minor announcement of her
arrival with her friends.

However, other men did take notice. Messages were
passed in to her from two of her Gsekk uncles. They
wanted to hear all about the new world and also about the
sad death of Chiknulba. She drew close to them, with just
the screen separating them.

"A delightful little thing, was Chiknulba," said old Hermeez. "Sorry to hear she'd died like that. Married some
awful naval sawbones I heard. Lived in Shasht, can you
imagine? Awful business."

Simona decided not to remind old uncle Hermeez that
she was a product of the marriage to the "naval sawbones"
and also lived in the city of Shasht. Some things were better
left unsaid.

Then there were other men, friends of her father's. "He

would have come," she said of Filek's absence. "He wanted to, but the work on the micro-scope is at a delicate stage. He cannot leave it. The Emperor himself has insisted that it be completed soon."

Describing the micro-scope to some of the older, and dimmer relatives was a trial.

"Look at things that you can't see? What's the point of that?" was a common reaction.

The gong announced the dinner prayers. A Gold Top appeared to say the prayers and blessings, then the slaves began bringing in the endless procession of dishes. Singers and musicians took their station in the "cradle," a cage to keep them separate from the women. The musicians played a different piece to herald each of the "great courses" as it was brought in. Each piece was selected to evoke something of the dish.

Thus the great pie of lark's tongues was accompanied by frantic flutes and a whistling tune evoking the timeless nature of the life of birds in the marsh reeds. Then for the great moogah of beef and chestnuts there was a song from a male choir in praise of He Who Eats.

During the dinner Simona was seated with her onetime "best friend" Jounni of Gsekk. Jounni was of the senior branch of the family, who still lived in the family heartland of Bilerr. For Jounni to take notice of a social nobody like Simona was unusual, and rather generous. Jounni's other friends, of course, were rather cool toward Simona, but Jounni took no notice of them. She and Simona had always been close.

"My dear"—Jounni had had several glasses of wine by this point—"I can assure you that being wedded is no bed of roses. Men are exactly the beasts we pictured when we were young."

Among Jounni's affectations was the idea that she was now mature, at the tender age of twenty. And had thus put a great distance between herself and the giggly teenage girl she had been when Simona and she had been rebels together.

Jounni was now securely wed to a young lordling of the

Hob clan, Rujus Imagger. She had spent the last few years having two children and enduring the passions of Rujus.

"Every night, ev-er-y night, for months he would come and molest me. It was appalling."

For Simona, who had never even known the touch of a man's hand in passion, it didn't sound quite so appalling, but she kept such thoughts to herself.

"I'm so sorry," said Simona, feeling out of place suddenly.

"Oh, Simona, sometimes I think you have the better life. Being alone and not having to endure the things that men want to do! Ugh. It's all so disgusting."

Simona sipped her wine. If it was all so disgusting, then why did she want to do these disgusting things? Was she a freak? She didn't think so. She'd read all the Love Sonnets, including Harumi's so she knew what was involved. There again she'd seen horses and dogs doing it, so it was clearly a universal thing, as it had to be if the creatures of the world were to reproduce their kind.

"Does it still, ah, distress you that you have to sleep with your husband?"

"Distress? Dear God, you have no idea. You have been protected, my child, you have been saved from, from . . . Well, I will have to whisper the details." Jounni moved closer.

But Simona was saved from these ignoble revelations by a sudden interruption. A wave of whispers hurried along the tables, across the room. Chairs crashed in the men's section. A voice was heard shouting, "Noooooo!"

"What?" Jounni was left hanging, unhappy at being interrupted in her complaint.

"What is it?"

And then came the words that ripped Simona's world apart. Jounni leaned over to Kedess Bemmertruben. A moment later Jounni leaned back, wide-eyed with shock.

"Aeswiren has fallen. The Emperor has fled Shasht. Aurook has been crowned."

A chill pierced Simona's heart. If the Emperor had fled the city, then her father was in great danger. Unless he, too, had fled. Unfortunately, there was no way to know. It could even be dangerous to ask too many questions.

The news from Shasht was fatal to Lord Iblesse's festival party. Some of the more important guests left at once, since they had military demands at such a time. Others drifted off as well, concerned about organizing an immediate move to the city. With a new Emperor on the throne, it paid to be close to the imperial court, ready to safeguard one's own position.

Lady Yeleelm tried to keep some sort of spirit going. For a while the tongues wagged furiously as the "I told you so" party had its say. Aeswiren had not paid enough attention to religious duties. He had not been seen in the temple for many years. The Great God would not be denied forever!

Others argued more gloomily that Aeswiren's real fault had been good governance, which had upset the priests, for it left them more exposed for the expensive, wasteful luxury that they were.

Those who were the most closely identified with Aeswiren and his grand project of repeating the prosperous era of Norgeeben had gone quiet, withdrawn into their own thoughts. A dangerous time lay ahead. Aurook was hardly the popular choice for the next Emperor. Repression would be intensified. Red Tops would visit households to seek out the impure of thought. Anyone with close affinities for Aeswiren's regime would be at risk.

Aunt Piggili caught Simona's eye, and Simona hurried to her side, where the table had partly emptied upon the astonishing news from the city. Piggili was plainly very worried.

"Simona, dear, your father . . ."

"I know, dearest aunt, I know. I pray that he had time to go into hiding."

"As bad as that, then?"

"Yes, Aunt. The priests do not want his work to continue. He threatens their grip on the Empire. He will be on their lists."

Piggili shuddered. She had been in the city once when the Red Tops went on a purge. It was before Aeswiren, in the time of Shmeg. The excuse was the hunt for the heretics of Xamf. Those same heretics that later challenged Aeswiren and were destroyed for it. But the Red Tops had used the excuse to burst into the homes of the well-to-do, who were known for their attachment to liberal causes. With malicious glee the Red Tops had smashed statuary and damaged wall hangings, letting the liberal lords and ladies know that the priests had their number and that one day, someday, there would be a reckoning. Piggili would never forget the horror of that time when she had hid from the rampaging young thugs as they tore up her parents' house.

"What will you do, girl?"

"I do not know yet, dearest aunt. I expect I will try and hide. But why would they come after me? I am not a scientist."

"But you are a heretic! Believe your ancient aunt when she tells you that they will want to kill all the heretics. This will be their best chance for years."

"What of yourself, dear aunt? Will you stay at the zob?"

"Only for the festival. Then I will go to Baldeberr to be closer to my other kin. It will be safer for me, I think."

The party ended early. Simona left when she detected signs that the main crowd was about to depart. She rode back alone in her carriage to the zob, thinking furiously the whole way.

The fact that she was at the zob for the festival had been accepted as perfectly commonplace behavior by everyone she knew. She caused less stir this way than by trying to hide at the zob and starting slaves' tongues wagging. The rumor mill was a constant fact of life among the zobbi. But if Aeswiren had really fallen from power, then everything had changed. If she stayed at the zob, she might draw the attention of the local priests, who would be eager to suppress heresy and deviation. If she hid herself too obviously, that would also cause comment and might even motivate some disgruntled slave to speak to the priests about her. Either course might be dangerous.

She would have to make a very careful decision. She

decided to sleep on it, and study it all carefully the next day before doing anything.

She could also plan to go into hiding, in case it became necessary. Faithful Shalee would help. Hilltop House would be the best place. Close, it was hidden in winter by miles of deep snow, but she would need supplies taken up there. Flour, oil, dried beans, sausage, all these things needed to be brought secretly. Gods, she realized, Shalee would be essential. Fortunately, Shalee could be trusted with one's life, the old eunuch was utterly faithful to Filek and Chiknulba, and by extension to Simona. But beyond Shalee, others would have to know: the drovers who took donkey loads up to Hilltop, the housekeepers who would clean and set up the rooms. The house had been shut down for winter, of course. It was only opened up in the summer. Simona could not do these things for herself. She would have to travel up there in the purdah carriage and stay hidden out of sight.

Preoccupied with these thoughts, she hardly noticed the dark clouds blowing in from the southwest. A wind picked up as they turned onto the road that ran alongside the Lake of the Woods. Now waves rolled across the lake, and the stars disappeared under the first tendrils of the clouds.

But when they turned into the zob and felt the sudden chill in the wind, she knew things were changing.

"There may be snow yet. Perfect for the festival," said Shalee as he escorted her inside the house.

Snow would keep the Red Tops in their chapter houses, for a while at least. It would gain her some time.

"A messenger has come from your father."

Shalee handed her the letter from Filek and discreetly left her alone.

She broke the seal and read the words, then consigned it to the fire as she was bidden. She knew how dangerous such a letter could be now.

"I will speak to the messenger," she told Shalee.

In his message Filek had expanded on her need to hide. Hilltop would not necessarily be enough.

She entered the purdah box and sat beside the slot. She heard the door open, and the young man was shown inside.

He took his seat on the other side of the inch-thick wood that protected her from view, or any other act of maleness.

"Thank you for bringing that message."

"My duty, ma'am."

"What will you do now? Return to the city?"

"Your father said it would be best if I did not. He suggested that I go to my own hometown, Turz."

"I see. Yes, that would be a good idea. The priests may come looking for anyone connected to my father."

"They will not find me in Turz. I will become a different person."

"What was my father's mood when last you saw him?"

"He was most determined to succeed, ma'am. He was sad, goes without saying, but I could tell that he did not intend to allow his work to be suppressed forever. He will have copies of the plans. I have copies, too. There are many copies now. The priests will never find them all."

"Take good care of them. We do not know how long it will be before the great work can be resumed."

Bidding young Pers farewell, Simona took some mulled ale and thought about the message from her father.

He urged to go into hiding. She should use Hilltop as a first step, and she should have the lodge on Mount Beegamuus made ready. She should use only the most trustworthy of the servants. Shalee was good, but others could not be trusted with this.

And so once again her life had been shattered.

Shalee knocked at the door.

"Mistress Simona, I must report there is a stranger, perhaps a spy, that's been seen on the edges of the zob for the past two days. Jokk the grounds keeper has seen him, but he says the intruder is wary and knows how to hide."

"A spy?"

"It could be, I cannot say."

"Shalee, I will need to leave the zob. I must go to Hilltop."

Shalee scarcely blinked. He was already primed for the emergency.

"Yes, Mistress Simona, I will see to it."

"Lips must be kept sealed about this."

"Only the most trustworthy will know."

That night it snowed, a light coating of feathery flakes, enough to bury the leaves and drape the branches in glittering white. When she awoke the day was clear, and inspired by the view from her window, Simona decided to take a ride in the park. Her favorite mare, Silvery, was readied.

After breakfasting and speaking privately with Shalee, she went to the stables. From there she rode out into the park, wearing the heavy hooded cloak of purdah, but daring to ride on a man's saddle, with her legs around the horse. The air was crisp and cold on her cheeks. Silvery was happy to canter along the path along the lawn, with the woods just to her right. She exulted in the freedom she felt out of the house, under the blue sky. The snow muffled Silvery's hoof clops and allowed Simona to imagine that the world was completely silent and that time had stilled its furious rush.

She reached the end of the long lawn, where the sloping ground had been terraced for a cut flower garden for the house. The path lead across the lawn and then either back to the main house, or on through a trellis that gave onto the riding trail out toward the Lake of the Woods. She was tempted to ride down to the lake, but she needed to go back and pack for the move to Hilltop. She still hadn't decided which robes to take.

Suddenly a figure appeared out of the snow-covered brush ahead of her.

"Simona?" it said.

She jerked the reins and pulled Silvery away, spurring across the lawn's smooth coat of snow. A Red Top, hiding there, waiting for her! Terror had exploded in her heart.

The figure ran after her.

"Simona!" it called again, and there was something uncanny about the voice. She knew that voice. She slowed Silvery and looked back.

The figure stood with hands outstretched. She turned back, cantered closer. It was a man, no not a man, a slight figure, a face that she knew. With stunning force it hit her, it was Thru Gillo.

Chapter 44

Nuza stood on the sterncastle of the frigate *Duster*. Away on her right, beneath a yellow crag, lay the city of Gzia Gi. The city of false hope for Aeswiren.

The land in view was harsh. All red and brown rock. Over the city hung a reek of smoke from the many chimneys. A chill wind from the east blew the smoke inland to pool beneath the crags.

Nuza remained astonished by the barren nature of Shasht. There was not a tree to be seen here. She thought back to the meetings at the Questioners that she had attended. Sometimes she had sided with those who had posed questions about the restrictions that kept the mots and brilbies from expanding their farms over more of the land. When so much of the land was left wild it meant that mots and mors had to restrict the size of their families. The whole culture of the Land was bent beneath such restrictions, or so it seemed to Nuza back then. Now she saw what could happen when a people bred beyond the limits of their land.

She turned back to the sea. In its profound vastness she sought comfort. Somewhere out there, far, far beyond the horizon, on the opposite side of the world lay the Land. Merely looking off into the distance like this brought up thoughts of her family, of Thru, of the troupe members, Toshak and old Hob, and indeed, her former life. Questions that could not be answered arose like serried tombstones. When she'd been captured, the war had reached Sulmo. Since then she had learned the war had gone badly for the men. Toshak had driven them out of Sulmo in complete defeat. How things went now, a year and a half later, was unknown, since no more ships had returned with news. She could only pray for victories for Toshak and his mots. Maybe the men had decided to leave the Land and either return to Shasht or to hunt for another place to colonize.

And then the sadness would well up again. For even if the Land survived, Thru Gillo did not. After the disaster at Farnem, Thru was listed among the missing. But his body was never found. Nuza had clung to the faint hope that he was still alive. Now, more than a year later, she had accepted that Thru was probably dead. That opened a void in her heart that she was sure would never be filled again.

Simona had described a little of what she had felt before her attempted suicide. Nuza looked at the waters below. Before, she hadn't really understood such a deep despair, but now she began to get an inkling of it. It seemed at times that her life had really ended on that terrible day at Bilauk. In the smoke of the charnel house of that village her future disintegrated. Everything that had happened since had been merely a step down toward the abyss that awaited her now.

Even her affection for the Emperor would be turned into a knife thrust into her heart, for as she stood there she knew that Aeswiren, her dear friend, was discovering the depths of betrayal from his supporters from the city.

Nuza had known from the first words of the city emissary, from the uneasy way he had spoken. Aeswiren's last bastion had been turned by the same treachery that had taken his throne.

Nuza had one last hope, but she was unsure if Aeswiren would be prepared to listen to her.

In the great room below, things went much as she had imagined. Aeswiren stood at one side of the rectangular table that filled the center of the cabin. On it was an unrolled map of Northern Shasht. Gzia Gi lay at one end of the map. Shasht itself in the center.

"No, my lord, the situation is more complicated than that." The speaker was the Baron Thruam, a close supporter of Aeswiren's. Thruam and three others stood on the far side of the table.

"You see, my lord, the priests began their preparations

here years ago. They have built up a network. Several of the richest landlords have gone over to them this year."

Aeswiren wanted to groan at this news. Grimes had blocked this information from reaching him. Or had Hesh been corrupted, too? In the aftermath of that horrific struggle with the former First Finger, he had to wonder. Now, with everything in ruins, Aeswiren would never know how deeply his organization had been penetrated by the priests. He did know that his positions had been smashed, and easily, too.

Another noble joined in, the Duke of Palia. "More important even than that, though, is this army marching here from Shasht. Bishop Bodo at its head, too, which does not augur well. Bodo is notorious for taking almost anyone for the knife."

Palia was feeling very nervous. His family had held their lands for many generations. Bishop Bodo was a noted tyrant. Many would be taken for sacrifice to the Great God when Bodo assumed control. The duke did not wish to be among them or to see his family lose everything.

Aeswiren looked around him, with eyes still filled with shock. To learn that so many had abandoned his cause so quickly had taken him by surprise. He had thought he might deserve a little support in return for what he had given the folk of Shasht for more than twenty years. But no, it was not to be. The bad news had followed him from Shasht. The Lords of Aeblan, Vemey, Darfola, and Gimms had all gone to pay fealty to the new Emperor, Aurook, who had taken the imperial name of Norgeeben II. He'd learned this before even reaching Gzia Gi, when a passing fishing boat had given them this news. Norgeeben II was now the advocate for the people with the Great God.

To take the name of Norgeeben? That was impious indeed. Norgeeben, the founder of the dynasty had been a sober, thoughtful man. It could not have been Aurook's idea. Aurook's thinking scarcely went beyond girls and gambling.

And what were Aeswiren's prospects? He was said to have died suddenly from pestilence, a curse sent directly from the Great God himself. After a few hiccups, the populace had taken it in stride. Aeswiren was popular, but in prosperous times the city was content to let his son step up. Aeswiren had ruled for a long time, and people had forgotten the chaos of Kisirim and Shmeg. Perhaps a change could be beneficial. Thus went the smug sort of thinking that ruled in the city's merchant class. Once things had settled down and enough hearts had been tossed into the maw of He Who Eats, then business would pick up again.

And now Aeswiren faced further betrayal in Gzia Gi. Lords Bizg and Faroon had withdrawn their support. The city merchants, seeing which way the wind was blowing, had quietly shut up their houses and gone inland. They would wait out the coming struggle and return only when Bodo had finished his work in the city.

Now he was confronted with these weaklings like the duke and the Count of Koluso. They were terrified. Though they were honor bound to heed his summons, they could not be trusted to muster their forces for him. Now came their whining apologies.

"There just isn't the time to make proper preparations," said the count, trying to keep the stammer out of his voice.

Koluso owed Aeswiren for his own rise to a title, but he saw that the Emperor's cause was failing quickly, right across the Empire. Koluso already feared the coming of the priests. They might have reasons for taking his heart anyway, since he was long associated with the Emperor. But they had no cause yet to confiscate his family's holdings. Yet if he took the wrong side then all would be lost and his sons and daughters would follow him onto the altar of the Great God.

"The priests were working on this long before we suspected anything . . ."

"My men are afraid of the Red Tops."

Aeswiren tried to rouse himself.

"Damn it, all I'm hearing from you is defeat. We can beat them. Give me twenty thousand men, and I'll take Shasht back in less than two years."

An uncomfortable silence ensued.

"Lord, I do not think we can scrape up twenty thousand men. Perhaps fifteen thousand."

"Not even that. I have but two thousand retainers now. At the most we could put nine thousand in the field," said the duke gloomily.

"My lord, face it, we cannot forge an army before the Red Tops get here with their priestly battalions." Koluso sounded almost frantic with fear.

" 'Tis said they have forty thousand on the march to Gzia Gi."

"They will burn the city, sell everyone into slavery."

"Not if we refuse to give them good cause," said the duke.

Everyone knew what that meant.

"Damned cowardice," said the baron. "What of our honor?"

"Baron, your title was a creation of Norgeeben no more than a century ago. My family has held Palia since the days of Kashank. We have learned a few things in that time, and one of them is that you don't survive by backing the wrong side against the priests."

"The priests! The fornicating, sodomistic priests! God, I hate them!" snarled the baron slamming his fist onto the table. "And all you want to do is kiss their goddamn arses!"

"We all hate them, Baron, but if our families are to survive and to keep their lands, we must bow to their will."

Aeswiren heard these words and knew that he was doomed. The noble families of Gzia Gi had been deeply penetrated by the spies and emissaries of the Old One. What Aeswiren had regarded as his bastion, from which to mount a counterattack, had been turned into contested territory. By the time he could bring all of Gzia Gi under his control and put together an army of sufficient size, he would be overwhelmed by the host that was marching from Shasht.

The meeting ended with no firm conclusions reached. Palia and Count Koluso could not contemplate raising their standards for the Emperor's cause. The baron had but a few hundred banner men with him, but he placed these at

Aeswiren's disposal. Aeswiren could barely speak. He turned and headed for his private cabin.

Inside, gazing out the narrow port at the distant city, he allowed his bitter thoughts to flow. He had been outwitted, just like so many men before him in the exact same position. The Old One had penetrated the Hand, the Old One had probably known all his plans from the beginning. The Old One had even given him his chance to save himself. Just hand over the female captive, and all would have been forgiven. But that would have meant condemning Nuza to die on the altar. Aeswiren would not do that!

He was ruined, there was no question about that. Gzia Gi had been his hidden card, his secret weapon. Alas, it had been no secret to his enemy. There was nothing left but to contemplate the end.

Quickly he wrote out his final orders. Captain Moorsh was to take the *Duster* around the world to the Land and see Nuza safely to the shore. After that he was freed of any further obligation. The men who had followed their Emperor thus far were to disperse, to hide themselves and their families, or to sail on the *Duster* if they preferred. He dried the ink, folded the paper, and sealed it with his heavy signet ring.

There was no choice, and time was slipping away. He could die by the hand of the Old One, or he could die by his own hand and deny that old bloodsucker the satisfaction.

Aeswiren pulled the sword from his belt and held it up before his eyes. It caught the tawny light of the day. A good Gzia blade, forged twenty-five years before in the aftermath of his victory at Koonch. He had wielded it in battle only once, at Kaggenbank, but he recalled that it had felt good in his hand that day. It still bore the marks of the fight, the scratches and a slight notch halfway down. Aeswiren had preferred to leave those marks on the blade, to remind himself that it was not the purely ceremonial sword of some prince who'd inherited his throne.

He turned it deftly and placed the point against his chest.

Now, how was one supposed to do this? The trick was to keep the blade straight against your ribs while you fell and drove it all the way through. That way your own weight die the work, and it was over in a moment.

It was not the end he had hoped for. He had tried to be a good Emperor, and to some extent he had succeeded. Restoring order and peace, he had overseen a growing prosperity. But he had lacked in religious fervor. He had not been able to truckle to the Old One. And so he had fallen and was left only with this final act.

"No!" A figure flew across the room. "My lord!" Nuza clutched his wrist, tugging the sword point away from his chest.

For a long moment he stared at her with the sword in his hand. Because of her and her outlandish, inhuman beauty, he had lost his throne.

"Leave me!" he grated. "It is time to die."

"No, my lord, you may not!"

Through a slight mist of tears he saw her, and then his anger broke to the surface like lava erupting through the ground.

"Begone! This is the work of men." He spun her away with a hard shove and then turned the sword, took it in both hands, and set it to his belly.

Far from being discouraged, Nuza sprang at him, her arms wrapped around his waist. He was borne back against the table, lost his balance, and fell to the floor with an oath.

She was sitting across his waist, leaning into his face, absorbing his fury.

"No, my lord, please, don't take your life."

"Who are you to forbid me! I am Aeswiren the Third."

"Exactly, and that is why you cannot waste your life."

"What?" He hurled her back. "By the purple ass of the Great God, get away from me. Don't you understand? I will not be taken to the altar alive. I will not look into the eyes of my enemy and see him gloat over my defeat. Do you hear me?"

He was roaring now, lost in miserable rage. He got back to his feet, seized her by the arm, and let the sword tip rest on her bosom.

She stared back into his eyes, unafraid.

"Sweet Aeswiren, Lord of Shasht, ruler of men, do not

take your life. Kill me if you wish, but before you do listen to my words."

He hesitated for a moment and recalled the strange silence at the field of Kaggenbank after the battle was over. That moment had always haunted him. It was then that he had known for certain that he would be Emperor. He swallowed, then shrugged.

"Speak, then."

"You can still save many lives. In my land, where there is still war. You can stop that fighting. You can use the men there to rebuild your strength. Take this ship. Captain Moorsh is loyal, he and his crew love you. You can sail to the Land. Announce yourself to the men there. They will stop fighting if you so order it. Live there in peace with my people. Together we could defeat any further attack from Shasht."

He stared at her. It seemed like madness. Sail off to the far side of the world. Ally himself with her people. They weren't even human!

He laughed for a moment, saddened by his own unconscious prejudice. They weren't human, but they were intelligent, soulful by all accounts, worthy of the name "people." But that wasn't what his race were brought up to think.

"Stop the war, eh?"

"And forge an alliance with Toshak and the Kings. You must meet great Toshak; you and he would understand each other, I am sure. You share the same kinds of power."

She had spoken often of this one, this Toshak, their general.

"It won't be quite so simple, my dear," he said.

"You are still Aeswiren. I believe you can defeat your enemy and regain your throne."

Aeswiren's mocking reply died in his throat. Her intelligence was penetrating. They had discussed many things now. He could not dismiss her idea so easily.

"Well, I must thank you, dear Nuza. Thank you for having such belief in me. Even if you are the last to believe in me."

His head was hanging slightly. It aroused a fury in her.

"No! You cannot surrender. You owe this to the world.

Your army has done much harm, but you can heal the wound. You and you alone have the power to do this. Yours is the name those men fight under."

He stared at her for a long moment. Did she know what she asked of him? Or how risky it all was? Nebbeggebben would not be pleased at the arrival of his father on the scene. Gaining the automatic allegiance of the army wasn't guaranteed, either. But he was Aeswiren. She was absolutely right. Those men had sworn their allegiance to him. They knew him as a leader in battle. They would turn to him.

And then, well, he pursed his lips. If he had an army behind him it would be a different world, because he would turn that army around, come back to Shasht, and use it as the core of a force that would rid Shasht of the Old One and the priests in one swoop. Once he had even five thousand battle-hardened soldiers under his command, things would be different. Then the Gzia nobility would find their courage, and they would rise for him and put thirty thousand Gzia swordsmen into the field. Give Aeswiren those kind of numbers, and he'd soon have Bishop Bodo's head on a pike.

"I don't care what you say about your Spirit, the Old Gods must have sent you." He enveloped her in his big arms and hugged her hard to his chest.

Chapter 45

For Simona the first few days were filled with constant apprehension. Thru was hiding in an empty stall in the far corner of the stables. These stalls had no horses but stored a few odd items. Thru made himself a tiny cave, lined with straw, behind an old broken chariot.

However, Simona knew that the stable slaves weren't stupid, and that sooner or later they would discover Thru. He had to come and go to find water and steal food. Each time he moved, he became more vulnerable.

Simona lived moment by moment, always expecting the cry of alarm.

Then, at last, Shalee reported that Hilltop had been provisioned and partially opened for winter use. The upper floors were still sealed. Simona was free to move up there whenever she thought best.

Of course, even with the crisis, the social round in the zobbi had continued. Keeping to her plan, Simona had attended two luncheons and a grand feast for the First Snow thrown by the Count of Ekshash. She had kept a bright smile on her face and ignored gossip about her father, as much as possible. Plenty of wounding jibes still came from the haughty, but ignorant, true-bloods. But she ignored the "sawbones" references and everything else, determined to be seen in society but only briefly, thus camouflaging her existence.

And back at the house she tried not to think about poor Thru, hiding out in the cold dark of the outer stables. He'd told her to trust him, he would not be seen, but still she felt pure terror at the thought that he would be taken by the stable slaves.

Shalee's report brought a blessed relief. That afternoon Simona was scheduled to ride, and after a brisk work out on the park she returned with Silvery to the stables. As usual she stayed to brush the horse and talk to her. They had been apart for far too long. Silvery was her favorite mount, and Simona had been so happy to find her horse in good condition. They shared a special bond. And now, once again, they would be sundered, for Simona would walk up to Hilltop, with a donkey to carry her things.

When the bell rang in the kitchen to announce the late afternoon meal, the stable slaves hurried off. Simona slipped into the darker, remote part of the stables. She searched the stalls, looking for the one holding a broken chariot.

One stall stored blocks of wood, another had some charred beams awaiting reuse, then a row of empty stalls. She was starting to lose hope, when at last, she found it, close to the end of the row.

She stepped inside. There was no sign of Thru, although she did see straw heaped along the back wall.

"Thru?"

No response. He was gone. Then she realized he would have timed his own movements for the moment when the stable slaves went to their supper. Disappointed, and wondering how she was going to get him a message without anyone knowing, she turned to leave the stall and almost ran into a slender figure waiting there.

"Simona?" it said.

"Thru, oh, thank the Gods."

Thru chuckled. Simona's Gods had nothing to do with it.

They embraced, she was transported by his hug. She hadn't touched a human being for so long. Or felt any love or affection other than the kindly benevolence of Aunt Piggili. But her warm emotions faded as she realized that Thru was thinner than she remembered and from his hard shoulders to the lean hunger in his face he was male.

It was a shock, because they had embraced before and she had spent many days and nights alone with him. However, back then he had been completely alien, and she had missed the masculine component. Now she felt uncomfort-

able and moved away with a little start. A life's training in
the mores of purdah brought on an inevitable reaction.

Thru let her go.

"I didn't mean to startle you. I heard someone coming
so I moved."

"I'm just so glad to find you. I was worried that you
wouldn't be here. Listen, the house at Hilltop is provisioned and ready. I'm going up there tomorrow. I travel
alone with just a donkey to carry the bags. Shalee is the
only one who really knows anything about this. But there
should be enough food for us to survive the winter."

"Thank you, Simona. I put my trust in you."

"Yes, well, the big problem will be staying warm."

"We will find what we need. As long as there is some
food, we will be all right."

His quiet confidence encouraged her greatly. They made
their plans, exchanged another, more formal sort of hug,
and she left well before the stable slaves finished their second cups of chai and were chased out of the cosy kitchens
by the house slaves.

She slept that night more soundly than she had in days.

After packing her things she met with Shalee to review
the plan. The zob would remain open, but invitations would
now be returned. Parties in these later stages of the festival,
after First Snow were much less important. She had shown
her face at enough events and said greetings with aunts and
uncles of the Gsekk clan. From here on she could safely
shut herself away and avoid seeing anyone. If anyone was
to ask, she had gone back to the city.

The donkey was loaded by Shalee himself, round the
back of the little private garden that he kept near the but-
tery. She went up the walled lane to the back road. As far
as they could tell, no one saw her leave.

In a few more days, when the festival was truly over,
Shalee would send a maid in a carriage over to Aunt Piggili's house and he would announce that Simona had left
the zob. Then the zob would be "closed down" except for
the slaves and servants' quarters.

Simona walked quickly up the north trail. She wore riding breeches under her heavy robe and leather boots with

felt bootees inside. Around her there was still a little snow on the ground, although much of the first fall had melted away. There would be more, and soon, and then this trail would be impassable.

The path wound past the woodlots. She paused beside an ancient ash pollard and looked back to the zob. The chimneys thrust up from the heavy roof, a glass window on the west side caught a gleam from the sun, and for a moment she saw a rainbow in the glitter. Leaving the house brought an ache to her heart. This was the place she had always been happiest. Now it was denied to her again, perhaps forever. Suddenly she seemed very alone in the winter landscape with nothing but trees all about. She went on.

And then, perhaps an hour later, she spotted him coming down the trail toward her. In the light of day she could see the changes that the past year had wrought in him. His face had fresh scars and a lean bitterness that had not been there before.

"I scouted up toward the house. No one is there."

"You went all the way to Hilltop?"

"No, only to the second ridge. The house is quiet."

Which meant he had covered about ten miles already that day. Simona recalled the endurance he'd shown during their week together in the Land, traveling alone, learning each other's language. It was the same Thru.

And he lived! But Nuza did not know.

Now, oddly, they went along in silence, with only the wind's soft howl through the bare branches. Simona was trapped with her dilemma once again. She had not told Thru about Nuza being in the city. She had not told him because she knew that if she did, he would go back to the city and try and find her. Simona had seen something of the passion in Nuza's heart and understood that Thru would be the same. Nothing except his own death would hold him back once he knew.

So she could not tell him, because if he left the mountains he would be killed. The priests would be tearing up the whole country, sifting out rebellious elements.

And selfishly she feared that if Thru left her, then she would be left alone on the mountain.

For Thru this was a happy silence. He had found Simona. His plan, ever since leaving the city, had been to find her. He strode along, impervious to the cold. He'd caught a rabbit that morning and eaten some of it raw. The rest was cached up a tree along the way. He planned to cook it that night. Back home it would have been risky to cache meat up a tree like that. Not that cats would touch it, but coons and grey foxes could both climb. However, scavengers like that did not exist in the bare woods of Shasht. With only the occasional fox, some small woodland cats, and distant wolves to the north, he was sure his kill would still be there when they reached the tree.

Simona seemed in reasonable spirits, although he knew she must be worried for her father's sake. She had described what was going on in the city to him when they were first together, in the snow that day. The Red Tops were out hunting for deviants and slackers, fodder for the altar of the Great God.

Thru had nodded. Now even the men of Shasht knew what it was like to be fugitive in this accursed land. It seemed fitting, somehow.

They came over the first ridgeline. The second ridge rose up ahead of them, higher than the first, flecked with patches of snow.

"I've been thinking," she said. "It might be best if we moved on to Mount Beegamuus right away. We can use the donkey to carry provisions."

"Beegamuus is the farther place you mentioned?"

"Yes. It is seven miles past Hilltop to Mount Beegamuus. The lodge there is small, just a couple of rooms, but there is a chimney. It is used in summer sometimes, but not much lately. I stayed up there once by myself, when I was fifteen. My mother was very cross with me when she found out. It was wonderful up there, though. I was completely alone, and I didn't have to worry about anyone watching me."

Thru marveled at such strange problems. The world of purdah and sexual exclusion was difficult for him to understand.

"So we stay in first house just one night?"

"Yes, then go on to Beegamuus, before the snow gets deep."

"You think they're less likely to go all the way to Beegamuus than to Hilltop?"

"If they come to Hilltop they will find nothing. They will not know about Beegamuus."

Not unless they tortured Shalee, of course. But if they found Hilltop empty, they would face another seven miles of travel through deep snow to reach the higher lodge.

Thru nodded. If the enemy learned of his existence, they would come all the way to the highest mountain in Shasht. But if they sought only Simona, then perhaps they would be deterred by more hard slogging through deep snow. It could work, but he would keep his eyes open anyway.

"We will have to make several journeys to take the food from Hilltop to Beegamuus."

"A donkey will be a help."

"We'll have to feed him through the winter, too."

"There must be feed for him at first house, yes?"

Thus engrossed in the details of their planning, they crossed the Spelt stream on the high bridge and then wound their way up the steep slope to Hilltop. Along the way they paused by Thru's cache tree. He astonished her by climbing into the branches and coming down with a small parcel tied up in hide.

"A rabbit I took this morning. We'll eat it tonight."

Soon they came in sight of the house. Thru whistled to himself. Hilltop was as big as Pern Treevi's showy house back home. It had two floors under a long roof, which he could see was steeply pitched to keep the snow off. Verandahs surrounded the ground floor, and the front steps were cut from white stone. It was lavish. Perhaps small compared to the zob, with its three separate wings, but impressive to a simple village mot.

The house was dark, but the door was unlocked. The shutters were not locked, either. They soon opened things up a little.

Thru examined the supplies that Shalee had had brought up. The old slave had been very thorough. The storeroom contained sacks of wheat, sacks of oats, two whole hard cheeses each three feet across, five wheels of dried sausage, a barrel of dried apples, another of dried prunes, two large crocks of cooking oil, a stone jar of salt, and a sack of black tea. There was even a sack of good tinder! Shalee had thought of almost everything. Thru judged that it would be just enough to get the two of them through the winter if it was augmented with a few rabbits.

For an hour or more they busied themselves gathering wood from the surrounding trees. Hilltop hadn't been used in recent years with Simona's family away in the Land, so a lot of fallen wood was available. They built a fire in the fireplace in the kitchen. Simona made griddle cakes, and Thru roasted the rabbit. Later they slept, rolled up in their blankets on the kitchen floor.

After Hilltop, the lodge on Mount Beegamuus was sturdy but less lavish. However, Thru saw that with a little work it would offer them shelter through the worst of the winter.

The good weather lasted another week and all the snow from the First Fall melted away. Thru used that period well. They brought over food and some fuel from Hilltop. They scoured the nearby woods for firewood, and they brought down hides from a storeroom and nailed them up inside the shutters. They filled cracks and gaps in the exterior walls with mud and mashed oak leaves. They cut and transported bundles of reeds from the pond a mile to the north and laid them across the floors on the second floor to help hold the heat in the ground floor. Thru trapped mice around the storage bins. Simona was not ready to eat mice, not even when they were cleaned and grilled thoroughly, but Thru had grown accustomed to eating just about anything during his life in the wilds of Shasht.

Day in and day out they worked. Mount Beegamuus lodge was set well above Hilltop at an elevation higher than most of the purple hills to the east. Only a few other small mountains to the west stood higher than Beegamuus. Up on the mountain Thru understood that their survival depended on getting all their preparations done before the snow really became thick. Therefore, every minute of daylight was precious.

Thru stacked the wood, but only split a small amount.

That was something that could be left to later. They bundled twigs and kindling, though, and stacked them as high as the roof on the west side of the house. They were fortunate in discovering some large limbs that had been on the ground for a few years. Dried out, cut, and stacked they would burn well.

Rummaging through Hilltop's endless storage closets, Thru found a small bow, with a quiver of a dozen arrows. Not a warrior's weapon, the bow was for a child or a young woman, and the wood and arrows were still good. For small game it was perfectly adequate for someone as skillful in the woods as Thru Gillo.

A light snow fell on the morning of the sixth day, and a nip chilled the air that night. Thru went over to Hilltop once more for a final search of useful things. Once deep snow fell, it would be very hard to get to Hilltop from Beegamuus.

Thru was already planning to make snowshoes and had found some tools in an upstairs drawer at Hilltop. He had also found a good supply of tight twine, waxed twine, and light rope. The rope interested him because it was woven of flax linen.

In another upstairs room at Hilltop he had found some thread and yarn. These were formerly used by the genteel women of the house, who would weave and embroider on the south gallery while Gsekk men rode the woods in search of game. The colors were faded a little, but kept in the darkened room, the damage was slight. He ran his hands over the spools of yarn. The red threads were still bright. The feel of the coarse thread under his fingers was similar to that of waterbush fiber.

That day he investigated the cellars again. Hilltop had been built seven hundred years before, by the Baron Gsekk of his day. Vast amounts of stuff was hoarded away. The attics were extensive. Beds, wardrobes, chairs of all sizes and shapes.

And in one room, underneath a pile of cloth, he found a loom. He recognized it instantly. It had a shedding stick and heddle rod. The frame was made of oak, the working parts were in lighter woods. Closer investigation revealed that the heddle rod needed replacing. He thought that he could do that with one of the straight rods he'd taken from the wood store in the carpenter's shop out by the stable.

Thru removed the cloth and debris that covered the frame. Then he pulled the loom to pieces. The oak frame was the only heavy part. He let the donkey bring that over to Beegamuus while he himself carried the thread, spindles, shed stick, and heddle, plus many other smaller items.

The next day heavy and moist southern air blew in. That evening grew colder and during the night heavy snowflakes began falling from skies covered in hurrying cloud. By morning it was a foot deep. By mid afternoon two feet had fallen. True winter had arrived.

Thru spent part of the day setting up the loom in a corner. He replaced the broken heddle rod and then added another pair. For the kind of work he had in mind, he would need a complex setting. Whereas he had usually worked with a weaving frame, or weighted warp loom when weaving before, he had been turning toward the use of shedding and heddle as a way of improving the consistency of his textures. Mesho had worked that way, and his art was the highest ever reached in those terms.

Simona sat nearby, sewing together a set of heavy underclothes. Thru had left her with no illusions about how cold it would be at this elevation. They would need many sets of underclothes, socks, gloves, and tight-fitting caps. Simona had learned her sewing from her mother and was good enough for these basic needs.

Fortunately they received good light from the windows, which Thru had been surprised to find were all glassed in on the ground floor. The Gsekk family had obviously been wealthy for a long time.

When all was ready Thru began to weave, working up a simple tabby pattern in pale yellow and red.

Simona put down her sewing and moved closer to watch. He worked from then to the end of the day, and was already enjoying the subtle differences of the linen from bushfiber.

Simona listened to the soft whispering sound of fingers on weft and warp with shedding stick opening and heddle closing the weave. Outside the silence indicated that the snow had stopped falling.

For a long while they were united like this. Thru established the warp and began to work in the weft. Excellent colors were available for another "Chooks and Beetles," and he was excited by the different feel of the thread.

At last he stopped, fingers cramping.

"The snow has stopped," said Simona.

"Let's take a look," suggested Thru.

They opened the back door enough to get out with shovels and clear the snow along a path through the back cloister. They would leave the snow at the front unmarked, in case anyone climbed up to the lower ridgeline to examine the lodge through a spyglass.

From above the rear court they looked out the gate to a world buried in drifts up to four feet deep. For now, they were safe.

Chapter 46

The water was warm, inviting, perfectly clear right across the lagoon. Palm trees waved past the glitter of the sands. Nuza rose to the surface, turned over, and languidly pushed herself toward the shore.

The island was five hundred miles from Shasht, uninhabited, marked on only a few charts. Captain Moorsh had anchored here to take on fresh water, fruit, and green stuff. Ahead of them lay a much greater voyage, with no habitable islands for several thousand miles, and the *Duster* had not been able to revictual in Gzia Gi.

Nuza was glad of the break from the sailing across endless ocean and very glad for the chance to swim. Another part of herself had come back to life. Since leaving Shasht, she had sensed a reawakening of things within herself that she had shut down during the captivity. She had found hope again, and strongest of all was the hope that she might see her homeland once more.

She turned over and swam down into deeper water. The lagoon was so clear you could see right across it to the banks of coral. A school of bright yellow and blue fish shot away from her. A larger fish followed them at a more leisurely pace.

She rolled, tumbled in slow motion, and touched the bottom with her fingertips, disturbing fine sediments into whorls of white haze. Now she swam by undulating her body, like a fish, legs kicking just from the ankles.

The water shallowed toward the shore, and she rose to the surface to take a breath. Her feet touched bottom. As she walked out of the water she shook her body, just like any furred animal, and threw spray all around her.

Aeswiren watched her. She sensed his eyes on her. She knew the look that would be in them, the strange emotions that she read there. He was in "love" with her, he said, as he had never loved a woman of his own kind. There was something troubling and oddly bewitching about this. Perhaps just because it gave Nuza some power in her life, something that had been missing for a long time.

But there was no sense of disgust. Even though she knew he was a "bare skin," even though he smelled "wrong" to her and had the strange "hair" that grew dark and long on his head. Despite all that, she felt no disgust at his touch. And she wondered about that. Aeswiren was like a father to her, or a favorite brother, or Toshak, who was like both. She had loved Toshak, but love was not enough for that intense, driven soul. Could she love Aeswiren?

He was not Thru Gillo, he was not even a mot, and she could not find sexual interest in him, but as a person, as a friend, she had great affection for him. And this made everything even more complicated.

When he held her hand or stroked her cheek, there was an emotional charge so strong and intimate that she could not pull away. Though she knew that it stoked an erotic flame for him. The thought was mixed with fear and fascination. Sometimes she thought she should forbid the contact, but it was the only contact she had with anyone and it was not unpleasant. Moreover Nuza had never been one to think anything intimate between male and female to be indecent or unpleasant, unless it was coerced like rape.

It was all part of the changes, she'd decided. Changes that had altered everything in the last few weeks. She had watched Aeswiren undergo a distinct change. He still seemed calm, but he had shed some layer of civilization, a veneer that had kept his real self in check. There was a controlled fury in him now that everyone could sense. Nuza was glad she was his friend and not his enemy. This Aeswiren was closer to the man who had mounted to the throne atop a mound of corpses.

She saw how this power flowed from him, invisible but unbreakable. The men who had joined him after Gzia Gi obeyed him without question. The Baron Thuam and the others were all ready to give their lives for him. Captain Moorsh was the same, as were his officers and crew. This was the man who had commanded armies and written campaigns of blood and glory across the entire Empire of Shasht.

And she knew that she had strange, mixed reactions to that power in him. Something in her wanted to worship it. Even wanted to take up the sword for him. But another side of her was distressed by that idea and wanted nothing to do with war. She'd seen the face of war and was not enamored of it. That side of her was disgusted by her positive response to that power he had.

And braided within these emotions was the knowledge that Aeswiren and his strength were the only thing that could save the Land. Nuza had seen Shasht. She understood the vast imbalance in might between Shasht and the small kingdoms of the Land. Toshak and his army might hold off the first invasion, but Shasht would keep coming and the Land would be overrun and lost forever. Unless, Aeswiren triumphed. In which case the course of history would be changed.

"My lord," she said, copying the form that everyone else adopted with him in casual surroundings, and took up the robe he had given her, which was hanging on a palm tree beside him.

"My dear, if they could see you right now even the priests would find it hard to contemplate killing you."

Indeed, Nuza was naked and unashamed of that fact. Her body was beautiful, her breasts like that of a young woman, but covered in fine soft fur, her nipples a paler color than was usual with women, her belly a lighter shade than her back, her thighs darker, with the clear outlines of the powerful acrobat's musculature that lay underneath. Aeswiren had seen more than his share of women's bodies, and he had seen none that were more lovely than Nuza's.

Now she wrapped the robe around herself.

"Do you think I should not swim?"

He laughed. "I think it's a good thing that my men are all occupied and cannot be witness to this." In fact, he was simply awestruck as she came closer, her hip swaying in a way that always captured the male eye. Gods! She was so beautiful, his desire for her was strong, but there was always that difference. In her face and in that fur that covered every inch of her, but for her face. She was not a woman. She was mor.

"The Great God Himself, He Who Eats, he could not cope with the sight of you, not in the least." His laugh had a slightly bitter edge to it.

Confused for a moment, she stared at him with slightly slitted eyes. He joked sometimes and she didn't quite understand the joke. It referred to things that she thought must be sexual and that was an area of discomfort. For they were of different kinds.

"My dearest Nuza," he said. "Forgive me. You rise from the water like the Goddess Canilass rising from the sacred lake. I was left giddy by the vision."

She smiled again, reassured once more by his playful tone.

Aeswiren thought to himself that really, he'd done the right thing. He'd lost his throne because he wouldn't give up this beautiful creature, and he'd be damned if he'd do anything different, even with the knowledge he had now.

Of course he'd been too slow. But he was awake now. It was as if the fog that had descended on his mind during the years of government had evaporated at last. In time there would come the opportunity to gain revenge. And when he had won and put his sword through the heart of that foul, old thing he would kill a lot of those who should have stood by him in the crisis. And every damned priest would lose his head and every image of He Who Eats would be smashed and burned. When Aeswiren III was finished, Shasht would be remade and the temple pyramid would be no more.

Aeswiren had realized that the struggle would be renewed in the new world. The Old One could not rest knowing that Aeswiren had escaped Shasht aboard a ship. The Old One would have to lead an army to find Aeswiren and kill him. And Aeswiren would be ready for him when he came.

"Let us walk toward the hill, there are some extraordinary flowers there that you will enjoy."

They wandered along the top of the beach, shaded from the hot sun by the palm trees. Small insects whined occasionally through the warm air.

"How long will we stay here, my lord?"

"Captain Moorsh thinks we'll be away tomorrow, as soon as he's filled all his casks."

"Seems a pity to leave this place."

Aeswiren chuckled. "It does, I agree. At times I have thought that we should abandon our quest and just stay here and live out our lives in peace."

She flashed him a look, saw that he was not serious, and turned away reassured once more. He thought again of how there was still a gulf in understanding between them, but that it was closing, day by day.

They came on a patch where a plant with dagger-like leaves had thrown up thick spikes, each of which hosted a large, orange bloom.

"They are extraordinary," said Nuza. "I've never seen anything like them."

Struck by a sudden thought, Aeswiren cut one of the flowers and held it up to her cheek. "Take it," he said.

She held it up and sniffed its scent, her eyes closed, and his heart jumped. Aeswiren blinked. There was too much beauty here for his old head. He found himself on the verge of tears, and he had no idea why, except that he couldn't stand to watch this for a second longer.

"These flowers are unknown in my homeland, but if they were I think they'd be very popular."

But Aeswiren had turned away and with a strange cry he went bounding down the sands, tearing off his clothes, and hurled himself into the lagoon. He swam out with powerful strokes, his kicks raising a high spray.

Chapter 47

It was a cold, clear day in deep winter. Recent snow had thickened the drifts on the north slopes of the mountain, but a few deer trails were still passable. Thru was working the little trapline he'd set along the bank of a mountain stream. His snowshoes made it possible to move about quickly despite the four-foot drifts.

He found a rabbit with its neck broken in one of his snares. With a silent prayer to the Spirit, he cut it down and placed it in his game bag. Earlier in the day he had been lucky enough to get close to wood pigeons foraging for loose grain and had taken one with one of the stone-tipped arrows. Between this rabbit and the pigeon they had enough now for a couple of days if they were frugal. He made a mental note to check the mousetraps again. One of the storehouses had some soft wood in the underflooring, and the mice had taken advantage of this opportunity. Thru planned to replace the underfloor entirely, but the work would have to wait until spring. Until then he had to maintain a strict regime with the mice.

Suddenly he caught a faint howl on the wind from the north. He stopped moving, held his breath, and listened carefully.

There, again, he heard another faint howl, to the north, probably on the other side of the high ridge.

He knew these wolves, of course. They were the small pack that denned somewhere just to the north of Beegamuus, perhaps on Small Hummock Mountain. In this poor country the wolves had to range over a wide territory to find food in winter. The deer in these hills were very wary beasts.

He moved back up the mountain stream, leaving as little of a trail as possible. The wolves were very rarely heard in the daylight. There had to be a good reason for them to call.

His other traps were unsprung, so he pulled them up as he passed and hid them. With the rabbit and the pigeon, he had no need to hunt for a couple of days.

He soon reached the black crag that jutted up from the southern face of the mountain. He had thoroughly explored all this ground and knew a quick route to the top. He pushed his game bag well over his shoulder and climbed a short steep stretch that let him into a gulley that hurried up the next fifty feet. Soon he hauled out onto the flat stone just beneath the top. Now he had a great view off to the north, toward the sun in the southern hemisphere. Lake of the Woods could even be seen as a silvery gleam on the horizon.

Directly to the north was the high ridge, which shouldered off Mount Beegamuus for three miles in a northeast direction before ending at the river. Beyond the high ridge was the second ridge, visible as a darker grey mass, and beyond that was Hilltop.

Hilltop House was hidden beneath the brow of the hill, but a faint finger of smoke was rising from one of the chimneys. He watched for several minutes, but there was no doubting it, he saw a thin white line of smoke.

Thru shook his head. The enemy had not given up on them after all. He studied the valley, but saw nothing more than birds on the move above the trees. He had made a few preparations for this development; now he would make some more.

Later, back at the lodge, he used only the driest wood, pine twigs, and well-seasoned hornbeam branches, so as to generate as little smoke as possible. Simona cleaned and skinned the rabbit, then broke it up into quarters. She worked quickly, although she had only done this kind of work for the last two months. When the rabbit was done, she turned to the pigeon, which she plucked and cleaned. Most of the meat she rubbed with salt and placed in a small, tight barrel sealed with a clasp. Thru grilled a couple of pieces of the rabbit, and Simona put flat bread on the griddle and poured tea.

Normally Thru would meditate with the first cup of tea. He could feel the power within his body, and renewed it spiritually before eating the last meal of the day. Thru had picked up the habit at Highnoth. Simona had been learning the ways of Highnoth, too, and she had come to like this moment when they were alone, in peaceful meditation rather than conversation. She had learned how to take hold of her appetite and control it. Even though she was terribly hungry, she was learning to disregard it in a way she had never managed before. She felt herself growing stronger every day she lived with Thru Gillo.

On this day, though, he was agitated and meditation was impossible. His news was too important.

"I saw smoke coming from chimney at Hilltop."

"Damn!" She felt her face go red immediately. It was unladylike to curse, so her mother had always taught her. But now the fear had returned to her heart like a hammer. "They are still hunting us?"

Thru was not downcast.

"We are strong, well fed. We have food. We will survive even if we leave this place."

Simona thought of the snow-covered mountains outside with dread. Thru had told her about his life in the small cave in the hills just to the east of Beegamuus. Just surviving in such conditions would take everything they had.

"I will be ready," she heard herself say. Thru had exerted some magic of his own. Her will had been strengthened by this time spent with him.

Struck by the same concern, they both turned to look at the loom. His first attempt at "Men at War" was there, while hanging on the wall beyond it was the first piece, another of his series of great "Chooks and Beetles."

The work had gone slowly at first, until he grew familiar with the feel of the linen thread instead of the slightly stiffer fiber thread from waterbush. The pattern, of course, was an old friend and these chooks were even more crazed than usual while the beetles were filled with a sinisterness that was both amusing and a little frightening. The piece was both funny and yet spoke of the seriousness of the chooks' annual war in the fields against beetles and other insect pests.

The new piece, "Men at War," was perhaps a third completed. He had filled in the helmeted heads of the three men, leading the charge, with a forest of spears behind them. They wore simple steel helmets, and the rendering of the steel was still a problem. He had worked with black, white, and grey, and had had some success, but was not yet satisfied. The faces were contorted with hate, the eyes blazed with fury. Thru had seen enough fighting with men to have caught perfectly the terrible beauty of war.

"We will leave the work. Let them look at it before they destroy it."

"Destroy it?" Simona stood up, aghast. "We can't leave the 'Chooks and Beetles.' It is too beautiful." Indeed, Simona had never seen such skill with material. Thru's work was a masterpiece, as detailed as if he'd painted it with oils and tiny brushes.

He shrugged. With a weary smile he said, "Thank you, Simona for your pure heart and the love you have for the work. I am sad to leave it, but when we leave here, we will carry only food and some tools. Believe me, after we have gone ten miles we will not want to be carrying an extra ounce, let alone the full weight of the mat."

"At least, let us hide it."

"But then it might serve no purpose if no one ever found it. If we leave it where it is, then whoever pursues us will find it. Perhaps they will take it back to those who command them. Then it will force them to contemplate it, even if only for a few moments."

She stared at him for a moment and then she understood. "Yes, I see."

Let the men who drove this hateful persecution, let them see this beauty. Let it fill their heads with its strange images, the leering chickens, the huge, ominous insects. Let them react as they would. Even if they burned it, they would still have the image of it in their minds. They would know that Thru was no less than they, that indeed he was more alive than they were, more connected to the Spirit that inhabited all the world than they with their ridiculous, cruel God of blood sacrifices.

They ate their meal with the usual hungry gusto. Living like this, cold most of the time, fueled a hearty appetite. As always Simona finished the last scrap, thinking she could eat the whole thing over again twice and not be full.

They cleaned up, scouring the plates with sand then wiping them with hot damp cloths. Thru lit two lamps and took up the weaving, and Simona came and sat beside him, and they talked of what they would have to do.

Even though he knew that his work was doomed, Thru put all of his passion into laying more lines of his portrait of human warriors.

To sit like that, as they had most nights since arriving up here on the mountaintop, was enormously comforting. She realized that it might not be so comfortable again for a long time. She marveled internally at how she'd adapted to this hard life.

She felt as though she'd become the wife of a good-hearted craftsman. Except, of course, that they did not make love like man and wife; however, Simona secretly had begun to wonder what it would be like. She had seen Thru naked, knew that he was just like men in those regards. Just looking at his body excited her, with the hard muscles so tightly defined on chest and shoulders. At times of frustration Simona would find herself aching to know what it was like to make love, to be gripped in the heat of passion. At times she thought that she would die without ever knowing it. Sometimes these feelings made her snap angrily at Thru or behave coldly, though she knew he deserved far better, and always ended up feeling guilty and remorseful.

And she had often reflected that Thru was better to her than most men would ever have been. He was thoughtful, unfailingly kind and patient. Without him she knew she could not have survived on Beegamuus. Someday, she hoped she could repay him, somehow. But she did not like to think about the future. Too many threatening clouds hovered on that horizon.

She put her hand up to the "Chooks and Beetles" hanging on the wall.

"It makes me sad to think that someone might destroy this beautiful thing."

Thru did not seem fazed by the idea.

"If it makes them think, even for a moment, about what they are doing, then it will have repaid me for the labor of making it."

"What will we do about the donkey?"

"Well, we can't take it through the deep snow. We can wear snowshoes and make good time. The donkey will have to go back with the men. Don't forget, the Red Tops don't have snowshoes. They are probably digging a path through the snow to get here."

Simona nodded. She didn't want the men to get even the donkey. But it would solve the problem of the donkey's feed, which had been worrying her. There wasn't enough for the whole winter, not at the rate Thru was feeding the animal.

"They must hate us very much to go to such trouble."

"They need their hate. It gives them their strength. Without it they would have nothing."

They slept soundly, huddled together under the blankets, but in the middle of the night Thru awoke, hearing the wolves crying again. They were back at the den on Small Hummock Mountain, and they were calling back and forth with other wolves, much farther south and perhaps to the west as well, though Thru could not be absolutely sure of that because of the distance.

He rose, put on his outer leggings, boots, and tunic and went out to watch and listen more carefully. The moon was high in the sky and three quarters full, and by its light he quickly retraced his steps to the crag. Too dark to attempt climbing the quick way, he simply trudged up the long route. At the top he stilled his own breathing and listened intently.

For a while there was nothing but silence, then he caught it again, a faraway howling, wolves farther north than Small Hummock, deeper into the hills. He'd seen that pack once, there were seven wolves, but he did not know where they denned, except somewhere much farther south.

While he strained to hear the distant cries, he studied the northern approaches to Mount Beegamuus. Under the moonlight the dark slopes of the high ridge were dappled with brilliant streaks of snow, while the valleys were rivers of darkness under the trees.

How long would they have? He had packed food, warm clothing, and the most essential tools. Even a bundle of dry pine twigs. In the morning they would set off, and head east, back into the hills that he'd explored before. The cave would serve the two of them. Not a comfortable life after living in Beegamuus lodge, but they did not have a choice. At least they had food and snowshoes.

The snow in the stream valleys was very deep now. The Red Tops would have a difficult march getting up to Beegamuus. While they struggled along, he and Simona would go the other way, southward, then curve around to the west on the Yellow Canyon River until it reached the wider river valley. Then they would strike out down the river. By his calculations that would take them to the edge of the country where he had lived when he first entered the hills. He knew those hills well enough.

Then a motion on the ridge caught his eyes, and his heart sank. Coming over the high mass of the ridge was a light, a torch. Another joined it, and another, and more. Beneath the torches he could just make out a dense struggling mass of men, wielding shovels, digging their way through the drifts. By the Spirit, there was an army of them! When the count reached twelve torches, he turned and hurried back to the lodge. The Red Tops had decided not to wait until daylight. The enemy really wanted to make sure of them.

Simona came awake in a moment and they hurriedly packed the rest of the food they planned to take plus all the blankets and an ox hide that Thru had rolled up and tied in a tight roll. They boiled hot tea, ate meal biscuits, and washed them down with the tea, then set off.

When it was all on her back, Simona realized just how heavy it was going to be. Flour, beans, the meat barrel, it all added up. She took a breath and renewed her determination. She would survive.

Thru had the escape route worked out in his head. They went out down the east chute, a steep little vale that opened onto a rock-filled canyon, deeply drifted with snow.

The drifts were crusted and firm, they had no difficulty in staying on the surface in their snowshoes and made relatively good time considering their burdensome packs.

Thru wondered how the Red Tops would pursue them here. If they didn't have snowshoes, it would take them a long time to get down this streambed. The moon fell below the horizon, and movement became more difficult for the final hour before dawn. The stars glittered brightly in the vault above in the bitter cold. Red Kemm was below the horizon.

Dawn found them on the lower slopes of Small Hummock Mountain at the opening of the Yellow Canyon, so named because of the ocher sandstone that lined its northern side.

They were well beyond Simona's family zob now, on land that belonged to another family, the Zempatti clan. Their big house was at the far end of the Yellow Canyon, where it opened out into the valley of the River Esk. Simona had been to Zempatti zob several times when she was a girl. The Zempattis were good friends of her parents. However, the big house would not be open at this time of the year. Elgh Zempatti was a lay deacon of the pyramid. He had to be in the city for the festival season.

Thru asked Simona questions about the land ahead, especially the crossings of the River Esk.

"There are two bridges that I know about. One carries the Emperor's road, and it has a guard post all year-round, because they collect taxes on that bridge, and the other is a bridge on the road to Yamich, a small village."

Thru was impressed. "You must have been observant when you were young."

"You don't know what it's like to be shut up in the purdah wagon. I always wanted to know everything about the places we visited. When we went to Zempatti, there was more purdah than in our own home. So I was not allowed outside the house and the women's garden. It has a high wall, and any woman of noble birth found outside it has to be impaled and her remains cremated and scattered in the wind. It says so right on the wall, carved there by the men who built it."

Thru's eyebrows rose involuntarily, as they did so often when Simona told him about the strange way of life called purdah. To have one half the population permanently locked indoors, restricted and kept almost useless, struck him as fundamentally insane. It was so strange that he could not comprehend why men would live this way.

They halted to eat some hard biscuit with cheese and dried herbs. They washed it down with water from the stream; Simona broke the ice with a rock to get to it. The water was so cold that it stung her hands at first, but she warmed the tin cup against herself until the water could be drunk.

While the cold was still causing an ache in her throat, she marveled at herself for a moment. Here she was talking of purdah and she was outside all restrictions, wearing men's clothing and accompanying a single male. Not exactly the way of life her mother had brought her up to enjoy!

She laughed. Thru's eyebrow rose in question, but she couldn't tell him what she was thinking.

"It's nothing." She put her mittens back on. "You said we would turn west here, and go down the Yellow Canyon."

Looking due west they could see the canyon wind through the foothills, on its way to join the river in the broader valley beyond. Much farther away, silhouetted against the strengthening light of dawn, were the hills on the far side of the Esk.

"That is where we go, to those hills."

Simona nodded. "I have never been that far, I don't even know what they're called. I do know that Shesh lies beyond them."

"Yes, I have seen it from those hills. We have a long walk ahead of us."

Now they went on up narrow trails cut in the same yellow sandstone that they saw glowing ahead of them in the early morning light. The canyon was steep-walled and stark.

The river splashing its way down a bed strewn with boulders and slabs of the same rock buried under snow. Dense thickets of alder grew here and there in the valley, making it almost impassable in places.

But Thru always found the deer trails. These weren't the easiest trails to follow for the two of them, burdened by their heavy packs, but they got through each barrier, no matter how impenetrable it appeared at first.

Later, hidden in a grove of aspens and small pines they stopped to eat more biscuit and cheese. The canyon had broadened out dramatically, and the River Esk was not far off.

"The big house is not far from here I think." She pointed south and east. I think it is over there, above the river. We always came in on the road from the south, which runs up along the riverbank. We could see the yellow canyon and then we would turn into the gate that leads to the house."

Simona wondered what her earlier self would have made of the way she was visiting the Zempatti zob this time. She shuddered slightly. She didn't want to think of it either. But it was hard not to contrast this visit with those summers of long ago. Riding up in the screened wagon, wearing her favorite summer dress made of silk the color of apricot, sitting with Mother and sometimes Aunt Piggili, and talking about the wonderful parties they would be attending for the next five days. Simona would be enjoying mango ice cream and meeting all the Zempatti girls, who she really liked. She shook her head to erase the vision. That life seemed so far away now, as if it belonged to another person. The Simona of the past had never planned on being snatched away to the new world to witness war and a multitude of other horrors. That little girl in her apricot silk dress had been so innocent, so naive, so protected that she was almost like another person. Even though she'd known that her world rested on the shoulders of a million slaves, she had thought that as long as she obeyed the rules and kept her head down, she would be allowed to live out her life in relative comfort, surrounded by books and art and intelligent conversation. Fate had not been so kind.

Thru, meanwhile had more practical concerns. The first

one of which was the river. Was it iced over? The fast-flowing stream in the Yellow Canyon was only partially iced, which worried him. The water was freezing and too cold to swim across. After studying the broader valley view very carefully, he turned back to her. The house was not far away, the pencil lines of smoke from its chimneys were visible.

The river was not yet iced over. The crossing would be difficult.

"Which of the bridges would be the nearest?" he said.

"The Yamich Bridge. It is much smaller than the imperial bridge of course. We always passed close by it when we came up toward the house."

"Is it in view of the house?"

"I don't think so, but I only came here in the summer, and then it's hidden by the trees from the main house."

"But it is unguarded?"

"As far as I know."

Chapter 48

With great care they worked their way through the ornamental shrubbery in the outer park of the great house. From the distance of half a mile, Thru thought that this house was not quite as large and showy as the great zob of Simona's family, but still it impressed him with its turrets and upper balconies. These country houses were all the size of the King of Dronned's palace. Just another indication of the difference in scale between Shasht society and that of the Land.

They left the house behind and went on through the woods, keeping parallel to the road, which was traveled by a few wagons, occasional parties of slaves and once, by a messenger on horseback who kept his mount to a fast trot and soon disappeared.

At length they reached the Yamich Bridge, which was wide enough to take a village cart. Across the bridge, tantalizingly near and yet so far, was the village of Yamich, visible as a cluster of dun-brown roofs.

Unfortunately, standing on the near end of the bridge was a party of six Red Tops. Wrapped in heavy robes with thick socks under their sandals, they chatted together while stamping their feet and swinging their arms. Now and then they looked up and down the road.

Clearly crossing this bridge was out of the question, at least for now. With a sinking feeling in his heart, Thru guided Simona farther downstream. At least the woods along the road were filled with dense underbrush so it was easy to stay out of sight of the Red Tops by the bridge.

A mile or two farther on, at the large stone imperial bridge, Thru's hopes of an easy crossing evaporated completely. Four more Red Tops stood guard alongside the two soldiers normally posted there.

Giving up for the moment, they moved farther south again and came to a low-lying area where thick beds of reeds lined the bank and the road moved inland for a ways. They made their way down into the reeds, and Thru pushed on to the water's edge to study the riverbanks.

The water was on the verge of freezing, fragile sheets of ice had already formed in the quieter sections. There were no boats to be seen on the river itself, but with a great feeling of frustration Thru observed a dozen boats of various sizes pulled up on the far shore.

Disconsolate, they ate some biscuit and cheese, drank from a small running stream, and hid themselves in the woods. They huddled together under their blankets in the cold. Simona rested her head on his shoulder, as she had done so many times and thought to herself how very normal this had become for her. Denied all contact with men of her own kind, she had been thrust into intimacy with a "man" who was not even human. And though they had traveled together before, spending more than a week on foot in the hills of Creton, they had not been forced into this desperate kind of intimacy. Now they held each other, just to get a little warmth into their bodies. For Simona, a well-bred girl of the upper class, this had been a considerable adjustment. No man other than her father had stroked her cheek or marveled at the color of her hair. But Thru Gillo had done these things often, and she had responded with occasional strokes of his own fur, usually on the back of his neck.

Thru waited until the sun was well down in the sky. Then they gathered up their burden and made their way cautiously back to the Yamich Bridge.

Thru's hopes rekindled. Only two Red Tops remained. The rest had either gone across the river, or up to the big house. Still, two Red Tops would not make this easy. He studied the bridge, watched the young men in their brown robes with their shaved and painted pates aglow in the late afternoon sunlight. His hopes became tempered by his determination to live.

After carefully studying the bridge, he turned to Simona. "Better we wait until dark. Perhaps when they get tired we can take them."

Simona felt her eyes widen. Take them? She knew that Thru, for all his gentle demeanor with her was well versed in violence. His face was covered in scars from combat. She'd been there when he'd killed a mot in the river in Creton. She, on the other hand, was not so trained. She doubted her ability to kill anyone, even a Red Top who wanted to kill her.

"Is there no other way?"

"No. We cannot swim, the water is too cold. All the boats are on the village side."

Thru understood that they were in a race against time as well. They had come all the way down from the deep snows of Mount Beegamuus on their snowshoes in just a few hours. But by this point the Red Tops would be getting close to the lodge on Beegamuus. The snowshoe trail would be still visible, and when that was reported, there would soon come an increase in the watch on these bridges. These Red Tops on the bridge at Yamich were clearly a precautionary move. The Red Tops might be searching for many people, after all. This was a "time of danger," as the folk of Shasht called it, a time when political enemies were likely to kill or be killed. So all bridges would be monitored as a matter of course. But once the Red Tops from Hilltop got here, the guard on the bridges would be massively reinforced. Thus, it was now or never.

From their hiding place, Thru keenly watched the Red Tops. The daylight waned. Thru estimated the Red Tops must have reached the lodge on Beegamuus by now. The word was being taken back to Hilltop, then down to the zob that the fugitives were no longer there.

A pair of ox wagons came down the road from the house and passed over into the village. With the wagons came a fresh pair of Red Tops who replaced the daytime pair. They went on into the village. That suggested to Thru that they had lodgings there somewhere. But the fact that the replacements had come down from the big house indicated that that was where the main group were based. Which was good news, because it was at least a mile back up the road.

Thru and Simona ate more biscuit and cheese and settled in to watch the bridge from concealment. Night fell, a wind blew down the valley. The Red Tops whistled, stamped their feet, and rubbed themselves against the cold. They talked longingly of warmer surroundings, of having a brazier, and of drinking something hot and alcoholic to ward away the chill. They were bored young men from the city, who until very recently had been loafing about the temple pyramid and enjoying life in general. Now they were far from home and far from warm.

Darkness grew complete. The moon had yet to rise above the central hills. The Red Tops lit a single torch that they raised on a torchère at their end of the bridge. It threw a flickering, uncertain light over their end.

Thru licked his lips. Thru had two arrows that were stout enough to kill a man with a good shot. And he would have to kill them, or else give up and move back up the Yellow Canyon and into the deep snowy hills. Into country that he had not explored before where it would be much harder to locate a cave and drinking water.

He explained his plan to Simona. She was to wait in the shadows while he went forward with the bow hidden under his cloak. If he succeeded, she was to join him. If he failed, she was to go south into the hills. They both removed their snowshoes, which would only be an impediment on the bridge.

With a deep breath he tried to calm his nerves. Then he stepped out of concealment onto the paved road and headed over it toward the bridge. The Red Tops were both looking the other way, toward the village, where a few amber lights glowed with an inviting warmth. They were wondering aloud about taking turns to go and get warmed up in the inn, leaving just one guard on the bridge. They wondered if they dared to risk it. If they were caught, they'd both get fifty strokes of the lash.

Step by step Thru went on, always expecting them to turn around and see him. He was well onto the bridge, moving into the sphere of light projected from the torchère.

Still they muttered together while looking toward the village. Now they were grumbling about the quality of the accommodations that had been set aside.

"A crib next to the damned pigs is what I heard, that's all."

"Typical, isn't it? The Gold Tops are on linen, and we're in with the fornicating pigs."

Thru's approach had grown stealthier now that he was past the halfway point. Each step without a challenge seemed like a miracle. He knocked the arrow, still kept beneath his cloak in front of him. Ten yards to go, then eight, then six, and now he was so close as to be absolutely sure of his shot. He shrugged away the cloak, raised the little bow, drew, and released in a single swift motion.

The left hand Red Top pitched forward with a sudden gasp as the arrow drove into his back. The other spun around, saw Thru, gave an inarticulate cry, and snatched for his sword.

Thru released, but his second arrow went a hairsbreadth wide when the Red Top slipped and went down on one knee. The shaft passed harmlessly past his nose. Drawing his knife Thru leaped toward him, determined to finish it quickly. The youngster came back up and flailed at Thru with his free hand. He'd forgotten to unclip the scabbard lock on the sword and was still tugging on it.

Surprised by this awkward response, Thru's killing thrust went awry and Thru slammed into the youth chest to chest. The Red Top got a hand on Thru's face and with a scream of fright shoved him away.

Thru came back immediately, ducking low and bringing the knife around in a killing stroke. This had to be ended quickly, in case the village was awoken.

Again the young man tried but failed to draw his sword, instead he snapped out a right hand jab that caught Thru squarely on the nose just before he could cut the man's belly. Thru sat down hard. The young man kicked him in the ribs, and he was knocked onto his side with the breath driven from his body.

The Red Top, still crazed with fear, finally realized why the sword wasn't coming free and slipped off the catch guard. He pulled the sword and turned back to kill the hairy thing that had attacked him.

And then there came a scream from the right and across the bridge came another figure, holding a bundle above its head, running right at the Red Top with mouth open and teeth gleaming in the torchlight.

The young man turned away from Thru, who was still struggling to draw a breath and faced Simona, who had started running as soon as she saw that Thru's second shot had missed. She was close though, barely six feet away, and now she threw her bundle at the Red Top, and with the momentum of her mad charge it tumbled right into his face.

With an inarticulate cry he fended it away with the sword arm and that gave Simona the opening to throw herself at him, grappling around the waist. The man was driven back a step. He was howling with fright as he struck down hard with the sword. Simona felt something hard and heavy strike across the pack cradle on her back and stumbled to the ground still clinging to his legs. Meanwhile the sword had sunk fast in the green wood that Thru had used for the pack cradles.

Still screaming thinly, the man kicked at her while he heaved on the sword to free it. She felt the thing release from her back, there was a foot pressing down on her head, and then she heard another scream, with a different timbre. The foot was removed. She turned her head and saw Thru holding the young man around the throat while he worked his knife back and forth in the Red Top's chest. Blood bubbled from the young man's mouth, he shuddered violently, and Thru let the body sag to the bridge.

She noted that Thru had blood running from his nose and spattering down onto the front of his robe.

"Go on," he mumbled thickly, "I have to get my pack . . ."

First, however, he bent down and took the young Red Top's sword.

She waited for him at the edge of the bridge, her heart pounding, her limbs trembling. She had done the unimaginable and physically attacked a man! For a woman of Shasht, this was an incredible thing.

Thru rejoined her and they ran, stumbling at times through the snow in the narrow lanes. Luckily for them, the shrill screams of the young Red Top hadn't yet brought much of a response. A few dogs barked while they scrambled through the narrow streets but they were almost out of the village before they finally heard some loud voices, and the first real calls of alarm—loud, prolonged hoots and hollers, didn't come until they were well outside the village and hurrying away up the dark road as fast as they could go.

After covering another mile on a road that was little more than a track paved with flints, Thru found a gap between walls and trees on one side and they pulled themselves up and into deeper snow. Behind them the village had many lights lit, and there was a constant, sustained barking of dogs. To Thru it brought on chilling memories. In the darkness, working with cold fingers, it was difficult to reattach the snowshoes, but in the end they managed and moved off deeper into the forest, heading in an easterly direction.

"Do you think they will chase us?"

"They will try."

"I wish that we had not had to kill them."

"I wish that, too. And I must thank you, Simona, you saved my life. That was very brave of you."

Impulsively she moved to hug him, though her arms could not go around the huge pack on his back. She kissed his bloody lips and drew back, startled for a moment by what she had done. She had never kissed a man, like this, not even her father.

Then Thru turned quickly and put his feet on the trail. The contact had ignited a combustible sea of longing. They had been both physically close and yet alone for too long. The thoughts that came up made him uncomfortable. He forced them out of his mind and concentrated simply on walking over the snow wearing the clumsy snowshoes while carrying a heavy pack.

An hour passed. Thru pushed them on, past simple exhaustion, though with pauses every so often to eat a little more of their precious supply of cheese and hard bread.

Then they went on again, still chewing, moving across snow cover that was often several feet deep. Only men with snowshoes could follow them here, and with the falling snow their tracks would soon be buried.

The sound of pursuit had faded away, and they continued to push on across the deep snow, keeping eastward, while Thru searched the gloom for landmarks that he might remember from his days of living in the cave.

They walked for hours, while the sky clouded over, and it grew even darker. It began to snow, gently at first. Eventually Thru called a halt in a rocky gorge where they found an overhang that offered a degree of protection. They pushed some of the snow out of the way and wrapped themselves in their thick hide blankets and fell into an exhausted slumber.

When they awoke it was snowing hard, and they were covered in two to three inches of fresh white powder. Thru got up and did some stretching exercises. Simona didn't move. She found herself shivering so deeply it was hard to move a muscle. A chill went right through her insides. Her legs were numb. She felt like just staying where she was. Why bother? Said a sweet little voice in her ear. Why not just lie here until the end?

But Thru would not let her be. Seeing that she was blue in the face he stopped stretching and crouched down beside her. He called her name. There was no response. He shouted at her and pulled her hair sharply. Still nothing. He slapped her, and she gave a little scream of anger. He pulled her up to a sitting position and rubbed her face forcefully between his hands until she wriggled and put her arms up to stop him. Then he forced her to eat a mouthful of cheese and hard cracker while he rubbed on her hands and feet.

"You are dying, Simona. Your heart is cold. This happens to mots, too, especially if they fall into cold water for too long. We have to get your heart warmed up."

In principle, this sounded fine, but she couldn't imagine how they were going to do it. She could barely chew, hardly swallow.

Thru dragged her to her feet. She could hardly stand

without help, her legs were useless, but then he made her dance in place, clumsily lifting one foot after the other with his own feet under them while he held her up. It felt as if her limbs had turned to lead. Her breathing was harsh in her throat as she struggled, and all the while Thru was jerking her arms up and down and whistling in her face.

Blood had dried down his chin and the front of his coat, and in the poor light his face had taken on a fiendish appearance. She wondered if she had already died and this was all some elaborate dumb show that the demons performed before they took you off to hell.

On and on it went, and she was dancing like a trained bear, and all the time he kept exhorting her in a harsh voice to "Lift your feet, lift your feet, breathe hard, blow it out, lift your feet."

And slowly, terribly slowly, feeling returned to her limbs, accompanied by a bout of pins and needles that made her twitch and scratch at her legs, though it did no good.

Thru never let her stop, not until the glassy look was finally gone from her eyes, and then he sat her down and fed her more cheese and hard flat bread. The terrible sense of cold in the pit of her stomach had faded, and she realized that she'd come perilously close to death.

"I'm sorry I had to hurt you Simona."

"Oh, Thru, I almost died."

"It is dangerous to be out in this kind of cold. We have to keep moving. Find the cave. Then we can keep warm enough to survive."

Thru cleared the snow out of their little space, and they tied on their snowshoes once more, took up their heavy packs, and went on, moving through a silent landscape filled with whirling snow.

Dawn found them several miles into the central hills and well past the last signs of human civilization. Thru thought he heard wolves howl to the south, but in the muffled conditions of heavy snowfall, the sound was too faint for him to be sure. He hoped they'd kept to their westerly course, but there was no way to be sure. And then off to the right of their line of motion he recognized a certain hilltop. It had a curious kind of tip, almost like a hook, and he had, indeed, called this place "Hook Hill." He gave a shout and jumped up and down in jubilation.

"What is it?"

"There, you see that hill with the sharp rock at the top? The cave is close by it."

Simona saw the distant hill and swallowed hard. It was several miles farther on. But she told herself, at least they now had their destination in view.

They broke for more hurried mouthfuls of food. Then they pushed on, struggling through the fresh snow as they climbed up the valley and into the hills. It was an arduous trek. Even with snowshoes the loose snow was hard to negotiate in places, but after several hours they were right beneath the hill with the hooked tip.

And now, at last Thru could point to a long streak of grey rock that outcropped all along the base of the hooked hill.

"The cave is at the far end of that outcrop. We will be there soon."

They went along the rock ledge, the snow had not drifted here, and progress was easy. The dead tree still lay against the cliff face, and past it they found the narrow little cave.

Thru drew the sword in case there was a bear, but the cave was empty, nothing had lived there since he'd left it. The remains of the brush he'd dragged in to make a bed for himself were still there.

The narrow space was crowded for the two of them, but Thru took out the ox hide he'd brought from Beegamuus and wedged it over the entrance and held it in place with a pair of branches broken off the dead pine.

They placed their packs at the front of the cave and lay down under their blankets, huddled together for warmth. Time passed, Simona realized that she was getting warm under the covers, the first warmth her body had felt since they had left Beegamuus.

"Oh, Thru, you were right, I can feel a little warmth."

"This is a good cave. I'm surprised that it's still empty. In my land it would be home to a bear."

"Oh, Thru, I don't think there are any bears left in Shasht. They were all killed long ago."

"We can live here, then. And they will not find us."
"But we don't have enough food for the whole winter."
"Thru will hunt. We will live."
But even Thru knew that this was extremely optimistic.

Chapter 49

In the pyramid of the Great God, Basth brought tea to the Master. He found the Old One studying the curious rug that had been brought in earlier that day by a party of high-ranking Gold Tops. Lifelike chickens danced among a group of huge, ominous beetles. The work was exquisitely rendered for a weave.

The Old One was idly running his hand across the surface of the mat, apparently enjoying its texture.

"Tea, Master," said Basth, setting down the tray.

"This work, Basth, what do you think of it?"

Basth handed him the golden cup of tea. He had grown used to being asked questions like this. Always he answered truthfully, straight from the heart.

"It is remarkable, Master. I have never seen anything quite like it. The chickens are so lifelike."

"And yet so comic. Whoever wove it had a sense of humor, eh?"

"Yes, Master."

The Old One had another piece of weave spread on the table. Basth saw a row of soldier's heads, faces etched in a terrifying snarl beneath steel helmets. The Master lifted this piece so Basth could see it clearly. The strange, ancient eyes were studying him.

"The weaver has seen something of the edge of war, eh?"

"Yes, Master."

"Almost a pity that we have to kill them all."

"Twenty-eight days, Simona."

"I never dreamed that I might die in a place like this," she said, her voice hollow with hunger.

Thru had pulled part of the oxhide aside so they could peer outside. Snow had fallen all night. Now the landscape was sparkling under the newly revealed sun.

"It is beautiful," said Thru, maintaining perfect kyo of "acceptance."

Accept all things that come . . .

besides what choice do you have, exactly?

He had been meditating a great deal during the last few weeks as their food ran out and starvation took hold. Death was only another interlude in the life of the spirit. He knew this.

There is beauty in all things

Even the rose that is withered on the vine.

No two are ever alike.

"Twenty-eight days, Thru. I bet they didn't think we could live this long."

"Look, do you see them?" He pointed suddenly through the gap.

As usual she saw only the white mountains, the dark masses of forest in the valleys.

"No."

"The wolves are there again: four adults, two youngsters."

She looked again, but saw nothing. Thru's vision was far more acute than hers.

"Do they know we are here?"

"Oh, yes. Remember when someone cleaned off my trapline two weeks ago?"

She nodded.

"It was them. But they haven't come back. They prefer to chase the deer."

He followed the tiny dots as they crested a small hill and disappeared, seeking deer that might have been trapped in deeply drifted snow.

"Will you try and hunt today?"

Thru shook his head.

"We still have some of the rabbit from yesterday."

And that was all they had. All their other supplies had run out days before. They had salt and some dried herbs, and that was it. Thru had set traps, and had produced a meager haul, a few rabbits. He had put out smaller traps and caught mice. He hunted with the bow and took a few more rabbits and coneys, but they were in limited supply on this mountain.

Simona had found that starvation was all it took for her to shed her disinclination to eat mice. Thru skinned and cleaned them, then rubbed them with herbs and salt and roasted them on sticks across hot coals. The bones were tiny, and you had to be careful not to swallow them. The meat tasted like chicken, but there wasn't very much of it. Two mice did no more than stimulate her hunger.

And that was their problem. They could not find enough food to sustain their weight. They could keep warm. The cave was small enough to warm up just from the heat of their bodies, particularly when they had the oxhide pressed tightly against the opening. The narrow space remained above freezing, no matter how cold it was outside. Lying under the blankets, huddled together for warmth, they had survived. To conserve their strength, they spent much of the time simply drifting in and out of sleep. But they could not find enough food to survive much longer.

During these long days in semidarkness, Thru usually meditated. He had tried to encourage Simona to meditate, too, but she had not found a way of calming her inner voices. She could not settle herself and simply stop thinking. Her brain raced instead of slowing, and after a while she gave up and just sat there stewing in her thoughts; worrying about her father, worrying about Aunt Piggili and Shalee and the zob.

She always marveled at the stillness he achieved, sitting there bare-chested on a pad made from his overcoat. Sometimes he would be frosted with moonlight there, and she imagined that he was a statue, carved in stone.

And yet, his peaceful purpose usually affected her after a while by some mysterious process, and she would get under the blankets and think of her happy days of childhood, and be liberated for a while from her fears about the present.

However, the grim truth remained. Day by day, they were indeed starving and that could not go on for very long.

"I wanted to go back," he said once. "I would tell the Assenzi what I have seen."

"Oh, we will go back. I know we will, Thru."

But she knew she was lying. They would never leave this place. Their bones would eventually be found by the shepherds.

"I wanted to. I tried." He closed the ox hide across the narrow opening once more and cut out the bright light.

Their eyes readjusted to the gloom. The air was warm but not stale. They'd freshened their bedding before the storm's arrival, and Thru had put up bunches of wood mint, which filled the space with a fresh scent.

Simona felt the stone around them, felt it's imprisoning clutch, felt her spirit quail in front of its cold massiveness and the doom it spoke of for both of them. Instinctively seeking comfort she groped her way into Thru's arms.

The simple animal contact with his strong, young body, awoke a primal desire.

"I am dying, Thru. But I don't want to die unfulfilled. I have never had a man. I was denied that basic right."

Thru understood. He would not have liked to die without knowing what it was to make love to a mor. And beyond that he had felt the tension growing between them. It was strong, and tormenting. They were living as one, knotting together in this narrow, intimate space. He was male, she was female, and her shape was no different from that of any mor.

A sense of shame often overwhelmed him when he found his thoughts drift toward arousal by her presence. What would Nuza say? And he would pray that she was well and safe with her family in Lushtan. Most often this calmed him and allowed him to think about something else. But, the thoughts would return. He was male and in the prime of life, it was inevitable that this would gnaw at his mind.

"Simona," he whispered, wanting to stop her. But her hand slipped inside his jerkin and stroked his flank, enjoying the feel of the soft fur.

To Thru, her touch was like a stroke of lightning. A vast wave slammed against the dam built across his heart.

"Thru, you are so beautiful to me. I know we are different, I know how ugly I must seem to you. I wish I could have fur, too."

Thru felt the dam break. Her simple wish was so heart-breakingly impossible. He wondered which betrayal was the more fundamental. That of his love for Nuza, or that of his very being, as a mot.

"Thru," she whispered in his ear. "Do not fear this. We are alone, we may never see another living soul. Why shouldn't we taste this fruit?"

"Simona." He was poised on the edge of a precipice.

She came to him willingly, their lips crushed together. After the weeks of closeness and frustration, the physical passion broke free at last. He forgot who he was or where they were. He simply took her, bore her back down into the bedding as their hips became conjoined in the beast with two backs.

For a long time they were like this, for they had lit a fire between not only themselves but between two worlds, two races and two ways of being.

And in these flames Simona found answers to some of the questions that had haunted her these many years.

Afterward she lay there beside Thru, listening to him snore very softly. She reached out and stroked the soft fur on his back. What had she done? Was she "abomination" for this? If so, why? What was the difference between them that made it forbidden? Try as she might she could think of nothing, except the crude physical differences. She had hair, he had fur, she had full lips, he had thin ones. Other than that they were just people, and she saw that there need be no barrier to love between them.

She amused herself for a while by imagining that she might even be quickened with a child from their mating. And if she was, what would that child be like? Would she have both hair and fur? Simona laughed inside. It would be hard explaining all this to such a child.

"She will be gifted, I think. Like her father," she murmured aloud.

Her remorse died away. She felt very strong all of a sudden. If she truly had conceived a child, then she had a new reason to try and live. She was a bridge between two peoples. For a moment she was able to laugh at herself for this conceit. But then the seriousness of this possibility overtook her, and she lay there quietly, absorbed in her thoughts. Such a child would indeed be a bridge between the two kinds of people. She would demonstrate to both the fundamental equality between them. So Simona had to live, to allow this child to be born.

And, just as importantly, she understood that Thru had to live to take his message back to the Assenzi. It was the only way they could win the war. She couldn't let him die here of starvation. Suddenly she had an idea, and she sat up with a sudden rush of breath as it burst into her mind.

She prodded him.

"Thru, darling Thru, we have to leave these hills. We can't just die here."

Thru struggled out of sleep. He was filled with shame for what he had done, but Simona did not seem angry in the slightest.

"I am sorry, I should not have done what I did. It was wrong . . ."

"No it wasn't!" She seized his hand and bit it gently, then squeezed it between her breasts. "I love you, Thru, and what we did was not wrong. Even if we never do it again, it will never be wrong. We are different, but we are the same."

He blinked, stared into her eyes. His lips moved, but he said nothing. Her breast felt warm, inviting, just like Nuza's.

"If we leave, where will we go?"

"If we go to Aunt Piggili she might be able to help us hide."

"But that would endanger her. You said the Red Tops would go after all your relatives."

"Oh, don't say that." This was Simona's great fear. That she might have brought down the wrath of the priests upon her family.

"I'm sorry, Simona, I wasn't thinking."

He put his arms around her, and she rested her head on his hard, muscled shoulder.

"We can't just die here, Thru. You at least must go back

to the Land. You can tell the Assenzi what they need to know."

He nodded. "Yes, but how?"

"We have to leave this place."

"Wherever we go, there will be Red Tops."

"No. We shall go to the coast and buy a ship. We will sail back to the Land."

"Buy a boat?" he grinned at her in the dark. "We have no money."

"We do. Or I do. At the zob, years ago, my mother gave me the jewels she had collected for my inheritance from her. They were for my dowry. I buried them in the courtyard of the purdah house."

"And that would be enough to buy a boat?"

"There is an emerald there that will be enough on its own. My mother told me never to give that stone up, unless my life depended on it."

She squeezed his hand.

"And it does."

Thru's mind fairly spun at the implications of this.

"Then we can buy a boat. The next question is whether we can sail it."

"We will have to learn."

Thru rubbed his chin thoughtfully. He had been around fishing boats, had traveled in them and handled nets. "I have watched them setting the sails, I think I could do that."

"I will steer. I will help you with the sails."

But how would they navigate? Thru knew that navigation beyond the sight of land was very tricky.

"And when there is no wind?"

"Then I will row the boat."

Chapter 50

In the murk of a late winter afternoon, the big house was a dark hulk within the cold fog. From what they could see, only a single light glowed in the kitchen. They moved closer.

"There's hardly anyone here."

The windows on the upper floors were shuttered, no lights showed there at all. The Red Tops had already scoured the place.

"Poor Shalee," muttered Simona. No doubt her old friend had gone to the city, destined for the altar to the Great God; all her friends at the house, probably.

They had investigated the stables. Only a couple of horses there and a single small carriage were left. Otherwise it had been stripped. Simona had had to fight back tears at the sight. Poor Silvery, her beloved white horse had been taken. She hoped that Silvery had been given to someone who was kind to horses and not some brutal Gold Top with a heavy whip.

They moved closer to the house. Movement was much easier now, since the packs on their backs held hardly anything. They passed quickly through the shrubberies behind the grand lawn. The gallery at the western end of the house was shut tight. Wide windows that were opened in the summer were shuttered, and the door was locked. But Thru tested them and found one that was slightly loose at one hinge. He climbed up to work on the other one with his knife. The fastening pegs needed repair, and he dug them out quite easily.

With a careful heave, he and Simona were able to lift the shutter off the window and set it down quietly. Rather than leave their snowshoes there, they tied them together and slung them on a thong behind their packs.

They slipped inside. Thru had given the sword to Simona. He held the bow at the ready, with an arrow nocked. They listened carefully, but heard only the sigh of the wind around the upper gables.

Simona knew the layout of the house with the familiarity of a girl who had spent all her summers there. They skirted the grand salon, took a stair to a mezzanine floor, and flitted through grand rooms, all shuttered and silent. None of these rooms had been used for years. That was in the other life, the happy time before Filek received the imperial summons sending him on the colony fleet.

Simona had buried the casket from her father under a brick in the garden of the purdah courtyard. The mezzanine floor took them to a cloistered gallery overlooking the court. Rooms set back around the central space were for relaxation by women of the leisured class on hot afternoons. In the center, ten feet below this floor, lay the garden, laid out in a circle with clipped shrubs in terra cotta tubs set around the outer edge.

Simona pointed. "You see the statue of St. Gizan in the center? Beside it on the right is a flower bed. The flower bed is surrounded by ornamental bricks. The casket is buried under the brick closest to the statue."

Thru nodded, identifying the orange brick in question.

And then they jumped as a door slammed somewhere far off in the house. A reminder that they were not alone in the great zob.

They stepped across the hallway and pushed open the door to a room. It gave a loud creak as it opened, and Simona felt a stab of fear. What if they were detected here? She held the sword in her right hand, but she had no idea how to wield it. She didn't really know if she could even bring herself to kill another person.

Then she thought of Shalee and Silvery and all the other victims of the Red Tops and found renewed determination. If she had to use the sword then she would, or die trying at least. The Red Tops were responsible for so much misery. Her mother's face swam up in her memory. Her mother would still be alive if they hadn't been sent to the Land. Poor Chiknulba would have been appalled to see her country zob in the hands of these vicious swine.

They listened, ears straining for the slightest sound, but heard nothing. Thru was reluctant to open the door again, since it made that loud squeak the first time. He examined the hinge, moistened it with spit, and started working it slowly open. Suddenly, the door opened just a few inches, they heard loud voices coming closer. Another door boomed open and feet strode down the hall, passing right by the door behind which they waited. The two men went past without breaking stride, engrossed in complaints about the food cooked by Dzumbud, whoever that was. They were gone in a moment, and another door slammed behind them. Simona found that she was trembling. Thru laid a hand on her shoulder. She looked up with a start.

"Whoo! That was close, eh?" he grinned.

She nodded, wanting to laugh. The fear mastered once again.

Another door down to their right slammed shut. The voices receded farther away. Apparently, the pantries of the great house had been stripped by the Gold Tops.

Thru and Simona waited, crouched silently behind the partly opened door. But the men did not return. Now, very carefully Thru opened the door enough for them to slip out again. After a minute of so of careful listening, they felt safe enough to creep down the stairs that lead to the central garden.

On the ground floor the garden was surrounded by a pillared cloister. They hid themselves in the shadows here and watched and listened.

After giving the space a thorough study, Thru entered the garden. The little statue was of a robed woman, holding her arms up in supplication to the skies. Thru crouched down and dug around the brick. After a little work the brick came out, and he looked down on a small black box, no bigger than his fist, buried underneath.

He scooped it up, set the brick back in place, and turned to leave. Whereupon the door above them boomed open again, and the loud-voiced Red Tops came back, now carrying pillows taken from the furniture in the distant salons.

With no time to do anything but freeze, he stood next to the statue, just a darker shape in the general gloom, and prayed they didn't notice him.

The Red Tops looked right at him and kept going. They still complained about the damned flour. Apparently, they hadn't had meat in days.

The door pulled open. One of them said something and turned back. Thru knew instantly that he'd been spotted, he rose and ran for the shadow of the cloister, but it was too late.

"Thief!" snarled the Red Top, and the two men came hurrying down the stairs.

Thru and Simona ran for the far set of doors, but the doors were locked. They turned at bay, and the two young Red Tops charged straight at them with raised batons.

Thru had no time to nock an arrow. He pulled his knife and dodged the first wild swing of the truncheon. Simona swung the sword at the other Red Top, who parried it with his baton.

And then both Red Tops saw that Thru was not a man. And that Simona was a woman.

They sprang back with peculiar looks of hatred and horror on their faces.

"What!" said one of them.

Thru leaped on them with Simona right behind.

Thru pulled one of the young men down, he stabbed home with the knife, and felt the Red Top convulse. Then he turned. Simona was down, the Red Top was hitting her with his baton while screaming curses. Thru crashed into him, knocked him into a pillar, and then bore him down. The knife rose and fell, and the Red Top lay still.

Thru got to his feet. Simona uncurled from the fetal position. He helped her up. She sobbed. A bump was rising on her forehead. She held her side where she'd taken other blows.

Thru picked up the sword where it had fallen.

"Can you walk? Are you badly hurt?"

She shook her head. "I can walk. I think."

"Take one of their sticks. Follow me."

Now they moved toward the source of the light at the other end of the house. In the kitchens they spotted another Red Top, busy in the act of cooking dumplings in boiling fat.

The fellow heard the door open.

"Well, you two took your time. These zooba are ready."

He started to turn, but then Thru was there. The last thing the Red Top ever saw was the flash of the blade, and then Thru laid him carefully on his side.

Simona fished the hot dumplings out of the oil with a spoon. They ate them with hot pepper paste straight out of an earthen jar on the table.

"We can't stay here for long. These Red Tops will be visited by others of their kind."

Thru nodded. "The carriage in the stables has two horse animals."

Simona chuckled. "Of course, you have only donkeys in the Land. Aren't horses beautiful?"

"Yes, but I'm glad you have experience in dealing with them."

Thru gave Simona the little black casket, and she pulled the pin that kept it locked.

"It hasn't rusted, even after five years."

The casket was lined with dark blue velvet on which shone a handful of bright sparkling gemstones.

Thru whistled at the sight of the fiery gems.

"There you are," she said. "That will buy us a ship."

Chapter 51

The road winding around the crag was steep and iced in places, but the tower looming above promised security, so Thru had no hesitation in going onward. He shook the reins, felt the two huge animals shift their feet, and soon had the wagon rolling slowly up the slope.

Somehow, with only an hour or so of training, Thru had managed the two horses over a dozen miles of rutted wintry roads without sliding off into a ditch or bogging down, in half frozen mud—but it had been a close run thing on several occasions.

As for other traffic, they'd seen very little. A few carts, one or two men on horseback, a handful of others trudging through the snow and ice. Thru kept his head down and his hat pulled low over his ears.

Still, the tension of keeping the pair of horses—gentle old geldings—under control and avoiding the worst ruts had taken its toll. The back of Thru's neck and shoulders were stiff and painful.

"This is the Tower of Quarantine," said Simona in a hushed voice as they passed through the lower gate.

"Yes," said Thru, rubbing the back of his neck.

"It is forbidden. All my life this place was spoken of in hushed voices. No one knows who is kept here, but it is said to be an ogre."

"What is an ogre?"

"A hairy monster, like a bear but with a man's head. It eats children."

Thru thought about this for a moment.

"We do not have these animals in the Land. Long ago we had trouble with lions, and we had to drive them up into the hills. Anyway, I can tell you one thing that is certain. The man in the tower is not an ogre. He calls himself the "Eccentric." He is not like the other men I have met."

They had come to the inner gate, which was shut. Thru got down and smote the knocker.

They waited. Shortly they heard a door creak open in the tower and footsteps slowly descend to the gate.

"Who goes there?" said a harsh voice.

"It is I, Thru Gillo."

Silence, then the door peep cracked open.

"Is it really you? Come back with a carriage and pair?"

"Yes, Master Eccentric. And I have a friend with me. We need shelter once again."

But the gate was already opening, and the Eccentric welcomed them in with a smile.

"Well, well, come in, come in. I had not thought to see you again, my fur-covered friend."

Inside the tower the tall figure wrapped in his hooded robe went ahead of them up the steps to the door, but once they were in the small room, he removed his robe and turned to welcome his guests properly.

At the sight of him Simona almost fainted.

"Your Majesty, I had no idea you'd be here."

The Eccentric stared at her silently, as she stood hidden behind her veil and hood. Thru looked blankly back and forth between them.

"You know my brother?" said the Eccentric at last.

"Your brother? I . . ." and Simona's voice trailed off. Because now she could see the differences. This man had a slightly lighter build of jaw and forehead. The nose was identical, as were the somber dark eyes and hair, but the face had other differences. The chin, the width of the mouth, all were subtly different.

"Yes, my lord, I have been privileged to know your great brother."

"How? As a courtesan?"

Simona colored. She supposed she should have expected this. "No, my lord, I was teaching him a new language."

"What?" the man stared at her again. Then broke into a smile and lifted his head to laugh out loud.

"Well, well, so Ge is learning a new language at his age!"

"Ge?"

"You know him as Aeswiren the Third. To me he is Ge. I am Mentupah. Ge is the older by four years."

"You are brother of the Emperor?" said Thru, amazed at this discovery.

"Yes."

"But, why are you kept here?"

Mentupah, the Eccentric shook his head in anger.

"I was imprisoned here because I was eccentric enough not to want any of the power and glory of my brother's Empire. I was a fisherman, not a soldier. I lived a simple life while he rose to the purple. Then I became a problem. He was afraid that someone would try to use me as a puppet to replace him."

"And so he put you here?"

The Eccentric shrugged. "Most men in his position would have just had me killed, but he locked me away here for the rest of my life. He has told me many times that someday I would have an important role to play."

Simona, who had never seen anything but the gentle side of Aeswiren, was shocked by these revelations. How could the wonderful, intelligent man she had come to know and respect be so cruel? But, she reflected, all the history that she had read of the Empire demonstrated that Aeswiren was right to be so careful. The struggle for power was endless and protean. Any tool, any weapon that could be found would be used."

"It is my turn to ask a question," said Mentu. "How in the world did my fur-covered friend find you? And why did he bring you here? Why is a woman of noble blood outside of the purdah house?"

"Ah, well . . ." Thru began.

"It is a long story, my lord," said Simona quickly.

The Eccentric listened and asked questions until the answers satisfied him, then he sat down and shook his head in amazement.

"Truly, you have been blessed by the Gods, whoever they are.

"But, now I must tell you that circumstances here are

uncertain. Since Aeswiren fell, I have had very little news from outside. They have either forgotten about me, or they have simply not yet decided to kill me."

"And you are waiting here for them to kill you?" said Thru.

Mentu shrugged. "I know I shouldn't, but I don't know what to do. If I stay here, then I am obeying the Emperor's commands. If I flee, they will eventually track me down and I will have broken the Emperor's law and can be put to death quite legally."

"We are going to go to the Land," said Simona in a firm voice. "That is beyond their reach."

The Eccentric stared at them as comprehension sank in. "The Land . . . You mean, the land where Thru here came from?"

"Yes. My father gave me some gemstones to use in an emergency. I think they will be enough to buy and outfit a boat. We will sail to the Land."

"But, it's thousands of miles away."

"True. So we have to buy a big enough boat."

"How will you navigate? Are either of you versed at all in the sea?"

"No. But we will learn."

The Eccentric smiled.

"Then, I will have to come with you."

"You?"

"I worked as a fisherman for eight seasons. I know the banks, I know the straits, and I know how to navigate by the stars."

They looked at him blankly.

"You won't survive without me," he added.

To that they had no reply.

Chapter 52

Good fortune continued to smile upon them. For two weeks they drove the wagon westward into Gzia Province. At night Simona slept in the wagon, and Thru and Mentu wrapped themselves in blankets and slept on the ground underneath. As much as possible they avoided towns. For food they had a stock of hard biscuit brought from the tower.

They saw parties of Red Tops on the roads, but Mentu's beard had grown quickly enough to obscure his looks and a fancy purdah wagon was still enough to overawe most Red Tops. On the one occasion when a party of Red Tops demanded to know who was in the wagon, Mentu was able to bluff them, with help from Simona, who spoke up on cue.

"I am the Countess Furissen, a friend of the Emperor Norgeeben the Second. Why do you halt my carriage? Who are you?"

At these imperious words the Red Tops quailed and backed away.

The weather continued mild, and the snow cover was gone by the time they came over the domido and into the little village of Bafleu, snuggled against the red rocks of the Givi estuary. Now Thru put on Simona's spare purdah robe and hood. They had decided that the best disguise for him was to pretend to be a lady in waiting to Simona. Hidden by the conventions of purdah, he would be almost invisible to the men of the village.

Mentu had spent much of his life in the village. Despite his long absence, he found that little had changed. He drove the wagon confidently through the narrow streets and ultimately into the outer yard of a fish wholesaler.

"This is my friend Yomafin's place. Stay inside, I won't be long."

Mentu disappeared into the back of the rather ramshackle premises, which reeked of fish despite the cold. Thru, peering out of a slit inside the wagon, was mystified by the dilapidation he saw. The roof needed a lot of work, and there were broken slats and gaps in the exterior siding.

Mentu returned a little later accompanied by another man, full-bellied, with white hair combed loose to his shoulders.

"Greetings, I am Yomafin, friend of Mentu, who I never expected to see again in this life."

"You will have to excuse good Yomafin, he's still recovering from the shock," said Mentu with a grin.

Thru and Simona left the security of the wagon, both wearing full purdah dress, with hooded cloaks that came down to the ground.

"Come this way," said the man.

They entered another rambling structure set on the farther side of the yard. The stench of fish was replaced by the warm smells of cooking and smoke. They passed a kitchen, glimpsed an old slave beside the stove, and went up some stairs into a warm, poorly lit room.

"You can rest here, while Mentu and I make things ready for you elsewhere."

"Thank you," said Simona.

The men left them, Mentu came back in a few minutes, bearing a basket with bread and peanuts.

"We stay here tonight. Yomafin has sent a message to his brother. We will hide at his farm."

"And the boat?"

"He says there are two or three that could serve our purpose."

"What about the Red Tops?" asked Thru.

"The terror has passed on to the city. All the Red Tops are gone now. They will be back, but not until all their victims have been sent to Shasht."

"Why do they do this?"

"It happens at the beginning of every reign. The Red Tops seize the chance to settle scores."

"My father told me that the priests call it 'weeding out,' " said Simona.

"How many people have they taken?" asked Thru quietly.

"Two thousand from Gzia alone. The purge in Shasht was even more severe they say."

"And all will be slaughtered?"

The Eccentric nodded. "The masses love the ceremonies. They will watch the priests sacrificing victims all day. The steps of the pyramid will run with blood."

Thru shivered. "Seems a waste of lives."

"In Shasht life is cheap," said Mentu with another shrug.

The next morning they moved out of the village as secretly as possible and up the lane to a straggling farmhouse. Later, Yomafin and his brother Heldo came to see them.

While Yomafin was friendly, without reservation, Heldo was closemouthed and hard eyed. Between the two brothers there was clearly some ill feeling. Thru supposed that Heldo was unhappy at the risk that Yomafin had taken.

"Before we initiate contracts and risk our good name," said Yomafin, "we must know whether you speak truth about these gemstones."

Yomafin was clearly embarrassed at having to ask. Heldo's eyes glittered with something unkind.

"Well, of course you can."

Simona opened the little box and showed them the massive emerald, plus the smaller diamonds and rubies.

The fish dealer sucked in a breath. Heldo's eyes widened.

"This is wealth indeed. . . ."

"Enough?" said Simona.

"More than enough."

"Good, then, know this. I will give you all of it if we succeed."

"No, my lady, I could not accept so much."

Heldo blinked and flashed a look of disbelief at his brother. Yomafin took no notice.

"My lady, I help you because of my friendship with

Mentu, and because I hate the filthy Red Tops and all their kind." Yomafin's voice had suddenly turned hard.

"They killed our grandfather," said Heldo in explanation.

"They killed many people from this village, because Ge Vust had rebelled against Shmeg."

"I wish there could be an end to the Red Tops, all of them," said Simona.

"A good thought, my lady," said Yomafin. "I will take these smaller stones, the diamonds and rubies. They will buy a good barque with provisions. There is one in the yard near here that I think will serve. The owner is eager to sell, too."

"Thank you, Yomafin."

"But I will not buy directly with these gems. It is best not to arouse too much suspicion. So I will have to go to Gzia Gi to sell them. I know some wealthy men who like to trade such things. They will give me gold, and I will use that to buy the ship."

"Is it safe in the city?"

"Not yet, so we must wait a few more days. When the Red Tops sail to Shasht with their prisoners, then the terror will be over."

The days passed slowly. They remained hidden in a small room on an upper floor. Heldo brought them their food, but otherwise stayed away, as did his family, all of whom were terrified of the consequences if the fugitives were found hidden on the farm. Thru felt a certain tension in Heldo every time he appeared.

Every day, Mentu went to look at the boat, *Sea Wasp.* He reported on the progress at the evening meal.

"Won't be long before they float her again. She's in excellent shape now. I think we can sail her with a crew of four, though five would be better."

Thru questioned him about navigation, a matter on which he still had many concerns. Mentu explained the use of strict accounting of the positions of the stars, planets, and Red Kemm. By making observations every day at the same time, they could judge their general direction and position. The method was not exact, far from it in fact, but of all systems of navigation, this one had been found the best by many centuries of trial and error.

"As we travel, so we have to take into account the distance east or west we may have traveled, because that affects the time of our observations of the stars. It is hard to keep an accurate log, but one must try, and that means logging our speed several times a day. Sometimes that becomes difficult, in bad weather, say, when we are driven far from our projected course."

Thinking of all that was involved left Thru shaking his head.

"I'm surprised that any ship can actually hope to sail around the world and find its destination."

"Ships often go astray, and it may take months for us to find our course again, which is why we have to take as much food as the barque will hold."

One day Mentu returned brimming with excitement.

"They floated her today. Put in the masts and set her rigging. She will serve very well. But we will need more hands than just our own."

"Remember that I will work, too," said Simona. "I will not stay in purdah once we have left these shores."

Mentu had heard Simona on this subject before, but the idea struck him as outlandish.

"As you wish, Mistress Gsekk. I will not try and stop you. But you may find working a ship to be harder than you had bargained for."

"I can work hard. I will show you . . ."

Mentu chuckled. "Oh, I don't doubt that. We will all work hard, believe me. Wait until we've been in a hard blow. Out on the great ocean there will be waves as high as the tallest trees, and we will be hanging on for dear life a lot of the time."

The day finally came that Yomafin announced he was going to Gzia Gi to sell the gems. With their blessings and prayers, he set off on his two-wheeled buggy behind a smart black pacer.

The next day Mentu decided to travel, too, a few miles up the coast to another village where some relatives still lived.

"Most of the family went to Shasht twenty years ago. But there are still a few down here on the coast."

Left alone that evening Thru and Simona ate a quiet meal together. When Heldo brought the food, he set it down and ran from the door at the sound of Thru descending the stairs.

"Heldo is behaving strangely," said Thru as he broke a piece of bread.

"I worry about him. He seems unstable."

Thru nodded. "I think he is very stupid. He is afraid, but he is also greedy."

"That is a dangerous mixture, I think."

They ate in silence after that, each suddenly oppressed by the knowledge that though they were close to escaping their enemies, they were also still at great risk.

Chapter 53

The next morning, Heldo brought them their food for the day, but this time he did not run away. Instead he lingered until Simona came down to take the tray. Thru followed her, but remained on the stairs.

"You ladies eat well in my house, do you not?"

Simona did all the talking when Heldo visited, since Thru was disguised as her servant, hidden in purdah robes.

"We thank you for the food, good Heldo. Your brother Yomafin will pay you for everything in good time."

"Yomafin will pay, yes, that is good." Heldo was studying them in a way that made Simona uneasy.

"Yomafin is an old friend of Mentu," Heldo said suddenly, as if goaded beyond endurance.

"Yes. We are grateful to Yomafin."

Heldo ducked his head. The glitter in his eyes grew stronger.

"Heldo is not such a good friend to Mentu. Heldo want more money."

Thru and Simona had foreseen that this demand might arise. Simona was ready.

"We have only the great emerald that you saw. We can give you that."

Heldo was a little surprised to be offered the stone so quickly.

"Good. Give it to me now."

"No. You can have it when we leave. That way we can trust you until the end."

Heldo was unhappy.

"You give it to Heldo now."

"No, we can't do that. Not if we can't trust you."

"You must trust Heldo."

"You are ridiculous! You help us because you owe so much to Yomafin, your brother and great benefactor. He has told us what you owe him."

"You give it to Heldo!"

"No."

Heldo went away, his face full of fury.

"I fear that Heldo is stupid enough to be dangerous," said Thru.

"Nor is he trustworthy."

Thru made certain preparations before nightfall. While Simona slept he waited in the dark, not meditating, but not sleeping, either.

Shortly after midnight, he heard the door open and close down below. He woke Simona and she hid herself behind an old chest left in the corner. The stairs creaked. Thru took up a position behind the door.

Where they had been sleeping, Thru had left a bale of cloth and their packs with the blankets piled on top. In the dark it might be mistaken for their bodies.

Someone moved very quietly up to the door and opened it just an inch or so. Thru tensed himself.

Something flashed in the air, and an arrow quivered from the center of the bale of cloth. Another arrow flashed in and sank into the pack beside it.

Now the door was opened farther, and a figure entered keeping the bow half drawn in front of itself. Cautiously it approached the piles on the floor, each with an arrow jutting up from where their shoulders might have met if they were indeed Simona and Thru.

Thru stepped silently up behind the man and brought his knife up and set it hard against his lower back while slipping his arm around his throat to hold him.

"Don't move," Thru whispered harshly.

Heldo froze.

"Drop the bow."

Heldo hesitated, then Thru pressed his knife in harder, pricking sharply above Heldo's right kidney.

The bow clattered to the floor.

"Is there anyone with you?"

"No. Heldo is alone."

Thru relaxed his grip.

Heldo turned and swung a heavy fist. Thru had anticipated it and ducked it cleanly before striking Heldo in the center of the chest with his foot.

Heldo sat down with a gasp and struggled to breathe.

Thru crouched down nearby, keeping his face hidden in the purdah veil. Simona approached from the other side.

"You are a stupid man, Heldo."

Heldo would have agreed at that moment, if Heldo had been capable of speech.

"You have tried to kill us, and when Yomafin comes back he will be very angry."

Heldo gasped again. "Don't tell."

"Why not?"

"Heldo sorry."

Simona reached over and tore an arrow out of her pack.

"You tried to kill me."

Heldo hung his head.

"Why shouldn't we tell Yomafin?"

"Heldo will tell the Red Tops."

Simona snorted with contempt. "You are so stupid. You think the Red Tops won't take you as well? If they find us, they will take everyone to the temple."

Heldo looked uncomfortable, for he knew she spoke the truth. The priests were usually quite indiscriminate.

But Simona had another card to play.

"Listen, Heldo. If the Red Tops come here, I will tell them you spoke to us of the Olden Gods. I will say that Heldo worships Canilass."

Heldo's eyes bugged in his forehead. Anyone taken as a heretic would face a long interrogation while the priests hammered his hands and feet into pancakes.

"No!"

"Then you will have to keep silent. Besides, you will not get the emerald if the Red Tops take us. It will go to the Gold Tops."

Heldo saw this uncomfortable likelihood, too, and squirmed.

"Leave us, do not return. Send someone else with the food. Tell them to leave it on the stairs. Understand?"

Heldo nodded, his features contorted by relief and anger.

"Leave us now. Say nothing of this to Yomafin, and we will say nothing, too."

"You say nothing?"

"If you keep quiet about it, so will we."

"You give Heldo the stone?"

"If you stay away from us."

Heldo shook his head. The world was a more complex place than he had ever imagined.

Two days later Mentu returned. He noticed at once that Heldo was subdued, and that an old slave woman brought the evening food.

Under his questioning Thru told him about Heldo's attempt on their lives.

"He will not dare to speak," said Simona.

"I hope you're right. Heldo was always the weak link. He is a stupid man."

"We have observed this," said Thru dryly.

"But it was better to hide here than in the village. Heldo's farm is far away from prying eyes. As far as I can tell, they still don't know you're here, though they know about me."

"Will someone tell the Red Tops?"

"I don't think so. Not until my name filters up to the city. I don't have enemies any more in the village."

"We told Heldo we would keep his attack on us a secret."

"Yes, a wise move. But Yomafin should be told. He knows best how to judge Heldo's moods."

Mentu stayed with them after that, but Heldo was not seen again, nor did he go to the Red Tops.

Three days later, Yomafin returned from the city.

Chapter 54

The gold was in imperial crowns, heavy coins bearing the face of Aeswiren III.

"Enough here to buy the *Sea Wasp,* and provision her for a year."

"This is excellent, friend Yomafin," said Simona. "You have done very well."

"How was it here while I was away?" Clearly Yomafin had already noticed that Heldo was behaving as if guilty about something.

"Oh, uh, it was quiet, very quiet." Simona tried to keep her voice steady.

Yomafin was not appeased with this.

"What did Heldo do?"

They looked to each other for a moment. Then Mentu explained that Heldo had tried to rob Simona in the night. Yomafin looked sharply in Thru's direction.

"The 'lady' subdued my brother?"

"Ah, yes." Mentu looked up at the ceiling for a moment. Clearly, Yomafin did not believe this. "Actually, my friend, the 'lady' is not a lady."

Yomafin blinked. Thru let his hand rest on the hilt of his knife under the purdah robes.

"Mysteries upon mysteries, Mentu," muttered Yomafin. "What is this about?"

"I think we shall have to reveal ourselves more fully. I had hoped to spare you this, but I think you have to know the truth."

Mentu signaled to Thru, who after a long moment of hesitation withdrew his veil and the hood.

At the sight of the face covered in fur, with the huge

bushy eyebrows and wide-spaced eyes, Yomafin lurched to his feet in alarm.

"What is this?"

"Please, do not be alarmed. I mean you no harm," said Thru.

Yomafin whirled to Mentu. "What is this?"

"This is a stranger to our land, who found me in the Tower of Quaranine and convinced me that there was a way to escape my fate."

"A stranger," Yomafin whirled back to stare at Thru. "You are one of them!"

A silence fell.

"One of them?" said Thru in puzzlement.

"And you speak Shashti so well I was fooled."

"What do you mean, 'them'?" said Mentu.

"While I was in Gzia Gi, I met with an old friend. He says that he has been contacted by people in Shasht who need his help. There are some monkey men there, who have been hidden by rebel aristocrats. They want to get out of the city."

Thru jumped forward, Yomafin put up a hand to ward him off and raised his fist.

"It's all right, Yomafin," said Mentu hurriedly.

"They are alive?" Thru was close to shouting. He had long since given up hope that his companions from the voyage could still be alive.

"You know them? Then you are one of them."

"Yes. I was separated from them in the city. I traveled on the canal. But, Yomafin, our friend, we are not 'monkey men'; we are mots and brilbies."

Yomafin was still shaking his head, amazed at this latest turn of events. More than that there was a genuine horror in his eyes.

"Mentu, when I saw your face once again, I knew I would have nothing but trouble in store. But little did I know that it would bring me to this pass!"

"Yomafin, my friend, I told you with my first words that this would be a risky venture and that I would not hold you to it in payment of our old debt."

"I know, I know, but look at the position you put me in.

I thought we were just shipping out some runaway ladies of the aristocracy. Now I find that one of them isn't even a human being, but some kind of animal, or a monster even."

Thru's jaw tightened. Simona put a hand on his arm.

"Yomafin," said Mentu sharply, reaching out to hold his friend by the shoulder. "This is an 'animal' that can speak our language."

"But it is abomination! The priests have always told us that the world is ours and ours alone."

"You believe the priests?" Mentu murmured softly.

Yomafin looked around wildly for a moment, grasping at straws for an answer. Mentu knew his old friend too well.

"You're right, I don't. And yet I find the sight of this creature repulsive and threatening."

Mentu and Simona looked at Thru, who was several inches shorter than Yomafin and far less bulky.

"He doesn't seem so frightening to me," said the Eccentric. "I've spent many an hour conversing with him. He has some interesting things to say about the life of the Spirit and the Gods."

Yomafin was visibly struggling. His eyes grew troubled.

"I don't understand. I hear your words, but when I look at him I see a monstrosity, some creature made in the likeness of man. How can you trust it?"

"How can one trust anyone? What is the essence of 'trust'?"

Yomafin frowned not wanting to think about these things.

"And what of the other one? Is that, too, some kind of monstrous creature covered in fur?"

"No," said Simona. "I am Simona of the Gsekk, daughter of the Emperor Aeswiren's personal surgeon. I have had the honor to know the Emperor Aeswiren."

Yomafin colored. Automatically he bobbed his head and said, "I am an Aeswiren man myself, my lady, always have been. A good Emperor he was. But he is gone now."

"That is why we are fleeing. We will go to the land of Thru's folk. On the other side of the world."

Yomafin's eyes widened farther.

"A noblewoman of Shasht will go to live among these animals?"

"Yes. If the Emperor still lives, this is what he would want, too," said Simona. "I am sure of it."

Yomafin's mouth worked, but he was unable to speak. He looked back and forth between Mentu and Simona. He did his best not to look at Thru.

"All right! For the Emperor I will risk this. But as soon as I have purchased the barque, I want you to leave."

"What about the provisions?"

"There are some here, I will see they are loaded for you. But beyond that, nothing. You can obtain more somewhere else. I just don't want you to be here."

Mentu shrugged sadly. "I am sorry to hear these words, old friend. I had hoped for better from you."

"I am Aeswiren's man, and you are my oldest friend, Mentu Vust, but I fear that dealing with this creature is something you should have asked of another man."

Thru came down off the balls of his feet.

"The 'creature' thanks you, Yomafin. I swear that I mean you no harm."

"How can a man trust the oath of a demon creature?"

"Hold on there, just a moment ago I was simply a creature. Now you say I am a demon creature. What drives you to think so ill of me?"

"None but Man can have speech! It is forbidden to the rest of creation. This was the way the Great God planned it."

"Do you honestly believe in the Great God?"

"I—" Yomafin looked away, his face contorted in torment.

"I am sorry for you," said Thru. "It must be hard to think like you do. But please understand that I did not come here of my own free will. None of my folk would ever have come here. We had thought that Man the Cruel was no more. It was the worst day in our lives when we found that we were wrong."

Yomafin stared at him, completely aware now that he was speaking to an abomination and that it was speaking to him. Aware of this, but forced to continue.

"You say you were captured?"

"After a battle, yes."

"And brought here to be sacrificed to the Great God."

"I suppose so. It seemed a strange thing to me. Why would you want to take someone from his home halfway around the world and bring him all the way to your land to kill him in the name of your God?"

Yomafin couldn't answer.

"Come, now, tell me. Do you believe in your God, this Great 'He Who Eats'?"

Yomafin could not find the words to reply. He stared at them, one after the other, muttered "abomination" once more and left them. Mentu hurried after him, crying, "Yomafin. Wait, my friend."

Simona turned back to Thru.

"Don't let his evil words upset you, such men as he are blind."

"I believe that, too, but I have met such words before. They are common among your people."

Thru turned away. There was a different concern in his eyes. Simona knew what it must be and was suddenly afraid. Thru knew that his friends were still alive and in desperate straits in the great city.

Chapter 55

Sea Wasp was a well built little barque. Freshly repaired, still smelling of paint, varnish and tar, she floated beside the dock with sails neatly furled in the late afternoon sun.

Yomafin and Heldo, wearing winter cloaks against a chilly onshore breeze, waited as the wagon came to a halt and Simona stepped down. She reached up and took down her traveling bag. One of Yomafin's young fishermen was driving the carriage and pair, which would now become Yomafin's property. All in all, Simona thought, Yomafin was doing well in this deal.

"Welcome, my lady. The ship awaits you." Yomafin beckoned her toward the gangway. Yomafin was desperately eager to see them gone. Mentu, already aboard, waved to her from the stern-castle of the ship. She did not see Thru, but Simona knew that he, too, had already gone aboard.

"Thank you, Yomafin. When I see the Emperor next, I will tell him how brave and loyal you have been."

Yomafin licked his lips. His friendship for Mentu and his loyalty to Aeswiren had overcome his distaste for helping Thru escape the priests, but he obviously still had his doubts.

"Go in peace, my lady."

Simona stepped past Heldo in her purdah robe and felt his eyes, hot and angry on her. He almost blurted some angry words, but held his tongue as Yomafin shot him a sharp look. Yomafin had promised to beat him black and blue with a chair rod if he persisted with his effort to steal the emerald from Simona. Yomafin had done well from the deal, a profit of thirty percent already, without including the purdah coach and the fine pair of horses. His own sense of honor would allow no more plundering of the lady's purse.

Simona walked up the boarding ramp conscious that she might be saying good-bye to Shasht forever. As she left she felt her spirit soar. If she never saw her native land again, so be it, she thought.

"Welcome aboard," shouted Mentu from the stern-castle, which rose ten feet above the deck at the far end of the little ship. She waved to him and took a look back. Yomafin and Heldo were pulling the boarding ramp back onto the dock.

A gust of cold wind sent a shiver through her, and she stepped down to the cabins in the stern. Hers had been marked for her by a twist of red thread nailed to the door. Inside she found Thru waiting.

Since they were out of view of Mentu, they embraced, hugging each other in a mixture of triumph and relief.

"It is done," she said pulling back.

Thru did not reply. His eyes met hers, and Simona knew what he was thinking.

"I understand, Thru, and I agree. We must try and rescue your friends."

Her heart soared as she saw the instant gratitude in his eyes.

"Thank you, Simona. Can we convince Mentu?"

"I don't know, but we will try."

It wasn't long before there was a knock at the cabin door. Thru opened it to allow Mentu in.

"Well, they've gone at last. We'll pull the ship out on a warp line for tonight. On tomorrow's tide we sail."

"We've waited this long, I suppose one more night can be endured," said Simona.

"And once we sail, we'll be safe," Mentu said while casting a glance out the porthole.

"Yes, true enough, but first we have a final errand."

Mentu looked up sharply. "What do you mean?"

"Before we can sail to safety, we must go to the city. Thru has unfinished business there."

Mentu blinked. Deep down he'd feared that this was coming.

"Then we sail into danger all right. All of us could end on the temple altar."

"There is danger, yes," said Thru, "but you, yourself, said the harbor will be crowded with ships."

"Yes, the festival will have drawn them from every port in the Empire."

"Strangers in great numbers will be out on the streets."

"Yes."

"And the terror in the city has passed?" said Simona.

"That, too, is true. The Red Tops will have withdrawn to the temple. Only the captives already taken will go to the pyramid. The people will be encouraged to jollity in the next few days, to bring the city into a good mood for the great day. I know how they do it."

"So there will be crowds in the streets, and the Red Tops will not be hunting for more victims."

Mentu nodded. He had made these calculations himself, but now he voiced a more critical objection.

"But how will you find your friends? If the priests can't find them how do you expect to do it?"

"That is where we need your help, friend Mentu."

Mentu let out a sad chuckle.

"Why did I know it would come to this?"

"I know your brother would approve of you, Master Mentu," said Simona. Mentu sighed. As if he craved the approval of the brother who had imprisoned him for twenty years!

His own self-respect was another matter.

"If the Red Tops do take me, you will never find your way across the oceans to your home."

Thru did not blink. "You will wear your cloak, it is winter, everyone else will be the same. Your beard has grown long. You will not be noticed."

"And yet, I fear there is something you overlook. Flattering as it is that you think old Mentu can find your friends for you, I must shatter your illusions. I only lived in that horrible city for a few years. I wouldn't know one rat infested wharf from another, and there's hundreds of them."

But Thru had the answer to that.

"Someone has to go to the house of the Erv Blanteer. He is a friend of Janbur of Gsekk; he will know where they are hiding."

Mentu nodded thoughtfully. "The Erv Blanteer? Any idea where in the city that would be?"

"It is a big house, with a wall around it. There are many trees in that part of the city. Gardens, too."

"Ah, in the outer Shalba, then. All right, Mentu can do that. I just hope that this Erv is willing to cooperate."

"I hope this, too. You will tell him you come from Thru Gillo, the mot who spoke to him and his friends in the vault beneath that house."

"And then what?" said Simona.

"Then I will go ashore at night to find them," said Thru. "And we will arrange a way of picking them up. Then we will sail to the Land."

Mentu was won over. "Well, I would say we have a chance, then. If this Erv that you spoke to has stayed true to his friends, then this could work. But we will still be taking a great risk."

"You said we needed more hands to sail the boat."

"I did. Sailing this barque with just the two of us would be difficult."

"I will help, I will be a sailor," said Simona.

"You will not need to compromise your honor, my lady. We will be able to handle the ship." Mentu spoke more sharply than he had intended. In truth, he was troubled by Simona's disregard for purdah.

"But more hands would help?" said Thru.

Mentu agreed.

"Perhaps we can also arrange to load more stores while we are in Shasht?" said Simona.

Mentu nodded. Yomafin had left them short in that regard.

"We have some coin; however, it exposes us to more danger."

"But to load a few sacks of grain would seem a normal activity," said Simona. Mentu had to agree.

Suddenly Simona stood forward.

"And now I wish to make an announcement. As of this moment, I, Simona of Gsekk, abandon the state of purdah."

She lifted up her veils, one by one, and pulled them back off her head.

"I will not live my life in hiding, as if I had committed some terrible sin just by existing."

Mentu's eyes bulged as she pulled the veils away and stood there, her face and hair openly visible. Only slave women were ever viewed thus.

"My lady!" He raised his hands as if to block the sight of her.

"I will no longer hide from view," she said firmly. "I learned before that I did not need to hide that way, and I will be free from now on."

She reached out, took Mentu's hands, and pulled them down gently.

"Look on me, friend Mentu. I am free."

Mentu was an eccentric from the culture of Shasht, but he found this moment difficult.

"You are free, but go uncovered. It does not become a woman in our culture to do this. When a woman goes uncovered, she is thought to be a slave."

"But I am free."

The determination in her voice made Mentu smile, despite his reservations.

"If you insist, my lady."

"Please call me Simona."

Mentu nodded. Then turned away with a sigh. The world had grown very strange while he had stayed in his tower.

After warping the boat out to the end of the line and making all secure for the night, they gathered in the small galley, set just in front of the mainmast, and ate a meal of flat bread, cheese, and pickles, which they washed down with thin wine. Thru and Simona spoke animatedly of the stores they needed. There might be as many as ten mots and brilbies to feed. Unfortunately, neither Simona nor Mentu were aware of the prices of meal and beans. Or whether oats were cheaper than wheat this year.

Mentu was largely silent, lost in his own thoughts. As they concluded, Mentu voiced another concern.

"We will have to keep watch from here on, and I suggest we change every four hours through the night. I will take the first watch."

Thru and Simona slept in separate cabins. Thru continued to distance himself from her physically. That strange, terrible day in the cave still haunted him and left him racked with guilt. An unnatural mating between the kinds. And an offense to his love for Nuza. And yet, he found Simona very dear to him, a great friend. Someone as close as family could be, and still not be family.

The guilt about his betrayal of Nuza often kept him from sleep, but on this night he slept soundly until he was shaken awake.

Mentu was leaning over him.

"My friend, we have a crisis brewing."

"What is it?"

"Come and listen."

Thru stumbled onto the deck while still pulling on his coat against the cold. A few clouds, silvered by the moon, scudded across the sky.

He heard a long wailing cry, then a furious roar of anger.

"It started just a few minutes ago. Some shouting, then this."

The cries had suddenly grown louder. A distant banging could be heard, more roaring and shouting.

"There are lights over there where the noise is coming from."

"That is Heldo's house."

"The Red Tops?"

"I don't know, but we should be ready to cut the warp line."

"I agree."

Soon afterward they saw a few people gathering on the dock. A voice called out.

"Mentu, my friend, will you help us?"

Mentu went up into the stern-castle.

"Yomafin? What has happened?"

And they learned the worst. Yomafin and Heldo had

fallen out. They had had a fight, and Heldo had run off. He had sworn he was going to the priests.

Yomafin thought his brother meant it, and he had brought his family, two adults and two children.

"I beg you to help us, Mentu, as we helped you. The Red Tops will come tomorrow and take us away. You are our only hope."

Mentu hesitated and turned to Thru standing beside him.

"What say you, my fur-covered friend? Are you prepared to take them?"

With a degree of foreboding, Thru shrugged. "Yes, they can come aboard."

Mentu called back. "Thru Gillo says you can come aboard."

There was silence on the dock. Then after a moment of inaction the people climbed down into a rowboat and pushed out toward *Sea Wasp*.

Climbing aboard the ship, Yomafin was greeted by Mentu, Thru, and a bareheaded Simona. The fish dealer was obviously in the grip of strong emotions.

"Mentu, my friend, how could you allow this?" He gestured toward Simona.

"Yomafin, this ship belongs to the lady. She has renounced purdah."

"I am a free woman, Yomafin," said Simona. "I will not wear the burden of purdah ever again."

"Abomination," said Yomafin in a thick voice.

"Do not say such things," said Mentu. "You owe her your life."

Yomafin's wife and children had withdrawn into a huddled group. He looked to them, felt the mute pressure of his wife's eyes from behind her veils.

"Of course, of course," he muttered. "It is your ship. You have the right to do as you please, you are no longer of Shasht."

"That is correct."

Yomafin shuddered as his eyes met those of Thru.

"But, you will excuse me if I stay below. I cannot . . ." Words failed him.

Mentu lead the group to the cabins in the forecastle.

On his return he found Thru visibly concerned about Yomafin.

I foresee trouble with this man."

"We could not, in honor, refuse him."

"Unfortunately that is true."

"We must be careful, that is all. Perhaps Yomafin will want to be left in the city. He is a dealer in fish, a good one, he can make a living there."

"I hope so. I do not think he would be happy in the Land."

Mentu gave a grim chuckle.

"The tide will turn well before dawn. We will be gone before first light."

Chapter 56

Sea Wasp proved to be a fine, stable vessel riding along very well with a light wind a point off her beam. Mentu had opened only the big triangular mizzen sail, since they were so shorthanded and inexperienced.

Thru was not a sailor, and yet Mentu was impressed by Thru's quickness to learn how to set a sail and tighten the rigging. Thru broke some fingernails the first day on the hard, cold canvas, but by the second day he was reefing and furling with reasonable facility. Simona, too, had impressed him with her turns at the steering wheel, or hauling on a line. Yomafin may have been shocked to see a lady of Shasht without her veil, working as a sailor, but Mentu could tell that Simona was quite capable of hard work, as well as being very determined.

Very old ideas were being overturned in his mind, something that left him bothered, but at the same time intrigued. Purdah had not always existed. But very little was spoken of those times in the history of Shasht. To see a noblewoman's face was a shock, but it was also a pleasant experience. Instead of being spoken to by a veil, there were lips, eyes, and visible emotions.

In the evenings when the stars had risen, they gathered on the high deck of the stern-castle to read the heavens and discuss the navigation.

From their log readings taken throughout the day, plus the plottings of the compass, they had some idea of their course, remaining west of north, and covering another hundred miles in that day. By using a quadrant to measure the sun's height in the sky at noon, they also had an idea of how far south or north they were.

"Always the great difficulty once you've been well out of sight of land," said Mentu, "is judging your eastward and your westward progress. The quadrant helps us find our latitude, but longitude is much more difficult. That's why we have to keep logging our speed and plotting our direction by the compass. If we know our direction from the compass readings and how quickly we are moving, we can keep an estimate on our position."

Thru and Simona both nodded. They were educated enough to know that the world was round and covered in vast oceans. They had both seen a geographer's globe, and in Thru's case they had made use of an astronomical telescope and had seen the disks of the planets and the bright colors of the stars.

"But equally important at night, we use the quadrant to measure the angle of the Red Star above the horizon. That angle varies throughout the year, and it has also been shown to vary by location around the world. That is why we carry the *Book of Variables*. It gives us the angles to expect for each observation."

They made measurements to great Kemm and checked them in the book. Then they examined the chart and plotted that measurement. They were a little farther east than their first estimate, made from their daytime readings with compass, quadrant, and logbook.

"Now we have two points. We might make an estimate between them, or we might go further and take a measurement on one of the planets."

"I see great Zanth has risen," said Thru.

"You call that one Zanth, do you? To us that is lgen the bright one."

"It is bright, because it is very big. I have seen it through the telescope of Utnapishtim."

Lacking any Shashti word for "telescope," Thru used the word from his own language, and had to explain further. Once more Mentu found his assumptions of innate human superiority challenged.

They measured the angle of Zanth's rise above the horizon, checked it by the time and date in the *Book of Variables,* and used it to derive a third mark on the chart, this time a little to the north of the other two and almost perfectly in the middle between them.

"We can assume that our position is somewhere between those three points."

Their position was plotted to within a few miles of complete accuracy. Thru was impressed. Among the mots it was rare that anyone sailed out of sight of land, for the land was what they used for navigation.

"How long until we reach the city?" said Simona, looking off to the west where the land lay.

"We should raise Shark Point, here, by early morning." Mentu pointed to the map. "Means we'll be in the harbor before noon if the wind remains favorable."

This prediction proved correct, which left all three of them feeling elated. Mentu was particularly relieved, since it had been a long time since he had employed his navigational skills.

The sharp tooth of the point came over the horizon an hour after dawn, bringing a loud shout from the Eccentric.

"Land ho!"

The cry brought even Yomafin from his cabin. He took a look and then caught sight of Simona hanging in the rigging, wearing no more than a tight jacket and sailor trousers with her hair blowing free in the wind. Yomafin turned pink in the face and had to go below.

They came smoothly around the point and into the bay of Shasht. Soon they made out the opening to the estuary and the glittering city.

Within the hour they had tied up to a buoy in the outer pool, surrounded by hundreds of other craft, from fishing boats to huge four-masted vessels with sides that rose up like wooden cliffs above their heads.

As expected, the city was crowded with festival goers, come for the coronation of Norgeeben II. A mood of elation gripped the people. There was a common belief that the stability that had existed under Aeswiren would continue under his successor, who had taken such a blessed name. Great Norgeeben I was still revered for ending the chaos of the last dynasty and reestablishing the rule of law.

Of course there were complicated feelings about all this.

Many folk retained good memories of Aeswiren's time. Added to this was the perennial dislike of the priests. The Red Tops were well fed and very numerous. Their yoke was heavy at times. Many of Aeswiren's followers were also heretics who had little faith in He Who Eats. So a certain feeling against the priests was abroad in the streets. The crowds felt their own power, and the Red Tops left them alone. Thus the streets and plazas were rather boisterous. The ruled became the rulers, and the rulers ventured out of their houses only with some trepidation on these days. Slaves, of course, did not count in any of these things.

For one who had had no human company in two decades, Mentu made his way through it with ease, dodging the worst drunks, even taking a cup or two of grog when it was proferred to him, and joining in the singing. Twice, men told him that he resembled Aeswiren, to which he replied with elaborate mock sorrow, "I have heard that one all my life. But, alas, it was not my lot to rule the world. I'm just a fisherman." On both occasions the men laughed with him, more grog was poured, and the dancing continued.

In the Shalba the crowds quickly thinned out. On the road to the Canalgate, he found the Erv of Blanteer's residence. The gate was barred. Mentu passed a message and traveled on so as not to arouse any curiosity. He walked up to the Canalgate itself and watched the two squads of Red Tops that were drawn up on either side. Ordinary folk flocked in and out, while the Red Tops stood there motionless. There was none of their normal preening and investigating. No one had to pay any bribes on these days, just before a coronation.

Mentu watched for a few minutes and then walked back down the road to the Blanteer house again and asked at the gate. This time he was welcomed in.

The young Erv was suspicious at first, but when Mentu passed on the things Thru had told him, he opened up a little. Mentu went on to describe how Thru had survived on his own, making a journey of hundreds of miles into the interior.

Still, there was the difficulty of Mentu's appearance. The Erv had seen the Emperor in person on many occasions of state. The similarity was too great for him not to remark upon it. When he persisted with his questions, Mentu finally revealed his own identity.

When the surprise had dissipated, the Erv pondered these things for a few minutes. He took a great risk even by meeting with this man, but he was impelled to take even greater risks by the dire situation they faced.

Moreover, he was assured to some extent that if he risked his life, then so did his visitor. As to his visitor's identity there was little question. The Erv could see the remarkable resemblance to Aeswiren, and he knew that Aeswiren's younger brother had been imprisoned long ago. Blanteer decided to risk it.

"In truth, I must tell you, because we are in a desperate strait."

And thus the Erv explained the situation as he understood it. An hour later Mentu left the house and returned to the harbor.

Aboard the *Sea Wasp* he passed on what he had received.

Four of the "strangers" had survived, Mentu had jotted down the names. Ter-Saab, Juf Goost, Pem Glazen, and Jevvi Panst. Also in hiding with the strangers was Janbur of Gsekk.

In the aftermath of his discovery, Janbur's family had felt the hand of the priests upon them. His mother had been questioned severely, and would never walk again without pain. Many friends had also been questioned, but none of those in the know had broken, and the secret had been kept.

Janbur had suffered a long illness, it was said, and had been nursed back to health by the strangers.

The current crisis was the result of exhaustion in the group that had come together to hide the mots. Of the original cabal about half had drifted away. They kept silent, because otherwise they risked themselves, but they no longer even spoke to the remainder of the cabal.

Each one of them had hidden the fugitive mots in his house at one time or another. But as time went on so the terror aroused by the priests frightened some of the young rebels into going into hiding themselves.

And so the remaining rebels had run out of hiding places. With the city packed like this, it would have been a great time to move the survivors. But no place was prepared to receive them.

Even the Erv of Blanteer could not help, so he said, because his mother had put armed men at the gates of his house to search any and all who might enter. She was determined not to allow her insane son to put the Blanteer family at risk. Everyone knew what had happened to Janbur's mother.

And so the survivors had been trapped in a small warehouse on the waterfront. The warehouse was one of those small, square buildings seen on many of the docks. This one was on the wharf marked with the sign of the Ram's Head and Two Barrels. All had been fine until a week before when the wharf had been sold to a new owner. The previous owner's mother had forced the sale, having become suspicious of her son and his friends. Everyone in her circle was also well aware of the fate of Janbur's mother.

The new owner had doubled the guard on the wharf and changed the policy concerning access to the warehouses. Food had become impossible to get to the fugitives, since the guards were searching everyone going in or out and the warehouse was locked at night.

After hearing all this, Thru took up the spyglass and went on deck. It didn't take long to find the wharf. All wharves were signified by a large sign, hung at the outermost point, combining animal motifs, barrels, and red circles.

"Tomorrow the sacrifices begin?" asked Thru.

"That is correct," Mentu replied.

Thru was determined to waste no time.

"I will go tonight."

As dusk fell over the city, a million lamps were lit. Fires soon blazed on the great plaza at the head of the avenue of the pyramid. Drums throbbed continually while great masses of men jumped and sang. On the pyramid itself the first lights of the festival were being lit from lamps filled with an oil rendered from previous sacrificial victims. The elite of the city were gathered below to witness the ceremony. All of their lives they would talk about the coronations they had witnessed, and central to all of them would be the tale of the First Lights.

Thru lowered the small boat to the water and then paddled across to the wharf of the Ram and Two Barrels. As far as he could tell, no one was watching his approach and without challenge he slid beneath the wharf. He tied the boat to one of the forest of support poles.

The cold water below stank, fouled by the city. The only sounds were the lapping of the waves against the seawall nearby and the throb of the drums across the water.

He climbed up onto the wharf and crouched there, listening. The wharf was twenty-five feet wide, and extended about two hundred feet out into the water. It was much like the wharves to either side.

Single-story warehouses were built on top of the wharves, each twenty-feet wide and forty long. Their doors were stoutly built and locked. At the end of the wharf, two guards were posted beside a brazier. Thru moved closer along the outer edge of the dock, a narrow space with no rail. From behind the warehouse closest to land he could see the guards sharing a pitcher of beer. A dog was asleep behind the guard post.

Thru moved quietly back along the wharf to the warehouse farthest from the guards. Using the handle of his knife, he tapped out the tune to "The Jolly Beekeeper" on the wall and then listened carefully.

Nothing but the distant sounds of the carnival disturbed the night. A huge fire had been built up on the Grand Plaza by the dockside. Even here, miles to the north, it cast a ruddy light.

He moved around to the far side of the warehouse and tried again.

"For who would be a beekeeper and suffer all those stings!" Still no response.

He moved across the narrow alley to the middle warehouse and tapped again. Still nothing. Then he turned his head, certain he'd heard something, but it was not repeated. He listened hard to his surroundings. Had it been a sound from someone creeping up on him?

He ventured a peek around the corner up toward the gate. The guards were still swilling from their jug. The dog slept on.

He went back along the alley, then around the back of the warehouse, on the narrow walk above the water. Once again, he crouched down and tapped out the tune of the Jolly Beekeeper.

He strained his ears to catch something, anything in response. But no knock came. So, after a minute, he went on to the far side, between the buildings. He almost didn't bother with knocking again on the middle one, but something nagged at him, and at the last moment he crouched down and tapped again.

Da Da da da da dadada da da dada da da. . . .

Silence. And then he heard a faint knock. He sucked in a breath and listened more carefully than ever. There it was—a knock! And then another knock, and he knew that someone inside was knocking out the same refrain.

He waited, then he knocked once more and listened.

The response came again.

Thru stood up. He'd found them. Getting to them was going to be the next big problem. The door was securely locked with three separate locks. To get to the door was impossible without attracting attention. It was in plain view of the guards. And the dog only a hundred feet away.

He surveyed the back of the structure. No weaknesses revealed themselves. The walls were solidly built of bamboo for its lightness, but then covered in a hard shell of plaster. To break them would make considerable noise. No obvious openings presented themselves, either. The roof was well constructed, to break in that way would also draw attention.

After a moment's thought he tapped again on the wall, reaching up to tap once, then tapping at waist height, and then bending down to tap again near the base.

A moment later he swung himself out over the cold, filthy water and climbed down the side of the wharf. He was in view of the men at the guard post, but their attention was riveted to the far-off fire and the dancing multitudes.

Underneath he progressed hand to hand until he reached

the pole that the boat was fastened to and slid down into the boat. Carefully he loosed the line and pushed the boat farther into the gloom beneath the wharf. After going perhaps fifteen feet, he stopped, tied the boat around another pole and shimmied up it to the juncture with the base of the wharf.

The wharf was made of wrist-thick bamboo poles woven together to make a strong, light lattice. On top of that rested the wooden decking and then the warehouse walls.

He reached up to the underside of the bamboo. Several layers had rotted and decayed. He was even able to break a pole and drag it down a couple of feet.

Reaching up he pounded on the underside with his fist.

An immediate response came. As he listened, he heard the sounds farther and farther away. They were trying to draw him on. He returned to the boat and pushed on, even farther into the stygian darkness. Again he tied up and climbed the pole. Again he thumped the bamboo matting as hard as he could.

Suddenly, he heard a splintering sound just behind his head. He turned, almost lost his grip on the pole, and saw a piece of bamboo the length of his forearm break and hang down under the wharf.

A hand came down through the narrow gap.

"Food?" said the voice, edged with desperation.

"No. Sorry, just me, Thru."

"Thru?"

The hand withdrew.

More bamboo cracked as it was broken and forced downward. A face showed in the gap.

A big hand came out to grip his own. He felt that rough kob skin.

"Ter-Saab! Good to see you, my friend."

"Thru! By the Spirit, but this is a miracle! We thought you were dead. you were running at the back of the line, we thought the priests had taken you."

"Is it really, you, Thru?" said another voice.

"Juf Goost, you old devil. I knew you'd still be alive."

"It is a miracle," said Juf's voice. Others were talking all at once in the space above.

"Listen," said Thru. "The big festival starts tomorrow. We need to get you out of there tonight so we can sail on the tide."

"You have a ship?"

"Close by."

"How can we get out?" said Juf.

"Right through the floor there, like you're already doing."

"We'll have to lever up another floor board," said Ter-Saab.

"Jevvi is very weak, we'll have to lower him down to the boat."

"We've had no food in several days," said Ter-Saab.

"I understand. Well, if this will help, we have plenty of food on the ship. Once we get on board, we'll get you something to eat."

"You've got all our bellies rumbling now," said Ter-Saab.

They now worked to widen the gap. More bamboo broke off, one piece fell to the water, and Thru cautioned them to be careful; there was a dog close by. Bamboo was pulled up, broken as quietly as possible, and stacked inside the warehouse.

Now one at a time they climbed down, swung onto the pole with Thru's help, and then climbed down the pole to the boat. It was arduous work, and Pern Glazen was only barely able to make the climb down to the boat. He and Goost took up position in the boat now, while Ter-Saab and Janbur lowered the unconscious Jevvi Panst through the gap on a line warped together from packing bales stolen from the warehouse.

Thru helped guide Panst's comatose form down, and Juf Goost took hold and pulled him into the boat.

Thru could see that the little boat was already full up. Now Janbur came down. He had lost a great deal of weight . . . Thru helped him get a grip on the pole.

"I thought we were done for," said the man, in muttered Shashti.

"So did I, on several occasions, but the Spirit moves in us, I am convinced."

"Well, I give thanks for that Spirit."

After Janbur came Ter-Saab. Finally Thru.

The boat was sunk within a few inches of the surface. It hardly responded to the paddle. Slowly, cautiously they pushed out through the poles supporting the wharf and into the open water.

Thru oriented himself by the huge blaze down on the plaza.

Suddenly, someone squeezed his arm.

"Look there, a light!"

Chapter 57

With a lamp raised at the prow, Red Tops rowed a cutter down the lines of vessels in the harbor. When they came to the *Sea Wasp,* they knocked on the ship's hull to get the crew's attention.

Mentu leaned over to ask them what they wanted. The whole harbor was lit up in the red glow from the fires on the plaza.

"We search for the enemies of the Great God, what else?" roared a bull-necked Red Top in the cutter.

"Ah, well, good luck to you," replied the Eccentric.

"So, what is your business here in Shasht harbor?" said the Red Top.

Mentu leaned over the side again.

"We need to hire some more crew, then we sail to the spice isles."

"And what port did you say you hail from?"

"Gzia Gi, this is *Sea Wasp*."

"Have you registered with the harbormaster?"

"The captain is ashore now, he planned to do that."

"If we find you are unregistered. We will have to come back and search the ship."

"Of course, of course, I understand."

"Have you given to the collections for the Great God?"

"I believe the captain intended to leave our contributions with the priests."

"I hope you gave generously."

"When you sail the oceans, you come to understand the need for the protection of the Great God."

"That is proper thinking. May He continue to guide you."

The Red Tops poled away, heading for the next ship along the line.

Mentu took a deep breath as he watched them go. The drums continued to rumble in the city.

Simona was crouched in the dark well of the cockpit. Her eyes seemed to glow.

"Congratulations, brother of the Emperor. I know he would be proud of you. Me, I'm amazed you could speak to them like that. I'd have trembled like a leaf."

"Thank you, young lady. I think my hands were shaking, actually, but they couldn't see."

"It's horrible to live in fear of them all the time."

"Yes."

Now they heard the bull-necked Red Top hail the next ship in the line.

"Your brother dreamed of destroying their power."

"I know. He was never much of a believer in the Great God."

They were interrupted by a rasping voice behind them.

"Have they gone? The redheaded devils?"

Yomafin stood there, wild eyed, his mouth working, having climbed to the cockpit atop the stern-castle.

"They have, friend Yomafin."

"Then we must be gone as well."

"We will be gone, very soon," said Mentu.

"No, now. Drop the sails, turn the boat, let us sail away while we still have our lives. Before they come back."

"Very soon, Yomafin."

"No. Now."

"We can't leave yet, not while Thru is still out there."

"Leave the monkey, it is but a freakish animal. Let the Red Tops take the monkey."

"No, Yomafin, Thru is my friend. You would dishonor us all. Thru is a very important person in this world; he forms a bridge between our peoples."

"Bah, you speak in riddles. How can there be bridges to abomination? Don't you understand? Those Red Tops will ask at the harbor office about us. Then they will come back here with a dozen more of their kind, and they will take us all to the pyramid! Where will your precious honor be then?"

"We'll be gone by then, Yomafin."

"You risk everything! My life, my wife's life, my children. You must go now!"

Simona had heard enough.

"Be silent! We took you aboard, we gave you shelter. We gave you gold. We will leave as soon as Thru returns."

Yomafin whirled around on her, eyes wide with rage.

"How dare you speak to me like that. I am a man! You are but a woman in man's clothing. A woman with her womb shut up against men. A woman that lies with the furred demon!"

Yomafin's voice had risen.

"Quiet, Yomafin, they will hear you." Mentu leaned over the fish dealer as if to muffle his harsh words.

"Then do as I say," hissed the fish dealer. "Cut the lines and let us take ourselves out of this harbor, and away from these deadly dangers."

Simona's anger was simmering at Yomafin's words.

"You have no right to say such things," she began.

Yomafin snapped completely. "No woman speaks to me like that!" he snarled and hurled himself at her. Their bodies collided, and Simona was driven back into the cockpit, where her head struck the rail.

In a mixture of fury and fright she struck out, and her hand clipped him across the face. He uttered a foul curse and punched her in the belly. Simona felt the air go out of her lungs, and she doubled up. He took hold of her hair, yanked her out of the cockpit, and kicked her to the deck.

Dimly, lying curled up on the deck, she was aware that the two men were fighting above her. Blows and curses followed in profusion, and several times one or the other of them trod on her and she cried out.

Mentu swung and missed, and the pair of them tumbled down the steps into the waist of the ship. She pulled herself to her knees and saw Yomafin's wife emerge from the galley holding a long knife in her hand.

"No!" Simona got to her feet. "Mentu," she cried. She

slid down the steps and landed in a heap throwing the woman off her stroke.

The men had hold of each other and struggled by the rail. If the Red Tops passed by now, they would see them fighting!

Mentu was the stronger of the two, and now he had hold of Yomafin around the neck and shoulder. He lifted him, swung him around, and shoved him hard against the mizzenmast.

Yomafin's wife stepped forward with the knife raised, Simona flung herself at the woman and slammed into her, driving her back against the galley door. They went down together in a tangle by the door to the galley. Simona tried to hold the woman's wrists, while she tried to bite Simona's hands. Fortunately her veils filled her mouth and got in the way.

Simona brought a knee up and rammed it into the woman's chest. Yomafin's wife gave a great heave with her hips, and Simona was thrown forward. The point of the knife jabbed into her breast.

They struggled there for a few moments, but Simona could not overcome the woman. The veils had been torn away, and Yomafin's wife's face was exposed, contorted in a snarl of rage.

Finally pulling up on the woman's shoulders, then pushing her down again, Simona got her own shoulder in past the knife point. She could lean down now and drive her forehead hard into the woman's face.

However, the pain that this blow provided brought stars to Simona's eyes. Then she saw that Yomafin's wife was done with fighting, having been knocked unconscious.

Simona wrested the knife away. The woman's nose was bloody. Simona's head was still ringing, when she turned around in time to see Mentu go staggering back into the stern-castle wall while Yomafin struck him with a heavy belaying pin, wrenched from the pinrail.

The bows kept coming, and Mentu collapsed to the deck.

Simona stepped forward and thrust at Yomafin with the knife. He saw her from the corner of his eye and stepped back with a growl.

"Abomination!"

He hit her with the belaying pin across her shoulder, and she almost dropped the knife. He swung the pin again, but she ducked.

He came on, swinging the pin with all his strength, keeping her tumbling backward. She backed into the stern-castle steps and almost fell in her effort to get out of the way. Behind her she heard the pin splinter wood as she spun and dodged away.

Around the waist they went, circling the mast. Mentu was struggling weakly to get back on his knees. There was no help there. She remembered the knife.

Yomafin swung at her, she tried to parry with the knife, but the end of the pin caught her on the back of the hand and the knife flew away while pain shot through her body.

Someone screamed as she ran for the steps. She got up the first three and then Yomafin's strong hands caught the back of her jacket. She clung to the rail, but he was too strong and her grip was broken as she was flung down, cannoning into the mast before falling to the deck.

Yomafin dragged her back onto her feet and held her up until his face was right before hers.

"Listen to me, you bitch. We will leave now. I will lower the sails. You will steer. I will kill you if you betray me."

Simona stared at him blankly, her head whirling while she struggled to find a breath.

But Yomafin was already busy releasing the lashings of the mizzen sail. He went about the task like the experienced sailor he was.

Simona looked around for the knife, but couldn't see it. She didn't know what to do. Blood welled from a cut along her cheekbone. Her shoulder ached where he'd struck her with the belaying pin.

The lashings were undone. Yomafin was raising the sail.

Mentu was still unable to stand. Simona watched in horror as the sail was raised and then Yomafin ran forward, holding the kitchen knife. In less then a minute of frenzied sawing, he cut the line holding them to the anchor buoy.

Sea Wasp came free, and the breeze immediately filled the big triangular mizzen sail.

"Steer, damn your eyes!" snarled Yomafin to Simona as he came running back from the bow.

The barque was alive now, the prow turning as the wind took her slowly sideways. Simona climbed the steps and took hold of the wheel, holding it hard over to the left. The stern began to pick up momentum, swinging the barque's nose back to the north and the open bay.

Yomafin came up beside her in a moment. He saw that she'd done exactly what was needed. The barque continued to swing smoothly around, her bow aimed for the ship channel. Simona turned the wheel slightly, adjusting the rudder's drag and slowing the motion of the bow.

Yomafin grunted, surprised somewhat by Simona's skill with the steering wheel after just a few days of handling it.

Yomafin adjusted the big triangular sail, letting the boom out. Now the light breeze would waft the ship straight out into the channel. The tide was running their way as well. Simona felt a very slight bump from the ship, but saw no obstruction.

Yomafin seized her by the shoulder and leaned into her face.

"Steer!" he snarled.

Terrified, she took hold of the wheel. Yomafin ran forward with the knife in his hand.

Someone clambered over the gunwale down near the bow. Yomafin surged up the deck and sprang on the intruder with an oath.

The two engaged for the briefest moment, and then Yomafin went flying outboard, arcing away from the ship's side to fall below with a heavy splash. Fortunately he fell on the side of the ship hidden from the Red Tops, who right then were studying the *Sea Wasp* with suspicion as she suddenly unfurled a sail and began to move out into the channel.

Yomafin had barely surfaced, spluttering, when Simona glimpsed another figure dive overboard, knife into the water with hardly a splash, and swim with strong strokes to Yomafin's side. There was a muffled cry, the sound of a blow and then the figure had turned back and was towing Yomafin toward the ship.

Simona swung the wheel hard back the other way, fighting the resistance with all her strength. *Sea Wasp* responded after a short hesitation, her stern swinging back, cutting the distance to be swum. Simona knew that the water was dangerously cold.

Another splash caught her eye, and a moment later she saw a second swimmer surface beside Yomafin. The two worked together to heave Yomafin's body toward *Sea Wasp*'s side.

Other figures had appeared on the deck all around her. A very large mot dropped in front of her. His face was marred hideously by some violence in the past. Then she realized with a shock that it was a brilby, except it wasn't quite, and she simply stared in confusion. She hadn't seen a brilby since she'd left the Land, and she'd never seen a kob close up.

Now, beside the kob, stood a man, very gaunt in the face. He wore clothes of quality, but torn and dirty. There was something vaguely familiar about him as well, but she could not place it. Perhaps it was the beard.

"Greetings, Mistress Simona," said this fellow. "I am Janbur of the Gsekk."

She put a hand to her mouth in shock.

"Janbur of the Prime?" No wonder. She had seen him many times at Gsekk clan gatherings.

"The same. But now a fugitive."

The "brilby" had left them to join two other mots throwing lines down to those in the water.

"Good gracious," said Simona with the instinctive manners of her class. "I am of the Gsekk as well. My mother was of the Shalba."

"I know, as soon as Thru Gillo told me about you, I knew who you were."

Simona felt a shiver. He meant no insult, she was sure, but she also knew that to him she was the infamous "red mark girl" that eleven men had viewed but none had bid for.

"All that is behind us now. I am simply Simona."

"Yes," he smiled. "And I, Janbur."

Simona saw friendliness in this man's eyes.

"Thank you," she said.

He nodded and turned away. Purdah still exerted its power, and Janbur was struggling with his feelings about a woman like Simona unveiled, wearing trousers, out in the open air.

Ter-Saab and the others had hauled Yomafin onto the deck and laid him out as wet and flat-looking as the fish he dealt from his slab.

The brilby immediately straddled Yomafin and began pumping vigorously on his chest. After a few hard compressions the fish dealer gave an explosive gasp and then began coughing.

Thru Gillo came over the gunwale, followed closely by the other mot. Both crouched down beside the coughing form of Yomafin, curled up, shivering, wet and cold.

"Better find him some blankets. He took chill from the water."

Thru left Yomafin to recover and stepped over to crouch beside Mentu, still lying against the wall of the stern-castle in a daze. After a moment's study he came up the steps to embrace Simona by the wheel. Janbur had taken over the wheel, though, for now all that had to be done was to hold to the course Simona had taken.

"I knew it was you who was steering." He spoke in the tongue of the Land.

"I knew it was you out there swimming," she replied just as if they were alone.

Janbur shivered when she spoke the alien tongue so smoothly. He tried not to think about the sight of a noblewoman embracing a mot like that. Abandoning purdah was one thing, but this hinted at abomination!

"Many men would have left Yomafin to drown."

"I am not a man. And if he had been seen by the Red Tops, it could have caused great difficulties anyway."

For a moment Thru reached up to her face.

"He did this?"

She tried to smile. "I'm all right. Nothing broken, I think."

Janbur coughed. The tenderness in the mot's voice dis-

turbed him. Janbur had learned a little of the tongue of
the Land, but not enough to converse like this!

Simona ignored the man.

"And you found your friends!"

"Those that survived, anyway."

Someone was up on the foremast letting down the
mainsail.

Sea Wasp had come around into the main channel now
and was gathering speed.

Ahead, no more than a mile distant, the estuary opened
out into the bay. Behind them the city rumbled to the
drums.

Somewhere back there some Red Tops were making in-
quiries about *Sea Wasp*, but too late, for she was out of
the harbor under sail with a good offshore breeze and a
running tide.

Chapter 58

In the end, after some argument, they put Yomafin and his family ashore on the northern tip of Cape Shebba.

The boat scraped onto the sand. Yomafin, his children, and wife got out and splashed up to the beach. A path lead up the ocher cliffs beyond. A dry wind blew off the land. The woman's veils fluttered about her head as she struggled up the sand. Yomafin made no move to help her.

"Yomafin, I am sorry that it has come to this."

"You destroyed my life, friend Mentu."

"But we let you live."

Their eyes met for a moment, then Yomafin looked away to where *Sea Wasp* rode at anchor.

"And now? You will sail away with the abomination on either side of you?"

"The lady gave you gold, Yomafin. She did not ask for your life. Many would have simply thrown you over the side after what you did."

Yomafin knew this, but his anger still ruled him.

"Abomination, Mentu, you cannot go against nature."

Mentu made no reply, then said, "Where will you go?"

"To Gzia Gi. I have friends there. They will help me. Perhaps I will become a dealer in fine arts. I have always liked that trade."

"A step up from fish anyway."

"Yes. Good-bye, Mentu. I am sorry we fought."

Mentu put a hand up to the bandage tied around his head.

"Good luck, Yomafin. Try not to let the hate corrupt your heart."

"Mentu, you should come with me. You do not belong on that ship of hell with the abomination and its queen."

"We should leave," said Janbur, still in the boat.

"Yes."

Mentu pushed the boat back, and Janbur worked the oars. Mentu sprang in, and they worked it back through the surf to open water.

"Do you think they will be able to hide?"

"Yes," said Mentu. "Yomafin has many friends. And the lady gave him gold enough to see him start a new life."

"She is merciful indeed."

Mentu nodded. "She has learned some of their wisdom."

Both men looked off to the *Sea Wasp,* now just a hundred yards distant.

"You and I, we have much to learn from them, I think."

After a moment, Mentu chuckled.

"We will have plenty of time to do that."